PRAISE FOR ASHLEY YORK

"If you love medieval, don't miss Ashley York." — *USA Today* Best-Selling Author Kathryn Le Veque

Praise for *The Irish Warrior*

"Ms. York's knowledge of the land's history lends to the excellently-crafted storyline interwoven with familial deceit, warring clansmen, conquered lands, and of course, the heated passion of the well-developed characters. The sharp banter and well-honed dialogue between Sean and 'Tommy' are an added bonus to this enjoyable read..." — *InD'Tale* Magazine

"Writer Ashley York is the best thing to hit Medieval historical romance in a long time!... A witty, strong hero paired with a spunky heroine prove a formidable force against Ms. York's trademark depraved villains. I can think of no better way to enjoy my time than hunkered down with a Ashley York tale and *The Irish Warrior* did not disappoint!" — Jenerated Reviews

"A true treasure! Ms. York is a consummate storyteller who writes fast paced takes of the Norman Conquest, the struggles, challenges, and finding a HEA, amidst turmoil, danger, betrayal and a country torn apart. Compelling and powerful." — My Book Addiction and More Reviews

Praise for *The Saxon Bride*

"This historical romance set in eleventh-century England is an intriguing read that grabs one's attention from the beginning and doesn't let go until the very end. Action filled with danger, betrayal, lust, murder, political machinations, and love, this entertaining story is hard to put down! The characters are likeable and engaging, and the plot moves at a good pace with many twists and turns..." — *InD'Tale* Magazine

"A beautiful first novel to lead off the Norman Conquest Series. I'm a big fan of Medieval political intrigue, and this novel had plenty. Well done!" — *USA Today* Best Selling Author Kathryn Le Veque

"A touching and at times heart-wrenching story comes to life with a hero and heroine who are fallible and multi dimensional, one cannot help but empathize with and like them. This author exemplifies how a book can combine history and romance effortlessly and hold its audience until the last page." — Jenerated Reviews

"Adventurous, dangerous and passionate. A very intriguing read! I read this fast paced, action packed tale in one setting. The characters jump off the page. The storyline is realistic, you could almost feel the tension between the Saxons and the Normans." — My Book Addiction and More Reviews

Praise for *The Gentle Knight*

"One will delight in the rich, colorful, and descriptive writings in this second standalone period novel. Some readers may initially become distracted with the convoluted list of characters, however as the storyline progresses in pace, one quickly discovers the much-needed necessity and added layer of depth that these individual personalities contribute..." — *InD'Tale* Magazine

"Superbly written with well-developed characters I could not put this book down. A wonderful hero, lovely heroine and wretchedly awful villains kept me on the edge of my seat till the very end. Looking forward to what this very talented author has in store next for her readers!" — Jenerated Reviews

"You gotta love this gentle knight with a fiercely protective heart and the lady who broke through his curse, to capture his heart..." — My Book Addiction and More Reviews

Praise for *The Bruised Thistle*

"How dangerous it was then for a woman is disturbingly perfect. The villain is more typical to history than readers may be comfortable with, but life was more brutal than we like to believe... the writing is clear and tight, the characters believable, and the accents are written well, which succeeds in making the overall story quite a good read." — *InD'Tale* Magazine

"Writer Ashley York brings it all to the table in her work *The Bruised Thistle* with a swoon-worthy hero, a gutsy heroine and hands down the best villains currently lurking in historical romance. This wonderfully written tale set in Medieval Scotland takes its audience on a reading experience filled with subterfuge, moral dilemmas and breathtaking desire." — Jenerated Reviews

"Powerful, and brilliantly written with engaging, and charismatic characters. The storyline is compelling, complex, and intriguing to say the least. A must read and a keeper." — My Book Addiction and More Reviews

ALSO BY ASHLEY YORK

The Order of The Scottish Thistle series

The Bruised Thistle

The Norman Conquest series

The Saxon Bride

The Gentle Knight

The Irish Warrior

The Seventh Son

To Chelley
Sláinte
Ashley York

The Seventh Son

Ashley York

DEDICATION

This book is dedicated to "Unkie" Uncle Forrest, my grandfather's brother, a gentle man I remember from my visits to New Hampshire when I was very young. He never married but was a good son to my great-grandparents who lived well into their nineties. When I got married, Unkie sent me a letter of best wishes and the advice to "always be kind to each other." His words of wisdom have carried me through thirty-five years and counting.

AUTHOR'S NOTE

The ancient people living in Ireland in 1075 had a very sophisticated social structure. The different titles they would use for "king" were specific to the amount of land they had and the number of people in their clan:

- The king of a *túath* (small territory and its people) = *rí túaithe* (later "clan land")
- The overking of several *túatha* (small territories, their people and kings) = *rí túath*
- The king of a *ruirech* (lordship, a huge territory, their peoples and kings) = *rí ruirech*
- The king of a *cóiced* (province) = *rí cóiced*
- The high king = *árd rí*

Although not historically accurate, I decided to simplify the system by using the term "chieftain" in all instances and ask for your indulgence. The authentic names may be enough of a challenge, and here is a short pronunciation guide to assist with some of them.

Aednat – a + nit
Aodh – ei
Aoife – ee + fuh
Breandan – bren + dun
Caireann – care + on
Darragh – die + ruh
Padraig – paw + dreg
Tadhg – tie + gue
Tisa – tee + suh
Ultan – ult + in

To hear many of these names pronounced by a true Irishmen, Frank McCourt, please visit this website: http://www.babynamesofireland.com

Ashley

Chapter One

Drogheda, Ireland 1075

"Is Brighit safe, Cormac?" Tadhg MacNaughton called to the lad stabling the horse.

All must go according to plan in delivering his sister to the Priory in England. He braced himself for any news to the contrary. So many things could harm her. Fear sat like a coiled snake in his gut.

Cormac had arrived nigh fifteen minutes earlier with the carriage. Tadhg clenched his teeth. He had to allow the boy to see to his duties before attacking him with questions no matter how desperate he was for answers.

"Ronan sent me off as soon as the curragh arrived to carry them across. The man was most anxious that I get ye the news that they'd arrived." The redhead approached, averting his eyes. "I dinna see them get on the boat."

Tadhg closed his eyes and offered up yet another prayer for his sister's safe travel. He should have taken her himself but his father had insisted she leave immediately. Even at death's door, the old man had a tight grip on the reins of power. Tadhg needed to remain by his side. A good son. He would not gainsay the great Padraig MacNaughton, not when the man still lived. Padraig had arranged for their Uncle Ronan to escort Brighit.

"Go see to yerself. There's food a plenty for now."

The mention of food brightened the lad's face. He started off toward the house then halted and turned back. His eyes rounded. "And the MacNaughton?"

Tadhg took a deep breath, his head slowly shaking. "He's gone. God rest his soul."

His gut tightened. Though intended to be respectful, it sounded cold

1

to Tadhg's ears.

"God rest his soul," Cormac repeated, making the sign of the cross at the same time.

Tadhg glanced toward the chapel where he'd said his last goodbyes to his father just that morning.

"Ye're chieftain now?"

"I am."

Cormac perused him as if looking for some visible sign of the responsibility now passed on to him. A small smile on his lips. An uncertain smile. "Ye'll be a fine leader, Tadhg. We all believe that."

He headed off toward the little cluster of thatched houses. Tadhg watched him go.

Sean O'Cisoghe came out from the direction of the largest building that sat at the highest point on the hill. He spotted Tadhg and quickly closed the distance.

"Is she safe?" Sean spoke as soon as he was close enough to be heard. His face compressed with worry lines, his warrior's body rigid with concern. "How did she fare?"

A show of Sean's fierce temper was not what Tadhg needed right now. He quickened his step toward the chapel and away from the other man. "Cormac saw her to the sea but dinna see her board the curragh."

The man kept pace with him but said nothing. The silence was telling.

"Dunna fash yerself. I've offered several prayers." Tadhg stopped and pierced the other man with his look. "Can ye say the same?"

The scruffy beard Sean wore, darker than the blond of his hair, gave him a hardened look. "Tadhg, ye're no saint. And dunna question me on my prayers. I wanted—"

"I ken what ye wanted, man. Ye wanted to be bedding my little sister."

He'd always had a yearning for Brighit, ever since they were very small. But she would have none of it.

"And why not?" Sean's blue eyes widened into a what's-wrong-with-that expression. "There's no better man here for her."

Tadhg tightened his jaw and continued toward the chapel. "Enough of yer damn pride. She's for the Priory now."

"Ye've got to call her back." Sean yanked at his arm to stop him. "I beg ye, Tadhg."

Standing at the wooden door to the church, Tadhg gave his closest friend a look of warning. Any other man would have gotten a hard punch to his jaw for such behavior.

"Let it go, Sean. Even if I were to work things out with O'Brien and bring her home, I'm not thinking she'll wed ye even then."

The man released Tadhg's arm and turned around in his frustration.

His long hair, pulled back at the crown, swayed with the motion. Tadhg recognized the signs of his friend's temper threatening to erupt and that he fought to keep control.

"Bring her home." Sean's lips flattened into a tight line. "Give me a chance to win her over. I'll kick the arse of any O'Brien that comes near her. Ye ken I will."

"Ye'd be here for her?"

"Aye."

"Like ye were here when she was leaving? She asked for ye." Tadhg was sure her mentioning Sean's absence had been a ruse to drag out the goodbyes rather than any desire to see him. "Enough. I've things on my mind. Clan business."

"Aye." Sean quirked his mouth. "Ye're chieftain now."

"I am."

"Ye have the final say. In all things."

Tadhg dipped his head.

"Ye can decide to call her back from the Priory."

"Damn it, man. I need to get us enough food for the winter. That's my priority now."

Sean crossed his arms, a speculative look on his face. "Are ye going to abide by yer father's break with the O'Brien? Even when it could mean deep suffering for us? Like the lack of food in our bellies? I had greater faith in ye."

"I will honor my father as I see fit."

"Even when it makes no sense? The falsehoods he told about the O'Brien coveting our land? Why would they when they have the better land for growing? He seemed to have an increasing hatred of Roland O'Brien ever since last winter. Ever since the death of yer ma."

Tadhg could not argue that. The treaty joining the O'Briens and MacNaughtons went back to before the battle at Clontarf.

"I dunna ken for certain why he chose to break it off with them but I need to think long and hard before I just cast it aside."

"Our clans worked side by side to prepare the soil. The soil that grows the food and fodder we've no claim to now. And look at all we've lost." Sean jabbed at Tadhg's chest. "All *ye've* lost."

"I am well aware of what a great loss this is."

"But Tisa, Tadhg?" His tone dropped. "Surely ye dunna want to let the lass go? Without even a fight?"

"Who would I fight? My ailing father? Nae. *He* gave the decree. *I* had no choice."

"The sickness that racked through his body? Maybe that was why he suddenly saw them as a threat."

3

Tadhg shouldn't make a quick decision. His heart could easily sway his mind. He'd grasp at anything to set aside his father's abandoning of their closest friends. Anything that would give him sweet Tisa again.

Tisa's lovely face as she'd looked the last time he had seen her flashed through his mind. They'd been betrothed since they were wee ones. The last time he'd seen her she'd been twelve. They'd kissed. Their first kiss. He'd towered over her but even then she felt right in his arms. Her soft lips against his. Despite the awkwardness, something had sprung to life inside him. The promise of the beauty she would become enraptured his senses.

Her father's rage when he caught them alone surprised them both. Roland O'Brien had jerked Tadhg away, throwing him to the ground.

"None of that. Not until ye're wed."

The throbbing in his loins had been unbearable. Many nights Tadhg awoke to dampened bedding and dreams of Tisa fully grown. And the wish for time to move more quickly.

Five years. She'd be ten and seven. And Tadhg had become very... restless. How long could a man wait? Many couples would have satiated their needs by now since the betrothal was as good as wed even for the church. No doubt that was what her father had been concerned about.

"I have much to think on." Tadhg gave him a sideways glance. "I could be using some wisdom."

Sean looked skyward before facing his friend. "Yea, Tadhg I will pray that ye receive wisdom." He took a few steps away, heading back to the house, and added in a loud voice without looking back. "And a set of balls."

Tadhg smiled. The man was the fiercest warrior in the clan. He had always been sorely infatuated with Brighit. Sean needed to get over her.

The relentless call of the birds became muffled by the thick walls when Tadhg entered the chapel. Through the dim light, he moved toward the table in the middle of the small room, a chest to one side, a bench on the other. His feet made a grating sound as he disturbed the dirt and dust settled on the stone floor. The book of the clan sat open. With the flint beside it, he lit the single candle on the altar and ran his hand over the stiffened sheet. The entire clan history was recorded on these vellum pages. Births. Deaths. Marriages. It was all here.

With the tip of his finger he followed down the list of memorable dates. The marriage of his parents. The birth of their first son. Then the second. Looking closer, he could see the smallest speck of ink along the list as if they had counted down from one to seven. The seventh son. Their greatest hope.

The legend over all of Eire was that the seventh son of the seventh son of the seventh son received a special blessing. He would be a man like none other. A powerful and wise leader. One who had great favor with God Almighty.

Padraig MacNaughton was the seventh son of the seventh son. A blessing went with this honor as well. Following the last drop of ink, Tadhg slid his finger along the line to the written words.

Brighit.

A daughter. And no more.

He traced along her name. Mother Moira the Wise. He jumped below for his mother's name.

Moira the Wise. Born at Tara. Wed to Padraig MacNaughton. Died 1075.

He touched the long, dry letters. His father's hand was always thick. Barely legible. The wind picked up outside. A storm would be there by nightfall. Reaching into the sack at his side, he withdrew the tiny flask of ink and quill. He searched out his father's name.

Padraig MacNaughton. Born at Clontarf. Wed to Moira the Wise 1050.

Tadhg held his breath for a steady hand and carefully completed the line.

Died 1075.

Unlike his father's hand, Tadhg's was thinner. More like his mother's. He glanced over the list of his brothers.

Cian. Mother Moira the Wise. Father Padraig MacNaughton.

Aedan. Mother Moira the Wise. Father Padraig MacNaughton.

Padraig's hand was near impossible to read. He noticed a lighter hand beside Brighit's name.

Brighit. Mother Moira the Wise. Father Roland O'Brien.

Tadhg paused on the words. He read it again.

The walls of the chapel closed in on him and he rubbed at his eyes. There was no mistaking what it said.

Brighit was the daughter of Roland O'Brien? She was not the daughter of Padraig MacNaughton?

Blood rushed in Tadhg's ears. His heart pounded faster and stronger as if trying to break free of his chest. How could his sister have been conceived by the O'Brien? Like oncoming storm clouds rushing forward, dread washed over him. There was only one answer. His mother had not been faithful to her husband. She had lain with another.

Tadhg dropped onto the bench, no longer able to stand. Did his father know of this betrayal? He glanced again at the death date for his mother. It was written in his father's hand and none other.

Tadhg rubbed his ice cold fingers. His heart slammed against his ribs.

Did his father learn of her betrayal after her death? Just as Tadhg was learning of it now? Could this be the reason for the break with the O'Brien Clan?

If Brighit had been wed to an O'Brien, she would have been marrying her half-brother. To avoid that sin they had instilled fear in Brighit about her treatment at their hands. At first, it had been their mother who discouraged Brighit. Since her death, Padraig had maligned them. Mercilessly.

Tadhg's mouth dropped open with an inaudible gasp. Clarity struck at his heart with the force of a hammer.

His mother had betrayed his father and his father never knew, not until he saw the entry. It must have driven him to lose all sense. It must have infuriated him beyond control. It must have made him want his closest friend's blood.

Tadhg closed the book tight as if the secret could somehow disappear if the words were no longer seen. He placed it in the chest before the table. The implications staggered his mind. He turned the key in the iron lock on the chest and placed the key in his sack with the ink and quill. No one could know about this betrayal. No one.

Chapter Two

Tisa O'Brien allowed the hint of a smile for her friend, Caireann, who stared at her with wide eyes. "I'll ken soon enough about the marriage bed."

"How can ye say such things?" The smaller red-headed woman's jaw dropped. "How can ye not be frightened?"

Tisa rolled her eyes, waved her hand dismissively, and turned to continue down the path that led to the little brook. This was where the fiddleheads they sought grew the best. "How else can I get with child, Caireann. Dunna be daft."

Caireann scrunched up her nose and her smattering of freckles shifted. "Ye do want a lot of children. 'Tis all ye ever speak of."

Tisa laughed, the sound blending with the trickling water as they neared the strand. "Well, ye've also heard me speak of my handsome Tadhg, have ye not?" She glanced toward her friend as they plopped down beside the stream. "He is a great warrior and will protect me... and get me with child, I am most certain."

Caireann swept her bare feet through the chilling water before facing her friend with a worried expression. "With yer Ma passed, who can tell ye what to expect?"

"My many married sisters?" Tisa sat tall beside her friend. Caireann did not need to know how little they actually spoke to her. "And I trust Tadhg will take care of me... in every way."

"Ye sound like an old married woman."

Tisa's eyes crinkled with her smile. "'Tis how I feel as well. We've been betrothed for a long while. Time has passed slowly. I've waited forever for this."

"Well, it will not be long now."

In companionable silence, they sat beside the brook, enjoying the last warm spell of the summer and taking a respite from the reaping that had begun in earnest at her father's word. Tisa would miss quiet times like these with her close friend when she moved to the MacNaughton's land. Perhaps her friend could marry one of the other MacNaughton warriors—like Sean. She glanced toward her friend. No, Sean was too... hard a man for Caireann. She would require a gentle touch, a slow coaxing, or she'd be running scared as a rabbit.

"I'll miss ye." Caireann spoke as if reading her thoughts.

"I'll miss ye. I was just thinking if ye wed someone from Tadhg's clan, ye would be close." She pushed a wayward strand of red hair from her friend's face. "I would like us to remain friends. Ye are closer to me even than my own sisters."

Caireann rested her head against Tisa's shoulder, hugging her arm, and looking down at the brook. "I will still be happy for ye to be with such a grand warrior. He's a handsome one, that Tadhg."

Tisa covered Caireann's hand where it rested in the crook of her arm. "Aye. He is that. His kind eyes." She impulsively kissed the top of her friend's head. "I could not love him if he were cruel."

Caireann tipped her face up and smiled. "True enough. Ye see a kindness in him for certain for ye to love him as ye do."

A call in the distance sent Tisa's heart to pounding. "What's tha—"

Young Liam burst through the trees, his breath coming in such great gasps he could not speak. He shook his head, bent forward, steadying his hands on his knees. "I... ran..."

Tisa stood, her breaths coming quicker. "Well, I can see that ye ran, Liam. What are ye about?"

Liam looked to the heavens, his chest heaving as he tried to catch his breath. His dark hair hung in limp clumps, soaked through with sweat. "Yer da—"

Dread tore through her like an arrow. She moved in closer. "What? What about my da? Oh speak!"

Her frustration grew with each passing second. Liam's face was blotched bright red from his exertion. She covered her mouth with her fingertips, trying to practice patience as she'd been trained. She tried to believe her father was fine. She tried to swallow the lump in her throat but it remained lodged there. Something was amiss and had been since spring but no one felt the need to share any news with her. She wasn't to question or speak until asked to speak but she could still listen and she did—to everyone. She'd learned nothing.

Tisa pressed her lips together to keep from prompting the boy to speak.

Looking toward Caireann, she saw her own fear reflected there.

"He's probably fine, Tisa." Caireann tried to reassure her but her widened eyes did little to ease the discomfort.

Tisa grabbed Liam's arm. "Is my father hurt?"

Liam shook his head, wincing slightly at the tight grip she had on his arm. "Nae." His breath finally returned. "Nae. He's fine, Tisa. Sorry I am that I frightened ye."

She released him and he exhaled a slow, steady breath. "I was sent to retrieve ye. He wants to see ye 'immediately if not sooner.' I ran the whole way."

Tisa's trepidation now shifted from fear for her father's well-being to why the sudden need to summon her when they would see each other after Vespers. Was she about to learn what had transpired the spring past? Her breathing was shallow. The axe was about to fall.

Immediately if not sooner—it meant only one thing. Her father was angry. Guilt nibbled away at her insides. Had she done something? No. It must have to do with whatever happened.

Standing erect, she proceeded with stately grace toward the village. She would remain outwardly calm as was expected of her. Caireann came up behind her, following at the same slow speed.

"Well, be sure yer da knows where I found ye," young Liam called. "I dunna want him to think I dinna hurry to locate ye."

Tisa did not respond. She looked neither left nor right. The view from the gradual descent to the little cluster of houses usually filled her heart to overflowing. A peaceful area of unmatched beauty. The water in the distance. The rolling, green hills. Not this time. Mayhap never again. The tension building in the pit of her stomach hardened like a rock. She'd been avoiding the uneasiness around her, the whispers of her father's trusted men, the glances from the elder women. Tisa could not even imagine what had happened but felt certain she was about to find out. Good or bad, her life was about to change.

The O'Brien's youngest took a brave step into the Great Hall but stilled. Her courage fled when she sensed the tension. She couldn't move another step.

"Please, Caireann," her voice quivered when she spoke. "Go to yer home and see to yer chores. I will find ye if I am allowed to."

When Caireann opened her mouth to speak, Tisa put a finger to her lips. Their eyes held and Tisa shook her head very slowly. Her friend backed out the way they'd come, her head hung low.

The stone in Tisa's gut doubled in size. Her feet refused to move. Across the hall, past the raised fire pit filling the middle of the Great Hall, and through the open door against the far wall sat her father. Waiting. She swallowed, forcing the lump back down her throat.

I have done nothing wrong.

Tisa closed her eyes, imagining herself again as a little child, still fair-haired and well-freckled. The look on her father's face as she dropped back down into his arms after he tossed her into the air. He was a strong, young man and loved her dearly. She needed to believe it was still true but things had changed as she'd grown. The flash of her father's expression when she'd found her kissing Tadhg set her heart to racing. She'd never seen him so angry.

Perhaps that's what this was about. Her father didn't like the idea of her being a grown woman and marrying. He'd even insisted Tadhg not see her again. Could this be the end of the banishment? Could her father be ready to finally see her wed?

Tisa exhaled, her shoulders rounding in relief. That must be what this was all about. Opening her eyes, she smiled. Surely that was what he was upset about. He may appear angry but he knew she must marry someday. The bond between the two clans would be secured by the marriage. The fulfillment of generations working side by side. With Tisa as the future chieftain's wife, the MacNaughton and O'Brien would be bound as one. Well, she may as well get on with this. She could admit she was sad to be leaving her home but she was also happy to be marrying the love of her life.

With more spring to her step, she crossed the hall. It was a moment before her father noticed her. He sat before a long table, leaning over vellum documents that were spread across it. Men surrounding him. Most she knew by name but one man sat to the side, separate. Men did not sit in her father's presence. This man must be his equal.

The unknown man was quite large in the chest and he did seem familiar. Strange skins she didn't recognize draped across his shoulders. Chieftain of some other clan, no doubt. A strange, dark material, stretched tight across his muscled legs that spread slightly at the knee. Her breath caught when she found him looking at her. His eyes tightened as he smiled.

"And is this yer youngest?"

She jumped at his loud voice and felt as if she'd been caught doing something she ought not. Roland O'Brien jerked his head up. He impaled her with his look. There was no welcoming smile. His irritation was all encompassing. Blood rushed in her ears as she moved past the men who opened a clear path to her father. She kissed his cheek.

"Father." She curtseyed and moved away slightly.

Her father grabbed her arm. It shook slightly. "Hasten not away, daughter."

The men beside her, her father's men, exchanged confused glances.

Perhaps they'd heard the anger in his tone as well. His grip loosened and he smiled at them.

"If ye'll excuse us, I have much to discuss with my daughter."

The captain of his men, Fergus, offered her a reassuring smile. His bushy, gray cheeks rose slightly with the movement.

"Of course, sir." He took her hand, kissing it lightly. "Ye're more lovely every time I see ye, sweet Tisa. Ye've grown into a beautiful woman."

Tisa felt nothing like a grown woman at this moment. She felt like someone who was suddenly drowning in guilt but she had no idea what sin she had committed. Attempting to smile back, bile rose in the back of her throat.

Fergus winked, almost as if sensing her trepidation, before leaving. His men followed him out the door. The stranger leaned forward slightly in his chair. His eyes surveyed her in a most intimate fashion, his thumb rubbing against his lower lip as if assessing her worth. She started to move away but her father held her fast, his arm now around her waist.

"Where have ye been?" He sounded more himself and the fierce look of anger had left his face.

She swallowed. "I searched for more fiddleheads beside the river."

"Tisa, they're long past now. Why do ye waste yer time?"

It was a reoccurring argument and her nervousness eased somewhat. No matter how many times she was able to find his much loved food still growing in tender shoots, he would tell her she would not. She secretly believed he deliberately goaded her so she would try harder to find it.

"I did find them, Father."

The O'Brien raised his brows in mock surprise. Then looking to her left and to her right in expectation, he said, "Where? I dunna see them."

A genuine smile at his silliness, she said, "Ye ordered my immediate presence. I put them all aside in my haste to do yer bidding." Her father's eyes seemed to cloud slightly at the reminder. She glanced at the other man.

"Ronan, I would have ye know my youngest—Tisa."

"Tisa." The strange man tipped his head. "It has been a long while."

Unsure of exactly who he was, she was unsure how to address him.

"Do ye remember Ronan?"

"I do not." She shifted against her father. "What is amiss, Father?"

He leaned back in his chair, his shoulders rounded as one in defeat. Alarm bells sounded in her head. When he motioned her to move to the other side of the table, her pulse quickened. That was where the villagers who came before him for judgment stood. Eyes downcast, her ears ringing, she took the place of dishonor and clasped her hands before her.

The chair scraped along the stone floor as Ronan finally stood. When he approached her, she held her breath. He was quite tall and had the look of an islander. That would explain the strange clothing. He circled her, surveying her, and glancing to her father occasionally with a slight nod and a smile. Her father steepled his fingers before his mouth, appearing merely thoughtful but she sensed his tension.

Fear replaced the rock in her stomach. Fear for herself. Fear for her father. Fear for whatever was about to happen. Something was very wrong—something to do with her.

"I think she'll do nicely." The words sounded loud as if he was used to speaking over the sound of the ocean. "Methinks we have an agreement."

The man reached across the table and her father stood to accept his outstretched arm. Each clasping the other at the wrist in solemn agreement. An unbreakable agreement. Then the man left the room without a backward glance or another word.

Tisa did not move. "Father?"

Her father strode past her to the narrow table beneath the small opening in the stone wall that faced the ocean to the east. He poured a generous amount of libations into a wooden cup. He didn't speak or turn toward her until he had refilled it a third time.

His eyes were pained. Something was terribly wrong. All other concerns fled. Her compassion for her father propelled her toward him but he held his hand up in a commanding fashion. "Nae! I will not allow ye to comfort me."

His tone was thick with regret. The way he sounded when he had to sentence one of their own clan to death. Was it her? Had she just been sentenced to death?

He sat in his seat, leaning back as if in exhaustion. She dare not speak. She dare not move. She dare not breathe.

"Tisa. Yer betrothal to the MacNaughton has been severed. Ye'll marry into the Meic Lochlainn Clan of Inishowen. They'll be here in two days' time."

The pain in her chest intensified with every word he spoke, like nails hammering into her heart, but her brain refused to understand his meaning beyond his first statement.

Yer betrothal to the MacNaughton has been severed.

Her betrothal to Tadhg? They'd been betrothed forever. They grew up knowing they would one day be wed. Tadhg was all she wanted in a husband.

Her father's eyes never wavered from her face. Surely he measured her reaction as if he cared.

"Ronan came here to make the agreement on their behalf. He has been a great help to our clan."

The kind eyes seemed familiar, but no. Those would have been the eyes of her father that loved her. A father that wanted her to be happy. A father that wanted her settled nearby. This? This was a man that cared nothing for her. A man that would rip away her future dreams of happiness. A man that would send her away from him. A man that would give her to strangers. Strangers that saw her as nothing more than… breeding stock.

No. She was more than that. She would not stand here and be handed off to a stranger without even a word of protest.

"Why?" Damn her eyes. The tears swelled and her father became a blurry figure. "How?"

He looked away. "The MacNaughton broke our agreement."

Her jaw dropped. A slap to the face would have hurt less. "Nae!"

"After Moira died, Padraig sent word he would not see his son married to an O'Brien."

"And ye did not think to tell me this?"

Her head reeled with the implications.

"And Moira? Tadhg's mother is dead?" Her breath hitched. Moira had been like a mother to her. "When was she buried? I wish to pay my resp—"

"Ye will not! Padraig would not allow us to come. None of us." Her father finally faced her. "We are no longer welcome on his land. He wants nothing to do with us."

"Nothing to do with us? They are our kinsmen."

"No longer."

"Ye canna just let him cut us off like this."

"I was given little choice in the matter."

"Then go to him! Beg his forgiveness for whatever ye have done!"

"I have done nothing wrong! 'Twas Padraig's doing. He chose to give me no reason. I will abide by his decree."

Tisa's mind struggled to make sense of what her father was saying. There must be something he was not saying. "Why would Padraig treat us like this?"

He looked past her. "It matters not. What does matter is that the O'Neill threatens us to the west."

"When will Seamus and Ian return?" Her only unwed brothers had been away going on two years now.

Her father's eyes rounded in pain. "I dinna wish to upset ye but yer brothers will not be returning. They died in battle against the O'Neill."

Tisa cried out. "When?"

"We received the news spring last."

"Again ye decided to keep this from me? Do ye think I am a child? If that is the way of it, 'tis because my own father kept me from the truths in life, shielding me as if I would break."

"Ye brothers went against my wishes. My anger was at them, not ye."

"Be angry then. Be sad. Be devastated! But dunna keep me from the truth."

"A great loss." Her father closed his eyes against the pain.

Her own heart cried out. They were much older than she was as were her sisters. The MacNaughtons were closer in age and felt more like family. Brighit was like her own little sister.

"I must make decisions that ye may not wish to abide by—but ye will. The O'Neill will not back down. We need an alliance with a strong clan. I need men I can count on, who will fight with me against them."

"The MacNau—"

"They will not fight for us now. 'Tis not their land that is threatened." He shouted the words, his nostrils flaring. "They have broken our agreement, Daughter. We are defenseless. Ronan was good enough to make a new alliance for us."

"At what cost to us?" Tisa knew the answer as soon as she asked the question. The way Ronan had looked at her, assessing her worth as a mate.

"Ye will marry their tanist."

"So I am to be exchanged for the promise of protection?"

"Ye will have a place of prominence in their clan."

"I dunna care about prominence! I want the life I had always been promised. The life I was raised for."

"That life is gone, Tisa. This is the life ye will have."

"I dunna accept this… betrayal."

"Ye have no choice."

She needed to be alone. "May I leave now?"

Her father's expression of shock quickly shifted to one of acquiescence. "Ye may."

Unable to take a deep breath for fear of the tears that would come, she walked with stiffened legs toward the door.

"I will see ye at Vespers."

She stopped but did not face him. "Ye will not."

"What?" He bellowed the question.

"I have much to see to in preparation for my impending marriage."

She continued across the hall and prayed she would see no one in the hall. Her face awash with tears, she bit her quivering lip.

"Tisa." Her father's voice sounded strained. "I've done the best I can by ye. Dunna doubt it."

Unable to respond, she made her way to the stairs that hugged the outside wall of the stone building. Her head turning toward each arrow slit as she ascended out of habit. She saw nothing. Numbness engulfed her. Her thoughts scattered. All but one—Tadhg would not be taking care of her.

Chapter Three

The aroma of cooking breads and roasting meats teased Tisa's stomach in to a loud growling.

Caireann glanced up from her needlework. "Are ye certain ye dunna want me to fetch ye some food?"

Tisa swallowed the water flooding her mouth. "Nae! I must make my father see reason. He canna marry me off to some clan I dunna ken, at a place I dunna ken, and to a man I dunna ken."

She grabbed at the tightening in her gut. Surely she must be starving to death.

Caireann frowned. "'Tis only been two days, Tisa. How are ye to outlast him?"

"By determination." Her words sounded like a sob. Her face heated and she turned away from her friend's concerned expression. "I have no choice. I canna marry that man. I canna."

The hearth was cold and the north wind blew about the room from the tiny openings along the beams at the roof line. She pulled the furs wrapped around her closer still.

"Without even warmth from a fire, Tisa? Ye're bound to take ill."

Tisa shook her head, forcing herself to appear stronger than she felt. "Nae. I will not be bartered off like some unwanted heifer. My father will see reason."

Caireann set the embroidery in her lap and sighed. "Methinks ye're wrong. The man is here now. He is below with his own father probably wondering about ye. Mayhap even thinking ye're daft? Or horribly disfigured to hide yerself away."

Tisa's vanity would not be piqued. "He is here so soon?"

"He was not a great distance when Ronan went to them. Methinks they waited for him."

"This will work. It must work. It worked for my sisters. It will work for me."

"Starving?"

"Nae, showing a strong objection by refusing to eat."

"Oh, Tisa, why take a chance? If this other clan breaks the agreement with yer father, he will be sorely vexed and take it out on ye."

"Surely not, Caireann. My father has never raised a hand to me."

"Methinks this is a very different situation. He begged forgiveness for yer absence from the feast at yer betrothed's arriv—"

"He is NOT my betrothed. Tadhg is my betrothed."

"It seemed a bit hard on yer father that ye dinna come down. He kept looking toward the stairs. These men from Inishowen are all warriors. Large. Strong. They come with many weapons. If yer absence offends—"

"Enough!" Tisa held up her hand. Guilt and fear for her father's well-being flooded her. "Yer making me sick with fright that my clan could be murdered if I dunna go below. I yield."

Tisa stood, the furs dropping to her feet. Her stomach growled loudly. "I will not bring shame to my father. I will meet the man."

"Yer betrothed."

"He is NOT my betrothed, Caireann, please." Tisa took her friend's hand in a tight hold, her face close. "In my heart, I will always be Tadhg's. I canna cast that aside. Not ever."

Caireann stood and helped Tisa dress for the occasion. The pale linen material did little to complement Tisa's sullen expression. The bell sleeves tight at her wrists fit perfectly with the tightness across her chest.

"Ye look ready to meet yer executioner."

"I feel as if my life is ending."

Caireann yanked Tisa against her in a tight embrace. "'Twill work out. I ken it, Tisa. Dunna be afeared of this man."

Tisa didn't trust her own voice as the tears gathered. "It was Tadhg I trusted and no one else. I *am* afeared of this man."

"Yer father would not give ye to a cruel man. He could not. Ye're too dear to him."

Tisa set her friend aside and hesitated before asking, "Have ye seen the man?"

Caireann glanced away, unable to meet her gaze. "He is tall but not overly broad."

Tisa forced down the lump in her throat. "My father did what he must for the clan—" She pushed her shoulders back. "I will do the same."

The last thing she expected to see upon her arrival in the Great Hall was a celebration. Celebration with abandon. Loud voices, raucous laughter, and discordant music drifted to her as she descended the last steps. The voices indicated a great quantity of libations had been consumed and probably continued to flow even at this early hour.

Unnoticed, Tisa took in the scene before her. Several long trestles were set up along the walls between the stone pillars supporting the upper floor. They overflowed with food and drink. Her father sat on his chair oblivious to all around him except for the man to his right. He listened intently, his head tilted close to not miss a single word. The man had gray hair and a beard of the same color that fell well past his chin. An unusual style. She prayed this was not to be her betrothed. Surely he was older than her own father.

At least twenty people, most of whom she did not recognize, were grouped in two circles and dancing to a tune she did not recognize. Unlike her own clan, these people touched repeatedly, both their palms as they passed and their shoulders as they crossed. Grouped in twos and threes, men and women huddled close at the far side of the hall. The iron wall brackets that hung along the back wall were not lit, creating a darkened area. Peering closer, Tisa thought she caught sight of naked flesh before her view was obstructed when the men moved closer together.

"And ye must be Tisa?"

A handsome man with bright blue eyes, blond hair, and a slender build with broad shoulders approached her. Perhaps three and twenty, he wore trews with his leine and appeared quite flushed. Behind him, a considerably younger man that she recognized as one of the cook's helpers, Breandan, startled her when he narrowed his eyes at her. That one preferred the company of other men but had never been so openly rude to her. He made his way up the stairs behind her.

Glancing past her, the man before her followed Breandan with his eyes. When he returned his intense gaze to her, he raised his brows in expectation of her reply.

"I am Tisa."

With a delicate touch and a sweaty palm, he brought her hand toward his lips and bowed slightly. "At least I have not been deceived regarding yer beauty."

Her stomach lurched. This was to be her betrothed?

His eyes twinkled as he searched her face for what seemed like an exceedingly long time before he finally spoke. "Ye do seem upset. And is that fear I see in yer eyes? Fear of me?"

She swallowed hard. "Nae! 'Tis just that we have not been introduced."

"Hmmm." He threaded her arm through his with a grip that seemed unnecessarily forceful. "Then let us see to it."

His body was stiff beside her as he all but dragged her toward her father. He was a foot taller than she was. She ventured a glance at the man's face. Tight lipped, his cheek twitched. She'd almost believe he wanted this match even less than she did.

"Look what the cat dragged in." The man beside her stepped away, dropping all pretense of pleasure at her arrival.

When her father turned away from the older man, his frown shifted to one of pleasure. "Daughter! I am delighted ye feel well enough to join us."

He closed the distance, kissing her lightly on the cheek and whispered. "They dunna need to ken of yer childishness."

She tipped her head with a tight smile. Searching his face, he appeared older and her heart quickened. "Are ye not well—"

"This is the Meic Lochlainn. Aodh Meic Lochlainn." Indicating the older man still seated with a sweeping gesture. Her father chose to ignore her concern but turned, instead, to the man beside her. "And I see ye have met yer betrothed."

"She appeared vexed that we had not been properly introduced." The man had beautiful eyes but an annoyingly high-pitched voice.

Aodh Meic Lochlainn's lips turned up at the corners as he took an overlong perusal of her from where he sat at the place of honor beside her father. "Aye. A lovely morsel indeed." He licked his lips and faced her father. "Well matched without a doubt."

"I believe they are indeed," her father answered.

Tisa glanced at her betrothed to find him rolling his eyes then turning back to the crowd behind them as if searching for someone.

He started when he noticed her watching him. He did not look pleased. "And can we be properly introduced before she turns tail and runs?"

"Mind yerself, son," the older man laughed out the warning. He approached, stepping in close to Tisa. His breath smelled of rotted teeth and ale. "Ye are a lovely one."

"Please, Father, we are not even wed yet. Can ye not wait before ye lust after my wife?"

Tisa's jaw dropped. Glancing at her father, she realized their voices had been too low for him to hear above the din in the room.

"Keep a respectful tone." The Meic Lochlainn turned toward her and winked. "Ye're a blessed lad." He turned toward her father. "Roland?"

The man used her father's name as if he'd the right. These are the men her father would create an alliance with? These are the men who would protect them from the enemy?

"Darragh, I make known to ye my daughter, Tisa."

Darragh's smile could have rivaled the loveliest sunrise. With slow deliberation, he brought her hand to his lips again, his eyes holding her own. Sky blue, beautiful eyes but not the eyes of a happy man. They were the eyes of an angry man. A livid man. A man following orders he did not agree with. Mayhap even a man who bided his time until he could make them all regret forcing him in to this position.

Her soon-to-be husband's soft lips touched her hand. A violent shiver jerked up her arm. He must have felt the tremor for his eyes widened as if he'd just been proven correct about something. The small creases now apparent at the corners of his eyes indicated this was a genuine smile.

"Mmm, a timid lass." He spoke softly, seductively. "I do find great pleasure in that."

Tisa dare not breathe.

"Perhaps I have been blessed." His words were for her alone before he turned back to his father. "When will the wedding take place?"

"Hah!" Aodh gave a hearty laugh and turned to her father. "What a sprite yer little Tisa is. She's won him over with a mere glance."

Darragh had stepped away again, placing a fair distance between them but laughed along with his father. Her own father's dark eyes were on hers. She'd swear she could read his regret but smiled back as cheerfully as she could manage. Her knocking knees and feelings of doom well hidden.

"This very night!" Darragh's voice pierced her through.

She gasped and turned to him.

No!

"Aye." Her father nodded and stood. "Let us meet with the priest and sign the contracts."

Darragh moved in closer, a keen eye measuring her reaction as he did so.

Her body quaked in response.

An eager smile now, he had the look of a cat playing with a mouse just before it was about to eat that rodent. He seized her hand. "Ye are not what I had expected from the woman I must wed. I dare say ye are very much to my liking, sweet little Tisa."

His eyes never left her face and there was a hardness there as if he looked on her not as a woman. Not as a wife. Not even as a prize. He didn't care to look upon her. Instead, he searched out her fear. He felt her dread. He recognized her reluctance to marry him as well and that gave him satisfaction. Great satisfaction.

"Come, son. Let us see to the signing of the marriage contracts."

Tisa's mouth went dry. "Father—"

Her father raised a hand to silence her. "I will see to it, Tisa."

The three men left her to stand alone in the middle of a room filled with many strangers.

A fluttery panic rose in her chest. Where were the men she knew? Where was Caireann? Fergus appeared at the far door, scanning the room. She willed him to see her. When he finally did, there was disappointment. Although he approached her, he had not come for her.

"No kiss of best wishes and blessing, my friend?"

Fergus brushed his lips against her cheek. He frowned. "Tisa, ye're cold as stone. Why have ye come down if ye are still not well?"

A simple kindness and tears flooded her eyes. She steeled herself to shield this man from her inner turmoil. "I was not sick. I reacted badly to the broken betrothal."

"My heart breaks for ye as well, Tisa. Ye and Tadhg should be marrying. It canna be easy to be set aside by him now."

Be set aside? She ground her teeth. Had he found another he preferred?

"Aye. 'Tis done. I have a new betrothed now and all these warriors," she indicated the men in the room who listed from side to side in their drunkenness, still attempting the dance, "who will see to our clan's protection."

Fergus' bushy eyebrows slammed together with his fierce frown. "Well protected we'll be. Yer father has told ye of the loss of yer brothers?"

She nodded.

"I told him not to keep it from ye but he thought it best."

"Their death has caused all this."

"No, Tisa. It was the MacNaughton that made this alliance necessary. They had always fought for us as if we were one clan. The loss of yer brothers pains me but 'tis the withdrawal of the MacNaughtons that puts us in danger."

She searched for any familiar face. "Are none of our own people coming to the celebration?"

"I dinna like the looks of these men. They were well into their cups upon their arrival. I dunna care for any unwanted attention paid to our women this day." He turned to her. "Do ye understand me?"

The dark corner appeared empty now. "I do."

"When our men are back from the fields, I'll ken we can protect our women better. Tonight they'll come around." He glanced across the sea of waving heads. "And tonight many of these will surely fall."

Tisa smiled thinking of the inevitable state of these drunken men. "They dunna appear to handle their drink very well."

"I have to agree with that."

"Although," Tisa paused and glanced around, "I also dunna see anyone dropping away."

"A couple of the men were headed to the stables. They must be hoping to sleep it off."

"If they dunna wake up any time soon 'twill be fine with me."

Fergus nodded. "Can I see ye to yer room? I'd not be wanting to leave ye here alone."

What sounded like a bellow of rage brought immediate silence to all in the hall.

"Never!"

It was her father. She started toward the antechamber where the men had gone but Fergus held her fast. "Ye best not interfere."

The men who had appeared deeply inebriated suddenly sobered, drawing their weapons, clearly unsure of where the danger lay. Doors slammed in the distance. Loud voices came closer. It was the Meic Lochlainn, not her father.

Fergus began to draw his sword but he was too late. The huge man closing in on her sank his dagger into the man's chest without missing a step. The captain dropped to her feet.

"We need to see this consummated." Aodh Meic Lochlainn replaced the bloodied blade and grabbed her by the arm, dragging her to the stairs.

Tisa looked behind her at Fergus, his blood spreading beneath him. She couldn't speak. She couldn't breathe. Her father came out of the anteroom. Darragh stood beside him.

"Father?" was all she could get out as she was dragged toward the stairs.

The crowd of strange men followed behind. She strained to find her father in the sea of heads but he was lost behind her.

"Nae. Stop. Where are ye taking me?" She pulled against the hurtful grip on her arm.

Darragh appeared on the other side of her and faced his father. "I will see to this, Father."

"Are ye sure ye're able to?" His words dripped with derision.

Tisa didn't understand this interplay.

"Please," she said. "My father."

They continued moving to the top of the stairs.

"Release my wife!"

Darragh's commanding tone brought a look of surprise from his father. They paused to face each other. His expression of surprise changed to one of respect. Tipping his head, he released his hold and raised his hand, palm out. Tisa rubbed at her arm.

"As ye will, my son. See to it then." His jaw tightened, he moved in close, his eyes widened in warning. "Let. There. Be. No. Doubt!"

"None."

Aodh glanced down at his daughter-in-law. Her cheeks heated at his blatant inspection of her bosom. He wrapped a hand around the back of her neck and pulled her flat against him, his wet lips covering her own. When he shoved his tongue into her mouth, Tisa gagged. With one large hand on her bottom, he jerked her against him. Evidence of his arousal hard against her. Just as suddenly he released her and she fell back against Darragh who thankfully caught her fall.

"Have at her, then I'll take my turn."

"Not this night." Darragh's commanding tone remained. He turned his gaze on her then smiled, moving in as close as his father had been. "So, show me to yer chambers, wife."

The grip he took of her arm belied the soft tone he'd used with her. She hesitated but a moment. Surely resistance would result in harsher behavior from them both. With her husband alone, she may be able to calm his ire, make him see reason. She led him to the far end of the hall and the stairs that led up to the single room. Her room.

"Please. Dunna—" Tisa said.

"Nae! I give the orders."

Mayhap not. She couldn't catch a breath. "But my father—"

"All contracts have been signed, sweet little Tisa. We are indeed wed. Ye are now mine to do with as I please."

She paused in front of the door at the top of the stairs. If he would but listen. "With no—no service or wit—witnessing, it seems—"

He shoved open the door. She didn't move.

"Witnessing? Ye wanted witnessing?"

"Yea. I had hoped for som—"

"Then ye shall have it." He gave her a radiant smile. "Of the consummation."

The crowd pushed up from below.

"Nae. I—The loud sound. My father objected—"

"Merely surprised at our terms."

Tisa couldn't wipe the confusion from her face. "I dunna understand."

"Ye're my wife now. Ye need not understand anything beyond that."

Darragh smiled for the benefit of those further down the steps, no doubt. The dirty faces of eager men leered up at them. Their eyes wide with anticipation. Tisa was going to be sick.

He pulled her unyielding body into the room that seemed suddenly foreign to her. The small bed with curtains pulled back—her bed—was his total focus. He released her to untie the material. Tisa wrapped her arms around herself. Her stomach tightening as each heavy curtain fell into place. The *swooshing* noise took on the horrifying sound of a sweeping blade. She should be glad they would have no one seeing the actual act but to have this man take her now, in her own bed, seemed a greater violation.

"Get on the bed." Darragh had dropped his voice but it was an order none-the-less.

Five men had squeezed into the room through the door her husband had left open. Their eyes glazed over with lust.

"Wait," Darragh grabbed at her although she hadn't moved. "Remove yer gown. Let them see *all* of my *wife*."

Tisa froze with fear. His hands were on her in an instant, turning her to face them as he unlaced her from behind. She pushed back against him, trying to turn away from the doorway. "Wait. Please."

She tried to stay his hands but they were adept and her gown was quickly falling away from her, leaving her all but exposed with the thin material of her chemise beneath. Cheers as even more men pushed through the narrow doorway for a glimpse.

"Please."

Tisa tried to cover herself with her hands but Darragh yanked them away. She closed her eyes against the assault. The cool air on her legs moved up her body. Her eyes flew open. He was removing her chemise. She held her arms rigid to her sides and clamped her jaw. She refused to loosen her hold even when he stopped and moved in close to look into her eyes.

"Shall I allow them to watch as I spread yer legs?" His breath hot on her face, he measured her emotions. "As I impale ye on my prick?"

Her breath stilled. Would he really do that? He smiled at her and removed the dagger from his waist.

As if in a dream, she watched as he used the blade to slice the material down the front. Sounds became muffled. The rending of the material. The cold on her bare skin. A collective groan from the onlookers. Shouts of congratulations. Lewd remarks on what they would like to do. Darragh stood to one side with a crooked grin.

"What are ye waiting for?" a toothless man shouted his encouragement. "If ye dunna take her, I will."

"My cock is stiff as a board just looking at her," another man added.

Darragh pushed her onto the bed and followed, the curtains closing around them. Entombing them. He shoved her flat onto her back, pressing her shoulders down. His face suffused with anger.

"Spread yer legs." He spat the words at her.

Tisa couldn't catch a breath. She did as he ordered.

He pulled his trews down to reveal himself then stopped.

"More." He didn't hide his irritation with her.

His legs dropped between her knees. He was fully clothed. Fumbling for something at his waist, he pinched at her nipple with his other hand. His upper body surging against her, the bed groaned beneath them. A look of triumph on his face, he held a small vial in front of her and unstopped the top.

The smile that creased his eyes was back. "Ye'll be a virgin no more."

He brought the bottle down between them, to the juncture of her legs, and arched his body away. A cold wetness seeped into her most intimate area, dripping down. Latching on to her shoulder, he bit down. She cried out in pain.

The others began to clap and cheer.

"Well done, man."

Darragh bounced on the bed. The creaking sound of the ropes below filling their small space and the men's imagination.

"That's it man."

"Give it to her good."

"Dunna hold back now."

Tisa watched as Darragh worked out the machinations of her wedding night. It seemed to be happening to someone else. The stickiness between her legs. The pain at her shoulder. The pinching of her breasts. Then it was over. He stilled himself.

"Deed done," he whispered the words. A shared secret. Hovering over her, he brushed her hair out of her face with a surprisingly gentle hand. "It wasn't that bad, was it?"

She cringed. He wanted flattery now? For a deed *not* done?

He pushed himself away, jerked down his trews and pulled out his limp length. With the vial safely hidden, he wiped some of the red liquid along his tarse. Spreading the curtains, he was met with cheers. He yanked up his trews with great, dramatic flair and raised his arms, allowing the curtains to close behind him.

"Another drink!" he announced.

More cheers and congratulations as they made their way down the stairs.

"Ye done well, man."

"How was she?"

Tisa dared not to move. The voices drifted further way until they were no longer heard. The men had gone back down to the Great Hall.

The curtain to her right was jerked opened and Tisa recoiled in fear. An old woman she'd never seen before began tying back the curtains. A tight covering over her hair, her eyes bulged as she moved about the bed doing the same at the other three posts. Tisa covered herself with her hands as best she could.

"The sheet," the woman said.

Tisa forced herself to sit up. Between her legs was a large, red stain. Her "virginal blood." She jumped away from the offending sight. Three other women stood between her and the door as if afraid she may bolt for freedom. None of them were familiar. One shook her head as if in pity. The bulging-eyed woman pulled the covering off the bed.

"I'll get someone to bring ye up warm water."

"Caireann." Tisa was relieved to hear her own voice. "Please send Caireann."

The woman shrugged and the four of them left, closing the door tight behind them.

Tisa stood naked beside her bed. The tears she'd been keeping at bay came in full force. She dropped to the ground. Humiliation. Dread. Fear. Relief. All of her emotions pushed against her brain making it difficult to think. It could have been much worse. He could have actually raped her as she was afeared he might. Instead, he'd barely touched her. She dragged the heavy, wool blanket from the foot of the bed and covered herself with it. Curling into herself, she slept.

Chapter Four

"The food stores will not last a fortnight."

Tadhg closed his eyes and took a slow intake of air before again looking at the dark-haired man before him. "And ye're just apprising me of this now?"

His ruddy complexion deepened. "I dinna want to burden ye with yer father so ill."

Lughaidh, a small man with a mop of brown hair that hung past his shoulders, had been appointed keeper of the stores ever since Moira the Wise had passed. He was a good, loyal kinsmen but Tadhg was convinced he needed a kick in the arse right about now.

"There was nothing ye could do about it with yer father breaking off from the O'Brien before we'd brought in our share of the harvest."

The man was right. Tadhg might have had some vague idea of approaching Roland O'Brien with a new alliance afore now. Now Tadhg knew the reason for his father's break. It was a little more difficult to go begging for food from the man.

"I need information, Lughaidh. Dunna be holding back from me for any reason. 'Tis what I need from ye."

The tall man nodded and accepted the seat on the bench beside his new chieftain. "Anything I can help ye with, Tadhg, ye ken I will."

Tadhg shook his head. "How many have gone off to the shore?"

"Twelve men. They've not had an easy time of it though." Lughaidh scratched his head. "Two of the men drowned in a storm. What the others brought back has been getting us through this fall."

"None was put up for winter?"

"'Tis been a vicious season. The ocean's near black with turmoil. The fish are farther out and harder to catch. Sending them out again will not do much good."

"They have to try. Who was it that perished?"

"Flann and his son. We've two widows now to care for with three wee ones between them."

The more desperate he was feeling, the more Tadhg refused to even consider going to Roland O'Brien. The more he resented the man for holding back on their rightful share of the harvest. The more he hated the man for seducing his mother. Certainly his mother would never have gone off to another man, not when her husband was here, seeing to all her needs, loving her. The betrayal stung like a vicious wasp. Tadhg had believed they were truly in love with each other. How could he be so naive?

"Tadhg?" Lughaidh's face was lined with worry.

"I dinna hear ye."

"Ye've a lot of worries on yer shoulder. I wish I could be of more help to ye."

Tadhg heaved a heavy sigh. "So there's no other choice in the matter?"

"Ye mean than to ask the O'Brien?"

"*O'Brien*—what a laugh. He's not great. Or a warrior. Never was."

Lughaidh pulled back as if he'd been slapped. After a pause, he spoke. "I've never heard ye be so cruel, Tadhg. Roland O'Brien is past his prime but he did his best. Having eight children and not a mighty warrior among them is a cruel life. That he's used his son's marriages to ensure peace with other clans was only possible because of our clan. He's relied on us to be his defenders. I dinna mean to be slighting yer own father, but to leave the man with no assistance when the western clans are making moves against them seems pitiless."

Tadhg's blood boiled but there'd be no explaining his reason. They needed to trust him. Lughaidh was a good man. He spoke out of desperation. Tadhg was finding he had less and less sympathy for others and an ever shortening length of patience.

"Methinks it best if ye leave me. Now."

Lughaidh nearly tripped over the bench in his haste to escape. No doubt Tadhg's expression was not as schooled as he had believed.

Damn. How was he to provide for the families depending on him? He knew they'd gone and helped in the sowing despite his father's proclamation that the alliance was dissolved. They must have thought he'd gone daft but knew they'd still need to eat. They had every right to what the O'Briens were storing away for the winter.

"Cormac!" Tadhg's bellow went far beyond the long hut he sat in.

"Aye?" Cormac was red faced and wheezing with the speed he'd run up the hill with.

Tadhg steadied himself before responding. "I need my horse readied. And find Sean. He'll be accompanying me."

Cormac nodded and headed for the door. The lack of questions from the ever inquisitive boy was a clear indication of the fear Tadhg's black mood was bringing to his clan. He just couldn't find a way out of it. He had been betrayed in the worst way. His father even more so. But the example of all that was good and gentle had been his mother. It was hard to reconcile the reality to his imagination.

"Where am I going with ye?" Sean's tone indicated his irritation at being called on unexpectedly.

"Wherever I tell ye to go with me."

"What kind of shite answer is that?"

"It's the answer ye get for showing disrespect to yer chieftain."

Sean lowered his head. He pursed his lips. "Ye want to try and kick my arse? Would that help ye with yer irritation at losing Tisa?"

"*Try* and kick yer arse?"

Sean smiled. His even, white teeth were clearly visible through his heavy beard. "Yea, try. Ye ken ye won't best me... unless I am ordered to yield to ye by my chieftain."

The promise of release the fighting would give him was quickly deflated. "I'd not need ye to let me win, Sean."

"But ye'll never know."

Sean's intense glare made Tadhg uncomfortable but Sean refused to ask again.

"We're going to the O'Brien."

His friend's face lit up.

"It's not to reinstate the alliance. That can never happen."

"Why not, Tadhg? What could have happened that was so unforgiveable?"

Ye'll never ken.

"Enough! I need to see if we can work out an agreement and feed ourselves through winter."

Cormac stood in the doorway but avoided Tadhg's eyes. "The horses are readied."

Sean glanced at Tadhg, a disgusted look on his face that seemed to ask do-ye-even-need-to-intimidate-the-boy but he held his tongue.

"My thanks, Cormac." Tadhg tried to sound less riled but the boy left without looking directly at him. Tadhg glanced toward Sean. "Well?"

"Ye're turning into an ogre. Scaring away little children. I dunna think ye'll be sweet talking Roland O'Brien with that fierce scowl."

"Enough, Sean."

The tall blond shrugged and Tadhg led the way to the horses waiting for them on the path. Cormac was nowhere to be found.

"He dinna get us any supplies for the trip."

Sean jumped onto his horse in one leap and grabbed the reins. "An ogre."

He urged his horse to the path leading north without a backward glance. Tadhg's blood ran hot in his veins. He'd like to take the man up on his offer of a fight. Kicking Sean's arse would give him a most improved outlook. But his clan still needed food and he still needed to go begging for it from that adulterous dog. Best to save his strength.

By midday next, they were approaching the large, stone castle that housed the O'Brien. Its building was attributed to Brian Boru himself and dating back to before the Battle of Clontarf. The king had great sons but many were lost in the battle. Roland O'Brien was the third in his line to sire many strong daughters but only feeble sons. It was as if they'd lost the favor of God Almighty. The treaty with the MacNaughton gave them the needed protection. So why jeopardize it by sleeping with his closest friend's wife?

A growl rose in his throat. Tadhg had to stop going over this time and time again. He had no answers. He had only the truth of the matter. Sean pulled up alongside him when he stopped, searching his face.

"Ye're clearly troubled, Tadhg. Come to new terms with the O'Brien and see this done with."

"Ye dunna ken what ye're talking about." Tadhg all but hissed the words. "Dunna be telling me how to handle this. Ye dunna ken all there is."

"Then tell me." Sean's eyes rounded in a look of vulnerability that Tadhg didn't often see on his stoic friend. "If 'tis not about Tisa, then what is it eating away at ye?"

Tadhg took a shaky breath, his nostrils flaring as he struggled for composure. His friend's unexpected show of compassion busted large holes in his defensive wall.

"I canna tell ye. Trust me. I," Tadhg glanced around, "need a bit of time for myself."

He jumped from his horse and led her to the small clearing. Sean did not follow and remained on his horse but his eyes followed his chieftain. Tadhg flexed his shoulders, working out the knots from the long, hard ride. The time had come. He needed to face a man he'd always respected and looked to for guidance. The man that turned out to be nothing but a lying adulterer. This wasn't helping. He dropped the horse's lead and continued down the path, between the oaks and maples just losing their leaves in preparation for the winter to come.

The path was familiar and led down to the brook. The same brook where he'd sat with Tisa many times and talked about their lives together. He continued to the river's edge and hunkered down to drag his fingers through the water's coldness. He could almost hear his love's sweet laugh with the trickling of the water over the stones. Bracken grew large along the banks, bleached golden from the morning sun.

That was where he'd confessed his love for her and taken her in his arms. He'd promised he'd protect her and provide for her. At ten years, there'd been nothing more he'd wanted from her. Any time they spent together after that, he would find a way to take her in his arms again. She felt so right there. Fitting perfectly against him.

When he'd held her that last time and her small breasts had pressed into him, his body had come alive. It became perfectly clear to him. She would grow into a beautiful woman, he would take her to wife, and he thought he understood what that meant. He would hold her against him at night with nothing between them. It wasn't until he was a bit older that he imagined what it would be like to lay with her. To take her virginity. To finally release his passion. A moan of longing filled the air around him. The need cried out from the depths of his soul. His Tisa. He wanted her still. Like an ache in his heart that wouldn't lessen.

Mayhap he could work this out with her father. Mayhap the past was something he could overlook and move away from. Mayhap they could build a new alliance based on a new understanding. A new understanding would make it possible for him to have his lovely Tisa to wife.

"Is aught amiss?"

Tadhg hadn't heard Sean come up behind him.

"Aye. I was thinking on the best approach with Roland."

"Ye sounded as if ye were longing for yer Tisa."

Sean never kept his thoughts to himself when it mattered.

"I suppose I was."

"If there's a way to overlook the offense, Tadhg, it would be best to do that." Sean paused. "I dunna ken what the offense was so only ye can decide if 'tis possible. I just ken ye have a deep need for her, a great love."

"'Twas a great offense."

If he hadn't learned of his mother's betrayal, things would be different. If his father had not spent the time in the chapel to look over their line as Tadhg had. Not knowing would have made things simple.

The far off cry of the puffins along the rocks drifted to them. Sean offered no more advice but waited behind him. A show of support for whatever decision Tadhg came to. Was it for the good of the clan that they starved through the winter? With the meat they were able to trap and hunt their only sustenance? No. That was not what was best for his clan. He needed to see this offense set aside. Did the O'Brien even know why Padraig had broken their alliance? Did the O'Brien know he'd fathered another child with Tadhg's mother?

Tadhg sighed and stood. He had much to discuss with Roland O'Brien. At least now he had a bit of peace. His father's betrayal may not be something Tadhg could set to rights. Tadhg needed to look ahead. What was best for all was what he needed to think on.

When Tadhg finally faced him, Sean's expression quickly changed from surprise to a satisfied smile. "Ye've come to a decision."

"Aye. I have. Let us see if we can get an audience with the great Roland O'Brien. We may have food in our clan's belly for the winter after all."

Tadhg patted Sean on the shoulder. They walked in companionable silence toward the horses.

In one swift motion, they mounted.

"We may even stay the night," Tadhg offered then urged his horse toward the wall surrounding the castle. Mayhap it would not be such a bad day after all.

Chapter Five

Roland O'Brien was at his wit's end with these pompous warmongers. If he'd had the slightest hope of making amends with the MacNaughton, he'd never have welcomed the Meic Lochlainn. He had no idea what had transpired to anger Padraig.

Moira had been distant as well these past years. When her brother, Ronan, came with news of her passing, Roland had been deeply saddened. There had been no communication winter last that she'd even taken ill. That had been the first blow but the man had brought more bad news. Padraig had dissolved their alliance even while his own people were working alongside the O'Brien clan. Tisa and Tadhg's betrothal was broken as well.

The news had been devastating. Ronan offered no further explanation but he expressed a certainty that Padraig MacNaughton would not be changing his mind. He was far too angry.

Roland sighed and glanced again at the hefty, gray-haired man beside him—Aodh Meic Lochlainn. It was Ronan that had suggested the alliance with the Meic Lochlainn. Ronan who had given his acceptance of Tisa as a match for Aodh Meic Lochlainn's son.

Aodh Meic Lochlainn had the manners of a wild beast and again took the most succulent meat from the platter before them. Ronan sat to his right, eating little, but keeping a watchful eye on all around him.

"Ye've a well-stocked castle, Roland," Aodh spoke as he gnawed on his food.

Roland waved his hand to pass the tray of food. His stomach was in knots. He glanced toward the stairs for the hundredth time and offered a prayer that Darragh had handled the bedding of his daughter with more consideration than his father displayed.

"And yer son has not come down yet."

"They've only just begun, Roland." Aodh slapped him on the back. Hard. "I doubt he'll be overlong."

Aodh laughed and took another bite of the near meatless leg. A strange man. The wounding of his guard had pushed Roland to the edge of his patience. Ronan had stepped in to diffuse the situation and minimize the affront. Their promise of even more warriors stationed within the castle had been an offer Roland could not pass up. The O'Neill had been coveting his family lands for generations. Word of the MacNaughton's withdrawal of support had quickly spread. The O'Brien was defenseless. He felt much like a wounded deer just waiting for the wolves to attack.

The loud clatter of a crowd making their way down the stairs had Roland standing. A shiver of fear worked down his spine. It wasn't his daughter but his new son-in-law. Aodh stood as well, wiping his greasy mouth on his sleeve and smoothing down his beard. Roland sensed the man's tension despite the wide grin on his face.

Darragh was surrounded by his men. Slapping him on the back. Shouting congratulations. Roland waited, his eyes fixed on the stairs, unable to take a deep breath. He needed to see Tisa. She did not come down.

Roland needed to see how she fared. He dropped the hand cloth on his seat preparing to leave but Aodh grabbed his arm.

"Is that any way to show my son yer support, Roland?"

Roland ripped his arm out of the man's grasp. "Was yer ushering my daughter up the stairs for her bedding before even a kiss of blessing from her father any way to treat my daughter?"

Aodh dropped his hand to the sword at his side. "I ken we do things differently in Inishowen."

"I ken that when ye said I had to commit my own warriors for *yer* battles." Roland stood his ground. He glanced again toward the empty stairs. Tisa was not there. "Conquering is not what we are about here. We are a peaceful people."

"Aye. Always defending. I ken it well." Aodh measured each word. A warning. "What I dunna ken is how ye managed to keep yer fine castle and all yer land for so long."

With the help of our allies.

Roland cringed inside. Padraig had been like a brother. They shared all things in common. It would have been their lands, MacNaughton and O'Brien, once Tisa and Tadhg were joined. Padraig's missive breaking the alliance had dealt him a serious blow. The offer of any of his sons to Padraig's daughter, Brighit, had been a ruse since he'd already married three of them off. It had been rejected.

Roland had waited and prayed that despite Ronan's beliefs to the contrary, Padraig would change his mind and honor their agreement. An agreement that went back three generations. Breaking Tisa's heart had not been an easy thing to do. Moira had kept her son away for so long, Roland had the small hope that Tisa might have forgotten him. That was not the case.

An elderly woman came down the stairs and into the hall. She held a large sheet in her hands and was followed by three others. Witnesses.

"My lord," she addressed Aodh in a loud voice so there would be no mistaking her words.

"Yes, Lilith?" Aodh said.

"The bedding cloth."

Darragh came to stand beside his father. He crossed his arms. His grin barely containable as he looked on. The woman shook out the bloodstained sheet.

"Ah." Aodh beamed with pride and glanced toward his son.

Roland's stomach churned. The man must have ripped Tisa asunder with that much blood. He moved to find his daughter but Aodh held him fast. He shook his head, a clear warning.

"We will stay and celebrate," Aodh said. "The bedding has proven yer daughter a virgin. We are well pleased. Our clans are now joined."

Aodh raised his mug, the special one he'd brought for the celebration, cast in gold and adorned with jewels. Roland relaxed his stance and lifted his own mug with a lot less enthusiasm. If he could but see his daughter and know she had survived, he could pretend to celebrate with these men. Now, he worried about the repercussions of his hasty decision. He should never have listened to Ronan.

Tadhg slowed his horse as he approached the castle. There were no guards visible from the signal tower or at the gate.

"This lack of protection surprises me."

"The hour is still early. Mayhap they anticipated no problems."

Tadhg snorted. "An attack is not usually anticipated, Sean."

The tall man tipped his head. "I was merely trying to ease yer angst."

"Hail." Tadhg called toward the tower. "We've come to see the O'Brien."

A small head popped up from the tower before dipping down again. Despite the distance, a loud commotion could be heard. Tadhg placed his hand on his sword as did Sean. After a moment a man stood, his helmet crooked on his head. Tadhg recognized him as one of Roland's men, Breandan. He was still in training without much hope of ever toughening up the last Tadhg had seen him.

"Greetings, Tadhg." The young man smiled. "Ye've missed the celebration."

Sean and Tadhg exchanged glances. The boy appeared inebriated. Another man's head popped up beside him then ducked again. The guard said something they couldn't make out before turning back to them. His smile gone.

"What are ye about?" The tone had shifted to one of aggression. "Ye have not been sent for. Why are ye here?"

"Breandan, what are *ye* about and who have ye got in there with ye?" Tadhg asked.

"Oh, just let them in." The whiny voice could be heard from within the tower now. A man's voice.

"Ye may come in. Open the gate." Breandan shouted to someone within the walls and the gates were opened.

Breandan's head quickly disappeared within.

"Breandan seems to be playing soldier with another man in yonder tower," Sean said in a quiet voice.

"Methinks ye're right." Tadhg's surprise carried even in his whispered tone. "I had my own ideas regarding the man and his unusual predilection but I'd never thought he'd be so blatant about his preference for his own sex."

Sean glanced behind them as they entered through the gates. "Or while he was on duty no less."

"Mayhap I should mention it to Roland."

Sean looked thoughtful. "Why is he not aware of the goings-on here? And where are the troops of his household with all this happening?"

His question was a valid one. Many of the soldiers they passed within the bailey, most which were not known to Tadhg, appeared intoxicated as well. Even the young boy who came to see to their horses was a bit shaky.

Sean remained outside while Tadhg followed yet another unfamiliar man into the Great Hall. Roland sat in his chair, staring far off as if deep in thought.

"A visitor."

Roland started when he finally noticed Tadhg. The smile that began quickly shifted to a frown.

"What have ye here?"

Tadhg forced his hands to his sides. A show of peace. His innards sloshed about in turmoil with the mixed emotions he felt. Rage. Betrayal.

Love. Respect.

"Roland. How fare ye?"

"Is that what ye've come to ask?"

"Be easy. My father has passed. I am seeing to my duty as chieftain."

Roland's eyes rounded at his words but quickly narrowed again. He worked to hide his feelings for Padraig, but he was not successful.

"My heart feels yer loss, Tadhg. I had great love for both yer parents."

The mention of his mother left a bad taste in Tadhg's mouth. He cleared his throat and unclenched his hands, forcing them to remain at his sides. This course of civility was harder than he had anticipated. Best to get to the point of the visit.

"My thanks. And how fare yer fields this harvest past?"

Roland's scowl did little to ease Tadhg's tension. He wondered if he would respond at all but then he began a slow nod.

"We have had a plentiful harvest. Our animals will not want for food. Neither will our people. Even a long winter will be of little hardship to us."

The blatant bragging caught Tadhg off guard. He hadn't expected Roland to need to twist a knife in his back.

"And ye?"

Tadhg nearly choked on his gasp. The bastard. He knew exactly why Tadhg had come and he was not going to make it easy.

"Tadhg," Sean said as he entered the hall. "Roland."

Roland tipped his head in acknowledgement. "Ye've grown, Sean, if 'tis even possible."

"Aye, I've grown several inches since last we met. And I train even harder now with not three but four opponents at a time."

The pressure of the knife eased a bit. The look of amazement that crossed Roland's face made Sean's boast well worth it.

"Roman got away from the lad. I need yer horse to get him back. Should I wait for ye?"

Tadhg glanced at Roland, measuring his increased anxiety before answering.

"Nae. See to yer horse."

Roland kept his eyes on Sean until he was out of sight. He spoke without looking directly at Tadhg. "So what are ye about, Tadhg? Yer da saw fit to break our alliance and the betrothal." The anger Tadhg saw in his eyes when he finally faced him was palatable. "Are ye here with yer tail between yer legs begging for food?"

A melodious gasp from the far stairs had both men turning toward the woman standing there. Tisa. Her face was radiant where she stood surrounded by the sunlight filtering through the single window. Her eyes, indeed, sparkled. Tadhg had begun to think he imagined that. Her young figure had blossomed into a woman full-grown. A woman of great beauty.

She took a step closer but stopped. Her lips parted. Her eyes wide. He drank in the sight of her from the long, dark tresses falling over her shoulders and hugging every curve, to her bare feet—yes, she was barefooted. His eyes met hers and he smiled. She'd always disliked having her feet covered, or her legs. Even foregoing warmer hose beneath her gown in the chill of winter.

"I like the feel of my skin. It's smooth and silky."

She had been ten years old and barefoot, hunkered down in a foot of snow beside the roosting chickens, rummaging through the straw for eggs hidden by the hens. He was three and ten and became obsessed with the need to touch that silken skin.

The sudden memory of her lips against his cheek hit him. Warm and soft. He'd dreamed of that kiss and much more over the years. Even imagined his own hands slipping up over those delicate feet, up her soft calves, and along her thighs to feel their softness.

"Tadhg." No doubt the only word she dare say without her father bidding her to speak. She sounded out of breath.

Tadhg had to force himself not to close the distance between them. Not to take her in arms that ached to surround her. Not to press her voluptuous length against his own and feel her breath on his cheek and taste her mouth anew.

She should be his. Surely she still could be. He glanced back to her father and licked his lips. If he used great diplomacy perhaps it could still work out.

"Yea, Roland. I have come to make terms with ye. Otherwise my clan will not make it through the winter. I dunna ken—"

"And I ken even less." Roland's voice boomed. "Ye come here begging for food? Well, there's a price."

Tisa moved closer, her head down. She appeared guilty of... something. Tadhg could not understand. He needed to speak to her. Alone. To tell her how much he loved her still. And still wanted her as his wife no matter the cost to his own pride.

"Name yer price." He glanced toward Tisa before facing Roland.

Roland grimaced. "Is that what ye want? Tisa? 'Tis too late. She has been wed to another."

The room shifted beneath Tadhg. His throat squeezed tight. He couldn't remember how to breathe.

"But if ye still want my food—"

Roland's mouth was moving and Tadhg struggled to make sense of what he was saying. How could she be married? She was his.

"—perhaps we can come to an agreement with ye offering all that we've ever needed from ye and yer clan—"

Air burst into his lungs and Tadhg took a deep swallow. Roland continued talking but the light around them dimmed. No!

"—ye and Sean and a score of yer best warriors will come to me spring next. Ye'll be my warriors to command until the Hunter's Moon. Are ye agreed?"

Tadhg turned toward Tisa. He swore he could see tears on her cheeks. He opened his mouth but no words came out.

Roland reached toward his daughter and she came to stand by his side, her hand white where she gripped his as if her life depended on it. Tadhg felt the knife in his back as it was shoved in deeper and deeper, piercing his very heart.

Tadhg stood erect. His face tight against the emotions he dared not show. "Aye, Roland. 'Tis agreed."

"I will see to yer provisions this very night."

Footsteps to the left caught his attention. The final blow. His Uncle Ronan stood in the doorway. Confusion overtook Tadhg as he counted through the days since his sister had left for the Priory. It wasn't possible for their uncle to be back from escorting her.

"Why are ye here?" Tadhg feared he was about to lose control. "Why are ye not with Brighit?" He was in the man's face in two strides. "What have ye done with my little sister?"

Tadhg swung a hard fist into the side of the man's jaw. Pain shot up his arm and he shook it off.

Ronan staggered back. Roland was there grabbing at Tadhg's arms, pulling him away.

"This is a powerful man of great influences. Dunna lay hands on him."

Tadhg jerked his arms out of the older man's hold. How dare that adulterous swine touch him?

"Why aren't ye seeing to Brighit's protection?"

Ronan reached toward Tadhg. "Settle down, boy. Brighit is fine. I found another to take her."

"How do ye ken she's fine? My father trusted *ye* to take her and none other."

"'Tis my own man, Ivan. He will guard her with his life. I swear it."

"Nae! *Ye* were to guard her with *yer* life. My father's dying request and ye lie to him?"

"Nae, Tadhg. A simple matter. She is safe."

His blustering assurances meant nothing to Tadhg.

"Without the protection of her family? Nae!" Tadhg struggled for composure. He needed to keep control here of all places. "Ye are no longer welcome on MacNaughton land."

He took a last glance at Tisa. Her shoulders back. Her head held high. Surely they had not been tears of sadness if there had been tears at all. This was a woman determined. Determined to make the most out of her situation. Whoever she had married, she would give him children and see to his home. She would live a life without Tadhg. Without even thinking about him. She would go on with her life. That's what women did.

"See to the provisions." Tadhg pushed past his uncle, shoving him out of the way, to the door.

If he never saw this place or these people ever again, 'twould be too soon.

Sean stood in the small bailey, casually wrapping an arm around Roman's snout.

"I thought ye had a horse get away from ye." Tadhg took the reins from the stable boy's hands but addressed his friend.

"I just wanted to see the old man. See how ye were doing." Sean followed Tadhg's lead and mounted his horse. "Not well."

Urging his horse toward the opening with a slow gait, Tadhg said, "We have food for winter."

Sean smiled, "Fine. And Tisa?"

Tadhg could barely spit the words out. "She has been given to another."

"Nae!" Sean shot up alongside him. "Who? Could ye not break the betrothal?"

"'Tis more than a betrothal. 'Tis already been done." His world was falling apart. "My Uncle Ronan was within as well."

"What?" Sean roared his disbelief. "Is he not the one accompanying Brighit?" He yanked at Tadhg's reins. "Tell me!"

"That devil's spawn had another bring my sister to the Priory."

Sean's eyes scanned the area. Tadhg could see his anger mounting and his assessing the situation. "I'll kill him."

"Nae!" Tadhg ordered with authority. "We will not spill blood this day. We will go find my sister and see to her protection ourselves."

Sean's face tightened in determination, but his eyes held a haunting disbelief. Clearly, Ronan was a dishonorable man but before they could take their revenge against him, they needed to get to Brighit, to protect her.

"But. Ken. This. If anything has happened to her, we will hunt Ronan down, and we will kill him."

Chapter Six

Tisa didn't dare to move. If she even breathed, her mouth would open and she would began a tirade at her father that may never end. Her body stiff, she turned toward the stairs.

"Wait!" Her father approached but stopped short of actually touching her.

Her hands gripped the material of her dress. She clenched her teeth to keep from opening her mouth. How dare he address her now? She had spent the entire night alone in her bed, rolled into a ball. Petrified. Imagining that every sound in the hall was her husband coming back. In the light of morning, she realized that was the most ridiculous part of this whole thing. Her husband would not come back. Her husband wanted nothing to do with her. He had no desire to be with her even to prove that she was chaste.

"I think we should talk."

Pain shot through her jaw. She would not be speaking to him now. Not ever.

Tadhg's face flashed through her mind. The look of betrayal. The look of pain. Then intense anger. Tisa was not to speak. Her father had trained her well. But she prayed with all her strength that her father would speak. That he would explain to Tadhg why she had wed another. Tell him how she had been forced to marry against her will. That her father had given her no consideration in the choosing of her husband, in replacing the man she loved more than life itself.

The tears had started as soon as she recognized Tadhg. A man full grown. Broad shoulders filling out his leine that hugged nicely across his chest. A heavy broadsword at his waist where she'd last seen a lighter, training blade. His strong legs strapped with leather ties over firm calves.

He was more handsome than she could have ever imagined he would be. And he was lost to her. Forever.

"Please, Tisa."

She whirled around to face her father. "I dunna wish to hear anything ye have to say—"

"I tried—"

"Not hard enough to spare me the humiliation I experienced at the hands of my *husband*." She spat the word at him. "He dinna care for shielding me from his men. He bared me in front of all of them and their... their leering... their taunts." She gulped down the tears that threatened. She would not cry. Not now. "I have been disgraced before the very people that I will soon be living among."

Her father's eyes widened. His mortification tugged at her heart. She tugged right back.

"And when the only man I have ever—*will ever* love comes to ye? Ye dunna even have the decency to tell him of my objections to this forced marriage?" Her nostrils flared as she pushed past the pain. "Nae. I have no words to alleviate yer guilt. Ye are dead to me."

With a stiff gait, she crossed to the stairs. Her *husband* had informed her they would be leaving within the hour. She needed to finish preparing. Alone in her room, memories assailed her. The happy times. The warmth of her father's loving embrace when she'd tumbled off the horse. The sweetness of her first kiss from Tadhg. All this she was expected to walk away from? Just leave it behind?

The impossibility of her situation pricked like pins into her skin. Tadhg had come. He was here. She got to the hall and ran to the other stairs that followed the back of the great room. She could not just let him leave. She nearly tumbled forward with the speed that she flew down the wooden steps.

Her breath caught in her chest, she wove around the men filling the narrow space behind the castle. If she could get through the crowd, surely she would be able to get to Tadhg before he left. The smell of unwashed bodies closed in on her as she pressed between men whose faces she ignored. Tadhg was the only face she needed to see.

Around the corner she spotted him. He had paused in the shadow of the passage. She moved toward him taking in the sight of him. The great height. The wide breadth of his shoulders. The solid warrior stance. Her young lad had grown into a formidable man.

"Tadhg." She but whispered his name and he turned toward her as if attuned to the sound of her voice. One riding glove on, the other grasped between his fingers, and a deep scowl on his handsome face. His fierce anger slowed her step. "Tadhg."

"Aye. So ye admit ye ken me?" His eyes held hers and she saw his pain.

His loss.

"My father would not allow me to speak to ye."

"Or yer husband, I would assume." It was painful to hear his biting tone.

Tisa glanced down, unsure what she should say. Or what she should do. He came to stand before her. She closed her eyes and breathed in the male scent of him, leather and horses. Her Tadhg. The lightest touch of his finger against her cheek, he caressed her. She opened her eyes. He cupped her cheek and she turned into it wishing she could place a kiss there.

"So ye've wed another?"

She longed to reach out, to place her hand flat against his solid chest, to feel his heartbeat beneath her palm, to know the touch of his lips if she could but lean closer. She did not move.

"Not by choice."

He dropped his hand and her heart lurched at the loss of his touch.

"Yer father ordered it."

The words would not come. How did she tell him she would never belong to anyone but him? That he would always be her love, the husband of her heart? And she would spend the rest of her life empty for want of him?

Tadhg turned and walked away from her. She watched him go.

"Ye go below and wait for me there." It was Darragh. He was coming into her room.

She wiped at the tears, her back to the door when he entered. "Ye're not ready yet?'

He huffed behind her. She turned to him, her eyes downcast, her hands folded before her.

"Beg pardon. I have been sorely troubled with deciding what to leave behind from a lifetime's worth of memories."

He barked a laugh. "'Tis simple." He pulled her arm and pushed her toward the door. "All decided."

He came up behind her, urging her toward the stairs despite her struggles against him. "What? I bring nothing?"

"Ye bring the clothes on yer back. 'Tis more than enough."

"But—" Tisa grabbed at the small basket that hung on a peg at her door. Her herbs. Her medicines. Precious cuttings were being knocked onto the floor as she struggled to take hold of it.

Darragh grabbed it at the last moment. She nearly tumbled down the steps with his shove but was able to right herself just as she entered the hall.

Her father-in-law stood there, a scowl on his face as he met her gaze. "What is amiss?"

"Darragh will not allo—"

"We are ready, Father." Darragh glared at her. "Let us be gone from this place."

Aodh puckered his lips in a disdainful scowl. "Ye need to settle yer temper, Darragh." He glanced around the now empty hall. "Be civil at least until we're on the road."

Tisa's stomach dropped. The reality of how bad her life was going to be slammed into her gut like a fist. Civil? Her husband was a cruel whoreson with not a bone of kindness anywhere in him.

"Damn it. Can ye stop taking exception to every word I say?" Darragh actually whined. God help her.

"Still yer mouth. Not another word until we have departed this place." Aodh's words left no room for disagreement.

Aodh turned his irritation on Tisa, glancing around her. "Have ye nothing to bring with ye."

"I—"

Darragh lifted the small basket. "She has this. Let us be gone!"

Aodh glowered at his son, no doubt for speaking when he'd just been told not to. It certainly had nothing to do with his treatment of his wife. Of that, Tisa was quite certain.

Flanked by both men like a prisoner approaching her death, Tisa felt nothing as she was led to the bailey. The villagers had come to say their goodbyes and filled the small space, spilling out through the open gates to the road beyond. Some had tears. Most had sad smiles. One little girl carried a small bunch of flowers but Darragh stopped her from approaching. It was Hannah. Tisa had seen her through a terrible sickness winter last. They'd become quite close. Her young eyes teared at his treatment.

Tisa stepped forward and smoothed the girl's locks, accepting the flowers. "Thank ye, Hannah."

"I will miss ye."

"And I ye." Tisa kissed her lightly on the forehead before standing.

"Say yer goodbyes to yer father." Aodh gave the command.

Tisa glanced at the man standing beside his captain. Fergus' side was well bandaged where her father-in-law had tried to run him through. She wondered who had seen to his wounds since she had not been called on. Fergus was tight lipped, looking neither left nor right. He was livid. No doubt he had voiced his strong objections to her father regarding his decision to marry her off to Darragh. That would have been in the privacy of her father's solar, with no unwanted listeners. Here, Fergus would display total loyalty and support to him even if he had to do it with a stiff back.

Tisa sighed. She would miss him. Searching the crowd, her eyes fell on Caireann. Her face puffy and swollen, probably from crying.

"One thing." Tisa withdrew in fear at the angry look her husband gave her even though she had addressed Aodh but she pushed on. "Please."

Aodh frowned his disapproval. Tisa quickly stepped toward the crowd. "Caireann?"

Caireann's eyes widened and she shrunk back at the sudden attention turned on her. Those closest pushed her forward.

"Come with?" Tisa clamped her hands tight. "Please?"

Caireann glanced to the men on either side of her. Tisa prayed she would consent but knew she couldn't blame her if she said no. Caireann's throat constricted with her hard swallow before she faced Tisa.

"I will come."

Darragh gave an exaggerated groan. "Well, then, let us get on with this."

Aodh lifted Tisa onto her horse. With his eyes on her face and his hands lingering too long about her waist, she was reminded of the man's earlier announcement. Tisa shoved the man's hands aside which got her a sharp look of disapproval.

Darragh's sudden concern when he moved in closer made her realize he may have been remembering the same thing. If her father-in-law did expect to share his son's wife, no doubt there'd be hell to pay for his only pretending to see to his husbandly duty. Repulsion shivered through her body. She would not be letting this man anywhere near her and she hoped Darragh was thinking the same.

The long line of Meic Lochlainn warriors surrounded the group as they set off. Caireann was tossed up into the small cart already packed tight with their weapons and supplies. Tisa was surprised to see Breandan riding up on a palfrey. He shot her a nasty look and faced straight ahead. With a start, she realized he followed close behind her husband. She also noticed that his features softened considerably when Darragh turned to speak to him. Her husband's laughter surrounding them at whatever Breandan had said. Uneasiness tightened her gut when her father-in-law glanced disapprovingly at his son.

Tisa closed her eyes and took a deep breath. Whatever mess she was being carried into, she could not allow it to overwhelm her. She would get through this. If Darragh had no use for her, and by all indications that was true, then she just needed to keep his father away as well. Darragh must want the same thing otherwise his little farce would be uncovered. She had no reason to want it known either. The only thing she would miss would be children. She had longed for a large family but that had been with Tadhg. Sadness settled into her chest and refused to leave.

By nightfall, they were stopping nestled among the evergreens, protected from the coastline they'd been following. Aodh again came to lift her off her horse. He was an older man but his strength was unquestionable.

"Father, can I not be allowed to see to my own wife?" Darragh's hand rested on his hip. He shook his head, his eyes wide, waiting for his father's response.

The older man set her beside him, an arm around her waist holding her fast. Tisa forced down the panic making its way up her throat. Surely her husband would win this battle. The men gathering around them would be reason enough. Certainly Aodh would want his son shown the respect due him.

"Ye can stop the pretense now." Aodh swept his hand along the many men surrounding them. "They ken yer disposition as do I."

The men around nodded in agreement. Their tight expressions showing their obvious disapproval of her husband's dislike of women.

Aodh turned a smile on Tisa who dared not breathe. "And as yer new bride does as well by now."

A few of his men glanced her way. One tugged at his tarse. Another licked his lips while he perused her up and down. Tisa shifted as far away from the man as his firm grasp allowed. They were a pack of wolves ready to devour her.

Tisa had one chance. She turned wide, innocent eyes toward Darragh. "Husband? I ken not what yer father is speaking of."

Darragh's crestfallen expression changed to one of scrutiny. "He believes I may not have done my husbandly duty by ye."

The hand at her side faltered just enough that she was able to break free and reach her husband's side in three steps.

"I dunna understand." She took his hand, her eyes pleading for him not to recoil at her touch. "Did he not see the bedding sheet? If I had not been there myself, I'd have believed ye'd killed me with all that blood."

The men around them laughed. She smiled toward them.

Darragh's hand gripped hers tighter, his eyes on her face. "Aye." He turned on his father. "Did ye not see the sheets, Father? She's well and truly bedded."

"And eager to have ye in my bed again." She dug her nails into his palm at his look of horror. His frown turned into an awkward smile but she feared he had taken too long to catch on. She refused to glance at Aodh and confirm her fears.

Darragh kept his eyes on her and looked like he'd stopped breathing as well. She wetted her lips and rose on tiptoe to kiss her husband on the mouth. Too shocked to recoil, Tisa prayed it appeared as a sincere indication of their feelings for each other. His tight lips pressed against hers unexpectedly. When she pulled back, the look of thanks he offered made her relax a little.

He pulled her against his side. "Please, Father, allow me to show my wife the courtesy she deserves from me."

Darragh's voice was lower this time, sounding more confident. His hold around her waist tightened a little too much. She struggled to stop the fear from showing on her face and smiled instead.

Aodh's bewildered gaze went from Darragh to Tisa and back again. The seconds ticked off. She waited and prayed the man believed the ruse. He cocked a brow and bowed slightly before answering.

"Well, then, ye've done well for yerself, Darragh." He glanced at the men around them. His men. "Dunna ye all agree?"

The men offered words of pleasure, agreement, and surprise.

Aodh stood before his son and placed his arm on Darragh's shoulder. "I am busting with pride for ye, son." He dropped his gaze to Tisa. "And busting to try ye out myself but I suppose I could wait 'til we've a firm pallet beneath us to cushion ye from my hard ride."

Tisa's jaw dropped but Aodh had already turned away and was addressing his men as they readied the camp.

Darragh released his hold with a lopsided smile. "Ye tried, sweet little Tisa. My thanks."

Breandan was quickly beside Darragh, shooting daggers at Tisa.

"Darragh, we must convince him!" She heard the panic in her own voice. "Ye canna take this boy off with ye and leave me here."

"And I think he can." Breandan said too loudly. He was dumber than she realized.

Tisa glanced at the men a distance away and lowered her voice even more. "Nae, ye canna. Please, Darragh, just stay with me while we are traveling."

Darragh made a look of disgust. "I dunna want to."

Tisa fought against the desire to roll her eyes. "But, Darragh, we are all sleeping in the open. They may give us a quiet spot to the side but it must just be ye and me. Breandan canna be near us. He has to stay with the other men."

"I dunna wa—"

"Shhh! I ken what ye want. Can ye not wait until we've arrived at his home?" She turned an imploring expression on Darragh. "If we can get to yer home, we can work this all out there. But here, where everyone can see us, we must continue to be happily wed. Please!"

Darragh smiled at Breandan. The young man's expression clearly revealed his distaste for having to wait for her husband's attention. Darragh stroked the hair back from his face. Tisa shifted to block the gesture from the view of any of the other men.

"We'll be at my home soon." He moved his face closer to Breandan. "I'll make it worth the wait."

Breandan's face lit up. Tisa glanced behind to be sure no one saw the two of them.

"Go with the other men." He winked. "Ye can wait. Aye?"

Breandan nodded then moved away toward the others. Darragh followed him with his eyes.

Tisa breathed a sigh of relief until Darragh turned an angry scowl at her.

"I'll not be putting him off again."

"'Tis fine with me."

"Truly?"

Tisa longed to inform the man she didn't want his hands on her. Ever! But that might be taken as a dare. She imagined her husband was stubborn enough to find a way to make her sorry for the seeming rejection of him.

"Darragh." Aodh's voice carried across the camp.

A large fire burned brightly. The men had taken up spots close to the warmth, their bedding behind them. One of the men had enlisted Breandan's help with the cooking which he didn't seem to mind. Tisa's quick scan found Caireann still sitting in the cart, empty now, and cast in shadows. She hurried to her.

"Why are ye here alone?"

Caireann's eyes widened as if she'd asked why she had two heads. "Because I dunna want these men's attention."

All the men looked to be keeping to themselves. One sat very close to the fire, mending a tear in his sleeve. Another man lay stretched out, his head propped on his folded arms, with a wineskin on his chest. The men around listened intently to his boasting. Three other men were playing some sort of game with sticks.

"Have they been bothering ye?"

"Ye should have seen them at home." She shook her head as if it were most unbelievable. "They jumped on anything that moved. Male or female."

"Ye jest!"

Caireann turned a very serious face her way. "I do not."

Tisa blew a breath. "I had my own challenges within. I dinna ken what was going on outside."

"Fergus had tried to keep us away but they all wanted to see ye wed." Caireann's eyes softened. "They care about ye."

"And I care about them."

"Are ye not hungry?" Aodh yelled toward her.

Tisa and Caireann exchanged glances before moving toward the cook. Breandan smiled at Caireann when he handed her a trencher drenched with a thick, meaty sauce. She blushed sweetly and smiled.

"Thank ye, Breandan. Nice to have a familiar man among these warriors."

The young man winked.

Incorrigible.

Tisa fumed at this cruel treatment of her friend. She did not believe for one minute that this man had any interest in any woman. His eyes glazed over as he watched something in the distance. She knew who it was without even looking.

The cook beside Breandan offered Tisa his best. "For ye and yer husband."

Tisa curtseyed politely, glared at Breandan, and headed toward the exact spot he'd had his eye on.

Darragh had the blanket pulled tight around him, his lips stretched over his teeth, and his eyes fixed on the roaring fire.

"Ye dunna look happy, husband." She sat down beside him, leaving enough distance between them so he may not need to shift away. She smiled up at him and balanced the platter on her knee. "Mayhap 'tis only food ye need."

He scowled at her before turning back to the fire.

"I think only of our own comfort, Darragh."

He shook his head in irritation.

"Please." Her whisper got his attention. "We need the pretense."

Darragh moved in close as if he might kiss her. She recoiled. "I dunna want to feed my *wife*."

Tisa glanced at the broth soaking into the crusty bread. She needed Aodh to stay away from her. From them. If she could not convince Darragh to play along, her life with these people would only get worse.

"I beg ye." She spoke in the quietest whisper. "I need ye to just remember yer part. Please. I want no more of ye. I swear it."

The tension poured out of him. He was wound up tight. Either he would let loose his temper right here or she would get a reprieve. She closed her eyes and offered a prayer.

The weight of the platter on her leg was removed and her eyes flew open. Darragh had a piece of meat speared on his dagger.

"For ye, wife." His blue eyes sparkled in the fire light.

She opened her mouth and accepted the meat. He smiled, even wiping her mouth with the cloth at his side. Her stomach gripped tight and she struggled to finish chewing enough to swallow.

"Ah, the couple enjoys their meal, I see," Aodh called to them from across the fire. "Methinks my son will enjoy ye as well."

"Save room for dessert," one of the men at his side offered.

Darragh's thigh tightened where it rested against her leg. She gave him a warning look.

"Methinks my son will do fine spreading his wife's legs for a sweet repast. Will ye not?"

Darragh stood beside Tisa. She held her breath, afraid of what would happen next.

"What I do or do not enjoy doing with my wife is not yer concern, Father." Darragh offered Tisa his hand. She stood with him. "But we will enjoy some privacy."

With a gentle touch, he led her toward a small outcropping of rocks. She was surprised to see blankets had been spread out along with the makings of a fire. All it needed was a spark and there would be both light and warmth.

Tisa sighed.

Out of sight of the others, Darragh plopped down to one side of the coarse cloth. She nearly laughed when she realized he was pouting again.

"Oh, my poor husband. Is this where ye had plans to meet with Breandan?"

"What do ye care? I've kept my father away from ye. And probably his men."

She gasped.

"'Tis true. He likes to pass women around to his men. Especially the 'good' ones. That's the way he's been as far back as I can remember."

Darragh struck the flint and the tinder ignited. Settling on the ground, Tisa took off her slippers and tucked her feet beneath her.

"Did he ever force ye to actually…?"

"Gawd, nae! He knew I wanted no part of it. One time he brought a girl just a few years older than me. Someone I'd conversed with on occasion. She had the prettiest green eyes. When he was done with her, he ordered me to take her. I refused. That's when he knew I was different."

Darragh's pain ran deep. Young boys always wanted their father's approval. That he couldn't force himself to do something that would gain his father's acceptance must have been a terrible blow.

"I dinna want to touch her like that." Darragh tucked his knees up and rested his chin there, no doubt reliving the painful experience. "Especially since her twin brother was very much to my liking."

He winked at her and she laughed.

"Oh, Darragh, methinks ye can be very charming."

Tipping his head to the side, he searched her more closely. "And I believe the same of ye."

Without preamble, he grabbed her chin and pulled her lips to his. The lips that had been soft were suddenly forceful and firm. He dropped a hand to her breast, a gentle hand that stroked and cupped. His other hand slipped up her foot and along the exposed skin of her leg. Tisa felt a scream rising up her throat.

"Well, well, well! Hard as a rock I am just watching ye." Aodh stepped closer to the fire and rubbed his aforementioned appendage.

Darragh pulled away. "Is this how ye leave me with my wife? Can ye not see we're on our way to giving ye the grandchildren ye desire?"

The confidence of his words surprised Tisa. She straightened her clothing but kept her eyes averted.

"Does he dampen yer nether parts with his touch?"

Tisa gasped and jerked her head up to look at her father-in-law. Darragh's eyes were on her as well, as if he also waited for the answer.

She stood, terror taking a foothold in her humiliation at the intimate questions. She didn't even understand what they were talking about. The last time she'd been in the arms of a man who pleased her she was only ten and two.

"I have just the right response to my husband's touch." Nice way to avert a subject she knew nothing about. "And I would take less offense at yer questions if ye were to allow us some time to be alone."

Aodh plopped onto the blanket. "I'd rather watch."

"Ye may not," she said.

"I dinna ask."

"Nae! Ye are not to watch."

Aodh arched his brow and glared at his son. "Darragh, are ye to see to this or am I?"

Tisa's terror spread across her stomach even though she wasn't sure what his threat actually was. She faced Darragh.

"Come to me." He reached his hand up to her.

No. No. No. She took his hand.

He pulled her onto his lap, hugging her close against his chest. "Shhh, do not fash yerself. What we do or do not do here and now is no one's concern but ours." Darragh dropped his warm hand to her bare ankle.

Darragh sat up tall and tucked her head against his shoulder, his hand stroking up and down her calf. "Quiet yerself."

He nuzzled his nose into her neck.

Tisa dared not breathe. She wanted to do nothing that might encourage this. Out of the corner of her eye, Aodh stroked himself as he looked on.

When Darragh's hand slipped up past her knee, she wondered how far he was willing to go with this pretense or if it even was a pretense. She shifted her bottom on his lap but felt nothing. Dropping her hand, her fingers spread in search of any sign that he was actually aroused. She found just the opposite.

"Shh, mmm, ye're a special one." Darragh's eyes were closed, his words low and throaty.

Tisa would swear he was thinking of what he might say to Breandan. When his lips clamped on to hers, there was no way out of responding. A groan of appreciation from Aodh's direction fortified her determination. She kissed Darragh back, even opening her mouth to his persistent tongue. How far was he going to go with this?

As if in answer, Darragh reached beneath her bliaut to rub his hand over one breast and then the other. Surely this wasn't necessary since his father couldn't even se—

"Oh, aye, Darragh, that's the way they like ye to touch them. And with a firm hand."

The man's hand moved more quickly over his own arousal.

Damn, was the man never going to leave?

Darragh moved in close to her ear. "Forgive me."

He whispered the words and his hand slipped up her inner thigh.

No! Tisa fought against the very strong urge to slam her knees together. The sure knowledge that this man preferred men to women was the only thing that kept her legs still. That and the need to convince his father once and for all that they were, indeed, intimate. When Darragh parted her legs even further, she was ready to scream.

"Well," Aodh stood. "Off to find me some relief myself."

He disappeared into the darkness. Darragh immediately withdrew his hand and pulled away from Tisa. He blew a huge breath.

"Good thing I've been forced to watch this enough times."

He rolled away and stretched out, propping his hands under his head. "I dinna think he would ever leave. I feared how far I would have to go to convince him—"

Tisa covered her face with her hands and cried. This was intolerable. She should be glad. She should be relieved that her husband had not forced himself on her. How many more times would Darragh have to touch her so intimately to keep his father away?

"Pardon, sweet little Tisa." Darragh was sitting beside her now, stroking her hair. "Ye have never been touched so?"

Tisa didn't want to speak to this man about how she had or had not been touched. She wanted to be off with Tadhg, having him touch her, having him kiss her, having him laying with her, and making love to her in truth. Damn. If Darragh had gone any further he would have found the proof of her treacherous body's response to his touch. Even petrified, she'd felt the dampness Aodh had spoken of. How could she have been aroused? She didn't want this man to touch her ever!

"Go on and cry." Darragh spoke quietly. "I will not tell a soul."

He took her in his arms, cradling her like she was a child, and she sobbed her heart out.

At some point she fell asleep. When she awoke, she was leaning on Darragh's bosom, his arm about her, covered with a heavy cloth. He snored softly. She dared not move for fear of waking him. A slight glow was just lighting the eastern sky. Unsure how far it was to her new home, she prayed she would continue to have this privacy. Mayhap his father had been convinced. She prayed it was so.

Chapter Seven

Tadhg and Sean traveled without stopping until they were exhausted. Brighit's safety was their only concern.

"Sean!" Calum was alongside Sean, catching the man as he was about to tumble from his horse. "We need to stop, Tadhg."

Tadhg shook his head to clear it. The man was right. No place nearby, they were hungry and cold. "Hell of a barren place."

"Methinks it has to do with their king's treatment of the people here. They burned it all down and let the people starve."

Calum stopped both their horses. He was barely able to help the huge man to the ground.

Sean's eyes barely opened. "We need to get to Brighit."

"But if ye kill yerself falling off the horse, ye'll be no good to her." Calum's voice left no room for argument.

Tadhg dropped from his horse, allowing it to graze. "I canna even think clearly. How much farther to the Priory?"

Sean settled against a tree, his arms resting on his knees. His eyes closed.

"Calum, get the man some water," Tadhg said. "Fool wouldn't eat or drink when last we stopped."

"He's smitten with her. Wouldn't even take that comely wench up on her offer." Calum held the skin to Sean's parched mouth. "Oh, just drink it and dinna be giving me any shite about it." Calum smiled toward Tadhg. "His loss."

Tadhg flexed his shoulders and threw his brat along the ground, following

53

on top of it. "I dinna think 'tis safe to just sleep in the open."

"I'll keep guard," Eoghan offered.

The raven-haired lad had been quiet most of the way. No doubt deep in his own thoughts having left behind his young wife who was heavy with child. That he'd offered to come along spoke of his own loyalty to both Tadhg and the clan.

"'Twould be much appreciated, Eoghan. Are ye up to it yerself?"

"Methinks I should get used to working on little sleep. I ken the wee bairns keep ye up most nights. Gael will need me."

Sean snored in answer. Calum had covered him with his own skins and settled beside him. "I've some time yet for those problems, Eoghan," he said. "Wake me when ye need to."

Tadhg smiled at the other man. They were the same age. Eoghan had lain with Gael as soon as they were betrothed and got her with child. She was a plump, little blond with sky blue eyes and an infectious smile. Tadhg would have done the same with Tisa. He had wanted her something fierce. Her father made sure that didn't happen by keeping them apart.

It was at the celebration of her sister's wedding. Finola marrying William. Just the week before, Sean had brought Tadhg into the barn to watch one of his father's soldiers with the woodcutter's widow.

"See how she's pressing against him like she'll die if he doesn't poke her? That's when ye ken they're ready for ye."

Tadhg couldn't take his eyes off of them. The man yanked down the widow's gown, her hefty breasts spilling out. The soldier's moan of appreciation accompanied him eagerly suckling her teats, pulling up her skirts, and settling himself between her spread legs. He yanked up his leine and impaled her.

"How do ye ken that's when she's ready?"

"Because that's what they always do before they take it."

The widow groaned and the man dug his toes into the ground for leverage while he pumped into her.

"See? She's not moaning in pain."

Tadhg glanced toward his friend. "I ken ye've been telling me 'twas so for quite a while now."

Tadhg couldn't be certain if it was the groans or the pumping that had put him into such a state but he was feeling quite confident of his own ability when he'd followed Tisa into the lean-to behind the house.

"Will ye kiss me then, Tadhg MacNaughton?"

He could still see her with her closed eyes and upturned mouth. She'd looked very grown with that dress of her sister's hanging on all her curves. Tadhg had licked his lips. He was more than ready to taste her, feel her lips on his but the closer he got, the more unsure he became. And then he froze like a twig stuck in the ice. She finally opened her eyes when he was a nose's length away.

"What are ye waiting on, my fine lad? I've a mind to have yer lips on mine. Will ye be disappointing me?"

She pressed her lips forward and didn't seem to notice how he was unable to move. She moved just fine. Her soft lips pressed against his, seemingly not even noticing the lack of response on his part. He took a breath for fear of passing out and she slid her tongue into his mouth.

For the flash of a moment, he thought of asking her where she learned such a thing but then he didn't care. He was eagerly responding. He couldn't stop himself from responding. His arms were enclosing her, heaving her against him as if his life depended on it. And that pleasant feeling traveled all the way down to his own hardened tarse. A tarse that sought out her warmth like a bee to honey, pressing at the juncture of her legs, his hips moving of their own accord. She wasn't repulsed. She didn't push him away. Instead, she wrapped her arms about his waist, hugging him just as tight. And when she withdrew, she smiled. His stiff rod bobbing against her but she said nothing about it.

"I love ye, Tadhg," she said. "With all my heart. Whenever ye're ready to take a wife, I'll be here waiting for ye. I dunna want anyone's arms about me but yers."

An owl sounded in the tree above him. An answering call in the distance. The large flapping sound filled the silence along with Sean's snoring. Tisa hadn't waited. Her father must have found another as soon as the betrothal was broken.

He had nothing to hold on to now. Both his parents were dead. The survival of a clan rested on his shoulders alone and he had no one to share that burden with. No one to warm his bed at night. No one to plan a future with.

When he finally slept, he had dark dreams. Instead of witnessing the soldier with the widow, it was Tisa who groaned in pleasure beneath him. Her large, pink nipples glistening from the soldier's mouth. Her eyes squeezed shut in her ecstasy. Tadhg had tried to stop them but she just smiled at him. A knowing smile that spoke of her own ability to continue on without him. To find pleasure in another's arms, just like his own mother.

"Tadhg, wake up. Ye're having a nightmare." Sean was shaking Tadhg's shoulder but he couldn't break out of the dream. "Come on, Tadhg. 'Tis fine. We'll see Brighit safe."

Tadhg jerked his body to a sitting position and ran his hands through his hair. He was breathing like he'd run a great race. Sean's worried eyes were red-rimmed from lack of sleep. He handed a cup of something hot to Tadhg.

"Ye were being chased by the devil methinks."

Tadhg drank the contents. "Aye. The devil."

"We've readied the horses." Eoghan offered. "Should we be off?"

"We'll stop at the first inn. We need to get food in our bellies. We're no good to her like this."

"Mayhap someone will have seen her," Sean said.

By mid-morning, they came upon a small village with a blacksmith and an inn. The others saw to the care of their horses and began asking around about Brighit. Tadhg went into the inn. Norman soldiers sat at a large table by the hearth. They paid him little attention as they played their game of wooden dice. The rest of the large room was still chilled by the outside air. A woman with long, blond hair brought him a mug. She was a tall woman but with the right amount of curves.

"Are ye here for food as well?"

"As well as what?"

She smiled. "As well as something to drink?" She lifted the clay pitcher she also carried then leaned in closer, frowning. "Or are ye after something else altogether?"

"Something else altogether." Tadhg needed to get this over with. He had no reason to wait. He'd been waiting forever.

She turned to the table with the soldiers, topped off their drinking vessels but left the pitcher at the end of their table.

Turning to Tadhg, she extended her hand. He took it and followed her to what he'd thought was probably the kitchen. Instead, there was a small pallet in the corner, the window covered with a cloth. She doffed her gown without preamble. She wore nothing beneath.

He hadn't expected it to be like this. He'd expected kissing and groping and something to be ignited within him. Her pert breasts were working on his desire so he concentrated on them. He opened his mouth and latched on to a hard nipple. She straddled him, pushing herself further into his mouth.

"Ye're one to take yer time, I see."

Tadhg ignored her comments, his hands slipped along her firm bottom, grasping and pulling. He was hard as soon as she dropped her gown. Her hands free, she worked at his rod, yanking and stretching through the material.

"A hefty one."

Again he ignored her comments but flipped her over to be under him. She spread her legs. His breasts were firm in his mouth and she pushed herself against his groin. He wanted to touch her between her legs. She was slippery and he prodded her, trying to see with his hand what he had never seen. She yanked up his leine with one solid pull. His length was right there, ready to press into her. Ready to feel the tightness he'd only imagined. To know the release that wasn't just in his hand.

"Well?"

One push and he'd be in. He could pump into her the way he'd longed to pump into Tisa. He could take her any way he wanted. She wouldn't complain.

She adjusted herself, widening her legs, her feet flat on the bed. He realized she wanted to finish and was about to see to it. He shoved off the low bed.

"What are ye about?"

Tadhg pulled his leine over his treacherous prick that convinced him he could do this with anyone and it would be just as good as if it were with Tisa. Wrong.

"I've changed my mind."

He dropped a silver coin on her naked chest.

Chapter Eight

The day Tisa arrived at her new home it was dark and stormy. They'd been keeping ahead of the impending rain the whole day. From the rise overlooking the sea, dark, angry clouds hugged the coastline, making it impossible to see the ocean. The sound of crashing waves pounding along the rocky shore made her stop. Her mount shifted beneath her as if wary as well. Darragh come up alongside and pointed out the little cluster of roundhouses nestled into the valley below.

"That is yer new home," he said.

Several small buildings surrounded a larger longhouse in the center. It appeared quite peaceful despite the many barren trees no longer protecting it from the sea breezes.

"It looks peaceful."

He snorted beside her. "Dunna be fooled. There is nothing about my father, including his clan, that is peaceful but ye've witnessed that yerself."

His father had been relentless in keeping track of their whereabouts. He'd continued to impose on them, making lewd suggestions when they separated from the group at night. Tisa would almost believe she had become dulled by his comments. Almost.

"Darragh!" Aodh barked at his son. "See to the ships."

Her husband sighed. "Father, I will see my bride settled before leaving her alone."

Aodh laughed. A cruel laugh. The belittling laugh he often used with his son. "Afraid to leave her unprotected?"

Darragh turned to face the man that had come up behind him. "Aye, I will have her well protected before I venture off to see to yer ships."

Aodh smiled at her. "But I've been so patient."

"Then be patient about yer ships!"

Darragh took the reins of Tisa's horse and led them both down the graceful hillside ahead of the others.

Tisa dared not breathe at this blatant show of disobedience. Once out of earshot, she whispered to her husband.

"Darragh, he is still not following."

"I've shocked him into immobility."

Tisa started to look over her shoulder.

"Nae! Dunna even glance his way. This is what he deserves for his treatment of me. Of ye!"

"Do ye not fear his retaliation against such defiance?"

Darragh was silent but continued toward the village at a good pace without letting up. Tisa said nothing else. Darragh knew his own father better than she did. She needed to trust that he knew what he was doing. He continued toward the smallest building set away from the rest. As he passed the longhouse, he finally spoke.

"This is where the next High King of Eire spends his time."

"High King?"

Darragh turned wide eyes on her. "My father, of course. Did ye not ken of his ambitions?"

"I had not heard. I ken very little of yer clan."

"Well, that is really the only thing ye need to ken. He has great ambitions and will not hesitate to take down anything, or anyone, that stands in his way."

Tisa had developed a great dislike of the man and this new information only deepened it for her. "How can he hope to ever follow in the footsteps of a man like Brian Boru and replace him as High King?"

Brian Boru's great leadership skills were legendary. He had made huge strides in unifying the clans along the fair island, a feat many had tried but fell far short of over the generations. It had earned him the title of High King.

"Oh, he doesn't hope to replace that man." Darragh had stopped in front of the small, round hut. He jumped off his horse and came to help her down. "He will surpass him."

The touch of his huge hands at her waist had become the norm once Darragh began taking on the duty of assisting her. Breandan had stayed with the supply horses and gave her only passing notice. She assumed her husband had spoken to the man to get him to change his blatant jealousy of her.

"This is where I pass my time. Out of the way of my father." He led the way into the cozy, round building and into a large center area. "We have an unspoken agreement that the man remains outside of this one place. Ye should be safe here."

Standing in the middle of the room, three smaller areas along the sides were separated from the larger hall by heavy materials secured along the wooden beams and reaching to the floor. With the entrance behind them, it gave the central hall a square shape. Darragh ventured into the alcove along the backside with the sack he'd carried in from his horse. He held back the corner of the curtain for her to see inside.

"This is where I sleep." He winked at her. "Not usually alone, I might add."

A small pallet was pushed against the curved, outside wall with a small chest to the right where he dropped the sack. He crossed in front of her to the area right of the door. He lifted that covering and revealed an even smaller area within. "We can set this area up for ye."

Tisa nodded and approached the area. "I appreciate yer kindness in giving me my own room."

A small chest and table were along the outside wall. There was room for a pallet. He stood alongside her.

"I promise not to bother ye when ye are in here." He smiled at her.

"I... understand."

The sound of horses and men reached them. Darragh shook his head. "We need to unpack the horses but certainly the most important unpacking is of ye."

She removed the heavy cloak she wore and he draped it across the coffer.

"Yer pardon, please, for not allowing ye to take any of yer belongings. I fear I was not at my best," he said in a small voice.

"Darragh!"

Tisa would swear Aodh's angry voice filled the entire village.

Darragh shrugged his shoulders. "I suppose I need to see what the man wants. Please rest yerself. Ye may use my pallet for now. None will bother ye here."

He left, closing the rough-hewn door tightly behind him. Tisa glanced around and assessed her new home. It wasn't very homey but she could easily remedy that. Picking up the corner of the hanging material, she found it finely woven. Adornment could easily be added and it would give her something to focus on. She would need to see about acquiring some supplies.

Tisa lifted the last curtain to reveal a third small area with a single table in the center. The curtain fell behind her and she went to the box placed in the middle of the trestle. It was inlaid with precious jewels that surrounded the depiction of a hunt, complete with a stag, three mounted men, and seven large dogs. The intricacy of the carving spoke of the artist's ability. Could there be someone in the village able to create something so beautiful? She would need to ask her husband when he returned.

She jumped at the knock on the door.

"Darragh?" It was Breandan's voice.

Tisa crossed to open the door. "Breandan."

"Tisa."

Breandan blustered past her but she could sense his own wariness at entering.

"Did my husband send for ye?"

He turned, the dark curls around his face shifting with the movement. "I have merely come as ordered to put this," he lifted the small bag she hadn't noticed in his hand, "away."

"And who gave ye these orders?"

Breandan's eyes darted around, refusing to settle again on her. He opened his mouth but she held her hand up before he could offer up his lie.

"Ye do not belong here, so please," she opened her hand, "give it to me and get ye to the kitchen before ye are missed."

The lad pouted but relinquished the property. With a lowered head, he went past her.

"Breandan," Tisa wasn't sure how to broach the subject with the man her husband clearly desired. "Let us be kind to each other."

His eyes widened but he said nothing.

"We... have the same... need for... privacy and... we will abide by... Darragh's instructions. Aye?"

"Aye." He kicked at the thick rushes covering the dirt-packed floor. "I am just a bit out of my element here."

"As am I." She placed a hand on his shoulder. "But we have come from the same place. Ye and I and Caireann. Surely we can find comfort from that."

Breandan brightened. "That is true. It makes this place seem less strange."

"So we will have a truce between us?"

"We shall."

Breandan smiled with pleasure as Darragh entered.

"We shall what?" Darragh asked.

Darkness seemed to fall over Breandan's face at the angry tone and he dropped his head as if he were ready to be scolded. He most certainly was not given leave to come here.

"Wife?"

Tisa's temperature rose at his tone. "Is something amiss?"

Darragh pressed his lips into a displeased scowl. "I ask. Ye answer."

"Why such a grouch? I believed ye were pleased to be here."

"Ye dunna ken what pleases me."

The comment stung like a slap.

Darragh ripped his leine over his head and went toward the alcove along the back. His room. The short braies he wore did little to mask his need for release. Breandan's face lit up again. He remained focused on the man moving about. When the lad glanced toward her, she could read his anger at her presence. So much for a truce.

"Please, Darragh. Tell me what has happened. How I can be of help to ye."

"The others lusting after ye is a problem. I dinna ken what to say to their taunts."

He turned toward them, oblivious of his own state, and shook his head. "I never wanted a wife."

Her heart sank. "I am aware of yer preference."

Darragh finally noticed Breandan's dreamy expression as he fairly drooled at the sight of his lover's solid erection. Darragh glanced down, apparently just now realizing his own condition.

A flush crossed his face like a cloud, his scowl gone, and he took a slow breath. Suddenly appearing quite contented, he smiled his appreciation at Breandan who fell into his opened arms.

Tisa felt a little tug at her heart and turned away from the sight.

"Oh, ye have been waiting a long while," Darragh's voice was smooth as silk behind her.

A tiny speck of disappointment settled in her chest. Mayhap because she could do nothing to ease her husband's discomfort. His happiness would certainly affect her even if they did not have sexual relations. It would be to her benefit to allow him time for his predilection without comment.

She crossed to her right with loud steps trying to block out the groans, the whispered words of encouragement, the guttural sighs of satisfaction. Avoiding the scene didn't stop her imagination. She could clearly see the kissing. The stroking. Tisa stoked the open hearth, adding wood with a loud bang as if this were an everyday occurrence for her.

The knock at the door startled her to turn around. Breandan was rising to his feet and Darragh reached for the same leine to cover himself. Both had turned toward the sound.

Darragh opened the door. His father's face was tight and suffused with color. His eyes went from his son, to Tisa, and lastly to Breandan. He was livid. Panic worked its way across Tisa's chest and her brain searched frantically for the words to placate the man.

"Why are ye here, Tisa, with this," he jerked his hand between Darragh and Breandan, "going on? Get ye to my house!"

Darragh's nostrils flared but he held his tongue.

Tisa swallowed before answering. "I am not certain I understand yer question. I had Breandan come here to assist me. He is the one man I ken. If he is not to assist me, I beg forgiveness. I did not realize it was to be so with him."

Tisa dared not breathe. Darragh squared his shoulders, a smug expression on his face. Aodh narrowed his eyes at her. She schooled her face and prayed there was nothing to see to confirm his suspicions. When he glanced at his son, he smiled. A smile that did not reach his eyes.

"I am glad to see mayhap I have been wrong about ye. I have called a gathering for this night. I need ye with me." He turned to Breandan. "Methinks ye are needed in the kitchen."

"Oh, surely he can be of more assistance to my wife."

Darragh draped his arm around Breandan's rounded shoulder. Tisa's stomach dropped.

Aodh glanced at her again. "Is that yer desire, Tisa? To have him close by yer husband... and ye?" His eyes dropped to her body, moving with slow deliberation. Her heart sped up but she held herself stiff against the assault.

"Aye. Breandan is quite capable. I have found him very helpful at home. I had hoped it would be the same here." Her voice squeezed slightly. She struggled to maintain an unconcerned attitude. "But however ye decide he can best be put to use is yer decision, Aodh. I would never gainsay ye."

Tisa prayed her acquiescent response would calm the man down. Her husband's overenthusiastic response to having his lover close had nearly undone him, of that she was certain. Darragh's reaction had not been uninterested. Not in the least.

"Father, yer choice is one we both will abide by, certainly." Darragh's tone had evened out but Tisa would wish the man be struck dumb rather than keep talking and confirm his father's suspicions. "I thought only to help my wife become more comfortable here. Both Breandan and Caireann are her own people. Their presence would ease the move for her."

Tisa's smile blossomed. Her husband had done quite well. Aodh again had that speculative look on his face. Now they waited. He went to the door and stuck his head out.

"Get that mousey girl here immediately!" He glanced back to his son, "Caireann?"

Tisa, Darragh, and Breandan nodded their heads.

"Caireann! Find her and bring her here."

Aodh moved in closer and smiled at Tisa. "So ye would never gainsay me?"

Tisa gulped. "I would abide by my husband's wishes. Methinks they would be the same as yers."

Aodh stroked his finger along her cheek. Her face heated but she said nothing.

"I want ye in my bed." The old man spoke in a low voice. She held his gaze. His hand dropped toward her bosom but Darragh placed himself in front of the man's objective.

"Father!" Darragh took her hand in his. "I wanted to speak to ye about that." He waited until his father turned his gaze to him. "I want there to be no doubt of whose child she carries."

Aodh frowned. Time seemed to slow down to a crawl. A spider at the top of the door frame danced along its web in the corner. Breandan's raspy breathing grated on her nerves. Her husband tapped his finger against her hand where he still gripped it.

"I will give ye six months' time to get her with child. If she does not, I will believe as I always have that yer preference is for boys. If she does," he winked at her, "I will even step aside as chieftain. Agreed?"

No one dared breathe. Tisa imagined hers was not the only mind frantically searching for a way out of this ultimatum.

"Agreed." Darragh stuck his hand toward his father. "And ye will keep yer distance from my wife and from our home here."

Aodh took his son's hand. "Yer wife, aye. But this will not be yer home, ye will move into the longhouse with me. So I ken ye are well protected."

"Nae!" Darragh whined, withdrew his arm, and stopped just short of stomping his foot.

Tisa's mind spun at the very idea of being constantly underfoot of this lecher. Would his word mean anything?

"Then my man, Malcolm, will move in here with ye. To see ye safe."

"Done!" Her husband gushed his approval and grasped his father's wrist in a solemn show of agreement.

Aodh turned his face toward Tisa with a smug smile.

"I will apprise Malcolm of the decision but ye need to come with me now. We have much to discuss before Ronan arrives with the Godwin."

When Darragh would have dropped her hand, Tisa pulled him toward her and kissed him on the mouth. "I will remain here, husband, awaiting yer return."

Chapter Nine

Breandan quickly lost interest in helping Tisa arrange the few items around the room.

"I have made a way for ye to stay here. Ye'll need to show some regard for me for the arrangement to go unquestioned."

She'd say he remained unconvinced by his lack of expression and listless eyes.

"I ken ye have great desire in ye, Breandan, but it canna be for my husband alone. Do ye enjoy cooking?"

He moved his head in what may have been a nod of agreement.

"Good! And gardening for a fresh supply of vegetables? Perhaps there are some nearby that ye can assist me with. Do ye ken yer herbs?"

He raised his shoulders, held them for effect, and dropped them again.

"Ye make this more difficult than need be." Tisa was ready to smack the boy.

If he was not of any use, other than to see to her husband's sexual appetite, he would not be staying. The realization came to her that it was all up to him. Breandan had to want to stay. He had to want to stay enough to want to serve some purpose for her.

She stiffened her back. "Along the slopes to the east is some winter grass. Fetch enough to cover the floors here."

Breandan wrinkled his nose at her. She held her hand up to stay his refusal.

"If ye wish to remain here, ye will do my bidding or I will have ye removed. Mayhap ye prefer the main shelter? Sleeping with everyone else?"

His jaw dropped. She crossed her arms, tapping her fingers impatiently, and waited.

When he narrowed his eyes at her, she knew she'd won. He did not have to be happy about his chores. He just needed to do them. He left without a backward glance.

Tisa dropped with exhaustion onto the pallet in Darragh's room. It was soft and smelled clean, as did the thick wool covering she pulled up to her chin. Her husband did demonstrate a propensity for cleanliness. Mayhap that would be something Breandan could see to without objection, the washing of her husband's clothes and bed linens. It had always been something she'd looked forward to seeing to for Tadhg. Her Tadhg. Her eyes drifted closed.

The aroma of cooked fish surrounded her. She opened her eyes to find she had fallen asleep in the tall grass alongside the fields of oats and barley that grew behind the castle. The sounds of celebration in the distance. Singing. Laughter. A rustling nearby had her flipping over to lean up on an elbow and peer between the thick blades.

"Hah!" Tadhg rushed her, pulling her atop of him. It wasn't the young Tadhg of her childhood memories but the grown man. His well-honed body solid beneath her while he held her, a hand on each hip, caressing her as he spoke. "Sleeping again when there's work to do."

Tisa covered his mouth with her own. Sweet, warm lips that moved against hers with a gentle yearning and parting her own with his persistent tongue. He ignited a deep longing in her. The warmth of the sunlight on her back. The birds singing their joy high in the trees beside them. Tadhg broke the kiss and smiled.

"Aye, my bonny lass. I want ye something fierce." His words moving like heat along her limbs. "When can we see to the bedding?"

She sighed and looked down on him, her hair falling around them. "I am aching to be held by ye, to have ye pressing into me, making me a woman."

With warm, strong hands he cupped her face and pulled her lips to his again. It intoxicated her. His fingers tracing her arm sending goose bumps along her skin, she moaned into his mouth.

Her eyes flew open and she bolted up in the bed. Darragh's bed. A tall, dark man with a heavy beard towered over her. He narrowed his eyes at her then broke into a huge grin. He crossed his arms about his chest.

"Aye. Having dreams about yer lovers?"

Tisa's face grew hot. She swallowed. "What do ye want?"

"Me? Nothing. I heard ye groaning."

Her gasp got stuck in her throat. That's what had awoken her from the dream. The sound of her own longing. She yanked the bed covering up tight to her neck.

"Then leave."

The burly man shrugged and turned about, the heavy material falling down behind him. Tisa leaned back on the pallet. Tears sprang to her eyes. Her dream had been so real. She could still feel Tadhg's warm body beneath her, his tender hands on her face, his firm lips. She buried her face into the coarse material to muffle her sobs. 'Twas all so wrong now. How could she go on without having any of her dreams fulfilled?

"I wait on ye, lady."

Tisa yanked the covers from her face. "Who are ye and what are ye waiting on me for?"

She sounded livid. A glint of satisfaction lifted her spirits. Good. Let him be intimidated by her.

But he didn't even respond.

Slowly, she got up from the bed and threw the covers back into place. With great stealth, she snuck toward the heavy curtain separating her from the central room. She shifted to the smallest slit of an opening where the edge of the material hung along the supporting beam. The man just stood there looking straight ahead. His hands folded in front of him. He was huge. Massive. His dark beard covered half of his face. He resembled a bear. He wore a long leine that was hiked up at the sides and tucked into the embroidered belt at his waist, exposing thick, hairy thighs. Legs as big as tree trunks.

He turned his face to look right at her. She gasped. A tolerant look crossed his face but he said nothing. She pushed the curtain aside and came into the room.

"Did ye not hear my questions?" she asked.

"Aye. I heard ye."

She raised her brows in that arrogant way her father used when laying on the guilt. The man refused to respond.

Tisa shoved her shoulders back. "Who. Are. Ye?"

"I am Malcolm."

The man Aodh was sending? The heat that had just begun to recede, rushed back into her face. This man would be living with them?

"Have ye come to make yerself known to me?"

"I've come because the Meic Lochlainn sent me."

"So ye just come in without my leave and watch me while I sleep?"

"I did knock. Ye dinna answer. I heard a noise behind the curtain so I went in to see if all was well. It was ye who was sneaking a look at me."

The heat spread down her neck as the embarrassment overtook her.

"I dunna think my husband would want ye in here without him present."

Malcolm quirked a brow. "And ye allow yer husband whatever he wants?"

Tisa heard the double meaning in his question. She took a deep, cleansing breath. "Who are ye to Aodh? Will he not miss yer overbearing presence?"

"I go where he tells me to go. I do as he tells me to do."

"Well, I prefer ye leave now. If ye must, wait outside for Aodh. Darragh assured me that none entered this place—for any reason—without his permission."

The man held her gaze as if he could see right into her soul. She swallowed. His gaze dipped to her neck then back to her face.

"If I make ye uncomfortable, I will wait outside. If ye want anything, ye need only call me."

"Want anything? What could I want from ye?"

Malcolm had started toward the door then stopped. He covered the distance between them in three steps. Not near enough to alarm, just near enough to ensure he had her total attention. "Ye'll ken when ye want it."

He crossed to the door, closing it behind him.

Tisa blew out a breath and covered her mouth. He'd heard her moaning in her sleep! It had been quite a dream. Tadhg was so handsome and his arms were so strong surrounding her. She'd melted against him and wanted so much more. She ran her fingers along her lips and formed a pucker. A total waste of her time.

Smoothing the material over the pallet, she again marveled at how clean it all was. The rushes here were showing wear. Where was Breandan? Her stomach growled. The light outside was fading. She had no idea where they took their meals. Darragh claimed he saw to her comfort surrounding her with people from home but thought nothing of leaving her here to starve. Now who was being a grouch?

She opened the door to find the bear of man sitting on the ground to the left, leaning against the thatched wall of the building. He didn't look at her. His legs were tucked up. His hands dangled casually over his massive knees. Since she didn't know what he was doing here, she didn't know what she could bother him with.

"Can ye tell me where the meals are taken?"

In an amazingly graceful leap for such a large man, he stood and faced her. "Most pleased to bring ye there."

He offered his arm. It felt a betrayal to Darragh somehow if she actually accepted this deferential treatment. Glancing around, no one else was about. She took his arm.

Rather than heading the way to the longhouse which she knew the location of, Malcolm weaved around the outside of the village. This gave her a good view of the backs of the houses. Some had openings she could see inside, others did not.

He led her up a small hill where two smaller roundhouses stood. One tiny house had a flat side facing the sea with a door that could be closed off. Hanging on the walls were iron implements that looked more like they belonged in the cooking area. She questioned him with a look.

"They hang the meat inside and stoke up a smoky fire then close up all the holes. The small opening betwixt the stones keeps it from bursting into flames."

"How much meat do ye eat?"

"Meat fills yer belly."

"As do the grains of the field."

"'Twas the Norsemen that showed us the importance of meat."

Her eyes widened. "The Norsemen? There are ruthless plunderers to the north."

"Our allies."

"Are those in yer clan ruthless plunderers as well?"

"If need be."

Her mouth hung open. That is not what she wanted to hear. This man looked like a trained killer. Like he could squeeze the life out of a man full grown and not even breathe heavy from the exertion.

"What are ye thinking now?" Malcolm asked.

The man may act like he didn't care what she thought but clearly he did.

"That I hoped it was no longer so. Our clan has been at peace for several generations."

"Because they had huge warriors ready to do battle for them at any time."

Tadhg! Her heart squeezed. He was a huge warrior that even this mountain of a man knew of. Her brave Tadhg.

How I miss ye.

"And what of this other building?" A larger, round building sat mostly obscured by overgrown trees and climbing plants.

"Our chapel."

Tisa gasped. "Why would yer chapel be in such a condition?"

Malcolm again shrugged. "Aodh is chieftain. He decides how things will be. We dunna use the building now."

"Who was the chieftain before him?"

"Eirnin. When he was chieftain, we used the chapel regularly."

Involved with the Norsemen. No regular Christian worship. What type of clan was this? Tisa feared she knew the answer.

"The food?" she asked.

"'Tis important for ye to understand the lay of the village." He indicated all the buildings around them. "Beyond the people that live in these buildings are outcasts that live in the woods."

"Outcasts? Are they lepers?"

"Nae. Aodh has exiled many. He would prefer they see to themselves rather than take away from what the rest of us have, what the rest of us have earned."

"*Can* they see to themselves?"

"Not always. But they are not able to contribute so they are cast out. Only the strong remain here within the village."

The weak could be children, sick, and older members. "Are there none that are weak that he deems worthy of his help?"

"The strongest children that can help with the meals. His mother until she passed but that was because she came to him when she was widowed." Malcolm shrugged. "It makes the clan stronger."

"By casting off the weak? That I do not like."

"That matters not." His eyes never wavered. "Aodh will have things as *he* wants them."

A rock landed at her feet. Malcolm was quicker than she was in retrieving it. He searched the darkening forest beside them as if seeking the source.

"It could have rolled toward us on its own." Tisa shrugged her shoulder.

Malcolm made a call with his mouth that sounded just like a baby puffin's cry. A response came. He turned toward her, his eyes wide in the gloaming. "I can see ye to the meal. They'll be waiting on ye."

Tisa frowned. "Did ye not get an answer from yer call?"

"Ye need not concern yerself."

His nervousness mounted and he began to pull her away.

"Malcolm." A child's voice called to him.

Tisa turned toward the sound then back at him. "Are ye not going to answer?"

He blew a breath. "Nae!"

"Please." The child was moving closer.

Tisa resisted his pulling. "Please, Malcolm. Someone is calling to ye. A child."

"Aye." Malcolm snorted his objection before turning as well. "Show yerself, little one."

An imp of a child with long, curly, brown hair limped out of the darkness, her dirty face bright with a smile for the big man. "I've missed ye."

Probably no more than four years old, she clamped onto Malcolm's tree-like limbs, her eyes closing in pleasure.

"I told ye *not* to come out. Did ye not hear my call?"

The girl smiled up at the huge man. "Aye. I heard ye. I just dinna believe ye."

Malcolm's eyes widened in warning and he glanced at Tisa. The girl did the same, her smile vanishing. "Oh." She turned to limp back into the darkness.

"Wait!"

Tisa reached toward the girl who continued into the dark of the forest. "Dunna leave." She turned on Malcolm. "Tell her not to go."

"But she should not be seen. If Aodh hears of the outcasts coming into the village, he sends his men out after them."

Tisa gasped. "For what purpose?"

"Methinks ye already ken."

"He would hurt his own people?" Tisa turned to where the girl went. "Please. Come back. I will tell no one."

"Mistress, ye canna be in this position. Aodh has great contempt for these people. Even more than his contempt for his son."

Her jaw dropped. Darragh knew his father's contempt? She'd seen glimpses of disapproval, but contempt? How cruel.

"Please, tell her she may come to me. I wish to meet her, learn her name. Please."

Malcolm's eyes stayed on her as if to give her a chance to change her mind. She would not. He called again but it was the call of the long-eared owl. Several shadows could barely be distinguished from the darkness as they moved toward Tisa.

Three children. Along with the girl were two older boys. The eldest had a filthy cloth wrapped about his hand. They were reed thin with sallow complexions.

Tisa tried to reassure them with her smile. "Hello."

Their wariness remained sharp. They waited for Malcolm.

"Tell them they are safe with me," Tisa said in her most demanding tone.

"Are they?" Malcolm's response gave her pause.

"I would never tell my father-in-law about them. Ye said it yerself. He belittles my own husband. I have no loyalty to him."

"He belittles yer husband with just cause."

Tisa's eyes widened. "Nae! There is no just cause. Darragh is a gentle, loving man. Ye will not speak so of him."

Malcolm lowered his gaze. "Forgive me, mistress."

She glanced at the three children. "And these children dunna deserve to be cast out." She hunkered down beside the children. "My name is Tisa."

"But ye canna call her that." Malcolm's firm orders riled her.

"Why not?" Tisa stood and turned on him with her anger. "If I am here among them in secret, why can they not call me by my given name?"

Malcolm rolled his eyes. "As ye wish, mistress."

The brown-haired girl pulled on her hand. Tisa went to one knee.

"My name is Aednat."

"Ah, little fire." Tisa took a curl between her fingers. "But yer hair is not like a fire."

Aednat's face widened into a smile, her eyes creased into tiny crescents. "My momma named me fire because of my strong spirit."

Tisa glanced at Malcolm for clarification but he averted his gaze.

Tisa asked, "Oh ho! A strong spirit?"

"Aye. One foot is not right and as a baby, I kicked the smaller one even harder than the first, as if to make it right by my spirit alone. Like I had a little fire lit in me."

The tears swelled but Tisa shook them away and faced the other two. "And yer names?"

"Will." The taller boy pointed to himself. "And Cad."

"Are ye the same family?"

Will stepped closer, "Yea. Now we are."

Tisa reached for Will's wrapped hand but he pulled it away to hide it behind his back.

"I will not hurt ye, Will. I swear it."

Will glanced toward Malcolm before putting his bandaged arm toward her. Tisa smelled the diseased flesh before it was completely uncovered. The hand had been hacked off and puss oozed from the wound.

"How did this happen?"

"I was caught stealing eggs." Will looked straight ahead, his jaw tight.

"Does this pain ye?" Tisa pushed at the swollen skin.

The boy refused to flinch. "Not overmuch."

If she could get it cleaned off, she may be able to save the arm which showed no sign of discoloration yet.

"Is there some water nearby?"

She followed the line of children as they went deeper into the darkness of the thick forest. They stopped alongside a bubbling spring.

"The Meic Lochlainn was so angry his eyes nearly popped out of his head," Aednat explained with great enthusiasm. "He could barely form words and then he was ordering his guard to seize Will."

"Enough, Aednat. She does not wish to be told all the details." Will sounded old beyond his years.

Tisa knelt beside the boy with a firm hand as she dribbled water onto the wound. Will hissed between his teeth. "It needs to be kept out of the dirt."

"They like to hunt for nests so he tries to climb the trees and then he gets it dirty—"

"Hush!" Will frowned at the little girl.

Aednat's eyes widened, her bottom lip trembling.

"I have a salve that will help this heal." A clean, thick linen was put in her face. She turned to Malcolm. "My thanks. Can I get the salve?"

"I can bring it to them."

Tisa preferred to apply it herself. "Mayhap I can come back—"

"Nae." Malcolm's face was unreadable.

Tisa faced the three children then smiled. She carefully wrapped Will's arm so that the wound was well protected. "I will be back again. Shall I bring sweets?"

"Oh yea!" Aednat exclaimed.

Tisa caught Will and Cad's quickly exchanged glances although they offered a more reserved interest.

"Good." Tisa stood up.

The mavis evening song came to them. All three faces clouded with fear. Malcolm hurried them into the woods then grabbed Tisa's hand, pulling her toward the road.

"What is amiss?" Tisa asked.

"Soldiers are about."

"Where? In the woods?"

"Aye. Mayhap 'tis nothing. Mayhap 'tis in pursuit of them."

Tisa's anger grew at the unjustness of the situation. "Aodh condemns them to live in the wild like animals and then hunts them down when it suits his purposes? Nae. This is not right."

Malcolm directed her back to the path. "And ye can say nothing about it."

She came to a halt. "What?"

"Aye. Ye promised or I'd not have allowed them to meet ye."

"But how can I do anything to help them if we act like they dunna exist?"

He took on the expression of a father explaining to a small child. "'Tis the way of it. If ye confront the very man who exiles them, ye will cause them more trouble."

Tisa harrumphed and pushed past the man to join up with the central path through the village. She hesitated but a moment. Surely she could discern where the meal was taking place on her own. Malcolm came up behind her, lifting her into his arms without a word.

"What. Are. Ye. Doing?" She slapped at his shoulder.

The beast refused to respond.

Tisa continued to slap and punch his chest. The man's grip never lessened. The sound of sloshing water made her quit her assault. Without so much as a pause, the man walked into a huge puddle that went from one side of the road to the other. There was no other way to pass than to go through it. She glanced at his face. He kept his eyes straight ahead. A stone visage.

He placed her on the dry ground in front of the opening to the longhouse.

The sounds of talking and music carried to them. Malcolm looked down at her, his face tight.

"Forgive my impatience and… abuse of ye," she said.

"Yer abuse was less significant than a fly."

She raised one brow and puckered her lips. "Not exactly what I wished to hear."

Tisa glanced about but saw no one around.

"Thank ye for trusting me. I would like to help if I may."

"Ye think on it." He gestured her through the door.

The smoke hung thick across the room. A large central hearth burned with dancing flames, giving off much heat. The smell of roasting meat tantalized Tisa's stomach but Darragh was nowhere.

"There." Malcolm pointed to the main table as if able to read her mind.

The cloth-covered table was raised higher and faced toward the other trestles that ran along the room. The place of honor. One couple she did not recognize sat at the far end, with perhaps enough room for six more although only five large, shiny drinking vessels were visible. Gold? And trimmed with precious jewels. Surely they were celebratory cups. Trepidation ran like a mouse along her spine. Malcolm gave her a gentle shove. She turned around to glare at him before sitting a distance from the unsmiling couple. Meeting others from the village did not seem like a good idea at present. Not when they narrowed their eyes at her and whispered behind their hands.

Malcolm stood alongside her then signaled to the man standing at attention across the far wall. He stood beside another she hadn't noticed. Mayhap that was the way Malcolm had planned on bringing her in rather than through the flooded road. The man, no doubt the cook, nodded and the rest of the room grew quiet. All eyes were on her. The woman who had retrieved the bedding cloth sat at the first table to her right but showed no sign of recognition. Two girls, perhaps eight and ten, approached and filled the cups with mead. A red-haired lass smiled sheepishly at her.

"My thanks," Tisa said.

Several younger, hale and hearty children processed in with trays overflowing with steaming meats, vegetables, and breads. They headed to her table. Tisa's stomach growled, her throat far too tight to eat. Malcolm stopped the server before he could present his offerings to her.

Tisa thoughts whirled. She could think of no reason for him to do this except to act in her husband's stead. That was not proper. Her stomach clenched tighter in anticipation of offending at her refusal to accept but she didn't understand the rules of this clan. She did not want to belittle Darragh in any way.

Loud voices preceded Aodh, Darragh, and Ronan before they entered the longhouse. She breathed more easily. But at the sight of her, Aodh's face brightened and he hitched up his belt. He settled on the long, hard bench between her and the other couple. Nodding their way, he faced front. A smug smile of satisfaction.

"Daughter."

Tisa cringed at the endearment. Did she have to respond in kind?

"Aodh."

He turned on her, his brows nearly touching his hairline. "Ye will address me properly, Daughter."

Darragh had stopped to speak to Breandan but turned at his father's outraged exclamation. Had Breandan been with Darragh this whole time? Ignoring the orders she had given him?

She glanced back at Aodh. There was no help for it. "Father."

He tipped his chin and his smile returned. Satisfied.

Darragh's face wore a mask of suspicion as he approached. He gestured Ronan to go before him. The man sat on the closer side of Tisa. Flanked by both of these overbearing men, this was not a meal Tisa would be able to participate in. Her husband sat next to Ronan without even a frown of disapproval on his face at being usurped from his rightful place beside her.

Aodh stood, lifted his bejeweled cup, and addressed the group.

"My loyal kinsmen, 'tis a day for great celebration. Yer tanist, my son, Darragh, has taken a bride." The gasps and mumbled words spread over the group. "Silence! Darragh has taken this lovely lady to wife. Tisa, I make known to ye yer new kinsmen."

Tisa gulped. Her face tight with fear, she smiled then nodded to the group. Cold eyes stared back despite the ear-deafening applause. Aodh sat, his thigh rubbing against hers, and accepted the platter Malcolm offered. His mouth glistening with grease from the food he had eaten.

"'Tis safe," Malcolm announced.

It took but a moment for Tisa to realize Malcolm was the food tester. Did Aodh fear his own people may poison him? Aodh held a piece of dripping goose toward her mouth. She had no choice but to accept it. His arrogant look rubbed against her last raw nerve. His hand sliding up her thigh at the same time nearly made her choke.

Tisa held her hand up before he could repeat the action.

"Darragh?"

Her husband's blank expression when he turned to her made her want to shake him. His gaze had been on Breandan. She grabbed at the food presented and offered the most heavily laden trencher from the stiffest upper crust, no doubt intended for Aodh, to her husband. The movement required her to lean and pass her arm in front of Ronan who decided at the same instant to reach for his mug. His hand moved open palmed along her breasts. He smiled without looking directly at her.

Tisa fumed at the violation. Her husband must have sensed something because, although he paid no heed to anything about his wife, he became aware of her anger.

"My thanks, wife." It sounded more like a question.

She fisted her hand for fear she may actually let loose her open palm on the man. "Would ye not care to sit beside me?"

"I do so enjoy yer company, Daughter," Aodh said, his voice sweet as honey on the comb.

"As do I." Ronan had the audacity to wink at her.

She glared at her husband. He appeared totally oblivious.

"Now?"

Darragh cleared his throat and faced the islander. "Mayhap ye could allow me to sit beside my wife."

"Darragh! Dunna offend our guest." Aodh's voice called more attention to the table.

Tisa tightened her jaw. All the eyes upon her were the eyes of censure. There was a problem with their chieftain and they laid the blame on her. Not knowing the custom of this place, she struggled with the best way to get out from between these two lechers.

Ronan glanced at Aodh. She had the sudden feeling they had conspired to push Darragh away from her and him none the wiser.

"Please." Tisa stood behind the bench and gestured to Ronan. "Would ye not prefer the seat of honor beside Aodh?"

There was no way for him to refuse without giving offense at her offer.

Ronan heaved a sigh. "Aye. I would." He stood alongside her. Peering down, his gaze traveled lower while his hand traced along her hip. "This time."

Darragh stood as well. He gestured for her to take his seat and put himself between her and Ronan. The apology she read on his face convinced her that he had seen the intimate gesture. She closed her eyes and prayed it was so. Appearing needy was the last thing she wanted. Darragh had no need of her at all. It was only in what she could offer him that he would see the benefits to being protective of her.

The rest of the meal progressed without incident while the mead flowed generously. Voices in the hall rose. Darragh took to his role as the dutiful husband, keeping his voice low as he spoke to his wife, pointing out who was who from his village. The rude couple at the far end of the table was simply referred to as Aodh's brother-in-law and his wife. Her nervousness eased a little despite Darragh also finding every reason he could to glance Breandan's way.

Breandan totally enjoyed the attention and flirted shamelessly with the man on his left who, like Darragh, seemed to enjoy his effeminate ways. She sensed her husband's increasing tension at the blatant attempt to make him jealous.

Ronan and Aodh spoke between themselves. Occasionally Darragh joined in their discussion.

"Will Leofrid arrive tomorrow?"

"Methinks he may not arrive for a few days more," Ronan slurred his words. He had been the most appreciative of the generous amount of libations.

Aodh took a long draw on his mead and gestured for more. "Good. And then we will finalize our plans."

"How much planning must we do, Father?" Darragh's voice took on that whining quality. "I would like to have some time to myself."

Tisa was certain her husband was about to turn again toward Breandan. With both Aodh and Ronan watching him, she kicked him in the shin before he followed through. The long coverings on the table hid the gesture.

Darragh jumped slightly, glanced at her, then finally smiled. A tight smile. Breandan's ploys were quite effective. Darragh was strung tight as a bow. She moved in to kiss him on the lips in the hope of hiding his obvious irritation with her.

First stiff and unresponsive, Darragh adjusted himself to turn toward her and kiss her more deeply. His hand snaked around her waist and he pressed her up against him. The movement startled her into breaking the kiss and pulling away from him.

He smiled, the corners of his eyes crinkling.

"I believe this meal is done," Darragh said without turning away. His eyes locked on to hers, he stood and reached his hand toward her. "Come, wife. Methinks we should spend some time alone."

Tisa dared not breathe. The room was silent. They again had everyone's attention.

When she began to stand from the bench, Ronan grabbed her other arm. His fingers pinched into her flesh. "Stay!"

The strength of his hold caused a ripple of fear in the pit of her stomach, radiating to all her extremities. She yanked against him. If this man chose not to release her, she doubted anyone could make him do it.

"Unhand my wife!" All whining gone from Darragh's voice, he used a formidable tone that brooked no interference.

Murmurings drifted to her from the onlookers.

Ronan's look of obvious contempt did not bother Darragh.

"Release my daughter." Aodh spoke as if Ronan was simply irritating, as if he'd only asked for the last piece of meat rather than assaulting his son's wife. "Let them be off."

Ronan dropped his gaze to her and pulled her hand toward his mouth. As if just noticing her clenched fist, he looked up at her with an expression of surprise. Surprise that she would not be welcoming his attention? He used his other hand to flatten her palm open. Despite the dread bubbling through her, she did not resist.

His sloppy kiss on her wrist was followed by one to her palm. "Lovely lady, I look forward to seeing ye again."

Finally released, Tisa quickly accepted Darragh's hand. He led them out through the center aisle, between the rows of tables overflowing with people she did not know. Each one of them watched as they exited the back door. As soon as it closed behind them, the hall erupted with conversation. Speculation, no doubt, at what had just transpired.

Tisa rubbed her wet palm on her skirt and followed Darragh who stomped toward their little house. She refused to look when she heard the door open behind them. If it was Breandan following, she would give him a piece of her mind.

Once within, Darragh tossed his belt and sword onto the chest in obvious irritation. "Why must that man always push me?"

"Yer father?"

"Nae, that islander. I dunna understand why my father took up with him."

"Nae?" Tisa was glad to be out of the hall and away from everyone watching them. It seemed like every husbandly gesture toward her resulted in murmurs throughout the hall.

Darragh dismissed her with a gesture. "Ye dunna understand how things work."

Tisa's stomach clenched. "Methinks *ye* dunna understand."

He turned on her, his mouth opened in a nasty scowl. "What do ye mean? Did I not wait on ye? And kiss ye? In front of everyone?"

"And watched as Breandan deliberately flirted with that other man just to make ye jealous?"

Darragh stomped to the fire, scattering the ashes when he dropped a heavy piece of wood into the center. "He does it just to anger me."

"But ye're not supposed to respond!" Tisa blew out a breath. "Darragh, ye must be more careful. I ken ye only want Breandan. I will not be demanding of yer time or attention but I am yer wife. I dunna wish to be accosted by yer father. Or that islander. To keep them away from me, ye have to pretend ye want me."

A heavy knock on the door that didn't sound at all like Breandan's gave Darragh something else to turn his anger on. Tisa pulled on his arm before he could get to the door.

"Please remember to act as if ye desire my attention."

A short nod and Darragh yanked open the door.

Malcolm stood there, his eyes narrowed as he looked first at her and then at Darragh.

"Yer father has sent me."

"For what purpose?"

Malcolm glanced at Tisa. "All that whispering and ye dinna even mention me?"

Tisa's face heated and she turned away.

"We have other things to discuss!" Darragh said. Clearly, he struggled to compose himself before confronting this newest threat to their arrangement. "I will not ask again."

Tisa knew Malcolm's eyes were still on her. She could feel them boring into her.

"I am to stay here," Malcolm said.

Darragh opened his mouth to protest but closed it just as quickly. He must have remembered the earlier agreement.

"Fine. Sleep there!" He pointed to the front of the room, not a curtained alcove. "And stay out of my way."

Her husband swept her up into his arms and carried her behind the heavy curtain opposite the door. His body was tight with anger and the pent up need for release. Release that he would no longer be able to see to with Malcolm present and he must have realized it. He dropped her onto the pallet and followed her, covering her body with his own. She dared not speak.

A new fear sprang to life inside her. The memories of their wedding night.

"Please do not. Yer anger is not with me," she spoke against his ear.

"I'll do whatever I choose. *Ye* are the wife. *I* am the husband."

He reached beneath her shoulders to pull at the ties of her bliaut along her back.

"Nae. Please, Darragh. I beg ye."

"Dunna beg. It does not become ye."

He shoved the shoulders of the gown down her arms. Then, as if finding it too difficult, he reached beneath her skirts.

She clamped her mouth shut.

Her chemise ripped at his insistent tugging.

Tears of humiliation dampened her cheeks. "Please. Do not."

Darragh stood. "Then just take them off."

He had not kept his voice quiet and his tone indicated he was not a happy man.

Anger seethed inside. She stood and yanked the gown over her head, followed by the chemise. Her feelings mattered not at all to this man. Despite her willingness to participate in his little pretense, he would use her to vent his own frustration.

Naked now, he didn't even look on her. Shame flooded her but she also feared how far he would go. When a man raped a woman, it had little to do with desire and more to do with control.

When he did finally look upon her, her stomach dropped. His gaze started at her feet then traveled slowly up her legs to pause at the patch of downy hair. "Lay down."

His words still loud enough for Malcolm to hear, trepidation filled the space where her stomach had been. She needed to stop him from taking them down this path. The path to their destruction.

"Those are not words of love, husband." Tisa spoke in a coaxing, playful tone, hoping to say the words that could still keep their true relationship a secret. "Touch me the way I like so that we may lay together."

He pierced her with his look, his forehead lined. Stepping toward him, she held herself nearer him but avoided his touch. She widened her eyes, wordlessly begging him to change his course.

"Oh, yes. That is my husband's touch." She spoke the words nuzzling into his leine but loud enough for her voice to travel. "Lay with me now."

She pulled him down with her. He appeared dumbfounded on how to react.

"Come quickly to me," she said.

Keeping his hands well away from her where she lay beside him, she bounced lightly against the pallet. Not really sure how long something like this would take, she stopped after a moment. Darragh's eyes widened as if affronted and rocked against the pallet quite a bit longer.

Darragh pulled the cover over her naked body. The tension in his body had lessened. His expression was sad and he put his lips near her ears. "Sweet little Tisa. I have mistreated ye again."

His tone had lost its sharpness. This storm had passed. She let out the breath that had been trapped inside like a cowering beast.

"Forgive me. Ye are verily correct. My anger is not yer doing."

She nodded.

The door opened. They both froze in place.

"Darragh!" It was Breandan. "What are *ye* doing here?"

From the contempt in his voice, Tisa would say Breandan was speaking to Malcolm.

"This is where I have been sent to stay. And ye?" Just as irritated a tone.

"I stay here as well," Breandan answered, his voice quiet.

"I am to stay here as well." It was Caireann.

Tisa sat up in the bed. "Caireann!"

She called out without thinking. Darragh dove beneath the covers before the curtain was lifted. Breandan, Caireann, and Malcolm stood there, looking in at them. She reached a naked arm out over the covers to reach toward Caireann.

"Come!" Tisa opened her arms and Caireann obliged but Tisa didn't miss the sad look on her face. "My dear girl. I am so glad to see ye."

Breandan's glare appeared over Caireann's shoulder as he looked down at her. Tisa pulled away. Malcolm stood there as well. She stretched her arm across Darragh in what she hoped appeared an affectionate gesture and leaned her head against his shoulder.

"If ye could give us a minute, we will be out anon. Malcolm, help Caireann get water heating."

"Aye, mistress, happy I am to help the lovely lady." Malcolm smiled at Caireann who averted her eyes, a light pink spreading across her face.

The curtain was dropped again. Darragh yanked Tisa's arm off him. "Ye go too far."

Angry again. No doubt because of the crestfallen expression of his lover. "We need to convince Malcolm. That is all. I will explain it to Breandan."

Darragh stood beside the bed.

"Wait." Tisa called out to him. It would not do for him to appear fully clothed too soon. "A kiss, my love."

She shrugged and motioned him closer.

"Methinks it takes some time for ye to don yer clothes," she said the words on a breath.

He appeared confused but then smiled. "My thanks, wife." He kissed the tip of her nose. "Has it taken long enough yet?"

She shrugged again.

Darragh made a loud yawn, no doubt for the listeners on the other side. "Breandan, see to a bath for me."

Her jaw dropped.

"Two can play at this game," he whispered with a wink and joined the others.

Chapter Ten

"That canna be too hot!"

Malcolm seemed ready to explode. He had been going back and forth with Darragh on the water temperature for his bath nigh on an hour. Just when it seemed Breandan had the right amount of cold added, Darragh would insist it was too cold. That required the whole heating process to begin anew.

Tisa couldn't help but think how feminine it seemed for him to be carrying on about the water. Being with the MacNaughton men from a very young age, she assumed men did not complain. When young Brighit found fault with the hotness of the water, they started making her bathe last. By that time, the water was so cold—and dirty—that she learned to not complain. Tisa assumed that was the way men handled things. But that was a very long time ago.

Brighit was a bit younger than her. They grew up together and were always close. When they were very small, they made mud pies at the river's edge while their older brothers, including Tadhg, played in the water. Even then, he had been protective of his own and that included Tisa. They had been betrothed much earlier. She knew what it was to be his. He'd punched his much larger brother in the face for teasing Tisa. She couldn't remember exactly what he had said but Tadhg had stood up for her. He'd demanded Aedan apologize. So strong and brave. She'd believed he would always be there to protect her. She had been wrong.

What made some men want to protect and other men just see to their own desires?

"Enough!" Malcolm dumped the last of the boiling water into the tub which was near to overflowing. "Yer bath. Do with it as ye please." He dropped the iron pot beside the hearth with a loud bang and went through the door the same way.

Darragh, who wore nothing but a cloth wrapped around his waist, burst into a smile.

Breandan fell against him, his eager mouth seeking his.

Caireann's jaw dropped. Her eyes widened. She appeared ready to scream.

Tisa held up her hand. "Do not!" She moved closer to her shocked friend. "Check to see that Malcolm does not return."

Bewilderment overcame her shock but Caireann opened the door the slightest crack to look out. She shook her head, her eyes avoiding the couple hanging on to each other beside the tub.

"Good."

Darragh's hands were all over Breandan, yanking at his clothes. His own cloth had already dropped, his hardened shaft quite large. His mouth slurped over Breandan's as if he were trying to eat him up.

The intensity of their emotions was singeing Tisa and the forcefulness of it was making it hard to breathe. "Please. Darragh, not here."

They were far too involved and desperate for relief to hear her. Breandan was going to his knees when Tisa pushed them toward the rear space.

"Go! In there!"

Darragh was only lucid long enough to give her a dirty look and then they tumbled behind the curtain.

Caireann watched at the door, her face a bright red at what they could hear taking place in the other room.

"Mayhap we should just put the bar to the door," Tisa said.

Caireann lifted the heavy board, dropping it into place. The guttural sounds of pleasure were overwhelming in the small space.

"He likes both men and women?" Caireann asked.

"Nae. He does not like women."

"But yer bedding. So much blood."

Tisa shook her head. "Nae. Darragh made it appear as if the deed had been done."

"Oh."

A loud, rhythmic pounding from behind the tapestry. Tisa did not exactly understand how men coupled and she'd prefer not to know. It took a minute for her to discern the sound of knocking on the door.

She went to the curtain but refused to lift it. "Darragh." Please hear me. "Darragh, someone is at the door."

No response except for Breandan's high-pitched moan of pleasure.

"Darragh!" She spoke louder. Damn. She closed her eyes and stuck her head behind the curtain. "Someone is at the door."

"What?" It was Darragh. "Quick! Get yerself covered."

Darragh dropped himself into the wooden tub, the water sloshing over the sides onto the dirt floor covered with the soiled rushes. He leaned back, a calm expression on his face. If not for his heavy breathing, one would believe he'd merely been soaking in the tub.

Breandan came in, his clothes righted, to sit beside the far side of the hearth, well away from the wooden tub.

Tisa sat on the stool beside her husband. She grabbed the cloth hanging over the edge and leaned forward to rub his chest.

Caireann pulled the door open.

Aodh paused at the open door. "Did ye not hear me knocking?"

"Beg pardon. I did not."

The man walked into the room and paused. With narrowed eyes, he surveyed the room, missing nothing. Darragh's breathing had eased and he ran his fingers through the water, a quiet smile on his face. Tisa glanced toward Breandan, also sitting peacefully. Apparently there had been time enough.

"Where is my man?"

"Methinks he went to see to nature's call," Darragh answered without looking at his father.

He missed the angry scowl but Tisa did not.

"And is that what ye were doing, son? Seeing to yer nature's call?"

Darragh shrugged. "Nae. Taking a soak is all."

"Ah, yea, yer soaks. I believe that was the very first time ye were poked. I ken I never should have trusted that man."

Darragh finally faced him. "Enough, Father." His angry expression matched his tone.

Aodh was again belittling his son but it was that flash of pain on Darragh's face that squeezed her heart. His father's words were meant to be cruel.

Tisa had the strong urge to protect her husband. "Father, what do ye here?"

Aodh stepped closer and traced his fingers along the side of her face. She stiffened.

"Ah, Tisa. Ever the dutiful wife. I wish to sit with ye awhile."

"Me?"

Aodh directed Caireann to bring the stool. Once settled, he stroked his long beard, running his eyes over her with slow deliberation.

"Yea, Tisa. We have much to discuss."

The man was going to break their agreement! Panic took a firm grip of her, heightening her senses. The scratching of the tree limb against the back wall. The water dripping from the iron pot tipped on its side where Malcolm had dropped it. The hissing of the fire as the sap escaped the bark. The rosy smell of the soap Darragh used. The scum on the water that clung to the wooden sides.

Darragh bent his knees up and took the cloth from her trembling hand. His kind eyes on her face, he smiled as if for reassurance. Did he not realize what his father was about to do?

"What trouble are ye about to cause now?" Darragh asked.

His undisguised irritation stiffened Tisa's back. Mayhap the man had a plan.

"Son. Ye dunna fool anyone with yer claim of enjoying women. Even Ronan can see through yer pretense."

Caireann's quick intake of air filled the quiet space. Tisa's eyes widened in warning and she gave a quick shake to her head.

"He believes whatever ye tell him! That man is a horse's arse." Darragh squeezed the water from the cloth, dispersing more soap scum to the side. "And I dunna claim to enjoy women." He rubbed the cloth across his hair-covered chest. "I need only enjoy one." He offered Tisa a sincere, radiant smile. "And I do enjoy this one. Quite a lot. Mayhap more than I should."

Tisa couldn't help but smile. Of course he enjoyed her. She enabled his trysts and even covered for him. "And I enjoy ye, husband."

Aodh's mouth curved into a disdainful grimace. He heaved a heavy sigh. "Ronan has brought up some things we need to consider before the arrival of the Godwin. I wish to speak to ye without his presence."

"Is that why ye encouraged him to over imbibe? Resulting in his accosting my wife?"

"The desire to accost yer wife does not require over imbibing."

Tisa stood beside the tub opposite his father. She tired of the man's inappropriate comments. "Am I the topic ye came to discuss?"

"Nae, but the mere sight of ye does, indeed, set my balls to tightening and my rod to grow stiff."

"Father!" Darragh sat up straighter. More water sloshed onto the ground. "We dunna care to ken about the condition of yer balls or yer prick. Get on with the reason ye've come."

Aodh gave his son a tolerant smile before turning to Tisa. "Do ye ken as a child, he was my constant shadow? And I? His hero." He shook his head in a defeated manner. "Now look at him."

Tisa dropped beside the tub, caressed her hand along Darragh's shoulders, and looked deep into his eyes. "Aye. He looks fine to me."

Darragh gripped her chin and pulled her in for a passionate kiss. She opened her mouth to him, even pressing herself against the tub as if she could not get close enough to him. His strong hand held her head, urging her closer still, moving his mouth over hers as if overcome with desire. Aodh cleared his throat. They parted slightly after a moment. Tisa would swear Darragh wore the expression of a victor. Then he winked and released her.

Confusion was evident on the older man's face. Doubt was a very good thing.

"What do we need to discuss?" Darragh followed Tisa with his eyes as she sat on the stool again, her needlework now in hand, before turning his attention to his father.

"The Godwin has much to lose if our plan does not come to fruition."

"That has always been the way of it." Darragh's voice was tight with irritation. He again glanced toward his wife, running his fingers through the chilling water. "'Tis not a new thought ye have. Even Ronan kens it is so."

"If his grand plan falls through, what then? We have stacked all our wheat against one wall. If the mice get in and devour it, where will we find food for winter?"

Darragh continued to watch her. His eyes hooded now. "Then we best find a cat to eat the mice."

Aodh tipped his head as if to ask are-ye-jesting?

Darragh smiled. He leaned forward, placed his hands on either side of tub, and stood with leisurely grace. Caireann turned away. His stiffened rod left no room for doubt. His father's jaw dropped, unable to tear his eyes from his son's solid erection. He glanced toward Tisa as if to verify that she was what he had truly been watching.

"Now, if ye'll bid us goodnight, we will talk again on the morrow. Anon, I would like to have time alone with my wife."

Breandan slept between the fire and the front door, a good distance from where Tisa lay flat on her back beside her husband. She had donned a heavy rail brought to her by Caireann who had spent her afternoon making friends with the villagers. Once Aodh had left, they decided sharing the small pallet was necessary while Malcolm stayed with them. He'd not returned by the time she drifted off to sleep.

Darragh's quiet voice came to her in the dark. "Tisa? Turn toward me."

Tisa fought against a heavy sleep and opened her eyes. Caireann's familiar snoring was the only other sound she heard. She turned toward him, unsure if he'd actually spoken.

"Were ye not pleased with me tonight?" he asked.

Even through a whisper, she heard his smile. He had been quite convincing with Aodh, indeed. "Aye."

He moved his mouth closer to her. "Have I made amends with ye for my anger earlier?"

"Ye have."

"Bestow a kiss upon yer husband." His voice held an urgency. Or was it just louder?

Darragh's hand, heavy on her hip, drew her nearer. When he started to move it as if to caress her, warning bells sounded in her head.

"Do ye need a kiss now?" she asked.

His face was cast in shadow. His white teeth showed clearly in the darkness. "I do."

She leaned over intending a quick kiss on the lips but he snaked his arm around her, pulling her on top of him.

Startled, she made to break the kiss but he held her head in place and devoured her mouth as if he had only one thing on his mind. His fingers ran along her back, slipping beneath her gown with little effort. She shivered. Hot against her cold skin, his hands stroked along her thigh, up and down, until he cupped her bottom. He pressed against her but his earlier condition was no longer evident.

She did not resist. Not his kiss or his caresses. He did not desire her. Even when she'd lain naked beneath him on their wedding night, and him between her legs, his body remained unaffected.

Darragh put his lips to her ear, his voice quiet again. "Are ye afeared of me? Of what I may do to ye?"

"Nae."

He held her still as he moved his hips against her. Again. And again. "Are ye afeard I may be getting stiff for ye?"

"Ye are not."

"Then kiss me like a lover. Pretend I am the man ye dreamed of."

Before she could react to that telling statement, he covered her mouth with his. How did he know of her dream? Malcolm had known. Why would he tell Darragh? He pulled back to whisper in the small space between them. "Nae, ye need to focus, lovely lady. I will be yer dream lover."

Perhaps she was not yet fully awake. Perhaps she had been affected by Darragh and Breandan but Tisa's dream and her own longing came swiftly back to her. The sounds of the birds. The smell of the grass. The feel of Tadhg beneath her. Darragh's warm tongue invaded her mouth but it was Tadhg and she kissed him back. Their tongues stroking and sparring. The hands tracing her bare thighs were Tadhg's firm hands. Massaging. Caressing. Spreading her legs. Rubbing against her.

She cried out.

Darragh's mouth muffled the single word.

Tadhg.

Her hips pressed against him, her knees on either side as he rocked into her.

"That's it, sweet Tisa. Dunna hold yerself back. Show me yer passion."

Tisa moaned into his mouth. Her hips undulating against him. Coming nearer.

He slipped a finger close to her wetness.

"Do not." Her only coherent thought.

"I can ease yer need," his words whispered into her ear.

And it was a true need. Deep inside. Growing. But she did not want him to touch her. The thought of Tadhg alone being with her, holding her, and her world exploded. She was swept away. Small tremors rippling like waves from the unanswered need at her core. The need only Tadhg could have met. The feelings slipped away like the morning mist, only partly remembered in the bright light of day.

She fell slack against Darragh and the tears came. He cradled her, turning her gently to lie beside him, her head on his chest. He held her tight, muffling her quiet sobs, and caressing her cheek. His breath against her face, he said not a word.

The sound of the curtain dropping worked its way into her thoughts.

Darragh wiped at her tears then caressed her arm with long, soothing strokes. "Wheesht."

She glanced toward the curtain. There was no one there. The sound of the door opening was unmistakable.

"I dunna understand."

"My father will trouble ye no more." Darragh kissed her forehead like a loving father comforting a hurting child. "My wife, ye are a lovely, passionate woman that deserves a man who can love ye back just as deeply. Thank ye for sharing with me what ye feel for this Tadhg. I am sorry I am not he."

His quiet heartbeat beneath her ear soothed her. The fears and frustrations floated away, only the memory of Tadhg's arms surrounding her remained. She drifted off to a peaceful sleep.

Chapter Eleven

Tadhg leaned back in the chair offered him by his new brother-in-law, Peter. Intended only for use by King William's half-brother, Odo, it was extremely soft and comfortable. That the man offered the seat to Tadhg rather than taking it himself was reason enough to be suspicious about this little meeting. He'd allowed Peter to wed his sister despite his men's objection to her marrying outside of their own clan. That she had found someone she wanted to marry warmed Tadhg's heart. He had always hoped it would be so for her rather than a life of seclusion as a nun.

The man was a Norman knight but Tadhg would not hold that against him. The Normans were of little concern to him. It mattered more that when the man looked at his sister, the intense love that he had for her was quite visible. Peter held her in the highest regard. Brighit brightening at the mere mention of his name had convinced Tadhg of the depth of her feelings for him.

"Is the mead to your liking? I've always found the best libations at the priories." Peter leaned casually against the wall of the small room off the chapel.

Tadhg sensed the man's unease. He took a sip of the dark liquid. "'Tis good," Tadhg said. "But certainly ye dinna take me from the celebration of yer wedding just to hear my thoughts on yer mead."

Peter glanced into his own cup and smiled. "Your sister told me not to be fooled by your seeming lack of concern with things."

"Oh, did she? I'll need to speak to her about that. How can I catch my enemies off guard if she warns them ahead of time?"

Peter searched his face. "Do you consider me your enemy?"

"Nae. Not an enemy. Just a man who allowed himself to be 'forced' into marrying the woman he loved. Tell me—if ye'd actually had yer way with her in that run-down house, would ye have taken her to wife anyway?"

Peter stiffened at the insult, stepping away from the wall. Tadhg had expected as much. He held up his hand to stay Peter's angry retort.

"Forgive me. My last taunt. I promise. Methinks ye are truly in love with my little sister. I can see that with my own eyes. I am well pleased. Why ye wish that she believe ye were forced into wedding her is something the two of ye need to work out. Hopefully, after I've returned to Eire."

The blond man's features softened into a genuine smile. "And we will work it out in due time but I did want to speak to you regarding when you would be returning."

Tadhg heaved a heavy sigh. He'd left the clan in such a hurry with so many things not seen to, even the thought of his return put him in a foul mood. And traveling back with Sean's heart all but bleeding onto the ground at having lost Brighit would make the traveling even worse.

"I canna tarry here. I've clan business to see to that requires all of my attention."

"Tadhg," Peter pronounced the name correctly for the first time since they'd met. "I fear for Brighit. The men she traveled with were unfeeling bastards. They treated her with contempt and although I cannot prove it yet, I believe they had plans to ransom her off. They fought hard enough to take her back from us."

The room became deathly quiet. Ronan, that impudent dog, had smiled and reassured Tadhg that Brighit was being well protected. Tadhg should have run him through.

"I ken she claimed it was not so but *was* she violated?"

"Not in body. In spirit. She was petrified. Had Mort and I not come upon them and realized something was amiss, I know not what would have happened to her." Peter's face softened. "Falling in love with the kind, gentle spirit walled up behind her fear was not difficult."

Tadhg felt the overwhelming weight of regret being added to his burdens of responsibilities. A heavy yoke. He should have stood up to his father, insisting Brighit wait until Tadhg could escort her. The realization that if he had taken that course, Tadhg would have, no doubt, reached out to the O'Brien as well. Mayhap even now have Tisa to wife. He cleared his throat.

"Then I owe ye a great debt, indeed. She recovers well under yer care."

Peter relaxed against the wall again. "Aye, if only I could spend all of my days by her side. King William has ordered me to take back his castle at York. I must leave immediately."

"Do ye believe battle will ensue?"

Peter shook his head. "We will lay siege and starve them out."

"What do ye need from me?"

"I would worry less about Brighit if I knew you were with her here."

Tadhg had so much to do but he had already allowed his sister to be in harm's way. That was an error in judgment he would not make again. "I will stay then."

"You answer me more quickly than I had expected."

"If I had chosen a different course earlier, she would not have been submitted to such treatment as ye described. I will not abandon her again. I can send Sean ahead in my stead."

Peter snorted. "I will not miss that one."

The man's obvious dislike for Tadhg's close friend was humorous. "Rest easy. He is all talk. Brighit would never have wed him."

"I do not understand."

"Sean does not love Brighit in the way ye love her. He just has not realized it yet. Brighit thought of him more like a brother and he would certainly have laid down his life for her."

Peter stiffened.

"He would lay down his life for any of us. Even for ye as her husband. Sean may be a nuisance to ye now but a more loyal man ye'll not find. God willing, he will find the woman for him and when he does, he will realize it was not love he felt for my sister."

"I know quite well what it is he feels for your sister—my wife!" The man's face brightened as if just remembering his newly married status. He moved toward the door. "And I believe I miss her company. Are we agreed then?"

"Aye. I will stay with her and care for her in yer absence."

Tadhg prayed it would not be overlong.

Sean's expression belonged on a surly, old man not a vibrant, young warrior.

"Cheer up." Tadhg offered to refill his friend's horn which he agreed to rather quickly. "Dunna be getting any ideas of getting yerself drunk and starting trouble on the wedding day of the very woman ye swear ye love."

Sean's eyes narrowed. A look intended to intimidate. Their dark depths like a turbulent sea.

Tadhg would not be stalled. "If ye truly love her, ye'd want her well cared for. Content." He gestured toward the table where Peter sat with his face close to Brighit's ear as he whispered to her. The pure joy on her face said all there was to be said. "Ye canna argue what yer own eyes tell ye."

Sean stood to his full height, inhaling a deep breath as he did so. He bent with a slight sway toward Tadhg who sat on the bench. "If ye can grant me a boon then? I'd like to take ye outside and throttle ye."

Tadhg gasped in feigned indignation. "Of what do ye speak, man?"

"I ken damn well ye kept me from her. All these years I could have been wooing her, winning her to me. Showing her what a grand husband I'd make. But ye," Sean stuck a pointed finger in the general direction of Tadhg's chest, "*ye* kept me away."

If not for the slight slur in his words, Tadhg would be taking offense at this condemnation. Mayhap even be willing to take the man outside and kick his arse, but this was the drink. When Sean sobered, he'd realize Brighit's happiness was what truly mattered.

"Well?" Sean listed toward him, his eyelids struggling to stay open as he tried to focus on Tadhg's face.

"Methinks ye've had enough to drink."

"Methinks not." Sean swallowed the contents of his horn, turned it upside down, and shook it before peering into it again. "*Humph.* I need a woman."

Sean glanced around the room. Tadhg was quickly blocking his view. The only women in the room were nuns.

"Ye dunna need a woman."

"But I *do* need a woman." His tone was turning belligerent.

"Sean, methinks ye can wait."

"Nae, I have no reason to wait now." He rubbed at the observable bulge beneath his leine. "I want to ease my misery."

"We'll go to the shelter around back."

"With the horses? For what purpose?" Sean smiled, his eyes barely open. "Aw, so I can beat ye? That would help as well."

"Something like that."

They started toward the aisle leading to the front of the Priory, passing Peter and Brighit who took no notice of them.

"She's the most beautiful thing I've ever laid my eyes on. I wanted to be the one to lay with her that first time. To put a light to that smoldering passion."

"Sean, 'tis my sister ye're speaking of."

"Aye, I ken. She told me nae but I wouldn't listen. Look at her. More beautiful than the sun rising over the bay. Damn, I wanted her beneath me."

"Sean, stop yer carrying on. 'Tis just yer prick talking."

Sean frowned, closed his eyes for a moment, then gazed down at himself. "Ye think ye heard my prick talking? Was it loud?"

Tadhg rolled his eyes and wrapped his arm around his friend's shoulders. "Come. Let us rest for a while. Surely later there will be more celebrating."

"Aye, after the bedding."

Sean headed more quickly toward the door but the mumbling continued.

"Damn, it should have been me."

Chapter Twelve

Malcolm sat on the floor beside the closed door, leaning against the inside wall.

"Do ye wait on me?" Tisa did not doubt for a minute that her irritation was apparent to all in the room.

"Ye ken I do," Malcolm said.

Darragh had gone on to his father's house but she was expected to join him. She had been successfully avoiding Aodh since the heavy rains began, making it impossible to leave their little house. Even for meals, the five of them dined there. That had suited her well enough. With the lightening of the rain came the need to venture out. The thought of seeing him now made her feel nauseous.

"Well, make yerself useful then." Patience was wearing thin in the small space and Tisa was the first to admit she was not fit for company.

Malcolm stood. "What would ye have me do for ye?"

She glanced at Breandan who sat beside the fire, working a small twig in and out from betwixt the moldy rushes. "Take that one to the winter grass so he can bring me some fresh rushes! Be sure they are dried."

The lad's eyes widened before he stood up. "Now?"

Tisa put a hand to her hip and shook her head. "Nae. A few days hence."

His face reddened. He took the fur covering hung over the bench to wrap around himself.

"And what will yer mistress be wearing if ye take that?" Malcolm asked.

Breandan shrugged, fear of the big man apparent on his face.

She may have been trying to give Breandan an excuse to earn a way to stay with them but she didn't want to speak of it in front of Aodh's man. He needed to do what she told him to do.

94

"Go on with it, Breandan. I am not for the celebration yet." She gazed down at the fine material she'd found in Darragh's chest, rubbing it betwixt her fingers. The need to focus on something other than her own fears forced her to go through his things to look for any mending that might need doing. Putting a needle to the trim of this elegant leine would be a perfect distraction.

She could feel the large man's eyes on her. "What is amiss, Malcolm?"

"Yer husband said not to tarry."

"I ken what my husband said."

"'Tis the Godwin ye're leaving waiting."

She refused to look away from the counting of the threads. They had been waiting on the man for weeks now but she decided not to share what he already knew. "I am not needed there."

Malcolm came to stand beside her. "But yer husband asked ye to be with him. He needed ye there."

Tisa had sensed a change in the way this man spoke of Darragh of late. "And yer concern?"

"Ye show he's a man ye respect by doing as he bids."

She searched what little she could see beneath his overgrown beard. He had heard about their night together. It could have been Malcolm who'd been watching. Darragh had said only that he knew someone was there but not who.

"I do respect my husband."

"Saying is one thing. Doing 'tis another."

Tisa glanced at Caireann who had looked up from her own mending. Her eyes were wide with concern. Learning that Tisa's husband did not even desire to lay with her had surely been hard enough for the girl. To see Darragh in a passionate embrace with another man must have sent her mind in a tizzy. There had been no time for them to talk of the events. Mayhap she would get a chance now if Breandan and Malcolm left them alone.

"Go on, Breandan. I've the wool to keep me warm. 'Twill be but a short distance. Go on now."

Malcolm shook his head but followed the lad out the door.

"Come closer, Caireann, so we can speak."

Caireann brought the stool and stood beside her.

"Sit!" The girl had been acting even more timid than usual. "Do ye not wish to speak with me?"

Caireann plopped down. "I do, but I wish to ken what ye have done with my friend."

"I dinna understand."

"Ye are not my dear friend. Ye are someone else. I swear it."

She clasped Caireann's cold hand. "Ye are still my dear friend. Please. Dunna say I have changed so much."

"Yer husband is a sodomite! And ye do nothing to stop him."

Tisa cringed at the condemnation. "What would ye have me do? He is kind to me. Do ye not see how he cares for me? Provides for me at our meal? Even while the one he would choose to be with looks on?"

Caireann's look of censure left little room for acceptance.

"His father wanted to take me the night of our wedding. He would have used me and passed me around his men so that they, too, could use me."

Her friend's eyes rounded in disbelief, her head shook. "Nae! He would not."

"He would! That is the way it is here." Tisa chose her words carefully. "Darragh sought to protect me from them. I am grateful to him. He is a kind man."

Emotions flitted across Caireann's face as she struggled to make sense of the situation she found herself in.

"Please. Do not think on what upsets ye. See the man for who he is."

"I will try." Caireann wrapped her arms around Tisa, holding her tightly against her. "I cry for ye each night that ye are away from the man ye love."

Tears sprang to her eyes but Tisa refused to give in. It was a waste of her strength. She cleared her throat. "I will do what needs to be done here."

Caireann pulled away, smiling at her friend. "Ye have such strength. I will endeavor to be the same."

Tisa kissed Caireann's cheek before standing to stretch her back. She blew a breath. Malcolm was correct that Darragh wanted her there and she did not want to disappoint Darragh. She should have just gone with him. Now she had to walk in while everyone was seated, all eyes upon her. Grabbing at the wool covering, she wrapped herself tight.

"Can ye gather the mending? I dunna believe this will be a short day for any of us."

The wind pressed against her so hard she had to shove the door closed behind them. Dark clouds were back, hanging heavy around the village where they drifted up from the cove. The Godwin had chosen a wild day to finally arrive. Loud music drifted to her the closer she got to the longhouse. The still damp earth sucked at her feet as she passed over it, the forceful wind doing its best to dry the area.

Lights flooded through the tiny openings of the longhouse and onto the road. Despite it being midday, the darkness required the aid of candles. The door was flung open by a young couple. They stumbled out, laughing and talking. At the sight of her, they stiffened, almost as if they'd been discussing her. What a silly notion. They rushed by without even a greeting. Tisa's stomach gurgled.

She was, indeed, far from the bosom of a loving clan that held her in high regard. Hoping to sneak in unnoticed, she hadn't expected the music to halt, cheers, and raised glasses when she entered. Darragh approached, pecked her cheek, and took her covering.

He had a relaxed smile and pleasure fairly poured out of him. "Ye took a long while."

Merely a statement and not intended as censure, she felt certain.

Glancing around, Tisa watched as Caireann joined the others then lowered her voice. "I was in no hurry to be here."

Darragh led her toward the head table but his eyes clouded with concern. "Are ye not well?"

She felt guilty at her churlish behavior and sighed. "I have not felt myself 'tis all."

Aodh stood and moved his seat so that she could join the group. "Daughter! Mayhap ye're with child."

He'd overheard her comment? Expecting a lustful gaze from him, she instead found him grinning at the dark-haired man beside him. The Godwin, no doubt. That he was settled in Aodh's seat of honor confirmed it. The young couple that usually sat at the far end was settled beside the older woman with the bulging eyes. The two had never found a reason to speak to her. Darragh's explanation that he was the old chieftain's son and to stay clear was a warning she heeded well.

"I dunna believe 'twould be so quick, Father."

"Ah, ye ken best." Aodh stood, cup in hand and addressed those gathered in the hall. "Now that my daughter has arrived, let us begin this celebration." The smile he sent her way seemed genuine. "Kinsmen, this is a proud time for our clan. Ye ken for generations we have opened our arms to any returning children, and children of children, who have left our shores to start anew elsewhere. Like the prodigal son, we welcomed them back to our shores with a fatted calf," he motioned to the meat roasting over the fire, "and a good mead," he lifted his glass, "and celebrate their fortune, good or ill. Today, we welcome back a Godwin, Leofrid, son of Tostig, and his lovely lady Abigail" He lifted the cup higher. All drank.

The dark woman beside Leofrid took a sip from her cup and made a face of disdain before returning it to the table. Godwin stood.

"Happy I am to be back among ye. My lady," it took quite a bit of coaxing to get Abigail to stand, "and I are here to celebrate yer good fortune with the joining of yer own Darragh and the Lady Tisa from of the O'Brien Clan." He turned toward her and raised his glass. "And a mighty clan it is. Welcome, Lady Tisa."

The applause burst forth. Many came to their feet and turned toward her, smiling. Darragh stood and encouraged her to stand as well.

"Welcome to ye, Leofrid. Lady Abigail." Darragh's loud voice carried over the cheers and applause. He exuded a new confidence. "And may this be the first of many more celebrations to come."

Aodh motioned to the cook and the procession of heavy-laden platters began, their table first. Malcolm had entered during Aodh's speech and stepped forward as taster. Darragh beamed with pride beside her. Aodh spoke with Ronan who sat on the far side of the Godwin couple. The woman appeared bored.

This warm reception eased her tension but Tisa couldn't begin to understand the sudden change. Breandan had settled at a table far to the left with several families who seemed to welcome him. He smiled and accepted the mead poured for him from the clay pitcher.

"Yer rushes have been seen to, mistress." Malcolm had come up beside Darragh and addressed her. When he placed a huge hand on her husband's shoulder, Darragh stiffened. "I have been remiss in not offering my well wishes on yer marriage these many weeks. The best to ye and Tisa, Darragh."

Darragh's surprise was replaced by a smile. "My thanks, Malcolm. Glad I am that ye'll be here to guard my lovely wife in my absence." He turned toward her. "She is not a treasure I'd lose lightly."

Malcolm bowed and withdrew.

Darragh turned his attention to the platter a lanky lad extended toward him. Perhaps seven and ten, the boy glanced at her husband again and again almost as if hoping to catch his attention. When Darragh had made his selection, he did finally notice him. The lad offered a coy smile and moved away.

Darragh's happy facade dropped, showing deep pain. Raw emotion. He struggled for composure.

Tisa put a hand on his arm. "Who is he?" Her heart quickened. "Is he not from this clan?"

"Aye, he is—he was… Father sent him with Leofrid the last time he was here. I have not seen him…"

A former lover? She squeezed his hand and he turned to her. "Dunna fash yerself." She kissed his palm and smiled. "Let us celebrate while we may."

Darragh exhaled a slow breath and attempted to smile. "He was just—he had been sent with another who was very dear to me."

The man Aodh had spoken of. His first. The pain was there again in his eyes.

"Dunna ye agree, Darragh?" His father was speaking to him.

"My thanks." He nodded then looked past her to his father. "Speak louder, Father. I dinna hear ye."

"When we go south, we will surely be seeing many heroes that day."

"Oh, yea, surely. Men who go willingly for glory into battle."

"And we pray ye will be among them that will return from battle unharmed to a hero's welcome," Ronan said, lifting his golden mug in the air. "Even in practice ye show ye have much strength, Darragh."

"He does indeed. Like his father."

Darragh smiled and raised his glass. "Victory will surely be ours."

"Aye." They all drank deeply.

Tisa couldn't manage to swallow her food for the lump in her throat. She gazed out across the room and noticed the number of occupants had increased. Tables had been squeezed in at odd angles to accommodate the huge crowd. Armed soldiers stood along the walls, eating as best they could manage.

A huge battle was planned. Planned with many warriors. A battle that would place Aodh Meic Lochlainn at the place of highest honor, High King of Eire. For the first time, Tisa wondered who this Godwin was. Why did he not expect the honor of High King over Eire? No doubt Darragh could explain. When she turned to ask him, she was startled to find Lady Abigail watching her.

The woman had a fair complexion and dark hair that hung around her like a mantle. She could see why Leofrid took this one as his lady. She was beautiful. A tight smile crossed her face before she turned away.

Tisa felt suddenly plain. She rested her hands in her lap. No one noticed. Leofrid saw to his lady despite her lack of enthusiasm for any of the food offered her. Aodh, Darragh, and Ronan continued with their incessant plans. Leofrid spoke little but any suggestions he made were accepted with little discussion.

A leather-clad man paused at the back door as if searching out someone in particular. He wore a rounded shield over his shoulder, a deadly looking sword as his sidearm, and an ornate, circular brooch at his shoulder, securing his brat. He removed his helm, approached the table and dropped to a knee before Godwin.

"My lord."

Leofrid stood to accept the man's offer of respect. No doubt, he was one of his own men. "Yea. What news have ye?"

"The clans to the west have laid down their weapons, my lord. Ye have won the day."

"Huzzah!" roared from all present.

Leofrid tipped his head back and smiled. A slow smile that started from some inner place of satisfaction for a job well done.

"Gerrit." Darragh's voice was a strangled whisper.

Tisa grabbed his hand. "Are ye not well?"

"Well done, Gerrit!" Leofrid said. "A better man-at-arms there has never been. Ye made a great gift to me with this one, Aodh."

Gerrit remained on one knee, his head lowered before his lord.

Darragh's eyes remained on the dark soldier.

"Gerrit! Rise! Join us for this celebration. Our reasons for celebrating increase yet again." Leofrid's happiness was uncontainable as he continued speaking to Aodh. "Not only do we have yer son's momentous marriage to Tisa O'Brien but now another victory. Music!"

The musicians who had stopped to partake of the food were quickly following his orders. Gerrit rose as well and turned his intense gaze on Tisa. She sucked in her breath, struck by the force of his attention as if the wind had been knocked out of her.

A handsome man. Dark stubble covering his strong jaw. His dark brows deepening the blue of his eyes. A small smile turning up the corners of his mouth, he quirked one brow then turned his attention to Darragh.

Darragh blanched. His shoulders slumped. His eyes rounded as if in pain.

Gerrit seemed to hold him mesmerized and neither turned away. Tisa cleared her throat. The spell broken, the leathered man faced the Godwin.

"My lord, I have just now arrived to give ye this news. I must see to my men and the horses. With yer permission, I will return when I have completed my duties and am in a more presentable state."

"So be it. Rest easy, Gerrit. I am more than well pleased with ye. Be off. See to whatever ye need to." Leofrid looked over the others dining. "Many a comely damsel here. Whatever ye like. Return whenever it pleases ye and we will hear the stories of our victory."

Gerrit just fell short of clicking his heels together and turned from the room. All eyes followed him including Darragh's. The sadness Tisa saw there was all she needed to know. This was the first man he'd fallen in love with.

Chapter Thirteen

Sean tucked his long, deer hide brat tight around his sleeping wife. That she lay naked against him and was well satiated did little to dissuade his own body's strong desire to take her again. He had time. They had their whole lives ahead of them.

Contentment settled on his chest like a purring cat. Being sent back to Drogheda ahead of Tadhg was the last thing Sean had wanted to do. Coming to the aid of this fetching lass along the way had certainly improved his disposition. Especially when that aid included taking her to wife.

His arrival home came with responsibilities he would rather not face. Not yet. This may be his last time to be alone with his new wife. He was no hurry to see it end.

Thomasina moaned beside him, seeking his lips even while not fully awake. He kissed her with all the passion she provoked in him. She was perfect in every way.

"Do we need to get walking again?"

They had quite a ways to go yet and the crossing had not been an easy one.

"Nae. Sleep. There's time yet. But first," even the smell of her roused his desire. Mayhap with the right persuasion... he nibbled her ear and whispered. "I want ye again, mo mhíle stór."

She smiled in his direction. "Mmm."

He moved to her shoulder, stroking with his tongue, nibbling more persistently. "Is that a yea?"

Thomasina stretched her neck. Running his hand across her chest, he enjoyed the feel of her nipples hardening against his palm. He grabbed a full breast, tipping his head to suckle a rosy peak. She arched into him.

One hand slid along her hip, gliding between her legs that parted quite invitingly.

"If ye insist." He traveled down her belly, smattering nibbles and kisses as he went. She rocked against his hand so hard that the vibration through the ground reminded him of a galloping horse.

Sean jerked his head up. That was a galloping horse. And it was coming very close.

"Stay here." Sean covered her, pulled his leine over him, and belted his sword at his waist.

A large tree was the perfect place to hide... and wait. If there was no need, he would not show himself but allow the rider to pass. He couldn't be certain if he was on MacNaughton or O'Brien land this close to the sea. The brown courser seemed familiar and the red head of the rider confirmed it. Slightly behind the redhead was the lad, Cormac. Sean had two choices. Stay hidden and enjoy feasting on his wife a little longer or let Calum know he had arrived safely home.

"Sean?" Calum Rua called out, his breathing heavy from his fast ride. He reined in the horse and the younger lad did the same. The light color of the brat was too bright against the dark brush. Sean hadn't thought of that. Calum's eye was drawn to it.

Damn. Sean licked his lips. He would have chosen to continue enjoying his wife if he'd had a choice but he did not.

"Dress quickly. I'll keep him from ye," Sean called to Thomasina in a hushed tone then stepped into the open on the far side of the tree, diverting the riders' path from where Thomasina donned her clothes beneath the large covering.

"Aye. Calum the Red."

Calum turned to him, his surprised expression shifted to a huge grin. "It's about time ye made it back. I thought ye were just shirking yer responsibilities."

Sean winced. He meant no harm but Sean would prefer his wife's first impression of how others saw him not be as a shirker. "Keep yer tongue in yer head, lad."

"Lad?"

Damn. Calum could never let anything slip past.

"Ye sound more like Tadhg than—" The man's eyes widened at the sight of something beyond Sean. He looked like a fish out of water with his mouth gaping and no sound coming forth.

With a deep sigh, Sean turned to Thomasina. He stepped close enough to yank out the bit of twisted skirt tucked into her hastily belted waist.

He kissed her pert little nose and whispered. "Sweet Thomasina, methinks ye intentionally reveal yerself to me so that I will not be able to keep my hands off of ye."

Thomasina smiled then peered past him to the men still atop their horses. "The redhead seems upset. Any chance he can be quickly dispatched so that we may see to that urge?"

"I will do my best." Sean turned back toward Calum. "Speak or be gone."

"Sean! What to hell are ye doing out here? And with such a comely lass and one I've never seen before?" The man was still out of breath when he jumped off his horse.

Sean smiled at the lass beside him. "Thomasina, my time alone with ye has come to an end it seems."

"Are these two from yer clan?" she asked.

Sean gave the men in question a withering look. "Aye, they are, but ken me well enough to ken not to bother me while in the company of a lovely lass even when 'tis my own wife."

"Wife?" Calum's face, already suffused with blood from exertion, may well have reddened with embarrassment. Sean certainly believed he should be embarrassed at interrupting his seduction of his bride. Their time in the tiny boat had left no time to spend in such pursuits.

"Aye."

"'Tis not Brighit!" Cormac blurted out. His face reddened as well.

Thomasina's face tightened. "Aye. I am not Brighit. *I* am the woman he loves."

Sean stood taller. Quite a lass who'd willingly married him and she'd not be regretting it any time soon. They needed to get back to what they were about.

"Thomasina, this is Cormac and Calum Rua. My wife, Thomasina."

"Pleased I am to meet ye, Thomasina," Calum said.

Thomasina had said her piece apparently because she only dipped her head in acknowledgement.

"Now go on yer way, both of ye. Tarry not here on my account."

"I need yer help, Sean. The O'Brien has not sent his supplies as promised."

"Nae food has come from him?" Sean's stomach tightened. While he'd been happily bedding the lass of his dreams his clan starved? "Explain yerself."

"Provisions arrived regularly and then no more. I'm off to see to the matter. I'd hoped ye'd be closer behind me than this." Calum glanced at the woman beside him, a skeptical expression still on his face. "But I see ye've been busy setting yer heart to rights."

"More than that. I've been learning how deep true love can actually be." Sean winked at Thomasina who smiled back. A beautiful smile. A smile that rivaled the loveliest sunrise. "So speak. What reason did they give?"

"Nae reason. I'd only just arrived and learned of the problem. Tadhg had set it up with the man."

"I ken that, Calum. I was there. Get on with it!"

"They may have met with a mishap. We'll soon be in dire straits."

Sean sighed. Responsibility had arrived. From where they stood, Sean was as far from the O'Brien as he was from his own home.

He took Thomasina in his arms. "Can ye find it in yer heart to spend a bit more time alone with me before meeting the rest of my kinsmen?"

Sean picked up the long, auburn hair that rested on her bosom. He twirled it around his finger.

"Time with just ye?" Thomasina asked.

"Aye. Can ye stand me any longer?"

"Methinks I may be able to."

Sean retrieved their few belongings and turned to Calum. "Give me the horse and head back with Cormac. If ye follow the river, ye'll see where the deer have been hiding from ye. At the big rock, a stone's throw east. Mayhap ye'll be bringing back some food." Sean mounted and reached an arm toward Thomasina, settling her in front of him. "Ration it as well as ye can. I'll return when I'm able."

Calum turned a wary eye on him. "Hold yer temper, Sean. We dunna need Roland O'Brien breaking the agreement because ye've offended the man."

Sean tipped his head. "What are ye saying about me, Calum? And in front of my new wife?" He turned the horse in the direction of the O'Brien. "If yer brash words find me in a bad light with her, I'll be kicking yer arse upon my return."

With a shake of the reins, they were off. Heading back toward the coast, Thomasina rested against his chest. Her arms held tight around his waist and she smelled as sweet as a meadow in spring. It would be a long ride. If he'd had a mind to take his time, he'd certainly be slaking himself in her arms but the clan needing food was not to be taken lightly. That Roland O'Brien might blatantly disregard their agreement was not something Sean even wanted to consider. There'd be hell to pay if that were the case.

Close to nightfall, Sean and Thomasina finally arrived. The full moon reflected off the still meadows surrounding this side of the castle. Movement within the tower silhouetted in the moonlight eased Sean's fear that the O'Brien had been attacked.

Thomasina shivered against him. She had said little. He thought her asleep.

"Are ye cold?"

"Aye."

She rubbed her hands together and blew on them. He brought her tighter into the folds of his cloak. "Better?"

She shrugged.

"Is aught amiss, mo mhíle stór?"

Thomasina shook her head but refused to look at him. Sean reined in the horse. With a fingertip, he lifted her chin up so the moon shone on her bonny face.

"Thomasina, tell me, what troubles ye? Is there discomfort?" He placed a hand high on her thigh. "I dunna mean to cause ye pain."

Sean adored this woman. She had the spirit of a young filly and the passion of an ocean storm. Nothing had ever felt as right as taking her in his arms, as if she were made for him alone. Their first time together had been pure ecstasy. She had, indeed, been a virgin. Unknown territory for him but he had kept his passion in check, choosing instead to open his wife to the intense fulfillment she could give as well as receive. He'd gone slowly, offering her pleasure before he took his own. The taste of her on his tongue, her responsiveness, etched in his heart. If he had caused her pain or if she were sore, he would move heaven and earth to ease it.

"And ye dinna." She again shook her head, more forcibly this time. "Sean, 'tis this Brighit."

"Brig?" He hadn't expected that. "What about her?"

Thomasina finally met his gaze, an imploring expression. "Ye loved her first."

With a hand on the back of her head, he eased her toward him. Her lips as sweet as wine. He tucked her in close, her soft breasts pressed against his hard chest. She smelled of the earth and the ocean.

She didn't resist. In fact, she kissed him back with much enthusiasm, wrapping an arm around his neck to urge him tighter still.

He reluctantly broke the kiss. He needed to look into her lovely, green eyes, let her see the sincerity. "My sweet Thomasina, ye are very wrong."

Frowning her displeasure, she closed the distance to his mouth again. Her heavy breathing matched his own.

"It matters not. I want to feel ye in me again." She spoke without breaking the kiss.

He took her shoulders and pulled her away.

She looked at him through hooded eyes filled with passion, running her tongue over her bottom lip. "What are ye about?"

Sean moaned at the lust-filled look, his own desire burgeoning. "Not when ye dunna understand."

Thomasina frowned. "Understand?"

"Ye said I loved Brighit first."

She shrugged as if it didn't matter and moved to kiss him again.

"Wait." He pulled his head back from her, struggling against his own desire to give her what she wanted. "I dinna ken what love was."

"Ah, this is love." She placed his hand over her breast and he caressed her, loving the weight of her in his hand. Her eyes closed and she leaned into him. Surly talking could come later. He moved closer to take her lips then jerked away.

"Wait! Hear me first. Carnal pleasure is not love. In the happiest marriages it is part of love." When she started to speak, he held his finger to her lips. "Love is when a man trusts all that he is, gives all that he is, in the keeping of one woman that he places above all others. When she cares for him, accepts his protection, shares his joy and pain, and honors him with her love."

Thomasina's frown deepened.

"Men can take their pleasure almost anywhere." He held up his hand. "Even by themselves."

She giggled.

"Some men even think this lass or that lass would be most pleasurable. 'Tis not love. 'Tis just taking the pleasure." He swiped her hair away from her face and covered her mouth with his, moving over her with the intensity of the love he felt for her. Pulling back, he sighed his longing. She was the most beautiful women he'd ever seen. "Ye, Thomasina, are the only lass I have ever loved. When my soul reaches out to ye and draws ye in close, just as yer own body takes me into yerself, we are truly one. Body and soul. That is the pleasure in the fulfillment of true love. That is the love I have for ye alone. None other. Ever. Mo chroí go deo thú."

She tucked her shoulder up, an endearing gesture she used when she was unsure of herself.

"I dunna understand then," she said. "What did ye feel for this Brighit if 'twas not love?"

"Until we met, I dinna ken love. Ye were right that I was afeared of ye."

"Afeared of me?"

"Aye and ye said as much."

"I said that?"

"Aye, in one of yer mouthier moments."

"I dunna have mouthy moments."

"Aye, ye do." Sean waited for her to respond. Although she said nothing, her eyes were focused on him. "So I thought I was just lusting after ye—greatly—but at the inn, I needed ye to trust me. To believe in me. To believe I had yer back whatever ye were about. None were going to hurt ye with me there."

"And if I trusted ye? And then ye left me?" Thomasina's eyes rounded with the pain she no doubt was remembering.

"I dinna ken yet that I loved ye and that ye could love me back. When yer brother arrived, it seemed ye had nae use for me or how strong I felt for ye. That was why I left."

Thomasina wrapped her arms around him. "I died inside when I saw how they'd beat ye."

"Wheesht, lass. I've been beaten worse by my own kinsmen."

Her tears dampened his shoulder.

"I'm thinking I've shared too much if ye need to cry so."

She clung tighter. "I dinna ken I could care so much as I do for ye."

Sean squeezed her just as tight. If he could but share the intensity of his love for her through his touch alone. Mayhap after a lifetime together.

"Then we are well suited, indeed. Destined to be together since before time began."

Chapter Fourteen

"Stand up slowly before I cut yer head clean off."

Sean's eyes focused on the tip of the blade at the end of his nose. He raised his arms above his bared chest to show he was unarmed.

"Where are ye going?" Thomasina spoke to him without opening her eyes.

"Wheesht. Go back to sleep," Sean whispered before responding to the mail-clad man before him. "I have nae weapon. Can ye draw down yer sword?"

With great effort, Sean worked to not reveal his true feelings to this unknown man but his blood was pounding through his veins. He could easily rip the man's head from his shoulders.

No response.

"If ye lower yer sword, 'twill be possible for me to stand as ye asked."

Thomasina picked her head up from Sean's shoulder with an irritated scowl. "What are ye about?"

The soldier lowered his weapon enough for Sean to stand.

"Wheesht. Stay down, mo mhíle stór." He urged her back to the ground. Her eyes were finally opening. She looked to be struggling to make sense of the commotion around them. Sean felt the same.

When he was standing to his full height, two more soldiers trained their weapons on him as if afraid of him. Their faces obscured by their helms, they shifted to a more defensive stance. Good. Waking a sleeping warrior was never a wise move.

"What do ye here?"

The soldier to Sean's left had noticed Thomasina's unclothed state. A greasy smile was making its way across his shadowed face. She yanked the brat over her shoulders and glared back at him.

"Back down!" Sean gave the man a menacing look. He could take these three and more if it were a matter of protecting her. "What do ye want with me?"

"Ye're not an O'Brien," the first soldier spoke but was also showing an interest in Thomasina now.

"And neither are ye." Sean moved right, obscuring their view.

"And how do ye ken that?"

"I ken these lands and their people. We've come to see Roland O'Brien. The gates were closed and we decided to pass the time out here."

"And we see what ye were passing yer time with." The greasy one wiped at his face.

The three soldiers chuckled.

"Back off." Sean jerked toward the man as if to attack him.

Greasy stepped back, dropping the tip of his sword before raising it again and giving Sean his complete attention.

"Roland would not like ye molesting his guests."

The first soldier ran his tongue over his teeth. "Ye're not a guest."

"'Tis just sun up now. We will be coming to him when the gates are open."

The same man glanced Thomasina's way. "They're open now."

"Yea, why dunna we help ye get in to see the man."

It was clear these men were waiting with bated breath to catch a glimpse of Thomasina as she dressed. That would not be happening.

"Methinks ye dunna ken Roland as I do." Sean eased into his storytelling voice, a keen eye on each of them. "There was a man who once spoke to his daughter—merely spoke—while she was out searching for her herbs one day. She told her father of the man. And what did her father do? Roland put the man to the spike."

The men shifted. One blanched but kept his eyes averted from both Sean and Thomasina. The greasy man rubbed at himself, flexed his shoulders and glanced back toward the castle as if gauging the distance.

"I'll make yer presence known to the O'Brien. What is yer name?"

"I am Sean of the MacNaughton Clan. He kens me well."

"And who is this? Will she be coming in with ye or was she only keeping ye warm for the night?"

"Hold yer tongue! She is my wife."

"Aye." The man tipped his nose perhaps in an attempt at a threatening look but all the men quickly withdrew toward the castle.

"Thomasina," Sean dropped beside her to take her in his arms, "ye handled yerself well."

"I dinna. I was scared." She pulled away to face him. "I need to get some guts."

Sean tried not to laugh. "Let us get ye dressed first. Then we'll see to the guts."

Roland O'Brien was abed, a priest at his bedside. Sean directed Thomasina to wait at the door and quietly approached the man. The room was dark and the smell of sickness permeated the air, making it difficult to take a breath.

"Is he near death?" Sean asked the priest who was putting away his vestments.

"He may be close. They sent me word that he was no longer aware of his surroundings."

"Has he spoken to ye?"

The priest shook his head.

"Sean?" Roland spoke in a strong voice. "Is that ye, Sean?"

"Aye, Roland. 'Tis me."

The priest shrugged and sat on the stool beside the bed.

"Tisa."

Sean felt a fist to his gut. If something was wrong with Tisa, he would have to send word to Tadhg. "Aye?"

Roland reached toward Sean. After a moment's hesitation, Sean took the man's hand. It was surprisingly strong.

"Please, Sean, go to her. See that she is well."

"Where is she?"

Roland covered his face with his other hand. "I have done her wrong, Sean. I have wed her to a cruel man. Cruel like his father. I have wronged my sweet Tisa. She will never forgive me."

The priest widened his eyes and shook his head. Sean locked his jaw. The church did not want to know about the cruelty of a man toward his own wife even when it violated their own beliefs.

"Do ye ken who she is wed to?" He directed the question at the priest.

"The Meic Lochlainn. A prominent northern clan."

Prominent meaning wealthy. Wealth they didn't need to take from the church.

Roland wiped at his cheeks. "She is wed to Darragh of the Meic Lochlainn. But I fear for her safety."

"Then why did ye allow him to take her to wife?" Sean fought to maintain his composure. A sick room was no place for a show of his temper.

"I could not sit here like a mole on a rock just waiting for the hawk to swoop down on me. I needed protection."

"Ye should have worked out an agreement with Tadhg when he came to ye." Sean's voice rose to the same level as Roland's. He seemed less at death's door and more racked with guilt.

Roland's eyes widened. "'Twas too late! Darragh had taken her."

Sean swallowed down the anger building in him. "Tadhg loves Tisa. He would have saved her from the man if ye'd but told him the truth. He would gladly lay down his life for her."

"I could not."

Thomasina came to stand behind Sean, a hand on his shoulder. He felt strength in her touch and took a deep breath before speaking again. "What would ye have me do?"

"Please. Go to them. See how she fares. Bring me back word that she is well that I may die in peace."

Thomasina squeezed his shoulder, a look of concern on her face. She nodded as if in consent. Sean didn't believe the man was anywhere near death, only that he was, indeed, overcome with remorse.

"Aye, Roland O'Brien. I will go and see that Tisa is well. And ye send the provisions to the MacNaughtons as ye promised."

Roland nodded his head. "'Twill be done."

Chapter Fifteen

York, England

With the short days growing even shorter, Peter and John were both wishing to be somewhere other than at the castle in York. No doubt, John dreamed of being back in Rowena's arms in Essex just as Peter dreamed of having Brighit to himself in that huge bed of Bishop Odo's.

"I do not believe there was much else we could have done that we had not done." Mort rubbed at the helmet gripped in his hand, polishing it before putting it back on his head. "I arrived in time and gave him your protection, my lord. Sean is, no doubt, home with his wife even now."

John nodded.

His wife. Peter snorted at the irony but remained silent.

"But they believed he had slaughtered Norman soldiers?" John asked.

"Aye. 'Twas a messy business."

"Did they have any proof of the offense?" Peter took a sip of his mead, thankfully fresh from the Priory.

"The best kind of proof. An eye witness."

Peter nearly spit out the mead. "How can that be?"

"'Twas our little friend, Ivan," Mort said.

"Ivan witnessed the slaughter? Then there is no doubt he was the actual perpetrator of the slaughter," Peter's voice got louder in his outrage.

"Indeed."

"Is this the same Ivan that was hired to see your Brighit safely to the Priory?" John asked.

"The same. A more loathsome scum I have never met," Peter said. "And that it was Brighit's own uncle who gave Ivan those orders was the worst offense of all."

"An uncle should be trustworthy," John said. "Although I have no uncles of my own that I know of."

Peter smiled at his friend, grabbing his shoulder before he spoke. John was desperate to learn who his sire was. "I wish you to be uncle to my children, John, for we are brothers."

"That would give me great pleasure." John's expression remained sad through his smile. "And you need not worry that your child will not be healthy as a horse. Brighit is a fine size for birthing."

"An expert are you?"

"I spoke to many priests after Rowena lost our daughter. They assured me 'twas Arthur's brutality toward her that caused the child to come too soon. She will have a fine birth this time and a healthy babe. I'm certain. If I had not that reassurance, I would not be here."

"Rowena is a special woman, indeed. You must miss her sorely."

John stared out over the muck, straw, dung, men, animals, weapons, trebuchets, and battering rams. Siege was hell, but considered better than hand to hand battles which ended with death.

"We have much to work out. Allowing her cousin to live when the king ordered his death puts me in a precarious situation."

"Only if Leofrid returns from Ireland." Peter laughed. "Saddling him with Abigail will surely make his life a living hell."

John nodded, a far off look on his face.

Peter could well imagine the thoughts and scenarios that worked their way through his mind. Abigail was the source of many troubles for John. She was from his past though, back when John had lived only for the next battle and William's approval. Now he had so much more to live for. His loving wife. The people that depended on him. The future of his family.

Learning King William was a self-serving tyrant rather than the selfless man John had believed him to be, no doubt, added even more trepidation. William taking John on as squire and away from the monks gave the boy the father figure he'd always yearned for. It wasn't until that father figure showed little regard for Rowena or her people that John's eyes were finally opened. Peter had no such attachment to William and he served at his pleasure.

"There was talk, my lord, that the slaughter of the Normans was only the first action and there would be more to come."

"Those against us will continue to be against us. Our only chance is to win them over," John said.

"Or see them dead," Peter said.

Peter and John had uncovered a plot within Rowena's own manor. A plot to keep the populace rejecting King William. The plan included dressing up as Normans and murdering their own. It was her most trusted man, a Saxon himself, who perpetrated the plot. Arthur. His father had lost everything, including his life, by refusing to swear fealty to William, the Duke of Normandy, once he was crowned.

Arthur had chosen a different path, hiding his hatred behind a benevolent facade. He did swear fealty to King William and was so convincing, he was placed in a powerful position watching over the king's ward, Rowena. Even after her marriage to John, Arthur had done all that he could to win Rowena over. He claimed he loved her. And yet, all that time undermining any attempts at peace that would have made her life easier. It wasn't until John returned from Normandy that Arthur's plot was uncovered. The price to both John and Rowena for Arthur's betrayal had been a high one. The life of their first born daughter.

"My wife had been escorted across England by Ivan," Peter said. "If he indeed used her transport as a ruse to ascertain the amount of support for putting a Godwin back on the throne again, Leofrid may have a reason to return."

"You have the right of it, Peter. Methinks this siege cannot end soon enough."

"Ye think 'tis best because ye have a soft heart, mo mhíle stór." Sean kissed the tip of Thomasina's nose. "And I have duties I must see to, but I will do as I promised the man I would."

She was again seated in front of him as they headed north to the Meic Lochlainn territory.

"And what is this Tisa like?"

Sean again saw the little girl Tisa had been. "She was headstrong. Had courage." He smiled down at Thomasina. "Methinks she is much like ye."

"Then I look forward to meeting her. Mayhap we will have much to speak of."

Something about the smug turn of her lips made Sean uncomfortable. "Now why am I questioning yer motives in speaking to Tisa?"

The corners of her eyes creased with her closed smile. "Because I want ye to always think of what I may or may not be up to."

Sean's mouth dropped open. He fought against smiling. "I yield, woman!"

She sat up straighter. "As well ye should!"

He kissed her cheek. She sat up tall, flexing her shoulders.

"Are ye uncomfortable, lass?"

She gave him a sideways glance. "Aye. My bottom is tired of this horse."

Sean grinned. "Oh, I can see to that as soon as we've a warm, soft place to set ourselves."

A snap of a branch and Sean jerked back on the reins. Too late.

"HOLD!" Five men with their bows at the ready and trained on them blocked their way.

Large men with broadswords and a few short-handled maces came out from the woods on either side. There were at least fifteen men surrounding them. Sean raised his hands up.

"I mean no harm!"

"Get down." A dark man dressed in black leather dismounted and swaggered toward Sean, tugging off his gloves as he approached. Their leader.

Sean slid off his horse and took a step away from Thomasina who remained mounted. He'd rather the men direct their weapons at him and not include her in their sights. He ground his teeth. This was twice he'd been caught off guard just since he'd arrived back home. He was thinking with his prick again.

"I've come from Roland O'Brien."

The leader tipped his head and circled him, his eyes traveling up and down as if working on the best way to handle him. If given the chance, Sean could easily best him. The man stopped in front of Sean. Nose to nose, they were of the exact same height. The man seemed pleased, his smile relaxed.

"My friend, ye are very far from home."

Sean did not avert his gaze from the bright blue eyes piercing him. "I am. I've come to see the Meic Lochlainn."

"And I see ye've brought entertainment." The man grabbed Thomasina off the top of the horse, the swords of his men keeping Sean from interfering.

She slapped at his hands. "Dunna lay hands on me, ye foul beast!"

The dark man smiled, clearly amused by her attempts to defend herself. With ease, he twirled Thomasina toward him and looked down into her face. His hips cantered toward her.

"A very nice playmate. Very nice, indeed." He shot a glance at Sean. "So nice that ye forgot ye were a warrior on a mission."

Thomasina scowled at the man.

Sean swallowed and tightened his lips, his nostrils flaring. More men were moving in. Sean had no chance for defense. "I have come to speak to the Meic Lochlainn."

The man kept his eyes on Thomasina. "Ye're a pretty thing. I might like a taste of ye."

He moved in close and closed his eyes. She pulled back as far as she was able.

"Hmm, ye smell like grass and ocean and swiving." He opened his eyes and stroked a leather-clad finger along her cheek.

She jerked her head away.

"Does this rather large man see to all yer needs?" His eyes on Sean now, he continued speaking in a slow, quiet voice. "Mmm, I bet he does."

The man seemed to savor the thought of what Sean did and did not do for his wife and again perused the length of him. A metal taste spread over Sean's tongue. His teeth had sunk into his lip.

"Ye were so wrapped up in her, ye paid no attention to yer surroundings. Tsk. Tsk. I would take ye to task for that if ye were one of mine."

Sean swallowed down the rage swelling in his chest. The soldiers around him never took their eyes off of him. Well trained soldiers, indeed. He would cut the man's hand off without a second thought.

"He bid me to come see his daughter, Tisa."

The man gripped Thomasina's chin and tipped her head back, his smile twisting into a cruel grimace. Sean shifted forward. Three burly men moved to intercept him. Sean bumped the first man's sword up. It connected with his face. Blood gushed from his nose. Ducking, one man tumbled over Sean's shoulder to land flat on his back. A step to the left, Sean fisted his hands and rammed his elbow into the man's back. He arched in pain. It was the soldier beside Sean that was able to plow the hilt of his sword into his gut, forcing the wind out of him. Sean dropped to his knees in pain.

Gerrit was unperturbed, keeping his focus on Thomasina.

"Yea, I do like pretty things. And I do like ye." He spoke in a low voice.

"I dunna feel the same," she spat the words at him.

He glanced toward Sean when he stood back up. "Is this one yers? Or do ye share?"

"She is my wife."

The man's eyes rounded and he removed his hands, palms out, as if he'd been scorched. "Wife? There seems to be an abundance of wives around here."

Thomasina ran to Sean's side, not giving the man a chance to grab her back.

"I will take ye to the Meic Lochlainn. Ye and yer *wife*."

Chapter Sixteen

The dark days of rain shifted to days of heavy snow. Despite their proximity to the ocean, a cold wind kept the air thick enough that their breath misted, their nostrils froze, and their fingers numbed. Tisa took to spending the days in the little house rather than to venture out. Melancholy settled in and she had little reason to push it away.

"I'll be needing to stay with the Meic Lochlainn for the next few days if ye do not object, mistress." Malcolm stoked the fire in preparation of leaving Tisa to her mending.

The warmth in the small area made her sleepy. Tisa shook it off. "If need be. How do the children fare in this cold?"

Malcolm scowled. He scowled every time she mentioned what she was not to discuss.

"We are alone," she said.

He bristled like an old woman.

"Do they have any needs I can see to?"

"Nae, mistress. Ye have done well by them. It is yer fair face they miss the most. Ye should have never started spending time with them."

"Why ever not? They give me great joy. I miss them as well."

With Leofrid's visit came frequent trips for both Aodh and Darragh to the other clans. Breandan complained of his abandonment when they were alone but managed to keep himself occupied. Sometimes she didn't see him for days. For Tisa, it gave her the time she needed to see to the needs of the outcasts. Many had difficulties that were eased with her teas and tinctures. Aednat showed a keen interest in learning about the herbs. In the spring, Tisa planned to take her out and teach her where to find the different plants. The knowledge would be very beneficial for them.

Malcolm hesitated at the door, displaying an unaccustomed shyness. Tisa became immediately alert.

"Tell me."

Malcolm's eyes rounded and she smiled.

"Ye so seldom seem at a loss for words, there must be something wrong."

He dropped his shoulders and his lips relaxed into a soft curve. "Ye have the right of it. Aodh has asked me if I have seen any strangers in our woods."

"Strangers? The dead of winter does not seem like the best time for strangers to be among us."

"'Tis not a stranger he speaks of." Malcolm paused as if to give her a moment to catch on but she had no idea what he referred to. "He has heard about ye."

"Me?"

"Yer visits to the outcasts. Someone has mentioned seeing ye with them."

Tisa's jaw slackened. "Who?"

"Aodh's own granddaughter is among the outcasts. Mayhap she got word to him."

"His own granddaughter? What a cruel—" She clamped her mouth shut when Malcolm's eyes narrowed in warning. The man's loyalty to Aodh surpassed what was deserved. Tisa could not begin to understand how men chose their loyalties.

"Methinks ye need to be more careful with yer ventures into the woods even when yer husband and father are away."

"So it appears." Her one reprieve through the dark days of winter had been her time with the children.

"Oh." Malcolm reached into his tunic. "For ye."

He opened his hand to show her a small figure carved out of wood. The strokes were more like gashes but she was able to make out the shape of a woman. She glanced up at him. "Is it me?"

Malcolm beamed. "Aye. Cad worked on it with Will. His ability is progressing quite well."

"Tell him how much I love it." Tisa sensed a ray of sunshine in her darkness and placed the sculpture beside the carved chest in the alcove. The chill within had her pulling back the hanging so the heat could reach the area. "I will treasure it. Mayhap I can go and thank him."

"Nae! Ye need to wait until they are no longer searching for the strange woman in the woods."

"They're searching for me? Are ye certain 'tis me they look for?"

He tipped his head. "Ye think I dunna ken exactly who is in these woods? 'Tis ye they search for and none other, so ye must remain here."

"Aye." The darkness was back. "Methinks I will rest until Darragh returns."

She lay down beneath the heavy covering on the pallet. Malcolm left without comment. Being with the children brought back memories of home. Of her time with Brighit and her brothers. Of Tadhg.

The blue sky was endless and the heat from the sun was soothing. Tadhg's handsome face. His warm lips pressed against her own then sliding across her cheeks, her neck. She shivered. Hands grasped at her hips, urging her closer. A sigh of longing. She opened her eyes. The room was dark, the fire nearly out. She must have slept for a long time but she felt as if she'd just laid down. The door opened.

"Malcolm?" Her foggy brain tried to remember when the man would be returning.

The curtain was yanked back just as she sat up. Gerrit stood there, his bright blue eyes taking in every part of her.

"What do ye want?"

"Ye have visitors."

"Who?" Tisa didn't dare come out from beneath her covers with him there. She didn't feel safe around him. It was as if he looked right into her soul. Darragh had never spoken of him but she was sure this was the man Aodh had said his son had first been with. Yet he looked on her as if she were a morsel he would like to eat. Surely the man could not have desires for both men and women. She forced herself out of the bed. When she made to move past him, he did not step aside but forced her to rub against him as she passed. A shiver of revulsion went through her at the contact and he grabbed her arm. His expression gave her the impression he was offended, as if she'd insulted him.

"Unhand me."

Gerrit smiled at her. His even, white teeth were visible in the dim light. "What do ye here? By yerself? In yer husband's bed?"

"I said unhand me."

"Do ye pleasure yerself? Is that why ye are here alone?"

Tisa gasped before she could hide her shock. His smile widened. He stepped closer, his body rubbing against hers. His fingers bit into the flesh of her arm.

"If I drag my finger between yer luscious nether lips, will ye be damp from yer own ministrations?"

Tisa held her ground. "Now!"

Gerrit released her, took a step back, and turned to move about the room as if he belonged there. His eyes taking in the lot, he paused beside the open alcove before entering to stand at the table. He slid his hand across the top of the intricately carved chest like a caress, as if feeling the detail of a lover's body.

"I wish ye to leave," Tisa said.

He faced her. "I've been sent for ye."

Darragh would not send this man to her for any reason. He avoided Gerrit at every turn.

"Who sent ye to me?"

He moved closer, sitting at the bench beside the table.

"Yer visitors."

Her heavy gown was not intended to be worn out and about. She needed to change if she was to see someone else.

"I've asked and ye've refused to answer me. What would Leofrid think of such open defiance?"

Gerrit's eyes widened, a clear expression of disbelief, before nearly busting with laughter.

Her indignation increased in direct proportion to her tightening lips.

"Do ye threaten me, woman?"

Standing suddenly, he closed the distance between them. All laughter gone. His face almost touching hers. "*I* have no fear. Or secrets to hide."

Secrets? Like her visiting the outcasts? Tisa did not want anything to happen to any of them because of her. Their lives were hard enough. This man may very well be worse than Aodh. A knock at the door made her jump.

Gerrit did not move away. He merely smiled, no doubt amused by her nervousness. "Will ye see to that?"

His arrogance left her speechless. It was only for need of another person in the room that she went to the door herself. The bar lay across the inside. She glowered back at Gerrit.

He shrugged. "I dinna wish to be interrupted."

She put the bar aside.

Breandan stood there. "Ye barred the door?"

When he noticed Gerrit, he glanced back at Tisa with narrowed eyes. She suddenly felt dirty. As if she'd been caught doing something wrong.

"He di—"

"I have been sent to retrieve the lady." Gerrit came to stand before Breandan.

Breandan surveyed the man, adjusting his head to take in every part of the imposing man. From his broad chest, to his narrow hips, to the size of his feet. He licked his lips and seemed unable to tear his eyes away.

Gerrit crossed his arms, his own lips slanting into an all-knowing smile. He leaned closer to Breandan.

"And what are ye about? Ye are Breandan?" Gerrit asked.

Breandan jerked his head up, his jaw slack, and searched Gerrit's face as if verifying the intent behind the question. "Aye, Breandan."

"Mmm, I ken ye. I've seen ye often." Gerrit's voice was soft, almost sensual.

"And I ye," Breandan answered, his breathing shallow.

Anger flashed through Tisa. Pushing Breandan out of harm's way, Tisa stood up to the man. Heat poured off of him and she blocked it out, refusing to allow him to disarm her.

"Ye may wait outside for me." She pointed through the open doorway.

Gerrit appeared taken aback but he regained his composure. "Take care how ye treat others, sweet little Tisa."

She locked her jaw to keep it from dropping at his use of Darragh's endearment for her.

His eyes twinkled in the fading light and he smiled. A knowing smile. A smile that promised much. She slammed the door shut behind him. Breandan heaved a shaky sigh from where he stood in the middle of the room. A sigh of pleasure, surely he was deeply aroused by the man's interest.

She closed in on him. "Breandan! Stop! Dunna be disloyal for an impressive body."

Breandan's lusty expression changed to anger. "What do ye ken of it? Ye're only a woman."

Her mouth gaped open. "Gerrit is playing some sort of game with us. Pray for wisdom, little boy, for ye surely dunna ken when ye have it good."

Tisa pushed through to the room that she now thought of as her own, her body shaking. If Darragh had been able to spend time with Breandan, he would not be acting this way. She doffed her gown just as the door slammed. Poking her head out, there was no one.

"Damn ye, Breandan." She had felt safer with him near. Yanking her dress over her head, she smoothed it down over her hips. She pulled her hair out and picked up the brush. "Spoiled little child."

Her mumbling did no good but it did feel somewhat reassuring to hear her own voice in the silence. When she went out the door, Gerrit was leaning his shoulder against the door support, facing her. He moved his eyes up her length, stopping on her face. The intensity of his gaze sent goose bumps up her arms. She knew as soon as he sensed her unease by the smile he bestowed.

"The visitor is from yer father."

"Hunh!" Tisa turned to run to the longhouse. Why hadn't he told her it was someone from home? Her heart filled with excitement, her lungs expanded with the exertion. She was so intent on seeing who was there, she didn't pause before bursting into the longhouse of her father-in-law.

Aodh turned toward her, an unhappy frown on his face. Darragh was not there. There was no one. Her eyes stung with tears. The door opened behind her and she turned to vent her anger on that blackheart Gerrit but it was Sean O'Cisoghe standing there. She fell into his arms with quite a bit of oomph.

"My Lord! Sean, 'tis so good to see ye."

It was the sweet sound of Tisa's voice that told Sean who had flung herself into his arms. She held him tight. He couldn't say for sure if the shiver that went through her was from excitement or fear. She did not seem inclined to release him but he pulled away enough to look into her face.

"How fare ye, little Tisa?"

Her wide eyes looked into his and she was a little girl again, hanging on to Tadhg's every word, begging for his attention. Sean's heart lurched at his own sentiment. She shook her head.

"Tisa. Show some dignity." It was Aodh Meic Lochlainn. Tisa stiffened in Sean's arms before stepping away.

She turned to the man who ridiculed her and missed Sean's attempt at a reassuring smile.

"Beg pardon, Father. I was overcome with joy to see someone from my home."

The man tipped his head and puffed out his chest. "Home? Methinks this is yer home. Is that not so, Daughter?"

Tisa dropped her head, accepting the reprimand. Sean swallowed down the need to come to her defense. She was wed to this man's son. Sean had no place in defending her.

"That is fine." Aodh smiled now. "Come. Sit by me." He gestured to the bench and Tisa dutifully followed his orders.

Sean came forward but it was Aodh who spoke. "Tisa. This man comes from yer father—"

"Is he well?"

The bearded man narrowed his eyes at her. "Have ye no manners?"

Tisa again bowed her head.

"Dunna interrupt me. Ye act like a child that I should take over my knee."

Aodh shifted in the chair, his eyes averted and a slight smile on his face. Sean sensed the man's excitement at his own words. Dread raised the hackles on the back of his neck.

"This man comes from yer father to see how ye fare." Aodh tipped her head up with his fingertips to look into her face. "Ye may speak to him."

Tisa's smile burst across her face when she turned toward Sean. "Oh, Sean. 'Tis wonderful to see ye. How is my father? And who is this with ye?"

Sean gently took Thomasina's hand to pull her to stand beside him. He didn't doubt she recognized the arrogant way this man treated Tisa. It was so much like her own father. "'Tis my wife. Thomasina."

Tisa's brows rose. "Ye, Sean? Ye have wed such a lovely woman as this?"

Thomasina giggled which eased his consternation at such a statement. "Aye. I have taken this lovely woman to wife."

Thomasina curtseyed. Aodh beamed at the gesture and sat up straighter. "Come, sit beside me."

He gestured to the bench on the other side of him. Sean held her fast. "My thanks, Aodh, but we wish to speak of old times with Tisa, if we may."

This man seemed to think he was king. Best to not cause any suspicion. The smug expression he received reassured Sean he had been correct to ask his permission.

"For certain." Aodh rose. "Please." He gestured to Sean to come up and take his seat. "I have duties to see to."

The man lumbered away through another door. Sean turned back to Tisa. She appeared thin with dark circles under her eyes.

Thomasina took her hand. "I am so happy to meet ye."

Tisa hugged her and Sean noticed a glistening in her eyes but then she pulled back and smiled at them both. "How is my father?"

Sean sat beside Thomasina. "He is not well."

Tisa's eyes widened.

"I mean to say, he is saddened at the loss of ye."

She sighed in relief. "I dinna even say goodbye to him."

"Why not?" Thomasina asked.

"He did not choose well in this match." She glanced toward the door Aodh had used and lowered her voice. "I took a while to become accustomed to not marrying Tadhg and of Darragh being my husband. I dinna act as I should have. I was not a loyal daughter."

Thomasina glanced at Sean. He took her hand and kissed her palm to reassure her. She had also parted on bad terms from her father. Surely, it was not the same. Her father had bartered her off to a man his own age.

"He misses ye greatly and wants only to ken how ye fare."

"I fare well enough. Have ye met Darragh?"

"We have not." Thomasina answered. "But we did meet Aodh's wife."

"Wife?" Tisa reeled back. "He has a wife?"

"Lilith." Sean shrugged. Strange Tisa didn't know that. "She is a small woman."

"She wore a tight head dress. Her eyes were... large."

"I canna say I have ever met Darragh's mother." Tisa's tone indicated her own bewilderment.

"Mayhap Darragh was from a different wife?" Thomasina asked.

Aodh burst in, a clay pitcher tucked under his arm and a horn in each hand.

"Come, Sean. Let us speak as men. Ladies," he put the items on the table, "if ye will give us some time."

Tisa and Thomasina exchanged glances but both stood. Sean's patience with this man was wearing thin. Thomasina must have sensed it and winked at him before turning to Tisa.

"Please. Can ye show me yer new home?"

The fact that his wife had no idea what her old home looked like made Sean smile. His sweet wife was doing her best to be the peacekeeper. A noble endeavor. He could do the same and accepted the horn. He followed Aodh's lead, raising it as well.

"Sláinte."

"Sláinte."

Tisa led the way through the hall and out the door.

Chapter Seventeen

"A peaceful place." Thomasina glanced around and followed Tisa who led the way to the small, round building set apart from the longhouse.

Tisa remembered Darragh's comment about how the village may appear peaceful but, in truth, it was not. She chose not to repeat the warning. It did no good for this woman or Sean to realize how warlike her father-in-law was.

"My thanks."

The fire was stoked and Breandan sat beside it, his own mending in his hands. He glanced up, clearly startled.

"Be easy, Breandan. This is Thomasina. She is the wife of Sean from the MacNaughton Clan."

"Sean has married? And to someone that is not Tadhg's sister?"

Thomasina tipped her head. "Men dunna always ken their own minds."

"Or what is best for them," Tisa added. "Brighit was a dear friend but not intended for Sean."

"Aye. Brighit was always kind to me." Breandan sounded wistful. "Do ye ken how she fares?"

"She has married a Norman soldier, Peter."

Breandan nodded, his eyes dropping again to the material in his hands.

Thomasina tipped her head. "What have ye there?"

"Mending," Breandan said, his tone quite irritated.

She settled beside him, sharing his bench without being asked.

Tisa draped her wool across the coffer. "Breandan is very particular."

"I've fixed this same hole every week for the last month. It keeps coming back."

"Truly?" Thomasina's eyes widened before she began laughing. "Oh, Breandan! Methinks ye need help with that then."

He smiled at her.

Tisa was a bit surprised at how kind he was being to Thomasina. She'd offered the same help but was met with a scowl. She sat on the stool opposite the two of them.

"I ken I'm doing it correct," Breandan's attention was again on the cloth.

Thomasina took the material from his hands, careful to hold it the same way. "I see. Ye have a thread here…" She prodded at the weaving with her fingertips before stretching it as far as she could then handed it back. "Try that."

Breandan frowned in concentration, made quick work of the stitches and smiled at Thomasina. A cheery smile. "Ye have the right of it. I dinna see that. My thanks."

A stab of jealousy pricked at Tisa. Breandan was never cheerful with her. But then again, Thomasina was not a possible rival for his lover's attention.

"What can I get ye?" Breandan stood beside her, ready to immediately do her bidding.

If only Tisa could get him to help with any of the chores with such willingness.

"Me? Nothing." Thomasina spread her gown over her knees, smoothing the material.

"Can I wash yer gown for ye?" Breandan's suggestion came with so much enthusiasm, Tisa's breath caught for fear Thomasina would not agree. Tisa did not want him to be disappointed.

"Oh, yea, Thomasina. A bath for ye," Tisa said.

"I'll see to the water!" Breandan dragged the tub out and left to get the water.

Thomasina smiled at Tisa. "That is very sweet of ye to offer. Are ye certain 'tis not a burden to ye?"

"I am certain. My husband is fastidious so we are very accustomed to bathing even while it snows outside. Breandan only need go to the next building for the heated water. Did ye see my father?"

"Aye. He was abed when we arrived but Sean felt certain it was merely fear for yer well-being that troubled him. We will let him ken ye are fine."

Tisa didn't feel fine. She was overcome with guilt for having left her father as she did. "My thanks."

The door flew open as Breandan entered with a bucket of water on each arm. "Nice and hot."

He dumped them into the tub then added cold water from the barrel beside the door. He left again, closing the door behind him.

"Let us see to yer gown." Tisa brought her into the alcove. "'Tis a lovely gown."

It may have been a beautiful shade of blue but looked more gray at present.

"My thanks. 'Twas my mother's. I wore it for my binding ceremony to Sean."

Another thing Tisa was not allowed to experience but it mattered little since it would have been to a man she did not love. She rummaged through the small chest for something Thomasina could wear while her gown dried.

"His face lit up when he saw me in it." Thomasina sounded as if she were reliving the event. "I had been dressed as a lad and when he saw me dressed as a lass," she sighed, "'twas a look of sincere appreciation I saw on his face, although he was more than eager to see it come off as well."

Tisa opened her mouth to respond and realized she had no words. She did not know what it was to be looked upon with love, with a man anxious to be your husband. She swiped at her eyes then worked to untie the bindings of Thomasina's dress.

"Beg pardon. Mayhap I should not say such things as that."

"'Tis fine."

"We are both women and 'tis very good to have another woman to speak with."

"Aye, Sean is a good man." Tisa repeated what she'd always heard said about Thomasina's husband, anxious to avoid any other revelations. "Although I have not seen him for many years."

"Why is that?"

Tisa shrugged and pulled the gown over her head. "I saw him more than my betrothed but not very often. My father kept me close."

Thomasina pulled up the chemise as she spoke, baring her body. "My father cared little for keeping me safe."

"Methinks we have had very different upbringings." A large bruise on Thomasina's shoulder caught Tisa's eyes. "Have ye been hurt? I have some salve—"

"Nae." Thomasina grinned. "'Tis a love bite from my husband."

"A love bite?"

Darragh's bite had left teeth marks. She couldn't imagine what Thomasina spoke of but she nodded her head.

"He likes to latch on as he rides betwixt my legs. I enjoy it as well."

Tisa's face heated.

"May we speak since we are both married woman?"

"If ye need to," Tisa said, hoping she would not.

"My mother died when I was very young and I have no one else to ask."

The heat spread down Tisa's neck and she turned away from her new friend, reaching for the wool to wrap her up in. She may be a married woman but she was not an experienced one. "I dunna ken if I can be of any help."

"Well, it's—"

The door blew open and Tisa heaved a great sigh of relief. "Breandan."

She went to the tub and helped him to dump in the water, leaving Thomasina to follow.

"Mayhap ye can see how it feels to ye?" Tisa asked.

Breandan and Tisa's eyes on her, Thomasina blanched pulling the ends of the cover closer. "I will not bare myself in front of another man."

"Oh, I do not li—"

"He will give ye his back." Tisa glared at him until he turned away.

Thomasina dropped the wool, swiped her hand through the water, then lowered herself into the tub. "Mmm, very good."

"I'll take the gown." Breandan went to retrieve the gown, not even glancing toward the narrow, wooden tub.

"Be careful with it. 'Tis very dear to her."

Breandan raised his brows at her as if she'd insulted him and left without another word.

"He is quite capable, I'm certain," Thomasina said.

"Aye." Tisa had no idea.

She brought out the soap from the carved chest. It had seemed a good place to store such valuables and Darragh had not objected.

"My thanks, sweet lady." Thomasina's smile appeared again when she accepted it. She took a deep sniff. "Mmm, ye treat me as one very special, indeed."

"I ken it feels good to soak. No doubt, yer husband will appreciate a clean wife as well." Tisa sat again. "Tell me how ye came to be wed to Sean."

Thomasina accepted the cloth Tisa offered and rubbed it with the rose-scented soap. "He came to save me from my father. A drunkard." Thomasina dipped below the surface to soak her hair. She spurted the water.

Tisa took the soap and rubbed Thomasina's long tresses with it, working it into her scalp as she listened.

"Quite a handsome man, my Sean."

"He is that." Tisa handed back the soap.

"He was on my horse and I needed to get her back."

"No simple task. Were ye not intimidated by his great size?"

"Aye, but I needed my horse. I was looking for my brother to aid me against our drunken father."

Tisa paused her scrubbing. "Ye said ye were dressed as a lad?"

Thomasina laughed. "Aye." She rubbed the soap over a long calf. "He said he knew I was a woman from the start. He fought against his need to protect me."

"You dinna find yer brother?"

"I did. 'Tis strange, but after I found my brother, he was no longer enough. Not after Sean."

"Not enough?"

"Niall, my brother, his protection was different. Sean's protection felt like his life depended on it. Like he would die for me."

Tisa's heart tightened.

"I liked the passion that flared in his eyes when he argued with me. And when he kissed me... I felt the heat singe me all the way down to my toes. I dinna want him to let me go. Ever."

"He must have felt the same."

"He told me he'd lusted after me."

Tisa longed to know Tadhg in this same way. To have him take her in his arms. To have him tell her he lusted after her. Listening to the details, her eyes drifted shut and she imagined Thomasina's story was her own.

"He took me in his arms and held me to his solid length. His arms like home. Safe."

So safe in his strong arms.

"His mouth on mine was as sweet as the summer sun after a storm."

His warm breath on her face. His lips on hers.

"He made me want him even closer."

Held so close, tight against his hard length.

"I fell in love with him."

Tisa sighed aloud. Thomasina looked back at her. "Are ye finished?"

She opened her eyes and dropped the damp hair. "Aye."

Thomasina ducked beneath the water then stood in the tub, sloshing the excess water down her body. Tisa held the wool for her to wrap herself in. She settled beside the fire.

"Will ye like to use the water as well? 'Tis still warm."

No one cared if she was clean. Darragh's baths had become the norm but she seldom had an opportunity for one herself.

Tisa smiled, a conspiratorial smile. "I would like that."

"Do ye need help with yer gown?"

Tisa snorted. She had become quite adept at removing her own gown and did so with no trouble, tossing it onto the rushes.

"Well done."

"Can ye assist me with my hair?"

"Certainly." Thomasina watched as she dropped into the water. "Ye have lovely skin. Methinks yer husband must enjoy its softness."

He had never said as much. Tisa dipped below the surface. "So ye were dressed as a lad?"

Thomasina sat by the tub, gathering Tisa's hair in one hand, rubbing the soap with the other.

"Aye. So no one would ken I was a woman."

"Did it work?"

"Sean said others dinna ken I was a woman."

"It must have been scary to pretend to be a man."

"It made me feel sort of free."

"Truly?"

"Except for the damn tying and yanking up and all that. Men look at ye not at all when they believe ye're another man."

Not all men. "Methinks it would be nice to go about unnoticed."

Thomasina became quiet. She rubbed Tisa's neck, scrubbing into her scalp. The water was getting chilled but Tisa was in no hurry to end the attention.

"Tisa. Can I ask ye something?" Thomasina's voice was quiet.

Tisa dunked under the water to rinse her hair. Thomasina was certainly persistent.

When Tisa came back up, she pulled her hair over her shoulder and said, "I will try to answer if I can."

"When Sean takes me... I want it to never end. I feel so vulnerable. Like he kens my soul. Is that bad?"

Tisa took a quiet breath, suddenly overwhelmed with the depth of her sadness. There was no one that cared for her. No one knew her soul. No one would ever know her soul. She would always be alone. And she longed for those feelings like she had never longed for anything in her life. She had no idea what Thomasina spoke of but she knew in her heart those feelings could never be bad.

"Methinks Sean treasures ye, Thomasina. He loves ye deeply and when he takes ye, he can show ye what words canna convey. He shows ye the depth of his love, how he feels about ye. Ye're a blessed woman to have a husband who feels that way about ye."

Thomasina teared up, her lip quivered, but she nodded.

Tisa forced herself to swallow down her own feelings and smiled. "I think ye are a wise woman. Return his love. Dunna hold back."

Tisa knew she would have done the same if she'd had the chance. She stood abruptly and stepped out of the tub. Darragh opened the door at the same time. Thomasina tightened the wool around herself. His eyes narrowed as if to figure out who she was before his gaze landed on Tisa's face. No wayward glance. No look of appreciation.

"What do ye here?" he asked.

"Does it not look like we're bathing?" Tisa responded.

"Then ye heard there's to be a feast tonight?" Darragh went past to the table without another glance her way. "I hoped to wear that leine ye stitched for me."

He poked around inside the chest.

"Are ye done with it yet?"

Thomasina's narrowed gaze sent off warning bells. Surely it couldn't matter if this woman noticed that Tisa's husband did not look on her with love or any other emotion. Totally bared, he hadn't looked on her at all.

"Here it is." His tone triumphant, he shook it out in front of him, admiring the row of leaves and elder blossoms she had embroidered around the hem. "'Tis lovely, Tisa."

He slipped behind the curtain and reappeared with the darker leine. "Father has ordered my presence immediately and ye are to come as soon as ye are able."

He flashed a smile toward Thomasina and went out the same way he'd come.

Tisa still stood beside the tub, the water droplets chilling her skin. "That was my husband. Darragh."

Thomasina nodded, a guilty expression on her face.

Chapter Eighteen

Sean leaned back against the wall behind the head table. The night had fallen quickly and he was anxious to see Thomasina again. Mayhap he needed to go out and find her.

"And then the man fell."

Aodh's storytelling had been going on for nigh two hours and Sean was tired of hearing this arrogant man's voice.

Sean emptied his wooden mug and stood. He was about to ask where he might find Tisa and Thomasina but the door opened. A tall man entered wearing a dark leine, etched with delicate flowers along the bottom. He recognized Tisa's handiwork. This must be her husband.

"Darragh! Come, come." Aodh approached his son with an outstretched arm. "I have someone for ye to meet." He urged him closer to Sean. "This is my son, Darragh."

Sean's unease deepened as the man's eyes traveled the length of him, taking in his imposing height and the breadth of his chest with a great deal of appreciation. Darragh's nostrils flared and he filled his chest. A small smile of pleasure on his lips when his eyes finally found Sean's face.

Sean clamped his jaw tight.

"And who is this?" Darragh's voice sounded breathy and his father turned a scowl on him.

"This is Sean. He comes from yer wife's father."

Darragh shook his head as if clearing his mind. He finally looked at his father whose fury was barely contained.

"Tisa's father? Is he not well?" Darragh asked.

Sean crossed his arms and did not cover his angry tone. "Methinks he will be much worse when I return to him."

Aodh turned his attention to Sean, reaching up to wrap an arm around his shoulders. "Come. Come. No need to concern Roland with events here. Let us relax and feast. Malcolm!"

Aodh struggled for some sort of control. Darragh had the decency to look away from Sean's intimidating glare. How could Roland marry his daughter off to a sodomite? He did not believe there was any chance Roland was not aware of it. The man did little to hide his interest. Breandan crossed into the room, saw Sean, and turned about to exit, setting off even more warning bells.

"Breandan," Sean called to the boy. Darragh immediately averted his gaze and followed his father to the head trestle.

The boy stopped as if deciding whether he would answer Sean. Sean made the choice simple by coming up behind him.

"Look at me."

Breandan's guilty expression shifted to irritation. "I have duties, Sean. Why do ye delay me?"

"I see ye have come to live here as well as Tisa. Who else is here from the O'Brien Clan?"

The young man sighed, his shoulders rounding. "Caireann has come as well."

"And do ye keep yer company with Caireann? Or only with Darragh as ye did in the guard tower?"

Sean was gratified to see the unmistakable reddening of Breandan's face.

"Think ye we dinna ken what ye were about?"

Breandan heaved his shoulders up. "Methinks it matters little here."

"And why would that be?"

"I have been well received."

"Have ye? And would this be to yer own mistress' detriment?"

"Sean! Come," Aodh called from his seat.

"We will discuss this later." Sean turned to the table. Aodh sat beside a man Sean had not met yet. Aodh directed Sean to take the seat between him and his son.

"I will await my wife."

"She'll be here anon. I met her with my own wife but a short time ago." Darragh spoke up, his eyes fixed on Sean's face now. His eyes wide and innocent.

"Methinks I will see what keeps her." Sean turned away, ignoring the assurances offered as he made his way outside.

Twilight was quickly taking over. The moon clouded over by heavy, snow clouds. No doubt, the return home would be delayed. Soldiers passed by. Sean recognized the leathered man from earlier this morning.

He swaggered toward the longhouse, surrounded by lesser men who all but bowed down to him. Definitely imposing.

Sean took a deep, cleansing breath. Snow would there by morning. He hoped there was a warm place for Thomasina and him to bed down. A light behind the longhouse drew his attention. A door opening. He went toward it. Thomasina and Tisa walked side by side in close conversation. His heart went out to Tisa that she had been wed to a man who found satisfaction in other men's arms. She deserved so much better.

"Mo chroí go deo thú."

Thomasina's face lit up when she saw Sean and he opened his arms to her. He had missed the feel of her beside him. She held him close then stepped away unexpectedly. A discreet distance.

"What are ye about?" Sean asked.

"We've been visiting," Tisa said.

"And I had a nice long soak with rose-scented soap." Thomasina winked at him. A rush of anticipation washed over him when he thought of finding all the places where the scent might have lingered.

"Lilith offered me the same," Sean said. He moved to stand between them, offering an arm to each lady. "Let us partake of the evening meal. They may start the feast without us if we dunna hurry."

They sped up along the path just as a light snow drifted down. The mavis evening song sounded in the distance. Tisa stopped. She searched at her side.

"Oh no! Please, go on without me. I have forgotten something. I will be but a moment."

Thomasina grabbed her hand. "We will go back with ye."

"Nae! No need. Please. Make my excuses. I will be but a moment."

Thomasina and Sean exchanged glances.

"If that is what ye would have us do," Sean said.

"It is. Go. I will be there anon."

Tisa headed back the way they'd gone but listened for the bang of the longhouse door. There it was.

She turned toward the forest and ducked low into the darkness.

"Hello?"

No answer. The bird call was the signal of danger. Soldiers were about. Mayhap there was something she could do to help. Whatever they needed, Malcolm would be at the meal with Aodh and unable to offer any assistance. The children would need her.

"Will?" Tisa whispered and moved deeper into the darkness. The moon was well covered by clouds. There was little she could make out. She closed her eyes and willed her ears to listen harder. A child sobbing in the distance. Her eyes flew open. It was Aednat.

She followed the direction of the sound, the cold air snapping the twigs beneath her feet. The sobbing stopped just as Tisa came upon her.

"Tisa?" Aednat whispered, her breath misting in front of her. She lay on the ground, the well-worn blanket Tisa had managed to sneak out to her wrapped tight around her. Her small arm held out in an awkward way.

"What has happened, sweetling?"

"There was a man on a horse. I could not get out of the way fast enough. I was knocked down."

Tisa picked up the little hand, feeling for the soundness of the bones within. "Did the rider not see ye?"

"I dunna ken for certain. 'Twas very dark. He did not stop."

Aednat cried out in pain.

"Oh, I'm sorry little one." The bone in her wrist was twisted at an awkward angle. Tisa lifted her into her arms. "Let me get ye to the others. Which way?"

"But, mistress, Malcolm told us never to show ye where we stay. He fears for ye."

"And I fear for ye!" Tisa's firm tone had to dissuade the little girl. "I will bring ye to safety. Here or my own home. But I will see ye safe."

Aednat pointed and Tisa followed the directions as she walked. A strong wind swept down the ravine at them, making it hard to keep her eyes open with the debris blowing into her face.

"There." Aednat pointed to the side of a hill.

Tisa continued forward not seeing the opening to the cave until the last instant.

"Will!" Tisa called and the boy quickly came out from the shadows of the cave.

"What do ye here? Malcolm will be angry with us." There was fear in his voice.

"Aednat has been hurt. Trampled by a horse. I had to get her to ye." She followed Will who disappeared through a gap so narrow she had to turn sideways to get through. It opened into a wider part of the cave. A small fire glowed in the center, warming the room. The eyes from those sitting in the darkness locked on to her, following her movements. There were maybe ten others but none of them spoke. Their faces obscured. Will directed her to a small blanket and she settled the small girl on top.

Tisa straightened the girl's arm in hopes of alleviating her pain.

Aednat winced.

"Do ye have anything cold I can put on her wrist? I think it may be broken."

A tall woman came from the shadows, bringing a wooden bucket for Will. "Fill this with water from the spring." She turned to Tisa. "That water is very cold."

"Grandmother!" Aednat cried anew and the woman hunkered beside her, stroking her hair.

"Shh, my dear. The pain 'twill pass."

She had long, black hair sprinkled with silver and bright eyes that reflected the firelight.

"My thanks. The cold water will ease her pain," Tisa said.

She glanced around for the basket of herbs she'd given them a few days earlier. Many had bone healing powers.

"So ye are Darragh's wife?"

Tisa stilled. "I am."

Their eyes met. "Aednat spoke of meeting ye."

Tisa grabbed the basket tucked under a low spot against the wall.

"I wish ye well with him," the older woman said.

"My thanks." Tisa rummaged through the basket, glad to not have to face the woman at this moment.

"He is my son."

Tisa jerked her head up, her eyes widening from shock.

The woman smiled. A quiet smile. "I am Aodh's wife."

Aodh's wife? The glow from the firelight revealed wide set eyes and high cheekbones. She was beautiful.

"His wife? But ye live here?"

Sean and Thomasina met her but she lived among the outcasts?

She dipped her head and swallowed as if choosing her words carefully, "I am Aodh's *true* wife. I stood beside him while he made his plans to take over as chieftain. Then I was set aside so that he could claim the chieftain's daughter as his wife." She sneered. "His attempt to placate the elders who would have chosen another to lead."

"I am... sorry for ye." Tisa pressed the small sack of leaves and twigs into the other woman's frail hand. "This can be boiled in water. It will help the bones to heal."

"I will see to it. Ye need to go back."

"I canna go back. I need to see to her wrist."

"Go before they come looking for ye." The woman moved toward the fire.

Will dropped the heavy bucket alongside Tisa. She ripped off a piece of her under dress and soaked it in the cold water. Her mind whirled.

This was Darragh's mother? She had so many questions for her. Giving the cloth a final squeeze, Tisa carefully laid it across Aednat's wrist.

"Mistress," Will said. He placed a gentle hand on Tisa's arm. "If they find ye missing, they will search for ye even here."

Darragh's mother returned with a wooden mug, the pungent aroma of the steeping herbs filling the small space. "Ye brought her to us. We will care for her now."

Tisa looked between the two of them then glanced back at Aednat, her face contorted with pain. She settled beside the little girl. "Oh, sweet thing. Can ye remember what the horse looked like?"

"It was the black one with the silver chain around its neck. The one the leathered man rides."

Gerrit.

"Thank ye. Rest," Tisa addressed the old woman, "what is yer name?"

"I am called Aoife."

"My thanks, Aoife. Aednat, I will come back to check on ye."

Will went with Tisa to the entrance of the cave. Even without Aednat in her arms the passage was nearly too narrow for passing.

She leveled her gaze on him. "Ye must let me ken if she gets worse."

"I will."

Tisa tried to feel some relief in that. "Will Aoife follow my instructions?"

"She will. Dunna fash yerself."

Every bit of her said to stay but she forced herself to walk away. If Aednat worsened, she would never forgive herself. She headed back the way they'd come. Slipping on the ice-slicked path, she fell hard to her knees. The snow came down faster now and she wrapped the wool tight around her, pulling it over her head to keep out the stinging cold. The wind whistled by, snapping the limbs overhead as they were tossed about. She stopped to get her bearings but found she couldn't be certain which direction she'd come from or which direction to take to even return to the cave.

The ground thundered beneath her. A horse. Tisa ran to a tall tree. Throwing herself flat against it, she wrapped her arms around its trunk. The horse came at her out of the darkness, silver chains tinkling, just missing as it passed. She sagged against the tree, her breathing ragged. The sound of the horse slowing a short distance away could be heard, then coming nearer again, picking up speed. Tisa held her breath. She dared not move.

The horse stopped, the dirt from its hooves pelting against her mantle. She turned her face away. Someone strong grabbed her shoulder, flipped her around and backed her against the tree.

"What do ye here?" Even in the darkness she recognized the biting tone of Gerrit. There was no attempt to control his anger. His leather-clad fist gripped her chin. "I could have run ye down!"

Tisa tried to free herself. He pressed his body against her, pinning her flat against the rough bark of the tree, planting one foot between hers.

"I will not ask again." He spoke through gritted teeth, his breath hot on her cheek.

"Nothing! I was lost."

"In the woods?" His bright blue eyes couldn't be visible in this darkness but she'd swear she could see them, piercing into hers, searching her.

"I was lost."

He released her chin and she jerked away. His body relaxed against her, a solid weight, making it difficult to take a breath. Time dragged by but she refused to look at him. Surely he would tire of this game and leave her.

"Meeting a lover?" His low voice startled her. It was the same seductive tone he'd used on Breandan. A ripple of fear slithered like a beetle down her spine.

She swallowed her fear and faced him. "I am not!"

"Oh, I think 'tis true. And who would yer lover be? Who would dare to take such liberties with the chieftain's daughter-in-law?" His voice quiet, Gerrit searched down the front of her. The devilish smile gleamed in the darkness as he removed the leathered glove with his teeth. "Ye're a comely lass. Pleasing to look at. I'd wager even more pleasing to touch."

He slipped one hand beneath her wool and she gasped, his hand hot enough to singe where he laid it flat against her. With his other hand, he guided her face back to him. A gentle touch this time, as if he needed to look into her eyes.

"Have ye never felt a man's hand on yer breast?" He cupped her breast and moved his face in close, his lips against her cheek as he spoke, "Or his mouth suckling ye here?"

She jerked her head away but he continued touching her, stroking against her nipple. He nuzzled into her hair, his breath coming faster. He slid his foot to widen her stance despite her desperate struggle against it. Skimming down the front of her gown, he pushed his fingers into the material and grabbed between her legs.

"Dunna." Her breath hitched, a sob in her throat she refused to release.

He began leisurely fondling her through the thick material, rubbing against her most intimate spot. When she grabbed at his hand, he caught her wrist and brought her hand to his mouth to kiss her palm. A wet kiss she couldn't wipe away. His shadowed face before her, he intertwined his large fingers with hers, bringing them above her head.

"Methinks ye've never had a man." With great deliberation, he did the same with her other hand. She struggled against his grasp but he pressed his stiff cock into her, simulating the act. "Pity yer husband prefers a tight ass to yer sweetness. All the better for me."

She swallowed again, unable to take a breath. She would not be giving her consent to this.

He stilled. Closing his eyes, he took a deep breath, as if smelling something quite pleasant. She smelled only his stench.

"Mmmm. Yer desire calls out to me. Begging me to take ye." He opened his eyes. A slow smile spread across his face. By handfuls, he dragged up her gown until he touched her bare skin, his hand slipping back between her legs.

"Cease!" Tisa yanked against his hand that held both her wrists motionless.

He remained unperturbed. "Ye need to slake yer passion." A probing finger stroked her. "And if I see to it, ye'll never be satisfied by another."

She squeezed her eyes shut. "Nae."

He slipped his finger deep inside her, moving in and out, rocking his hips against her to the rhythm of his hand.

"Yer body says yea."

He watched her as if able to measure her reaction.

"Methinks ye want to ken the pleasure I can give ye."

I do not.

"Ye long to be taken."

Not by you.

His mouth was hot on hers.

He broke the kiss and spoke against her lips, "Ye've done well, covering for yer husband." His shoulders shoved into her, holding her in place so tight that the jewels of his brooch bit through the material and into her flesh. He reached down to free himself. "Everyone questioning whether Darragh has, indeed, been able to perform for ye. Humph. I ken better."

His long, rigid tarse pressed into her hip, hot and silky against her naked flesh.

"I'm eager for ye." His breathing labored. He spread her legs wider still and angled himself at the juncture of her leg.

Tisa took a deep breath and stiffened against the inevitable.

"Release her!" Malcolm had an arrow trained at Gerrit's head. "And I mean this very instant."

Immediately released, she dared not move. Gerrit took a step back, his hands open, indicating no resistance. He took a deep, steadying breath and turned away from her.

"Now why did ye need to stop me?" Gerrit sounded sincerely disappointed. "She's a comely woman that deserves to have a real man."

"A prick does not a man make." Malcolm's voice was menacingly quiet. "Cover it up or I'll cut it off."

Gerrit adjusted himself and half-turned toward Tisa, a smile on his face.

"Another time. My apologies for having aroused ye so and leaving ye unsatisfied."

"There'll be no next time." Malcolm towered over the man. "Ye're not man enough for her."

As soon as Malcolm lowered his arrow, Gerrit swaggered to his horse and mounted. "Methinks I'll have to find another to quench the fire ye set in me, sweet little Tisa."

He galloped off into the night as if able to see right through the darkness.

"He's the devil himself." Tisa quivered in a breath. Intense emotion washed over her. Rage. Disgust. Humiliation. The jumble of emotions made a mockery of her attempts to right her clothing. And the tears came.

Malcolm took her in his arms. "Forgive me for not being here sooner. Darragh was worried for ye and sent me."

Gerrit had opened her eyes to things she did not want to know. Feelings she had no use for. She felt dirty. Thomasina had a perfect marriage and a man that cared for her in all things but Tisa had empty dreams with no future promise of happiness. Her body racked with sobs.

Malcolm remained silent. No doubt, he knew he wasn't the one she needed comfort from. Who then? There was no one to comfort her. Not now. Not ever. She hated herself for succumbing to tears and struggled for composure, pulling back from Malcolm.

"My thanks for coming to my aid. It was Aednat. She was trampled by a horse and broke the bones in her wrist. I tried to help her."

The big man's eyes widened. His anger, barely contained, was more intense than she'd ever seen it. "Mistress, I warned ye. Ye need to stay away. It was probably Gerrit who ran her down."

"Please see to her." Tisa wiped at her nose.

Malcolm stood his ground, his face tight. "Listen well. Their life has been decided by another and we canna change that fate. We may be able to ease their discomfort but their destiny will not be changed."

"Mayhap when Darragh becomes chieftain."

Malcolm barked a laugh. "Sweet lady. He is the same as his father."

"Nae. He can be kind."

"He does not question his father's way. He will be the same. The strong must stay together. The weak must be banished." Malcolm paused before speaking again. "Take care for yerself. The banishment of the outcasts will not be changed but ye may become a casualty as well if ye get in the way."

Tisa took a shaky breath, rubbing at the bruise above her breast where Gerrit's brooch had pierced her. Her fingers came away wet. "I need to go to my husband but I need to wash first."

"I will see ye safely home. They will not start the feast until ye are present."

At the entrance to the roundhouse, Malcolm opened the door for her but remained outside. She questioned him with a look but he gave no hint of what he was thinking. He only said, "I will wait on ye here. I will explain to Aodh that I will be remaining here with ye."

Chapter Nineteen

Tisa fixed a smile to her face and entered the hall. Everyone's eyes were on her. Thomasina made no comment if she noticed the change of gown.

"My sweetness," Darragh stood to meet her then lowered his voice. "Are ye not well? Ye look... different."

She tightened the smile. "All is well. Beg pardon for keeping ye from yer meal."

Darragh helped her to her seat then settled beside her. Sean's eyes missed nothing, she felt certain. Thomasina turned away.

Aodh stood. "Ah another celebration from our new allies, the O'Brien. Sean and his lovely bride, Thomasina, grace us with their presence. By the looks of the snow, they will be spending some time with us."

He lifted his golden mug and the rest did the same. Tisa took a hefty swallow and put down her empty cup.

Darragh's eyes on her, he asked, "What is amiss?"

She shook her head, the smile still stretched across her face. The dark man entering by the back door turned toward her. He assessed her with eyes a stormy blue. Her breath caught in her throat at the sight of him.

She motioned for more drink but shook her head at the clay pitcher. "Something stronger."

"Is there anything ye need to tell me?" Darragh's concern was beginning to irritate her.

"Nae." Her face felt ready to crack. Either that or she would stand up in front of all these people and scream until she could scream no more.

She accepted the golden cup filled with the same drink Aodh and Ronan enjoyed well into the night. Ronan was nowhere to be seen. "My thanks."

Tisa coughed on her first swallow but took another which went down easier.

Darragh continued to watch her. "Do ye wish me to stop asking ye? Ye need but tell me."

"I wish ye to stop asking me."

The liquid pooled in her stomach, radiating heat through her body. The sounds around her became distant. The watchful eye of the villagers and soldiers before her seemed of little consequence. Her body relaxed. It was just as well since all was beyond her ability to control. Happiness. Joy. Love. A life worth living. All were ethereal, at best. She raised her empty cup for more.

Sean could not begin to guess what had transpired since he'd last seen Tisa smiling with his wife but something certainly had. Her face was pale and tight as a bowstring. One wrong word and she would, no doubt, let loose.

"Sean," Aodh turned to him, "I would make known to ye our kinsman, Leofrid."

Sean's chest tightened. Leofrid? Certainly this could be a different Leofrid than the one Ivan—that miserable, little curd—had taunted Sean with. Even offering him escape from a promised beheading if Sean but joined in Leofrid's fight against the Normans.

"Pleased I am to make yer acquaintance, Leofrid."

"Nae, the pleasure is mine to meet such a fine warrior as yerself. Yer skills are legendary."

Sean was not fooled into smugness by the flattery. He tipped his head, "Surely they are exaggerations. No more."

"Oh ho, I think not. Not when any other warrior would be falling over himself to accept the accolades for the battles ye have been ascribed to winning. Yer ability is well known across this fair island and beyond."

He tensed. "Beyond?"

"As far as England."

Taking his glass, Sean forced down the mead and struggled with the best approach. "I have just come from England."

"Have ye? It has been some time since I was there." Leofrid looked at his lady, avoiding Sean's eyes. "But I hope to be there again before very long."

"Is that where ye hail from?"

"I lived there for a time just as I have lived here." He smiled at Aodh who also scrutinized Sean, stroking the length of his gray beard. "Truth to tell, I am at home in both places."

"Aye," Aodh said. "And what were ye about in England?"

"Rescuing my bride." Sean took Thomasina's hand and kissed her palm. There was no need to explain he'd left to rescue one woman and came back with another. "It made for a worthwhile trip."

Thomasina seemed to have little interest in the others at the table, barely glancing their way. Mayhap she was not feeling well. He selected the best beef for her, holding it to her mouth.

She smiled at him, her eyes shining, and accepted it.

"Is the cow to yer liking?" Aodh asked.

Sean moved in to kiss her, licking the bit of juice from her lips. "She is very fond of beef."

"Beef? Ye sound like a Norman," Aodh scoffed.

Sean's gut tightened but he kept his breathing even. "Aye. That is what they call the meat from a cow, is it not?"

"They do." Aodh held his cup up for more to drink. "Those arrogant Normans."

Sean shrugged, feigning an indifference he did not feel.

Ivan had spoken ill of the Normans at every opportunity just as Aodh was doing. Sean would not side against the Normans, especially not when Tadhg's sister was married to one of King William's favored knights. Peter had also come to Sean's aid when he'd been wrongfully arrested. Even offering his protection as well as that of Lord John, one of the most powerful men in all of England. "They are of little interest to me since they are there… and I am here."

Across the many tables, most were paying no heed to what the head table discussed but there were exceptions. The leather-clad man had come in late. Sean recognized him from their earlier encounter and his interest in Thomasina. Thankfully, Thomasina paid him no notice but the other warriors did.

The man had the eyes of all the soldiers scattered about the room. That he listened intently to their conversation was very telling despite his attempt to appear uninterested. Sean bristled. Liberties taken were not easily dismissed and if given an opportunity, he would gladly take this one down.

"Is that yer man?" Sean took a bite of the food, tipping his head to where the man leaned casually against the wall. A younger man brought him a platter and received a stroke to the side of his head and a smile.

"Aye. My man," Leofrid answered. "Gerrit."

Tisa dropped her platter, causing a disturbance beside Thomasina. Many servants came forward to assist with cleaning. Tisa offered apologies although her gown wore the brunt of the mess.

"So clumsy of me."

"'Tis fine." Darragh's concern seemed genuine. "Are ye not well?"

Tisa was visibly shaken and Malcolm came forward to offer his assistance. "May I see ye back to yer home so that ye can change?"

She scanned the faces of the hall. Everyone's eyes were on her. The faces were not kind but suspicious. Many whispered behind their hands. A surge of pity swept over Sean.

"Where is Caireann?" Tisa asked.

"She is not present, mistress," Malcolm said.

"Mayhap we can go back with ye." Sean stood then addressed Thomasina. "My wife and I are happy to accompany ye."

"The hour is still early. There is no need for ye to leave," Aodh blustered beside Sean.

Darragh immediately turned his attention to his father, nodding in agreement. "True. Surely ye can stay, Tisa? We have much to celebrate." He lifted his cup.

Sean offered his arm to Tisa and helped her from the bench. "If she is up to returning, we shall do so."

"Malcolm, my wool?" Tisa asked.

The big man held it for Tisa, wrapping it tightly around her. Sean was disgusted to see Darragh back in conversation with his father, all concern for his wife forgotten. Leofrid told his lady something that caused her to laugh. Sean was glad for a way to escape if only for a short time. The oncoming snow would ensure he was unable to quit the place any time soon. He would use that time to discover if this was, indeed, the Godwin who thought to take back England from John and Peter's King William and if so, was he a viable threat? What he would do with the information, he would have to decide then.

Chapter Twenty

Tisa breathed deep, filling her lungs, before blowing it out.

She addressed the man behind her. "My thanks, Malcolm, for convincing Thomasina and Sean that ye could see me settled here."

She reached toward the door then stopped. "My humiliation is deep enough without having to convince them I am fine."

"Mistress, the humiliation ye speak of is not on ye. Ye did nothing to deserve the treatment ye received."

"Will ye tell Darragh what ye saw?"

"To what purpose? The man will not be reprimanded for his behavior. But I will do whatever ye bid me to do."

She shook her head. "I thought... well, ye told him of my dream."

He shifted behind her. "I thought little of the man at the time and was belittling him. 'Twas wrong of me. He is not the man I had believed him to be. I beg yer forgiveness for my transgression."

But the man was exactly what Malcolm had believed. It was merely a tragic play she and Darragh performed for everyone's benefit. "Think no more on it. Ye have been a good and loyal friend to me."

Tisa pushed the door open and stopped at the unaccustomed blackness. A moaning sound came from the far left. Malcolm stepped in front of her, his dagger at the ready as he moved toward the sound. There was a scent in the air she almost recognized and struggled to name—blood.

"Someone is hurt!" Tisa said. "Who is it? Who is here?"

Malcolm kept her shielded behind him, the blade in his hand, despite her attempt to get by. She weaved her head back and forth to peer around him into the darkness. When he got closer to the sound, she gasped at the sight of the huddled body, moaning in pain.

"Caireann!" Tisa shouted and dropped beside the girl.

Malcolm came up from behind, the dagger replaced by a lighted lamp. He held it high enough that she could now see the blood on Caireann's ankle, her torn gown, and the tapestry that lay on top of her.

"Dearest, what has happened?"

Malcolm kneeled beside her, wiping the tears off her freckled face. "Caireann, where is the pain?"

"Malcolm." Her voice was a whisper. "I ken ye'd come."

He picked her up into his arms, cradling her against his bosom. His gentle touch seemed impossible for a man of his great size. Tisa's chest tightened. He cared for her. When had that transpired?

The heavy material fell open and the source of the blood on her leg became apparent.

"She's been raped," Tisa said.

Malcolm's face turned white, his eyes wide. He pressed Caireann's head against him. "My sweet, what can I do?"

Caireann shook her head.

"I will get some water heated," Tisa said.

Tisa busied herself with feeding the fire that appeared to have been dowsed with water. A dangerous thing to do with the biting cold temperatures and it took some work to bring back the flame.

"Sorry I am that I was not here sooner," Malcolm said, the second time in as many hours.

"My sweet Malcolm, it was a man in a rage. He would have killed ye," Caireann said.

"He would not! But it would be his blood spilled this night instead of yers."

She moaned. "There is pain. I think he ripped me apart."

Tisa came with a cloth. She glanced up at Malcolm. "I need to see her wounds."

He held Caireann tight against him, closing his eyes and turning his face away.

With great care, Tisa inspected the injured area. The man had been brutal, leaving small rips that continued to bleed but there did not appear to be anything torn within. Tisa held the cloth to the cuts. Caireann hissed in pain.

Tisa covered her friend then told Malcolm, "She's covered."

He tried to hide the great turmoil she read on his face.

"Who was it?" Malcolm's tone was strained.

Caireann shook her head. "I dunna ken. I was turned away from the door. He came in and shoved me. I fell onto the table. He threw my skirts up over my head—" She clasped her hand tight to her mouth. Tears coursed down her cheeks.

Malcolm kept her close, whispering soothing sounds and rocking her like a child.

Tisa went to her herbs, adding them to the water she'd heated. "She needs to drink this."

Caireann sipped at the liquid. It would help her to rest. Tisa saw no bruises on her face or arms.

"Did he say anything? Would ye recognize his voice?"

"Nae. He was quick. He said nothing."

Tisa and Malcolm exchanged glances.

"There are many soldiers here. It could have been any one of them," she said.

"Too many for me to even ken who belongs and who does not."

"Mayhap ye should rest on the bed?"

"Nae," Caireann's eyes opened, Malcolm's leine grasped between her white knuckles. "Please let me stay here. Safe."

"Happy I am to have ye near me and I *will* keep ye safe."

She nodded. Her eyes drifted shut. It wasn't long before Caireann was asleep.

Sean had not been convinced by Tisa's assurances that all was well. All was far from well here.

Thomasina hugged his arm to her. "Methinks we should talk." She glanced at the longhouse. "But not here."

Sean pecked her cheek. "Since we are sleeping as guests here beneath Aodh's nose, we should find a place to ourselves."

He led her a short distance, following the path that sloped up along the winter grass. It grew quite tall. Ducking down, he pulled her onto his lap. "We have made our escape. Have yer way with me."

Thomasina laughed, slapping at his shoulder. "I am serious, Sean."

Sensing her tension, he sobered. "Is there aught amiss, mo mhíle stór?"

"That man with the dark-haired woman. Leofrid? I recognized him and that woman."

Sean frowned. "Ye saw them afore today? Where could ye have seen them?"

"At the inn we stayed at. Where the massacre of the Normans took place." Her eyes rounded. "While I waited for ye to go to the room ye had rented. Do ye remember?"

He nodded. "Ye waited outside then snuck up the stairs and they were none the wiser."

"When I was watching that redhead rubbing her body all against ye, the innkeeper snuck up the stairs."

"I dunna remember her doing that."

"Well, I do and I hate to disappoint ye but 'twas just a ruse for the innkeeper to get upstairs afore ye. He came down leading *that* man!"

"Leofrid?"

"The very same, Sean." Thomasina glanced off into the distance as if rummaging through her memories. "They spoke of him returning— Leofrid—later that night and that the innkeeper needed to keep to the plan."

Sean's gut tightened. "Are ye certain 'tis the same man?"

"He came out the same door I watched ye from, passing right before my eyes! My heart jumping in my chest. I was afeared he would see me. And not only that Leofrid, but the same woman! She came down after him. When I saw her at the table, she was familiar but I could not remember from where. Then I smelled that flowery scent and remembered."

Sean blew a breath. Leofrid was the Godwin. If Leofrid crossed from Eire to England with such ease, the man may indeed have the ability to plan an attack against the Normans.

"Oh, aye, Sean! Leofrid and the innkeeper—they spoke of keeping the irons hot and then Leofrid said something about giving the usurpers what they deserved."

Sean had been arrested for the murder of those Normans. The lord who'd lost his son spoke of them being branded like animals. That only meant one thing. The overthrowing of King William that Ivan had spoken of had begun. It was Leofrid that had massacred the Norman soldiers. Sean needed to get word to Peter.

Hugging his wife to him, he said, "Ye've a good memory, lass, but it means we've not much time to get word to Peter and John. Do ye believe Niall will help us get word to them?"

"An adventure? He'd never say nae."

With the impending snow, no one would be coming or going soon but that included Leofrid Godwin. Once the snow ceased, Sean needed to find someone who could travel alone through the drifts, knew their way to MacNaughton land, and was willing to get a message to Calum Rua. He had an idea of who that could be and he may need to apply quite a bit of pressure to make Breandan leave this welcoming place.

Chapter Twenty-One

Over the next few days, Caireann was well cared for by Malcolm. He anticipated her needs before she spoke them. There did not seem to be any lasting injuries from the attack. Not on the outside, but mayhap on the inside. Malcolm's gentleness with her warmed Tisa's heart. She wanted the best for her friend. Tisa watched the blossoming romance from her seat near the fire as she worked on her needlework. The drifting snow made it difficult to travel to the longhouse which suited her just fine. Darragh was kept busy with his father and she was left on her own.

Malcolm came to sit beside her.

"Does she sleep?" Tisa asked.

"Aye. I worry for her sleeping so much."

"I've found nothing wrong with her body. Her spirit? Ye do much to help her with that. Ye are a very kind man."

She tied the threads on the final bird in her scene. The last of the hangings was done. A great sense of accomplishment filled her. She shook out the material.

"'Tis beautiful. Ye have a great skill," Malcolm said before taking it from her to reattach it to the beam.

Tisa paused to look around her home. The little house seemed more cheerful. "I am pleased to be able to improve my circumstances. So much is beyond my ability to change."

He stood beside her as if looking at the hangings with her but she sensed a tension in him.

"Is there aught amiss? Ye seem troubled."

Turning toward him, she noticed the gray at his temples for the first time. His eyes fixed on her and her stomach clenched.

"Is it the children?"

"It is not." He swallowed. "Caireann... she may be with child."

Tisa turned toward the curtain that blocked the view of her sleeping friend. "She canna ken that yet."

"Nae, but it could be."

His frown deepened. Something else was amiss.

She nodded and waited.

Malcolm straightened to his full height, looked past her and announced, "I wish to take her to wife."

Tisa's jaw dropped. Her chest filled. "Oh, Malcolm, I think 'twould be wonderful."

She threw her arms about his massive shoulders and hugged him.

He patted her back awkwardly. "I dunna ken what she will say."

Withdrawing, she searched his expression. "I believe she would be honored to be yer wife."

"I wish I had asked afore now but I wanted her to become more comfortable with me."

Malcolm had been thinking of marrying her dear friend? How could Tisa have not been aware of that?

"'Tis not too late." She placed a reassuring hand on his arm.

"But now she will believe I ask only because of what has occurred."

His point was valid.

"I would have asked earlier but for consideration of her gentle nature. I wanted her to learn my ways and mayhap see me as more than just a very large man." He faced Tisa, the frown gone. "I have loved her from the first."

Tisa put her hand to her chest where her breath fluttered like a butterfly. "Methinks ye should say just that to her."

He looked at her askance. "Mistress! Surely those are not the words she would want to hear. I could speak of her comeliness, of her gentle ways, or her—"

"Speak to her from yer heart. 'Tis all she needs to hear from ye."

"But ye are... not vexed at me?"

"Nae! I am well pleased. Methinks ye will make a lovely couple."

Malcolm's shoulders rounded and he let loose a great sigh. "My thanks. I have worried over this."

"Dunna fash yerself. Surely 'twas meant to be."

She collected the stray threads and moved about the area straightening this and that. Malcolm sat with his eyes fixed on the blue birds, an intense look as if rehearsing what his exact words to Caireann should be.

Tisa smiled to herself. "I need to see about retrieving Darragh's things."

He nodded his head without turning to her.

The air outside smelled of spring despite the snowdrifts and ice-covered lochs. Soon the snow would be but a memory. Long forgotten. Mayhap she was being wistful. The thought of her friend marrying stirred those memories of her own dreams not easily set aside.

The sky was a perfect blue without a cloud. At the next house, Tisa retrieved the items she had left for washing. Darragh's fastidiousness was a bit tiresome when it was too cold to wash. That his neighbor helped him out before Tisa's arrival made it that much easier. She knocked on the closed door.

"Hello?" she called, pushing open the door. "Hello? 'Tis Tisa."

No answer.

The clothing sat beside the banked fire, no doubt left for her. They may have decided to travel the icy path to the longhouse. She shook out the trews. No mending was required as yet but the knees were showing wear. The leine was tight across Darragh's chest. It was probably meant for someone smaller but it wasn't Breandan's. He had brought his old pair of cuarans for mending and she took those as well.

A thud at the door made her jump. When she opened it, she found a wooden object on the ground. A mavis called from the forest. Glancing about, there was no one this far down the path and she went around to the side of the house. She had not seen the outcasts since her encounter with Gerrit. Admittedly, it had left her shaken but she was concerned for Aednat and worried about how she was healing. Adding a twisted hand to the struggles she had with walking could make her situation so much worse. Mayhap something was wrong. The call came again but further away.

Her hands grew slick. It could also be nothing. She came back around to the door and picked up the wooden object. It may have been there and she hadn't noticed it. Turning, she crossed to her own home. Malcolm now sat leaning against the wall, not moving even when she closed the door. Looking more closely, his eyes were closed. He was fast asleep. No doubt exhausted. He had been up for many nights now seeing to Caireann.

Tisa dropped her armload onto the table and settled herself on the bench.

Malcolm had been right about not being able to change the fate of the outcasts. When she'd mentioned them to Darragh, he sounded much like his father. The strong ones must stay close. The weaker must be cast out. She dared not ask him about his own mother. Did he even know she was living with them? No, there would be no help for them even when Darragh became chieftain. The fact that she would not be getting with child any time soon—Not ever!—made the inevitability of the passing of leadership doubtful as well. The six months was coming to an end. The only good thing was that Aodh had not mentioned it.

If Aednat developed a fever, she would surely die from her encounter with the damn horse. What a tragedy. What a great loss for the outcasts. The little girl was very bright. Her ability to learn how to heal would certainly improve their lot. Tisa dropped down beside Malcolm. He needed to check out the call and be sure Aednat was well.

His breathing was heavy. He puffed his lips with each exhale. Between seeing to Caireann and still performing his many duties for Aodh, the man was worn out. Tisa was hard pressed to wake the sleeping giant. She returned to stand next to the table.

Darragh only wore the trews on the bitterest of days. The added warmth on his legs was frowned upon by his father. Naturally. She shook them out. What had Thomasina mentioned? She wasn't even noticed when dressed as a man? The pulling up of this and the tying off of that? Tisa eased off her slippers and slid one leg in, then the other. They did feel strange, difficult for her legs to move.

Tucking the balled up gown under her chin, she secured the tie at the waist. They were a bit tight in the seat but it could work. If no one knew she was a woman, no one would notice her. The chances of seeing anyone in the forest were not good. They were not the only ones keeping to their houses and if any were to venture out today, it would certainly be to see others within the village and not to go traipsing off into the woods.

Going into Darragh's room, Tisa doffed her gown and donned the leine. Her breasts were, unfortunately, quite prominent. She perused the small area around her. The fine cloth she'd recently discovered at the bottom of Darragh's chest would be perfect. She'd planned to surprise him by making a longer leine in the hope of placating his father and still keeping him warm. She could still do that but right now she had other uses for the material. She wound it tight around her chest. Much better. With her hair braided and tucked inside at the neck, Tisa discovered Breandan's shoes fit well enough. She wrapped her fur tight around her, pulling it over her head, and went off for the woods. She'd be back before she was ever missed.

Sean had not been approached by either Leofrid Godwin or Aodh Meic Lochlainn regarding King William. He was unsure what part, if any, Aodh Meic Lochlainn played in the Godwin's bigger scheme to overthrow the Normans. Although the two spent much time meeting, no one discussed any plans and they certainly shared nothing with Sean.

It had turned out to be a simple thing to convince Breandan to travel to MacNaughton land with Sean's missive. Apparently, Breandan missed his mother and his sister had been with child.

"For Calum Rua's eyes only and Breandan, he will give ye something after he reads this message. Accept it as my thanks and bring it to yer sister. I will pray daily for a safe delivery and a healthy nephew for ye. Godspeed."

That the lad had not returned yet only meant he'd wanted to stay with his sister and mother. If he ever chose to return, it would be his own choice just as it had been to come here.

Sean was more than ready to quit this place. He needed to get away and the melting snow now made it possible. These men acted more like the Norsemen he'd always heard stories about. No woman was well treated. Getting Thomasina away from them was a good enough reason for him to want to leave. If he could get Tisa away, he'd be even more relieved.

"I dunna see that 'tis necessary. Ye are the messenger. Bring the message to her father that all is well here," Aodh blustered.

Sean cleared his throat. "Mayhap he has worsened during my time away. Bringing her to him will be no hardship, I assure ye."

Aodh shook his head, his son meekly sat at his side. Sean couldn't be sure he was even listening.

"What say ye, Darragh? Will it not do yer wife good to have her see her father?"

The man shrugged. "If she wishes, she may go."

Aodh scoffed. "Nae. She needs to remain here. She may be carrying yer child even now."

Sean searched the older man's face but found only sincerity. How could he not realize his son preferred the company of males? No child would come from their union. Yet another reason for Sean to try and get her away from the place.

"I will take great care of her. My wife will be with her."

"As I said, we shall ask Tisa what she would prefer," Darragh said.

"She would prefer to be home as all women do with their fathers coddling them rather than seeing to the needs of their husbands. Mark my words, Darragh, she will not return on her own if ye allow her to leave."

Darragh's eyes widened. "'Tis not true. She would return to me. I will allow her the choice."

The finality of the statement was quite impressive. Sean tipped his head to the man. "Fine. She has expressed her interest in accompanying us and I will let her ken she has yer consent."

Darragh smiled and stood. "Nae. I will address my wife myself and learn her preference. I will return anon."

"I will miss ye being by my side."

They were alone in their house but Darragh seemed ill at ease.

Tisa smiled in the hopes of reassuring him. "Ye're very kind, Darragh."

"We also have clan duties to the west so we will travel with ye. See ye have a safe arrival."

Darragh glanced toward the door, fidgeting.

"Is aught amiss?"

He came to stand in front of her, took the clothes out of her hands to lay aside on the chest, and held her hands in his. "I just want ye to ken how much ye mean to me."

The sentiment surprised her. "'Tis kind of ye to say."

Darragh shook his head and glanced away before turning back to her. "My father seeks my counsel now."

The idea of asking him about his mother crossed her mind but she quickly dismissed it. "Ye're a married man. Does that not always happen?"

"Ye ken what I refer to, Tisa. I am not a lover of women and never have been. My most intimate desires are fulfilled by other men."

Tisa placed a hand to his cheek. "I ken that, Darragh. Ye are still my husband."

"Do ye not wish for more for yer life?"

A warning bell sounded in her head. There was a look in his eye. The sudden need to tread lightly overwhelmed and she paused before speaking. "I have all that I need."

"Good. I would not give ye up lightly."

"Dunna fash yerself."

He let loose a breath she'd swear he'd been holding. "My thanks, sweet little Tisa."

She cringed at the endearment. "Have ye ever spoken of me to others?"

Darragh averted his gaze. "I have no reason to."

"They dunna wonder how it is with us?"

"There is nothing I would repeat to another about ye."

"Even yer lovers?"

"Nae! They ken ye care for me. That is enough."

Not nearly enough but she smiled.

"We will take ye to yer father and return by sowing time."

Chapter Twenty-Two

Tadhg took a deep breath, savoring the smells of home. Despite the unexpected snowfall, he had made good time in his crossing. Brighit was happily wed to a good man and he need no longer be concerned for her well-being. He hoped Peter had been sincere when he offered that they may come for a visit. Mayhap after the child was born.

The path leading home was a mix of snow, mud, and brown grass. It sucked at his feet, making passage difficult. The sound of children playing carried to him. The mother's scolding tone was a boon to his ears.

"Mildred!" Tadhg called to the woman by the thatched house closest to the forest.

Her eyes widened and a smile burst like a sunrise across her face. "Tadhg! Ye're home!"

She ran to him, grabbing the hands of the wee blond girl beside her as she went.

Tadhg accepted the heartfelt hug.

"A sight for these tired eyes ye are."

"My thanks, Mildred. And I am happy to see ye as well."

"And how is our lovely Brighit?"

"She is with child and happily wed."

Mildred lifted her hands in a prayerful gesture. "Thank the Lord for such a blessing."

"Aye." Tadhg had not offered many prayers on his journey home. Instead, he'd spent his time with dark thoughts, trying to reconcile truth to pretense. He'd always considered his mother the epitome of all that was loyal, gentle and loving. He thought the same about Tisa. The truth was he was wrong.

"How are things here?" He continued walking toward the main building, taking in the state of all around him. "'Twas a rough winter?"

"Aye, but we managed." Mildred picked the child up into her arms. "Enough food in our bellies and warmth in our homes."

Tadhg caressed the little girl's cheek. "Ye are growing so big! That is good to see."

"Well, back to work for me." Mildred waved, encouraging the little girl to do the same.

That was the hardest part. Knowing there would be no children. His decision to continue alone had been a difficult one but the only way to protect himself from more pain. He didn't need pain like he'd had these past few months. His mother's betrayal. Tisa's abandonment. No. He'd best be on his own and focusing on his responsibility.

Sean trotted around the chapel, a smile on his face, before he noticed Tadhg.

"I'll get ye back," a woman's voice called to him just before a lovely creature came up from behind the building, wrapping her arms intimately around Sean's naked chest.

"What have we here?" Tadhg put his hands to his hips. "Are ye choosing the younger lasses for yerself now?"

Sean narrowed his eyes. "Shh."

The auburn-haired woman peeked at Tadhg from around Sean's torso. Her smile dropped and her eyes widened.

"Tadhg, ye look like hell," Sean said, pulling the woman beside him. "This is my wife, Thomasina."

Tadhg reeled back. "What? Wife?"

Sean rolled his eyes and looked at the woman. "He's such an arse."

"Is this Tadhg then?" She smiled up at him.

He returned the smile and kissed the tip of her nose. "Aye. The same."

Sean pressed her closer and dragged his hand along her length, leaving no doubt of the intimacy of their relationship.

"I canna believe ye were able to trick her into marrying ye."

"Close yer trap, Tadhg! Come, mo chroí go deo thú." Sean and Thomasina walked back the way they'd come.

"Hey, where are ye off to?"

"None of yer concern." Sean's voice carried even after they'd disappeared behind the little, stone building.

"I need to ken what I've missed."

"And I need to bed my wife. I'll see ye at Vespers."

The thought that Sean had taken a wife took hold like the talons of a hawk biting into him. It prickled his mind, making him feel things he didn't want to feel. It brought back his own desires for his future with the force of an ocean gale. Desires he wanted dead.

He veered off the main road to the outbuilding he used as his own. The place had been looked after. New rushes, fresh herbs, water beside the glowing fire. It appeared the bed had been used as well. He pulled the covers over the straw-filled mattress. The scent drifted to him and his eyes closed. Like a punch to his gut he could see her again. Tisa. The gentle slope of her neck to the swell of her firm breasts to the length of her soft thighs to her tiny, bare feet. Desire flooded the length of him.

Tightening his jaw, he opened his eyes. He'd thought he'd mastered this. There was no need to keep going over it. It was done. She was wed to another and he was incapable of settling for anyone else. Not even for carnal satisfaction. She was too ingrained in him. Too much a part of all he had desired his life to be.

"Oh!"

Tadhg swallowed, unable to move. The one sound had been so familiar. He'd come home to demons haunting his waking hours. He forced himself to turn toward the open door. His body tensed in preparation, his mind struggling to dismiss the burgeoning hope of seeing Tisa standing there in the doorway.

"Tisa."

Her hair was pulled back, her eyes sparkling with life. A cluster of herbs overflowed a small basket she held to her breast. And her feet were bare.

"What do ye here?" Tadhg asked.

She dropped her head and walked past to put the basket on the only table in his small room. His room.

"Why are ye in my home?" His tone was hard.

His gaze shifted to the pallet. It hadn't been his own longings that left her scent in his bed. She'd lain there. Lain there as he'd dreamed of her laying there far too often. Had she lain there alone? He turned back to her.

"Where is yer husband?"

"He will be here anon. I was to wait for him with Thomasina and Sean."

Tadhg's chest tightened. He couldn't take a full breath. He strode to the door. "I will find another place." He grabbed the small sack he'd dropped upon entering and left.

"Nae. Please." Tisa followed him out.

Tadhg refused to turn toward her. He did not need to see her again. "'Tis not a problem, Tisa. Ye and yer husband may continue to stay here.

I will find another place."

"I have not—my husband dinna—"

Tadhg whipped around to face her. "What? Yer husband dinna what? What do ye have to tell me? What pain do ye wish to inflict on me now?" His eyes dropped to her waist. All thoughts ceased save one. She could be with child. "There is no need for words here."

Her eyes never left his face but she did not reply.

"Stay." He held up his hand to stop her from following. "I will find another place."

Tadhg slammed into the longhouse, the children looking up from their chores of kneading bread, mending clothes, kirning milk, to stare at him with wide, fear-filled expressions. The adults working alongside them looked much the same.

"Why are ye not in the kitchen with all this? Out!"

"The kitchen was flooded by the storms," young Moira said. The little boy at her side gathered his work into his little arms. He'd grown quite a lot.

Tadhg just wanted them gone. "I need the hall."

He went to stoke up the fire, giving his back to the workers, and refused to turn around until they were gone. The door shutting was the signal for him to drop onto the bench, his head in his hands. He didn't realize how hard this would be and he'd never expected to have to see Tisa.

"Did it not go well with yer sister?"

Tisa's voice, as sweet as in his dreams, came to him. He set his jaw and raised his head but refused to face her. The sight of her would weaken his resolve. It would rip whatever was left of his heart right out of his chest.

"Aye, it went fine. She is married to a Norman knight who holds her in high regard."

"Sean told us that much. Ye're so angry, I wanted to ken if something else had happened. Did she lose the child?"

Sean had told her all it seems. "Nae. She is hale and hearty. 'Twill be an easy delivery like with our own moth—" He had a hard time referring to that adulterous woman with such endearments as mother. "Like with Moira."

"I've removed my things from yer house. Beg pardon for being in yer way."

"Did I say ye were in my way? I will no longer be staying there now regardless."

She shifted behind him. She was probably anxious to get back to whatever she was doing.

"Ye need not stay. I prefer to be alone."

"Aye. I wanted ye to ken is all."

Tadhg would not speak again. He waited but didn't hear her leave.

"What are ye about?" Sean's irritated tone forced Tadhg to turn around.

"Where's Tisa?"

Sean shrugged, a frown on his face. Tadhg waited but he said no more.

"Are ye done with yer lovely wife?"

"Never done with her. I just gave her time to do other things. Did ye wish to hear what has happened during yer long absence?"

The jab was not missed. He had been gone a long time. Too long. "Let us sit."

They moved to the table at the far side of the room.

"The O'Brien followed through with his promise to provide food. We are well stocked and able to get through 'til harvest. We've plans to plant along the riverbeds to the east which have been dry these five years past. The soil there is rich and good for growing. We should be fine for next winter, God willing."

Tadhg raised his brows. "God willing?"

Sean didn't smile. "Aye, God willing."

"Well, that's a bit of a different tune ye're whistling."

"Nae, 'tis not a different tune. It's just one I ken better than I did afore."

"Taking a wife change that for ye?"

"That and her being with child."

Tadhg's jaw dropped and quickly shifted into a smile. "Well done! Congratulations, my friend. How soon?"

"Methinks she is at least two months along."

"And what does she think?"

"She does not ken yet."

Tadhg looked askance, unsure if he'd heard his friend correctly. "Ye ken afore she does?"

Sean grinned. "Aye, I ken when I am not able to take her because of her courses. She hasn't noticed yet."

"That makes it a winter birthing."

"A mild winter. God willing."

Tadhg let the comment pass. "Why is Tisa here? And in my bed?"

"There was no place else for her. She said she did not mind and preferred it to being with Thomasina and me."

"Aye, the scent of her in my bed? But *she* did not mind? Methinks ye're an idiot, Sean. And who is this Thomasina?"

"My wife."

"And that is all I ken."

Sean reached into his tunic and withdrew a silver object. He laid the intricately designed knife on the table. "Yer knife."

"Aye, I see that. How did it come to be in yer possession?"

"I took it from ye at the inn on the way to save Brighit. I used it to rent a horse. It ended up being Thomasina's horse so I took her to wife."

Tadhg picked up the knife, traced the etched design with his thumb, and turned out the blade. "It is none the worse for yer care but yer story needs some details."

"It is enough to say I am well pleased with her as my wife and I believe she feels the same."

"Well then, I suppose that is enough."

The big man grinned at him. "We have only been here a short while with Tisa. Her husband has gone off with the chieftain and Leofrid—"

Tadhg's head jerked back. "Leofrid? As in Godwin?"

"The same, although he was never introduced to me as such. My lovely wife recognized them. Leofrid and his lady. Before I came back to Eire, there was a Norman massacre at the inn in town. It seems to have come about at Leofrid Godwin's command."

"Mort spoke of some trouble. He also said ye had been wed though I dinna put much stock in such stories."

"I was arrested for the massacre but Thomasina's brother got word to Peter. He sent Mort forthwith to stay the executioner's hand. I would do no less to save Peter and have sent word that Leofrid Godwin was responsible for the massacre of Normans in Black Poole and that he is in Inishowen making plans with a powerful, warring clan and we would send more information as we received it."

"And does the Meic Lochlainn have aught to do with any of it?"

Sean shook his head. "I dunna ken for certain. They did allow me to escort Tisa to her father although they acted as her guard."

"What is amiss with Roland O'Brien?"

"He is not well though much improved since seeing Tisa. She chose not to stay there."

Tadhg got to his feet. "My head is reeling. I need something to drink."

Sean refused when offered libations. Another first for the man. Tadhg poured himself a generous amount before sitting again.

"Who is Tisa's husband?"

Tadhg would have preferred not to ken but it was better if he did.

"She has married into the Meic Lochlainn Clan."

Quite impressive. Roland was able to work out an alliance with such a powerful clan and so quickly. No doubt the man she married was older, mayhap even infirmed and dried up, to be available for the match in such a short amount of time. Tisa's life would be a hard one. She was a beautiful woman that deserved so much more.

"It is unclear to me why O'Brien would have need of so many MacNaughton warriors when he had made such a treaty."

"Mayhap we are hired thugs now?"

"Nae, a clan without enough food for winter. O'Brien demanded we come to him this spring or he would not provide food."

"And who is 'we'? 'Twill be difficult to prepare the soil and plant if 'we' are all at his disposal."

"A score of warriors to do his bidding. We were included by name."

Sean's face tightened.

"Mayhap if we go while he is still weak, he will release us from the agreement and ye can return to the arms of yer wife."

"'Twould please me if it were so."

Tadhg shook his head in amazement. "I have never seen ye avoid fighting. Is this coddling?"

His friend's expression did not change. "We will bring Tisa as well. That is where they will come to collect her. No doubt 'twould please ye to see her gone."

"'Twould please me to not see her at all."

"Do ye wish to wait a few days?"

Tadhg was exhausted. He'd been away for a long time but he would rest easier if Tisa were safely away and his time under the command of Roland O'Brien, a thing of the past.

"Nae. We will leave at daybreak."

"I will let her ken."

"Did he raise his voice at ye?" Thomasina glanced up from her kneading, her forehead lined with worry. "Although I dunna ken the man, I had no thought he would behave so churlish."

"He may have cared for me once, but no more. He dinna want me there and especially not in his bed." Tisa gazed off, again seeing Tadhg's anger. "He looks like a bitter man. Dark. Foreboding. His intense anger surprised me."

Her own sleep had been sweet. Being in his bed, surrounded by the smell of him. She had dreamed of him each night. Of him taking her to wife. To a new life where she could be a whole woman, completely loved by the man she would never set aside. Tisa pounded down the loaf.

"Lovely maidens." Sean swaggered in, a smirk on his face at his own choice of words, no doubt.

"Nothing but matrons here."

He glanced toward Tisa before chastely kissing his wife's cheek. Thomasina must have told him to control his ardor in front of Tisa. Very thoughtful girl but not necessary. Tisa was becoming quite used to it, living with Darragh and Breandan. And then Caireann and Malcolm but they just held hands. Although since the formal betrothal was announced, Tisa did wonder about their disappearances. She beat her fist into the bread.

"Thomasina, ye will always be my lovely maiden. And what of ye, Tisa?"

She gaped at him. Did he ask if she were a maiden? "Beg pardon?"

Thomasina slapped his chest. "He is asking how ye are, 'tis all."

"Fine." She turned the two ends and flipped the bread to punch it again.

"Well, we need to be traveling back to O'Brien land tomorrow."

She ceased her movements, her irritation switching to overwhelming disappointment. "So soon?"

There was no reason for her to stay but going back to her father meant Darragh and Aodh would be taking her back to Inishowen and her very sad existence.

"Aye." Sean's eyes narrowed, no doubt hearing the desolation in her voice. "Tadhg will meet with yer father."

Tadhg was coming with them? "About what?"

He raised a shoulder. "Clan business."

Tisa nodded, wiping her hands on the cloth beside her. "Methinks I will collect my things."

"Mayhap ye should rest. Use our bed." Thomasina took her hand. "Traveling is so tiring and ye've a long trek ahead of ye."

"Aye. Methinks I will."

"I will wake ye for the evening repast."

Tisa headed out the door. Her heart heavy, she avoided the children playing in the yard, choosing the quiet path that led behind the little, round buildings. Seeing the children upon their arrival had lifted her spirits, reminding her of when she and Brighit had played in the same area. That was ages ago. The passing time was even more evident now.

Brighit had wed a man who "held her in high regard" and even gotten her with child. Surely their future would be a happy one. Tisa stretched out on the pallet tucked close to the wattle and daub wall. It would be best for her to return north without delay.

It was good to be back among the people who knew her well. Fergus had been kind to her and again wished her the best. She had been able to see little Hannah who was growing like a weed. Mayhap she had thought of this as an escape but she did not belong here either. Not anymore. Her father seemed strong, even ready to meet with Tadhg. There was no reason for her to remain.

'Twas not a terrible life she returned to. Not the life she had thought she would have, but a life where she was needed. Time spent preparing clothing, food, and herbs for the outcasts was time well spent. She'd only seen them twice since her encounter with Gerrit but it had warmed her heart to spend time among them, like she belonged. They appreciated all she did for them. She enjoyed her conversations with Aoife, Darragh's mother, as well. She told of many things including how Aodh had poisoned the last chieftain, Eirnin. Eirnin was Lilith's father.

Thomasina had been correct. Dressing as a man did give her a certain freedom. Once she'd learned to smear her face with ash and her clothes with fresh dung, she learned people kept their distance and her disguise worked even better. No one noticed her. It would be good to be back and check on them.

Chapter Twenty-Three

In the Great Hall of the castle at York, John dropped a hefty log onto the fire. Sparks flew high into the air. It was good to be within the castle at last rather than freezing outside. Peter squared his shoulders and pressed into the high-backed chair with its ornate carving, gold trim, and cushioned seat. Ralph de Gael had certainly never missed an opportunity to surround himself with luxury. No wonder he fought so hard against King William getting his share.

"What troubles you, John? King William is still a week's journey from here. He will not travel in haste when the siege is over and the castle has been won."

His friend nodded but continued to gaze into the fire.

Peter surveyed the unusual greenish-yellow vessel he held in his hand. Something he'd never seen even at William's court. "Is it Rowena you miss?"

"Of course. I miss her greatly."

"But that is not what concerns you now? Is it Leofrid?"

John put his hands to his hips and turned toward Peter. "They are both one and the same. William was wrong to order me to kill my wife's only surviving family. The life she knew was ripped from her hands when we came here. She had nothing left. I could not very well kill her cousin. Mayhap if I cared nothing for her but I do care."

He walked to the trestle table made from the same heavy wood as the chair and poured more of the cloudy liquid into a similar chalice before he continued.

"Her thanks for my decision to spare Leofrid's life was more than I deserved. Her father falling on my sword was something I had tried without success to avoid. I owed her that much. That the man has to come back here to start trouble after his life was generously spared convinces me he must be mad. Look at all the havoc William has reaped on these Saxons. His need for absolute power knows no bounds. And Leofrid dares to return?"

"The missive from Sean of Drogheda said as much."

John's face lined with worry. "So now I must do what I had tried to avoid? And then tell Rowena her cousin is now dead?"

"Rowena knows of power struggles. Her uncle was king before William came and now he is dead. Surely she will not blame you."

"How am I to help William with the unrest among the Saxons when he continues to view them as irrelevant, tossing them aside or trampling them underfoot while he grasps for more and more power?"

"And will your Saxons pledge fealty to him as he required from you?"

John gave a heartfelt sigh. "My dear friend, they swear fealty to me alone for they know I care for Rowena and them. If they do as commanded by the king, 'twill be out of deference to me and I do not accept the gesture lightly. I *must* see to their protection and that includes Leofrid."

"John! Surely you're not proposing to battle the king for Leofrid's life! That would be foolish. His life is not worthy of the sacrifice."

"I would not but my life will be forfeit when William learns of my betrayal to him. I disobeyed his orders."

"My lord." Mort came in from the front hall with great bluster.

He had traveled to the Priory without stopping to return with Peter's most treasured item. Prickles of excitement danced along his skin. Mort paused, bowed, and stretched his arm beside him in presentation of who followed.

Brighit, red-cheeked and still well-covered from her journey, stopped behind him.

Peter's breath caught. Brighit had arrived! He jumped from his seat to cross to her and took his very pregnant wife into his arms. The smell of her roused him, the feel of her pressing against him a boon to his time from her side.

"Sweet Brighit." He whispered the words into her hair paying no heed to anyone else. "I have missed you, greatly."

"It has only been a few days, Peter!" John said.

John's exclamation left little doubt to how he felt about this display.

Mort coughed and shifted behind them.

Peter ignored them both.

"The child is growing well." He spoke against her ear, not releasing her even when the babe inside kicked against him. "Hmm, I wish to see what this movement looks like."

Peter pulled away just enough to turn her toward the stone stairs leading to the rooms that ran along the floor above.

"Peter!" John voiced his loud objection. Mort broke into laughter that followed even as Peter gently pulled her by the hand.

"You look lovely," he said the words over his shoulder.

He led her up to the room. That room's previous lord had snuck off into the night, leaving his young wife to face the siege of the castle alone.

Brighit merely smiled. It was a tolerant smile that reminded him of his improper behavior but he didn't care. He needed his wife naked and in his bed. Now.

The burning fire warmed the small chamber and Peter's burning need had him pressing her up against the closed door and tracing kisses along her neck.

"I'm a thirsting man in need of a drink." He yanked up her skirts. She shifted away to free the material tucked behind her. "I am a man dying of hunger and you alone are my sustenance."

His hot hands finally on her flesh, he stilled. Stroking up the length of her thigh and along her waist, he exhaled a slow, steady breath. "I have been too long with neither food nor water." He moved to her mouth. "Give me what I desire."

His hand slid over her rounded belly and dipped between her legs finding blessed moistness that spoke of her desire.

"The nectar I crave." He kneeled right there before her and nosed his way into her most intimate spot. Dropping her hands to his head, she spread her legs, giving him full access. Her hips quickly rocking to the rhythm he set with his tongue as he stroked her. He gripped her bare flesh, enjoying the feel of her nakedness.

With an answering moan, she pressed him closer into her.

In one swift motion, he swept her up in his arms and deposited her onto the biggest bed ever built. He cupped her breasts with greedy hands. Squeezing and stroking, his head tucked into the curve of her neck.

"I have longed to have the taste of you on my tongue and more." He rubbed his hard need against her hip.

She lowered the material from her shoulders and he wrestled her breasts free.

"I have longed to have ye inside me again," she said.

He stopped, his nostrils flaring while he scanned those mouth-watering mounds. He grinned down at her. "Forgive my repeating myself but you do have the most lovely breasts."

Gripping each from the underside, he ran his tongue over one with long, firm strokes, circling the hardened nipple before suckling her deep inside his mouth. Her deep, throaty sounds of her own need nearly undoing him. And when switching to the other breast, the sight of her with her eyes closed and her head pushing back into the bed challenged his willpower.

"Oh, my love. You push me to the edge showering me with such blatant desire."

She pulled his mouth back to her bared bosom.

Peter obliged, continuing his assault of her breasts.

"Please. I have a great need for ye." She sounded out of breath.

Peter's prick ached to meet her need and he moved away to yank her gown up and over her head. That she had nothing at all underneath made him pause. He looked down into his lovely wife's face, his brows high.

Her lips curved into a satisfied smile. "I know what my husband is about."

Peter lowered himself between her legs, careful of the swell of their child between them. Brighit widened her legs to accommodate him.

"Mmm." It felt so right to be there. Peter had some vague idea about saying how much he loved her, how many times he'd dreamed of taking her just like this, how he believed he was the most blessed man alive to have her. He couldn't find words. His mind was full of overpowering need. He pressed himself into her slick sheath, its tightness overwhelmingly pleasurable.

He would show her how he felt by his awareness of every detail of her pleasure. Surely she would know by his loving what his words could not convey.

Opening his eyes, he watched her as he moved into her with long, slow movements. Her breath quickening. Her lips slightly parting. A deep groan of pleasure met his ears. Raising her hips, she met him thrust for thrust, her moans becoming more intense. Higher. Louder.

She tensed against him then sighed, her muscles pulsing around his engorged cock. He impaled her deeply. And again. Her guttural cries of fulfillment speeding him to his own release.

"Oh, Peter. I am such a wanton." Her words were panted as she struggled to catch her breath. "I dreamed each night of ye taking me. It must be that I am with child. I cannot get enough of ye."

"Sweet Brighit," he nibbled her neck, stroking it with a firm tongue, "do you hear a complaint from my lips?"

"Nae. And ye do see to my every desire." She blew a breath then sighed. "I am never satisfied. Not for long."

Peter rolled onto his back and tucked her in close beside him. "You need but say the word and I am roused to readiness."

"I fear ye will tire of me too soon."

"Never."

He covered them both with the heavy, woolen cloth then kissed the top of her head. "Welcome home, my love."

Mort poured himself a generous amount of mead. He took a sip and smacked his lips several times. It was, indeed, quite good. No doubt brought up from the Priory. But he was avoiding the unavoidable with digression and inconsequential matters. The problem at hand? How best to approach such a touchy subject as treason with the Earl of Essex.

Having been sent by the king to follow John when he'd first returned to England, Mort was given the task of seeing how the man was adjusting. The king knew full well that John had left his Saxon bride rather quickly and despite being given nigh five years, never felt compelled to return to her. That left the king with no alternative but to order his return.

Mort knew the man's past. A bastard of unknown parentage being raised by a cruel man with a hard fist. William, then Duke of Normandy, learned of John's plight and, no doubt, his parentage, and brought him to the monastery. Though he never spoke of John's father, Mort assumed it was one of William's closest friends if not William himself. It wasn't until the death of the Duke's dearest friend, William FitzOsbern, that William took John in to train as his squire, keeping him close at hand. Mort was no simpleton. Obviously John was the bastard son of William FitzOsbern. It was confirmed when John and Rowena were called in for an audience with the king and Mort was told to ensure John and Emma, FitzOsbern's only daughter, did not spend too much time alone. 'Twas John himself who informed Mort of the attraction he'd felt for Emma and that he'd even asked to take her to wife. William had been mortified which had surprised John but not Mort. They had the same father.

Mort found in John not someone he needed to keep an eye on but a man trying to do the right thing for all involved. The Earl of Essex was a good man. A man Mort genuinely liked. But that was not the information William required. William would want to know the details of how John had defied the king by allowing Leofrid Godwin, the king's enemy, to live and merely exiling him to Ireland.

Since Mort had decided against informing the king, the seemingly inevitable return of the exiled man was creating problems for all. They would need to get their stories straight, preferably before the arrival of the king to the castle at York.

"My lord, do you agree with Peter that monasteries and priories have the best libations?"

John paused and settled himself on a stool beside the fire before responding. "I believe I was the one who made that observation to Peter. Do *you* agree?"

"I do!' Mort removed his hat with the new peacock feathers, righted the tiny bell around his neck, and sat opposite John. "I really do. Why do you suppose that is? Is there aught they do, some knowledge that they may have—being men of God—that is vital and unknown to the rest of us? As if, mayhap, being in league with God Himself and striving to do the Lord's work, they are privy to some great secret? A secret that may not even be knowable to us mere mortals. And yet would it be right for such grand knowledge to be bestowed on any mortal man? Saint or sin—"

"Mort!" John's face was tight. "Speak with me about what is bothering you. I cannot listen to one of your tirades right now."

Mort bowed his head.

"Forgive me, my lord. You know me well." He took another sip of the mead. "Still—"

"No!" John cut him off. He turned his head to one side and then the other, his eyes never leaving Mort's face. "Speak of what is on your mind."

"The king will be here and we must decide what information to give him regarding your wife's cousin."

"So he has not yet been informed that the man still lives?"

Mort held his gaze a moment, surprised at the question. "I did not deem it necessary to inform him."

"My thanks for that."

Clearly the man did not understand how Mort felt. "I do not believe the decision was made to defy the king but rather to keep peace. If I am questioned, I will convey as much."

"You mean if he discovers the truth and wants to know why you kept it from him?"

"Yes."

"We both know the king. If he discovers our treachery, we will pay the ultimate price."

Loyalty was something akin to the blood that runs through the veins, not something you took up only when it suited you.

"My lord, I have no regrets. The decision to not relay the information was mine and mine alone. Your time with the Saxons was bearing fruit. The men were accepting you as their lord. It would have been wrong for you to be removed for such a minor offense."

"That places you in the position of judgment, my friend. God help you if the king feels your judgment was in error."

"My judgment was not in error. You and your lovely wife have done much to mend the chasm between the Saxon and Normans. The end result being a more peaceful place for King William. Granted, he may not see it that way. And if he does not? I will gladly take the punishment."

"You would die for me?"

"I would."

"A plea of ignorance could save you."

"I will not lie."

John would prefer Mort save himself if the truth were discovered? Just claim he was unaware of the decision John had made to allow Leofrid to live? Never! Mort would stand beside this man whatever the outcome.

John's eyes pierced him through, his face tight with emotion. "My thanks for your loyalty, Mort."

Mort dipped his head. "I am at your service, my lord. Always."

Nodding his head, John left the room. Mort followed him with his eyes as he ascended the stone stairs. Peter would be returning with the lovely Brighit any time, her head held high and no offer of apology for their quick exit. That one's passion matched Peter's perfectly. Just as Mort's own wife matched his. Myra was, no doubt, busy with the children, planting the garden, seeing to repairs. Mayhap this fall, Mort would be there to help them with the harvest, prepare for the cold weather, and even be home for the cold, dark days of winter.

It had been many years since Mort had seen his own lovely lady. Even in his dreams, she appeared indistinct as if he were forgetting how she looked. When he awoke, try as he might, he could not recall the dream or her face. Or remember the touch of her hand in his. His chest tightened. He feared he could no longer remember the sound of her voice. Her beautiful voice. His sons would be mostly grown. What kind of men did they turn out to be?

Brighit's laugh traveled down to him. Mort wiped at his eyes, refilling his mead. Now Peter and Brighit! Their lives would be full. No doubt, the king would be honoring the man's work in settling the disruptions here in York and taking back the castle. If the man could also put to rest any Godwin plans for an overthrow, the king would be deeply in his debt.

In *their* debt.

Mort smiled.

John and Peter. And Mort. The idea of having the king in his debt was a pleasant one. Mort would need to approach Peter with it in such a way that he believed the idea was his own. They could travel west, sail to Ireland before the cursed man even set foot off his place of exile. They would demonstrate, once and for all, that King William of Normandy was the rightful heir and it would be his children and his grandchildren who held the throne into perpetuity.

Mort could be home by fall. A pleasant thought indeed.

Chapter Twenty-Four

Tadhg pushed to the head of his mounted group. He avoided looking at Tisa, both when he'd headed to the back of the line to speak to Cormac and upon his return. That he was unsuccessful turned his mood even blacker.

Sean moved up alongside him. "Yer foul mood will not stop me from asking for yer assurances."

"What are ye about?"

"I want yer assurance that ye will not agree to another commanding us if Roland is unable to. Being under his command was the agreement, was it not?"

"His to command. Aye. We will wait and see what he tells us upon our arrival."

"We'll be there anon, Tadhg. Give me yer assurance."

Tadhg made his most disdainful expression. "If this is what marriage turns a warrior in to, I'm blessed to have none of it."

Sean snorted. "Aye. Ye tell yerself the lie but I dunna believe it." He glanced toward Tisa. "Her husband does not appreciate her."

"Cease! I dunna wish to hear of her plight. 'Tis not within me to change her situation, as well ye ken."

"Giving fair warning." Sean reined in his horse to fall back behind Tadhg.

Four armed warriors approached from the meadow. They must be O'Brien men but Tadhg didn't recognize even one of them. He held his hand up for his group to stop.

"Tisa! Come forth," Tadhg called to her without turning her way.

She moved her palfrey forward, stopping beside Tadhg. He sat with his hands crossed before him and waited for the approaching men.

"Hail," a leathered man called out as he approached, not stopping until he was quite close.

"I come with Roland O'Brien's daughter. She wishes to see her father," Tadhg said.

Without warning, the man turned his scowling face on her and yanked the palfrey's reins, jerking Tisa away before Tadhg could react. "Yer father takes exception to yer absence."

Tadhg drew his sword, the metal cold in his hand.

"Stay yer hand, friend, unless ye wish to draw blood."

"Release the lady and there'll be no need to draw blood," Tadhg said.

"The Meic Lochlainn arrived three days ago and was not happy to have his daughter not in attendance."

Tisa paled. "I will come to him at once."

She dug in her heels and sped toward the castle.

The leathered man remained motionless as did Tadhg.

"We've come to see the man as well," Tadhg said. "He is expecting us. Shall we yet draw blood?"

"And who are ye?" The piercing blue eyes took in the party of warriors, pausing on Sean. A smile played on his lips.

Tadhg sheathed his sword in disgust. "Roland O'Brien bid us come and come we have. If ye turn us away, 'twill be on yer head."

Tadhg reined the horse about. Let O'Brien rot in a hell of his own making.

"Yer name!"

The leathered man's bellow caused Tadhg's mount to rear. He struggled to settle her without being unseated.

"Gerrit, ye ken who I am," Sean said. "Allow us to pass."

His friend's demanding tone surprised Tadhg as did the response the man gave him—a graceful sweep of his arm. His mount again under control, Tadhg and the rest of the men followed behind Sean.

"Pompous arse." Sean muttered under his breath.

Once within the bailey, they dismounted and were escorted into the main hall. Music and a blazing fire greeted them. The room was full of people drinking and eating.

The sight of a man other than Roland in his seat of honor startled Tadhg. "Where is Roland?"

Sean approached the gray-bearded man, still impressively broad in the chest despite his advancing years.

"Roland is visiting with his daughter. My thanks for her return though 'twould have been better for her to stay here, among her *own* people."

Sean faced Tadhg, his flaring nostrils the only visible sign of his annoyance. "This is Aodh Meic Lochlainn, their chieftain."

Aodh stood and nodded, his hand resting on the ornate hilt of the sword at his side, the gold trim of it glistening. His eyes perused the length of Tadhg, missing not a thing. When the man's eyes finally settled on his face, Tadhg raised his brows. "Have I passed yer inspection?"

Sean turned away, no doubt, to hide his smile. Aodh reddened and glanced beyond them at the others with them. "Ye must be the warriors Roland has on retainer."

Tadhg and Sean exchanged glances but neither answered him.

Aodh settled himself. "Roland will be down anon. Please," he indicated the table against the wall with a shake of his hand, "make free of the food and drink. We celebrate!"

The men crossed to the table, their eyes wary. Tadhg took a long draw on his mead, watching Aodh in deep conversation with a fair-haired man now seated beside him.

"They do like their celebrations," Sean said. "'Tis not the way I remember Roland O'Brien."

"Methinks Roland has little say over what happens here," Tadhg said in a quiet voice.

Sean drank from his horn as well and nodded. "Something is amiss. 'Twas the same when we came with Tisa which is why I dinna press her to stay here."

Tadhg looked away not bothering to hide his irritation.

Sean stiffened. "I am not speaking of her except in the most general way, Tadhg. I ken what ye said. I will abide by yer wishes."

Tadhg blew out a breath and refilled his mead. "So why would a man as rich with land as Roland just step aside for someone like this?"

"He said he feared he would be easily overrun if he dinna find protection."

"Protection such as this is not what the man needed. Where are the strapping sons he was so proud of? The ones whose arses we kicked with little effort."

"Dead."

A deep sadness welled within him. Tadhg knew loss. "I dinna ken."

"Methinks he dinna even tell Tisa."

Sean's eyes narrowed as if assessing how much he should say. Tadhg hardened his resolve, standing tall. He wanted Sean to say nothing more about Tisa.

A glimpse of a blond man ascending the stairs drew Tadhg's attention. The music became more lively. Couples moved about, lining up for some sort of dance. The blond reappeared and Tadhg's mouth gaped open. He pulled Tisa behind him. Her eyes downcast, a small smile on her lips. She wore a dark blue gown that hugged every generous curve. Large, amber stones on a chain hung around her slender neck. Tadhg wetted his suddenly dry lips and took a deep, slow breath.

Tisa smiled up at the tall, young man who grinned down at her. He was impeccably attired in the same blue. Her husband? He was neither old nor feeble. Pain pierced through Tadhg's heart like an arrow but he could not tear his eyes away as the handsome man led her through the dance.

They touched, palm to palm, after every clap with the slow beat of the song. When Tadhg expected them to pass by shoulder to shoulder, they, instead, wrapped an arm familiarly around the other's middle, holding close as they turned. Then crossed. And did the same to the left. Then crossed back again. Each time Tisa's bosom pressed into her husband's chest, Tadhg felt her against his own body. His own hand around her slender waist. Holding her tight. Her cheeks pink with exertion and a smile just for him.

Tadhg turned his back to the room, his breathing heavy. His groin tightened with need. He reached for the clay pitcher for more mead, downed the liquid then closed his eyes.

Someone slapped his back and Tadhg nearly exploded.

"Wonder what they're celebrating." Lughaidh smiled as he looked across the sea of bodies.

"I'll be seeing to the horses," Tadhg said, his throat tight. "Get me when the O'Brien shows himself."

Tadhg stomped out of the hall and into the chilly night air. He didn't stop until he was hidden in the shadowy darkness of the stable. Leaning his back against a post, he closed his eyes and struggled to steady himself. The mere sight of her made a mockery of his feigned composure. He ached to hold her against him. To touch her. To smell her. To taste her. She should be his.

Moving within the small building, he stretched out on top of the scattered straw and hay. Need raged through him like an uncontainable fire. Seeing her was killing him. Seeing her with a man able to satiate her needs, give her the children she'd always wanted, was even worse. He could not be this close to her.

"Ye've not eaten." Sean towered over him.

Tadhg rolled away from the tall man. "I dinna want anything. Is the O'Brien about?"

"Nae. Aodh said he would not be available until the morrow."

"Fine. Let me rest."

"Ye're not resting. Ye're torturing yerself."

"Sean, get yerself away and now!"

"I've no mind to leave ye to yer own vile thoughts."

Tadhg refused to respond to the jab. He recognized Sean's ploy for what it was. Talking would not lessen the need or the loss or the pain of his miserable existence.

"Ye're in a hell not of yer own making."

"And that makes it no easier to take." Damn. He wasn't going to respond.

"Nae and it won't."

"Won't?"

"Make it any easier." Sean hunkered down a few feet from him. "I want to remind ye of the legend."

"Ye dunna even believe in legends so speak no more of it, Sean!"

"Ye're the sixth son. That means ye'll have nothing but trouble."

"Thanks for that."

"Do ye want to lie down for it? Or do ye want to prove the legend wrong?"

Tadhg bolted to his feet. "I dinna want to live a life of trouble. Not ever but look—" he pointed toward the castle. "The love of my life is married to another. What am I to do?"

Sean's somber expression didn't change as he waited and watched and eventually Tadhg sat back down.

"I will not speak to ye of her again," Sean said. "Ye have my word. But please dunna let yerself get swallowed up into a pitiful life that has no meaning, where ye have no happiness, where ye have nothing to get up in the morning for. Will ye promise me that?"

How could Tadhg deny that was his life? He certainly could not promise it would get better. By all indications, it would not but he forced himself to respond with an even tone. "Aye, Sean, I promise ye. Now let me get some sleep."

Tadhg forced a smile for his friend and went back to lying down in the hope that Sean would feel better about leaving him there.

At daybreak they received word that Roland O'Brien would receive them.

The man sat in his own chair. His cheeks sallow. Dark circles beneath his eyes. He looked like death warmed over.

"Tadhg." Roland did not smile. His voice low. "So ye've come to offer yerselves to me?"

Tadhg was not offered a seat so he stood before the man, his hands joined behind his back.

"As we agreed," Tadhg said.

He'd left the others in the bailey so that he could speak privately with Tisa's father. No witnesses were necessary to his groveling before the adulterous swine. "I appreciate that ye saw my clan through the winter from yer own provisions."

"I dinna wish to see them starve."

Tadhg said no more. He'd said all he needed to say. Now he waited. Roland sipped from his cup, his eyes fixed on Tadhg. The moments plodded by.

"Ye will head north to Inishowen with the Meic Lochlainn and go where Aodh Meic Lochlainn commands. He has need of more warriors and I offer him only the very best."

Tadhg might have found pleasure in hearing such a compliment from this man earlier in his life but not now. Now, he didn't care what Roland O'Brien thought of him. He remained silent, uneasiness shifting inside him like a bear waking from a winter's sleep.

"Ye will fight with them until the Hunter's Moon and then ye will have fulfilled our agreement."

The bear roared into wakefulness and his arms fell stiffly to his sides. "To what purpose do they fight? Do they defend their home? Are there raiders they wish to curtail?"

"Nae." Roland answered in the same low tone. "They fight for conquest. They fight for Leofrid Godwin, son of Tostig Godwin, against the Norman invaders. They fight for the throne of England."

Chapter Twenty-Five

The trip north was not an easy one. Winter held a firm grasp as they headed along the coast to the Meic Lochlainn village. Frozen roads and driving snow made everyone miserable. Traveling with more than two score unhappy warriors at a fast pace made each stopover a raucous occasion. The mead flowed, the talk was bawdy, and the tempers flared. Being unfamiliar warriors to the Meic Lochlainn, Tadhg and his men were not included in their nightly disorders. He'd not even been introduced. Their attempt to send someone back to O'Brien land and get word to Peter was thwarted by a sudden need to count their numbers. Sean was correct; they were indeed hired thugs.

Tadhg kept his distance and avoided Tisa whenever possible. She and her husband slept away from the group. At night, Tadhg was beset by wild dreams where he was the husband, receiving her generous bounty. Each day he struggled against the darkness that threatened to overwhelm his thoughts.

"There is an inn down the road where we will stay our last night. We will push home on the morrow." Aodh made the announcement astride his mount at the front of the group.

The grumbling he received in response indicated they still had quite a distance yet to go.

Tisa rode near the back of the Meic Lochlainn group but just in front of Tadhg and his men. Gerrit was the only one who stayed behind when they arrived at the inn. Almost as if the man were to keep an eye on them. It seemed strange that after her husband had stayed by her side the entire trip, he would spend the day mingling with the men. She didn't seem to mind, hunched as she was with her husband's long, fur wrapped around her against the cold. Her mount, at least, seemed mild with an easy gait that probably made the travel easy.

Tadhg forced himself to turn away. What did he care of her comfort or why her husband had seemingly abandoned her?

"Is aught amiss?" Lughaidh came up beside him.

Tadhg swallowed down his angst. "There is not."

"'Twill be good to be sheltered this night. My fingers freeze right through my gloves."

Tadhg did not respond.

"Have ye ever been this far north?"

"I have."

"The frigid wind is relentless." Lughaidh finally faced Tadhg. The man's eyes widened. He ducked his head and returned to his place in the line.

From atop his horse, Tadhg watched as Aodh and Darragh went inside the inn. A large out building in the back, mayhap there would be room for all to be warm this night. A slither of something shivered up his spine. He turned in time to see Gerrit nudging his horse forward, his eyes locked on Tisa. When she noticed him, the look of fear that flashed across her face could not have been Tadhg's imagination. Without forethought, he jumped from his horse and hurried to her side. The leathered man pulled back and avoided looking at him. He moved toward the outside of the group as if it had always been his destination.

Tisa frowned at Tadhg, no doubt for his sudden appearance. He cleared his throat. "Can I assist ye?"

"With what?"

He raised stiff arms toward her. Confusion furrowed her brow but she leaned toward him. His hands at her waist, he lifted her down with ease. All ceased around him and she became his total focus. The earthy scent of her filled his senses. He breathed her in. Her dark hair brushed against his cheek like a caress. He turned into it. His fingers spread at her waist. He pressed against her ribs.

When her feet touched the ground, she stared at him with wide eyes, her bottom lip caught between her teeth. Heat surged through him. Did she feel the heat as well? He ran his tongue over his lips, his breath caught in his chest and he moved his face in closer. Just a taste of those luscious, red lips.

"Tadhg." Sean's forceful tone broke through his passion-induced fog.

Tadhg yanked his head back. His breathing labored. The knife burned where it sliced through his gut and he stepped away from Tisa. He gave her his back and faced Sean.

Tadhg closed his eyes, struggling for composure against his

overwhelming desires.

"My thanks," he said as he passed Sean.

"They've food and ale." Aodh's voice carried over the men. "And a warm building for the night."

The men cheered. Tadhg inhaled, a long, steadying breath, and turned back toward the group.

Darragh stood smiling beside his father who scratched at himself. Tadhg watched with narrowed eyes. Tisa's husband had no thought about leaving her out here unprotected among all these men. He'd given her no thought at all.

"Stable yer mounts in back, they've fresh water and fodder," Aodh said. "Gerrit!"

Before Tadhg's very eyes, Darragh seemed to cower where he stood, turning away from the leathered man when he approached.

"Aye?" Gerrit asked.

"Can ye see to our mounts as well?" Aodh asked.

"I'm not a stable boy."

Aodh pressed his lips together before he answered. "And well I ken it. I'm getting us some wenches." He glanced toward his son. "Or were ye hoping for something else?"

Darragh looked away when both men turned to him.

The bearded man's lowered voice carried to Tadhg but it made no sense. No one else seemed to hear, they were talking amongst themselves.

"A wench with a large arse would suit my needs fine," Gerrit answered.

Aodh gave a hearty laugh and slapped his son on the back. "Come. Ye've a wife to see to."

Darragh moved with his father toward Tisa. He kept his face averted. It certainly appeared to Tadhg as if Darragh were hoping to not be noticed by Gerrit or, at the very least, not to be spoken to directly by him.

"I dinna bid ye to dismount." Darragh's tone was harsh when he approached Tisa.

Her eyes darted toward Tadhg before answering. "Beg pardon. I meant no harm."

Darragh turned to Tadhg and puckered his lips in a thoughtful manner. Tadhg moved to follow his men.

"Ye!"

Not quick enough.

Tadhg faced Darragh. "Aye?"

Darragh closed the distance, leaving Tisa to follow. Her obvious discomfort tugged at Tadhg's heart.

"I dunna believe we've met," Darragh said.

Aodh came up behind his son. "This is one of the O'Brien warriors."

"I ken that." The blond rolled his eyes. "I want his name."

His father scrunched his face. "They're here to follow our orders not become kinsmen." He grabbed Darragh's arms, pulling him back toward the inn. "Ye concern yerself with things ye should not. Come, Tisa."

Her head down, she followed behind the two men who paid her no mind. They didn't offer an arm up the stairs. They didn't open the door for her or allow her to enter before them. Instead, she scrambled up behind like a stray dog hoping for scraps.

Tadhg closed his eyes. He was seething inside at her treatment and at himself. Had he really been ready to kiss her? Right there in front of all those men? Damn. He still longed for a taste of her lips. How much longer would this trip take?

"Tadhg."

"What!"

Sean backed away, his arms open in submission.

Tadhg struggled for a controlled tone. "What?"

"Mayhap ye can get a room within? The building is not as warm as they would have us believe."

Tadhg blew a breath of frustration. "Better to be in the cold than alongside that rutting man."

"Aodh?"

"Nae, his son!"

Tadhg stomped past, shoving Sean aside, to catch up to the rest of his men. The best he could hope for was that Tisa would remain far away from him for the duration of his stay at the Meic Lochlainn. He didn't know yet how much information he'd get upon his arrival or how quickly he could dispatch Cormac to update Peter in England. Mayhap waiting to learn their plans for attack would be helpful. He prayed for Peter and Brighit's safety.

Tisa prayed for patience. Being in closer quarters than usual with Darragh was trying her patience.

"Does it make me look... formidable?"

She looked again at the way he'd belted his sword to his side. "Ye are formidable."

The man snorted and smiled. "I have worked with great diligence to become the warrior my father requires."

"It shows."

He tipped his head and glanced her way. "Ye notice such things?"

"How can I not? The other men step out of yer way. They keep their eye on ye."

Darragh slowly nodded. "Hmm, mayhap I could be chieftain."

Tisa's shoulders rounded, the breath knocked out of her. "Methinks ye have forgotten what is required in order for that to occur."

Darragh shrugged. "That ye must get with child within six months? Some women are barren. Mayhap we can convince him 'tis the case with ye."

Tisa nibbled at her lip. Aodh had kept his distance but six months was quickly coming to an end. He did show Darragh a certain respect that had been absent previously.

"Think ye he will not wish to prove 'tis me who is indeed barren? And not yer lack of trying?"

Darragh stiffened. "How would he do that?"

"By laying with me! By forcing himself on me. By doing the very thing we have worked so hard to keep from happening, Darragh."

"Then we will convince him of our trying... at every opportunity." He adjusted his sword again.

"The other way." Tisa rubbed the damp cloth under her hair. Despite the cold temperatures, riding for so long made her sweaty.

"Hmm, maybe formidable is not appealing."

Tisa took a breath and stood in front of her husband. "Ye wish to be appealing? To someone in particular?"

Darragh reddened, a sly smile on his face. "Mayhap."

"What of Breandan?"

He put on a pout. "I ken not when he will return. Am I to pleasure myself?" Darragh's eyes drifted closed and his nostrils flared before he met her gaze. "I have a great need this night."

"What are ye about, husband?"

He dropped onto the single stool allotted to their tiny room above the inn. "'Tis hard for me to be around Gerrit. He upsets me."

Tisa's chest welled with compassion, like an overflowing loch, and she dropped to her knees before him. Her hands warm on his. "My poor Darragh, did he hurt ye?"

"He did." Darragh faced her, unshed tears on his lashes. "I *loved* him very deeply."

Her heart went out to him. She wrapped him in her arms. "Did he not return yer feelings?"

He pulled back to see her, his eyes widening as he spoke, "He did, Tisa. He wanted me. He pursued me as if I were a great treasure to him. He said he wanted me like he'd never wanted anyone and if I just allowed him to take me... I would never be satisfied by another."

In one motion, Tisa gasped, dropped her arms, and drew back. "Nae."

Darragh stood. "What? What is amiss?"

"Nae!" Shaking, she turned away from him. "He said ye would never be satisfied by another?"

"Forgive me, Tisa. I should not speak so to ye. I forget myself."

She turned back to him. "Those are the same words he used on me."

Darragh's body turned rigid. "When did he have occasion to say such a thing to *ye*?"

Tisa fought against the intense need to turn away so that she could think clearly and not say the wrong thing. She didn't move. "He came upon me in the woods."

"The woods? Ye were alone?"

She swallowed. "I went in search of my herbs."

His eyes narrowed. "Winter kills the plants this far north, Tisa. Is it not so where ye come from?" The question required no response, not when suspicion tightened his features. "Tell me true, wife. Why were ye in the woods?"

"I needed to take a walk, to think about the spring and where I may find my herbs. I was restless. 'Tis no more than that."

He tipped his head up and down. Slowly. His eyes intent on her as if considering the truth of her words. Her own face was hot with the lie and she felt certain he saw it.

"Gerrit came upon ye in the woods and what did he do?"

Tisa turned aside, she needed to think. She took a shaky breath. "He... he made moves against my person."

"How so?"

"He said he would give me what ye could not."

His gasp drew her eyes back to him. "And was he successful?"

"NAE! Nae, he was not successful. Malcolm cam—"

"Malcolm?" Darragh threw up his hands in disgust. "And why have I not have heard of this before now."

"Malcolm stopped him."

"Malcolm stopped him. Malcolm protected ye." His face darkened in anger. "As if yer own husband was not able to see to yer protection?"

"'Tis not the way of it, Darragh."

"Nae? The man who has caused me so much pain was able to approach my wife—Did he touch ye?"

Thoughts flew about her head as she struggled with how much to tell him.

"Answer me!"

She jumped at his tone. "He touched me."

Darragh recoiled. "Where?"

"He came close to—to forcing himself on me."

"How close?"

Unbidden fear washed over her and tears swelled but Darragh's rage did not lesson. He locked his fingers around her wrists when she didn't immediately respond, pulling her tight against him. "Tell me. How close did that whoreson come to raping my wife?"

"He was stiff between my legs, about to impale me, and Malcolm—"

Darragh dropped her hands, the impetus shoving her away as if she were worthless. "—and Malcolm came to yer aid."

Her entire body trembled but she took a step closer. "Forgive me, Darragh, for not telling ye. I believed he sought to scare me only. I thought he was like ye."

Darragh turned his scowl on her. "Nae. Gerrit is nothing like me. Gerrit likes to use his prick wherever it can be accommodated."

"I dinna ken."

"He used ye to insult me further." Darragh settled on the stool, his hands fisted on his legs. "And me none the wiser. How he must be laughing at me."

Tisa's stomach tightened like she'd been punched. She'd earnestly tried to not allow her husband to be disparaged. She'd failed miserably. His pain so deep, he masked it with fury.

"I fought him, Darragh." She spoke quietly, kneeling before him, and he looked down into her face. "He was very cruel."

Her husband's eyes rounded ever so slightly. "Did he hurt ye?"

Gerrit had been as seductive as a lover. "He would not release me despite my struggles against him."

"I asked if he hurt ye?"

"He refused to hear my refusal!"

"Tisa! I asked if he hurt ye!"

She bit her trembling lips. "Nae."

Darragh searched her face before he spoke again, a small smile on his lips. "He tried to seduce ye."

He knew the man quite well it appeared.

"The bastard stroked ye and whispered in yer ear and kissed ye in those intimate places and he tried to get ye to give yer consent. He wanted ye to fall into his arms."

Tisa was afraid to answer, afraid of Darragh's response. "I dinna want him to touch me."

"Ah, my lovely wife, ye fought against even the great Gerrit." He cupped her cheek with a cold hand. "Many have fallen before ye."

Her short breaths puffed in and out with little sounds of relief. "I will not."

Darragh pulled her into him, her head resting on his shoulder. "And we have no shortage of assailants against ye, trying to take me down."

Rubbing his cheek against her hair, Darragh comforted her. Her breathing steadied. Darragh held her closer, his body tight with emotion.

The door opened behind them. She'd swear she heard a groan of pain from behind. Tadhg stood in the doorway. His face bright red. "Beg pardon. I.."

He turned to leave.

"Stop!" Darragh stood and ordered in his most commanding tone, all of his deep emotional upheaval set aside.

Tisa jumped up at his voice but wiped the tears from her cheeks before pasting a smile on her face.

"Come in." Darragh said, all charm and easy manners.

Tisa had a terrible feeling deep in her gut.

"Please. Sit." Darragh directed Tadhg to the stool.

Tadhg remained at the door, stiff. His face stricken.

Overcome with concern, Tisa moved toward him, reaching a hand toward his head. "Are ye not well, Tadhg?"

"Tadhg?" Darragh said the word like a curse. "*Ye* are Tadhg?"

Tadhg pulled his head away from her touch, not allowing her to feel his brow.

"I am."

Darragh's intense gaze stirred up the quaking barely settled in her gut. He squared his shoulders and approached Tadhg but glanced toward her before he spoke.

"I've heard yer name… even as far north as Inishowen."

Tisa did not move. She did not breathe.

Tadhg's eyes narrowed. All sound ceasing around them.

Darragh said, "Is there a reason ye're here?"

"Wrong room. Beg pardon."

Her husband glanced at her, his face an unreadable mask, before he turned again to Tadhg. "Methinks we best see ye below, Tadhg. I would like to have some time alone with my wife." Darragh smiled widely then winked. "Ye understand."

Tisa's mouth nearly fell open. The implication of them having an intimate moment now, here, and in front of Tadhg stung like a hard slap to her face. Tadhg's jaw tightened and she didn't miss the flash of pain. He tipped his head and was gone.

Tisa shut the door, emotion welling up inside of her like an ocean gale. Great sobs threatened to erupt. She leaned her forehead against the cold wood, fighting to just take a breath.

"So that is the lover ye dream of?"

Darragh's contemptuous tone left little question of his true feelings toward the revelation.

Tisa whipped around, ready to confront her husband but his eyes were on her, dark with rage. She fought down the urge to cower and stood her ground. Darragh ripped the belt from his waist. The hissing sound filling the room as he slid the leather scabbard down its length.

"A handsome man, yer Tadhg." Darragh placed the sword on the table but kept hold of the belt, playing with the thing. Doubling then snapping it as if in a silent threat. "I, too, would have fallen for a body like that but he is not like me, is he, Tisa?" He faced her. "He requires a woman's touch, no doubt."

"I dunna ken."

Darragh tipped his head in a blatant expression of disbelief. "Ye dream of him making love to ye but ken not what pleasures him?"

"We were very young when last we met."

"Ye just imagine 'twould be ye that could pleasure him? Or would ye enjoy him pleasuring ye?"

Tisa closed her eyes and shook her head.

"Come now, Tisa. I'm yer husband. Ye can share with me yer deepest desires."

She would not discuss her feelings for Tadhg with Darragh.

"Nae? Then answer me one question."

She looked at him.

"Did ye confirm to Gerrit that we have not been together as husband and wife?"

"I dinna!"

"Is there anyone ye have told?"

"Of course not! I have never spoken to anyone of such intimate details."

Caireann did not count. She would never tell anyone what she knew.

"Then ye must understand 'twill be the same in front of everyone. *All* must believe we are truly husband and wife."

No! Not Tadhg! She struggled with the urge to slap him. Repeatedly.

Darragh closed the distance between them, caressing the side of her face with a gentle touch. "No one need ken it is in word only."

"Yea."

He dropped the belt beside the sword. "Make haste to go below. I will wait outside for ye."

Chapter Twenty-Six

Tisa dropped onto the stool, her legs shaking, and stared at the closed door. Darragh's anger sapped her strength and made her afraid. As her husband, he had the right to do whatever he chose. No one would gainsay a man's decision about how he treated his wife. Aodh had set his own wife aside for another.

She filled her lungs to help ease her galloping heart. The mere sight of Tadhg was like fresh air blowing against her face on a sultry, summer day. She longed to bask in his presence.

And when he'd helped her off the horse? That intense look of longing? His lips moving in closer to hers? She wanted his kiss. She longed for his kiss, to be held in his arms, to feel his solidness against her. Her desperate moan of longing vibrated in her chest.

A solid rap against the door startled her.

"I'm waiting on ye," Darragh said.

Her husband's intense anger must come from his knowledge of her feelings toward Tadhg. And it scared her. She needed to hide her feelings away, keep them buried deep inside where no one else would see them.

Tisa wiped the cloth over her cheeks erasing any sign of tears. She opened the door. Darragh faced her, his hands resting over the doorframe. He cocked his head to one side, his eyes scanning her.

"Ye're wearing that?" His disdainful tone would have been the same if she'd been covered in dung.

"I thought ye liked this gown."

He flattened his lip. "I would like my wife to look fetching at all times."

"Beg pardon. This is what I am wearing."

Darragh leveled his gaze on her, the anger still there.

She refused to look away.

He took her hand, pulling her flat against him. She gasped.

"And ye look beautiful, wife."

His mouth on hers, he kissed her deeply, even leaning her against the door frame as he pressed into her. She didn't resist. There was nothing he wanted from her, just the show of an intimacy that didn't exist.

Finally, he pulled away and smiled, his face still close. "Now that is the look of a woman well ravished... her lips anyway."

He led her down the narrow stairs to the room below, tightly packed with their soldiers.

"Ah, Father," Darragh said in a voice loud enough to carry above the din. "Apologies for my tardiness." He pulled her alongside him, tucking her against him when he stopped in front of his father. "I had a difficult time tearing myself away from my enticing wife."

"And a fetching wife, she is, Darragh." Aodh led them to the table before the fire. "No grandchild yet? Ye just keep trying, son."

"Oh, I am, Father." He kissed the side of her head. "I certainly am."

Tisa sat beside her father-in-law, Darragh so close beside her that their bodies touched. When the food was brought out, many settled down at the few tables around them, the rest stood against the walls of the small inn. Darragh brushed her hair away and kissed her cheek before offering her a trencher, heavy with meat juices.

"We'll keep up her strength in preparation of the event." His eyes locked on to hers when she didn't immediately take the bread. A warning. Tisa accepted the food from Darragh.

"And keep up her strength for the making of it." Aodh laughed, his mouth full of food.

His father believed all that Darragh told him. His father wanted to believe him. She lifted the bread to her mouth, catching sight of Gerrit where he stood against the far wall, his eyes fixed on her. He smiled, that tilted smile he had when he spoke of his own prowess. She hesitated before biting into the bread and looked away. With difficulty, she swallowed. The mead was passed but she reached for the same that Aodh was drinking. Darragh blocked her hand, allowing the cup to pass them.

"Do ye need this? We would not want ye too relaxed." He gave her his own mead. "This will do for ye tonight, wife."

She swallowed down the liquid, her eyes closing, then lifted it for more. Darragh covered the hand that held the mug with his own, forcing her to bring it down to the table. He moved in close and kissed her again, his tongue invading her mouth before he ended the kiss. "Dunna get any ideas about becoming drunk, sweet little Tisa. More slips happen when drunk."

Her eyes filled in her humiliation. "Why are ye doing this, Darragh? Few couples display such blatant, unquenchable desires. Have I given ye any reason?"

Darragh dipped his head and took a drink from the now full cup. When he looked at her, his own eyes were bright with suspicion.

"There are many seeking my downfall, that would lure ye into their web of deceit. I dunna want to learn the hard way that ye succumbed by finding yer legs spread with someone else betwixt them."

Her jaw dropped but she quickly recovered. "'Tis ye alone that go to someone else."

He moved in close, hissing her silent. She searched around those closest but saw no one's eyes on them.

"I'll admit that I've often wondered why that was, why ye never objected to my preferences, or why ye allowed it."

Tisa moved in closer, her words for him alone. "Because I want my husband happy!"

He raised his brows expectantly, his eyes on her, and waited but she did not understand. Humiliation washed over her. When she tried to stand, he grasped her hand to keep her seated. "I dinna bid ye to go. Ye need to stay with me this night."

Aodh frowned in their direction.

"Yer father is wondering if something is amiss," she said.

"And ye will stay and convince him it is not."

Tisa tipped her head in acquiescence. Darragh handed her his cup of mead and turned to his father. As soon as they started talking, she downed the cup. It was not very good and it did not numb her as the other drink did. She glanced out over the men's faces, they were deep in their cups able to drink much more and much faster than she was. She envied them.

Darragh leaned toward his father, speaking with great gusto to the man on the other side. Mayhap that was the man he'd dressed for, not Tadhg. She searched him out. He was not in the room. There were only Meic Lochlainn men as had been the way of it the entire journey. The MacNaughton warriors were kept away. She heaved a sigh and looked down at her sopping bread.

A gold cup appeared next to her. She followed the hand to find the innkeeper standing beside her.

"For ye."

The amber liquid in the cup was a boon and she smiled at the man. Darragh was paying her little attention now.

The liquid went down smooth and he refilled the cup.

"My thanks."

"Not me, my lady." The innkeeper directed her to the far side of the room. Gerrit raised his cup to her. The innkeeper stepped away to disappear in the crowd.

Sweat broke out on her forehead and her breath tightened in her chest. She put the cup down with trembling fingers.

"I need to leave, Darragh," she said.

He swatted at her and kept his eyes on the man he spoke with.

"Now, Darragh, I am not well."

"Ye ken the way." He spoke over his shoulder at her.

So much for his show of interest in her. On shaky legs, she stood. The man on the other side of Aodh was a soldier she often saw Darragh in conversation with. Ronan's commander of the guard. The room shifted beneath her, her arms flew out to catch herself. She lowered her head closer to Darragh.

"Please, I am not well. I think—"

"Then return to the room." Darragh turned his angry eyes on her. His mouth was a tight, thin line. He turned back to the captain.

Aodh had moved to the other side of the captain, a hefty wench on his lap. Her large breasts close to his face. The room dimmed then brightened. She could not stay here.

Groping along the wall, she made her way through the hall. Men pushed against her, only moving at the last minute. They paid her little heed. When the stairs came into focus, she struggled to move closer, her legs heavy. A firm hand gripped her waist, giving her aid through the men that now stepped aside. The steps were but a few feet away when she turned to offer her thanks. Gerrit's bright blue eyes looked down at her, a huge grin on his bearded face.

"Did ye wish to offer yer gratitude for my assistance?"

Fear lurched in her chest but settled back down, leaving her numb. He lifted her into his arms. No words came out. The scream trapped in her throat.

"Allow me to bring ye to a place where ye can show me proper gratitude."

Gerrit carried her away from the stairs, taking her out and into the darkness. She lurched forward, trying to break free, but her movements were awkward. He held her tight against him.

"With what have ye poisoned me?" she asked.

"Poisoned? Never. Relaxed ye only. I wished for ye to enjoy our time." His eyes twinkling when he looked down at her. "Yer first time."

Out in the night air, he strode toward the trees. Then she was on a blanket, the smell of horse dung surrounding her.

"Nae." She pushed herself up before Gerrit pressed her back, flat, with little effort.

He lay beside her, looking down at her, a hand caressing her cheek. "Oh, yea, sweet little Tisa. Did ye think I'd not have my way with ye?"

His bright blue eyes hovered over her before his lips brushed against her cheek then moved to her lips, pausing there. "I always get what I want."

Tisa tried to shake her head but he clamped a hand to her chin, his tongue pressing against hers with feverish strokes. When he broke the kiss, he was breathing hard.

"I've a great need for ye. I want to be the first to master yer comely body."

"Nae." Her voice sounded so small.

"Oh aye." His lips shifting to her neck, his hand groped at her breasts. Then her dress was laid open, the cool night air on her skin. She'd foregone the chemise that reeked of body odor.

"Stop."

"Stop? Why would I stop?"

Gripping her breast, he sucked at her nipple, drawing it into his hot mouth and stroking it with his tongue.

"No one will stop us this time." His hot hand grazed her skin, working its way between her thighs. His hand stopped and he lifted his head. "Ah, sweet little Tisa, ye disappoint me."

Covering her, his huge body forced her legs far apart. His hips dug into her, no doubt bruising her. He rubbed his stiff shaft against her. "Where is my passionate lover?"

Tisa spit at him. "I'll not be yer lover. Ye defiler of all innocents!"

Gerrit drew back, wiping the spittle from his cheek, an odd expression on his face. "I defile no one. I give them what they want."

"I dunna want this!"

The herbs were wearing off. Anger surged through her and she fought him, straining her legs against the invasion. He slapped her hard. Her head jerked back.

"Methinks ye do."

"Then ye ken ye're raping me, not taking me willingly."

"I just ken ye like it rougher than I first believed."

"I dunna want ye at all."

Gerrit frowned. "Ye did when I found ye in the woods. I smelled yer desire. Ye were wet with desire."

"Ye're wrong. 'Twas not ye I wanted."

"Ye're lying to yerself." He yanked down his hose and lowered himself. The tip of his tarse hot against her skin.

"Dunna." She turned her head aside.

Gerrit did not shift to the juncture of her legs as she expected. Abruptly he stood and covered himself. A horse came up behind them and he strode toward the rider.

"What is amiss here?" Tadhg's sweet voice carried to her. She stood up and pulled her gown to close, wrapping the tie around her.

"There is naught amiss. A lover's tryst is all."

Tadhg searched beyond, his eyes fell on her. "Is that so?"

"Aye."

"Then I will speak to the lady and hear it from her mouth."

"She does not wish her husband to learn of this."

"And I will not be dissuaded from hearing it from her mouth." Tadhg dismounted. "Come forth."

Tisa walked toward Tadhg, her lungs filling with cool, night air and exultation. He examined her closely before he spoke. "Are ye here willingly?"

"I am not."

Gerrit roared. "She plays me false! She came here of her own accord."

Tadhg reached his hand toward her, his somber expression never changing. Heat rippled through her at his firm grasp and she went to him. "Do ye wish to leave?"

"I do."

Tadhg mounted and caught her up, settling her in front of him. She wasn't sure if her shallow breathing now was from fear, the herbs, or her closeness to Tadhg. He was rock solid beside her. An anchor in the storm that was her life.

Gerrit fisted his hands at his hips, an inscrutable expression. He said not a word but she could feel him following them with his eyes.

An arm on either side of her, Tadhg urged the horse forward. She dare not move. She dare not speak. She dare not look at Tadhg or he would surely know the joy in her heart at being so near him. Her hero. His scent surrounded her. She longed to wrap an arm about his waist, to snuggle her head against his chest and hear his heart beating, to feel his lips on hers.

"Do ye need a moment before I return ye to yer husband?"

Tadhg's voice held no emotion, no hint of what he was feeling. Tisa exhaled quietly to calm her pounding heart before she answered him.

"I do." She could not say more than that, not without revealing her inner turmoil.

Leading his mount down the road, he veered off toward the coastline. The moon disappeared behind the clouds, the surf heard but no longer seen. Tadhg dismounted and reached up to help her down before crossing to the water, leaving her behind.

The night birds called in the distance. The water crashed against the rocks. She wished she could speak of her longing to be his but Tadhg gave no indication he felt the same. He seemed cold now. Unapproachable. Not the man she remembered. She missed his ready smile. The way his eyes twinkled when he laughed. The way he held her against him.

Tears fell but she did not approach him. He stood stiff beside the water, gazing off toward the horizon.

"When ye have composed yerself, I will return ye." He spoke without facing her.

"Thank ye."

What could she have done to deserve this life? What great transgression had she committed to be ripped away from the man she loved, the man she would give up the rest of her life for just one night in his arms, to be completely his?

Oh God, please forgive me. I beg for yer mercy, Lord. Allow me this moment. Let me ken again his gentle kiss, the feel of his arms safely surrounding me.

Tadhg faced her. "I do need to return to my men."

Tisa dropped her head. "Aye."

He mounted and reached down to her, placing a hand at her waist to steady her. His hand was hot. The horse was not urged forward. His breath fanned against her face. She closed her eyes and imagined things were different. This was her love and they were headed to their own home where he would take her in his arms and make love to her. They would talk of their future and make plans for a family.

She opened her eyes and turned to him. "Is aught amiss?"

His eyes were on her. When his gaze dropped to her lips, she held her breath, wetting her dry lips.

"Nae." He looked past her and urged the horse forward, his hand dropping away.

She stiffened against the tears. Loud noises carried to them, the men had moved their celebration outside. Her gut tightened. She couldn't be found with Tadhg. She put a hand to his chest and he took a quick breath.

Tisa turned to him. "Ye can let me down here."

It was a moment before he responded. "Nae, ye are not safe here."

"The men are about." Panic rose within her as did her voice. "Please. No closer."

She made to get down on her own but he halted the horse and assisted her. She moved toward the throng, searching out Darragh or Aodh. They could not see her with him. Not now.

"Tisa!" One drunken soldier addressed her.

Her body tensed.

"Is the privy that way?" Another man scratched at his head, a thoughtful frown on his face.

She slipped past without responding.

"Tisa!" Darragh called to her from closer to the building, the red-headed captain close at his side. He could not have seen Tadhg. "I will be up anon."

Fury gripped her innards.

She stomped past them and into the building where a good many warriors still sat, some playing games, others making moves on the wenches that Aodh had supplied. All of them looking quite exhausted.

Gerrit's solid frame blocked her way to the stairs.

"Move aside," she said in a loud voice. When he reached to grab at her arm, she jerked it away. "Nae! Ye'll not touch me again! Ever!"

"Oh, a fire in ye now! Now that ye got the handsome MacNaughton warrior on yer side."

He could not learn how wrong he was. She moved her face in closer, the anger rippling through her, tightening every muscle on her face. "Ye have the right of it. Now step aside!"

Gerrit's bright blue eyes flashed, a look of admiration. He quirked a brow and stepped aside. Tisa nearly ran up the stairs, throwing the door shut and barring it tight. Darragh would not be back anon unless they were interrupted. He'd been too long unsatisfied to not want to go at it all night long.

She ripped off her gown and threw herself on the pallet, covering herself with the thick, coarse blanket. It scratched at her skin and the discomfort somehow felt right. Somehow she deserved it. She drifted off the sleep.

Chapter Twenty-Seven

Darragh remained by the captain's side for the rest of their journey home. He spoke to Tisa only when his father was present or if he noticed Tadhg nearby. In all other ways, it was as if she did not exist. When they arrived home, Darragh helped her down and again left her to fend for herself.

Caireann approached as soon as he was gone.

"I've missed ye." She held Tisa close.

"Is aught amiss? Has something happened?"

The redhead's eyes were filled with tears. "Nae. All is well. I have just missed ye so."

Tisa headed toward her home, her small sack of belongings in her arms. "Has Malcolm been seeing to ye?"

"Aye." Caireann blushed. "He sees to my every need."

Tisa pushed open her door, the smell of home greeting her. "Of course he does. He cares for ye."

"He loves me so. Sometimes I dunna ken what I did to deserve such happiness."

Tisa dropped her sack onto the chest in the alcove. "Do ye ken when ye'll make yer pledge to the man?"

"We would like to do it whenever ye think 'twill be best."

She stopped to face her friend, her hands at her hips. "The morrow? 'Twill surely be a fine day for it."

Caireann's mouth dropped open. "So soon?"

"Why not? Ye should be together."

"Malcolm has said as much but I dunna wish to leave ye."

"Ye're not leaving me, lass. Ye'll be here to help me as I need ye.

Dunna fash yerself. The joining will be on the morrow. Go to see the man. Off with ye now!"

Tisa shooed her out the door. Waiting to wed was begging for trouble if Caireann was, indeed, pregnant from the rape. Who would do such a thing? Even that bastard Gerrit showed himself unwilling for such an atrocious act.

Aodh always had women around for the men although Tisa kept her distance from all that. After what Darragh had told her about him sharing the best wenches, she did not care to witness what type of women did not mind being passed around. Or mayhap they were not willing. That could easily be her. A chill of fear passed over her. She had avoided it thus far. She needed to continue to do so.

Tisa yanked back the coverings from the little bed but they needed cleaning. She ripped them off and headed toward the door. Darragh burst in, laughing, and nearly collided with her. His head turned away, his attention on whoever was behind him. The captain followed.

"Oh, Tisa! I expected ye to be at the longhouse."

Tisa did not smile. "I dunna choose to be at the longhouse. I choose to be at my own home."

"My home."

"And as yer wife, 'tis my home as well."

The slender redhead smiled at her. A glowing smile. A smile of condescension. "Tisa."

"Ian." She pushed past and continued out the door.

Tisa followed the short path to the washer woman's house. She had acquired a lotion for her. So much time in the filthy, hot water made the woman's hands red and chafed. Surely the woman would appreciate it.

"Siobhan?" The house was empty so she deposited the bed linens on the bench beside her ever present wash water. Tisa grabbed the trews and leine, freshly cleaned, that were neatly piled there.

A rustling behind her made Tisa jump. When she turned, her smile froze on her face.

Tadhg stood in the doorway. It was a moment before he spoke. "I was told I could stay here until we depart."

Tisa shrugged and shoved down those warm feelings that threatened to overwhelm her every time she was near him. "I dinna ken. 'Tis not my place."

She went through the door but he stuck out his arm at the last moment to stop her.

Fighting against the ripple of hope that swept over her, she locked her jaw. He wanted nothing to do with her. She would not fall against his solid chest and wrap her arms about his middle.

She turned to him. "What are ye about?"

"Are ye well?"

Well? No, my husband has no use for me and my father-in-law wants to slake himself on me. My father is sick with guilt and giving up his family heritage to warmonger that want to conquer some Godforsaken country.

"I am well."

She looked away to pass by but he did not drop the arm. She waited. She did not need to look on him again with that growth of dark hair on his chin making his dark eyes even darker, even more alluring.

"Has Gerrit bothered ye again?"

Anger gripped her, pushing every other emotion aside. She faced him. "Oh, so ye believed me? Or did ye believe him that I would go out to meet such a man as that on a dark night?"

"I dinna ken. 'Tis yer life, Tisa."

"Nae, Tadhg. 'Tis not been my life for quite a while. Will ye please step aside?"

Tadhg removed himself. Stopping on the path, she was torn between returning to her husband rutting with another man at her home or heading to the longhouse and being lusted after by everyone else. Looking up to heaven, Tisa blew a breath and headed to the longhouse.

Tadhg kept a watchful eye on Tisa as she moved along the path toward the longhouse. He closed his eyes. Her scent lingered, reminding him of his latest dream of her. It haunted him. The taste of her neck where he nibbled along her shoulder. Her groan of longing and the feel of her breasts when he ran his hand over her chest, cupping and squeezing. Her bottom pressed back against him, rubbing his hardened prick. He groaned aloud. He was past the point of pain with his need for her.

Dropping on the bench beside the fire, he sighed. Fiddling with the material beside him, he realized her scent was drifting up to him, surrounding him. He brought the cloth to his face. A bad idea. He shifted uncomfortably.

"Hello?" An older woman stood in the door. "Are ye Tadhg?"

He dropped the material, fighting to keep from appearing guilty. "Aye."

"Good to have ye here. Surely Aodh's plans will be fruitful with such a fine warrior as yerself beside him."

Tadhg stood. "Well, not exactly beside him."

She pshawed, waving his comment aside. "Not the wisest of leaders then. Here," she set out a pallet from the corner, "ye can sleep here."

Taking the material that he'd dropped, she made up the bed for him.

"Ye'll be warm enough in here. In winter, there's an unending amount of work for me. Water's always heating."

He moved closer, wishing he could figure out a way to not have Tisa's scent surrounding him while he slept. "Can I help ye?"

"My thanks for yer offer of help. No need. Aodh expects all his men to be seen to."

Tadhg stood uselessly beside the fire. 'Twas a small room with the wash water the center of all activity. No other table or chests and a single candle secured beside the door.

Finished, she stretched and faced him. "Methinks Aodh may have been looking for ye and yer men."

"Oh! My thanks, mistress. I'll go to him."

"The Godwin arrived nigh a week ago and his lady is none too happy here. Yer bed will be waiting for ye whenever ye're released from duty."

Tadhg headed out again, glancing behind the little house. The roundhouse set back from the path had been the house he'd seen Tisa come from. It was tucked into the side of the hill, separate from the rest of the houses. Without knowing exactly why, he approached the door. Grunts of exertion carried to him, he put his ear closer to the wood, trying to discern the sound before knocking.

"Oh aye!" Darragh's moan of pleasure.

Tadhg jerked back. He stared at the wooden door, questioning his own hearing. The sound came again and Tadhg turned away, trotting back to the main road. He felt his ears were on fire and in his mind, flashes of Tisa the way he'd imagined her in his dream flooded his mind. Her eyes closed in passion. *Her* groans of pleasure.

The sharp sting of frosty air helped to clear his mind. The wind along the shore, covered with fog, gusted a brisk breeze over the village. The longhouse was crowded even this late at night. No doubt, Aodh sent word ahead to put off the evening repast until his arrival.

Situated with tables lined up on either side, people worked to prepare the meal. Aodh sat at the head table drinking with another man, not a man Tadhg recognized. The opposite door lay open and the heavy smoke drifted out. His fingers and toes tingled in the toasty warmth.

Tisa passed by the door. Tadhg paused. Surly he was mistaken. He strode to the door in time to see her round the corner. It couldn't be her.

"Tisa!" Tadhg followed after her.

Tisa stopped a few feet away, a pile of material wrapped in her arms.

"Did ye call to me?"

Tadhg wasn't sure what to say. If she wasn't in the house with her husband, someone else certainly was. Mayhap that wasn't her home.

"Is that yer home beside the meadow?"

"Aye. Darragh's home."

She looked tired. Tadhg had the strong urge to smooth out the worry line between her eyes. He imagined her response, a peaceful expression of appreciation for his concern. His breath quickened. Then he would grab her chin with gentle fingers, pulling her in closer for a passionate kiss on her full lips. His eyes darted to her lips. He forced himself back and swallowed. "I dunna believe I will be here over long. I wished to get a lay of the land."

Tisa nodded, her lips tight, then continued down the path toward her home.

What if she walked in on Darragh with another woman?

"Tadhg! Yer men need to be in here," Aodh called from the door.

"Aye. I'll collect them."

Aodh scowled but went back inside.

This would not end well if she walked in on what he'd heard happening with her husband.

Tadhg walked back down the path, moving to spot where he could see Tisa go inside the small house. A tremor of excitement settled in his belly. She would need comforting. He took a few steps closer. He waited. Nothing. Tadhg scratched at his cheek, a hand resting on his hip. He frowned, certain of what he'd heard.

The door suddenly opened and the red-headed captain of the guard came out of the house. Tadhg turned toward the woods, feigning interest in… something.

"Good day, Tadhg," the man said as he passed, a pleasant expression on his face.

"Captain." Tadhg nodded then glanced back at the roundhouse. His eyes narrowing.

"Tadhg." Sean called to him from further down the road. "Aodh bids us come at once."

Tadhg waved, then turned to follow a few feet behind the captain. The man swaggered, even whistling a tune. Very odd.

Aodh stood at the front of the longhouse when Tadhg entered. His hands crossed about his chest, he had an air of great importance as he spoke to the gathering.

"Is he sharing his plans with us finally?" Tadhg whispered to Sean once he'd made his way through the group to stand beside him.

Sean nodded without turning to him, an irritated scowl on his face.

"Well?" Tadhg asked.

Sean wouldn't need much nudging to share what was bothering him, as disgruntled as he appeared.

"He's not said much."

"And what is wrong with ye?" Tadhg asked.

Sean finally faced him. "Ye ken I dinna want this man ordering me about."

"Aye. O'Brien knew it as well. He was careful in the command he gave me."

Sean dropped onto a bench with a thud. His elbows banging on the table, he rubbed at his bearded chin. Disgruntled indeed.

Tadhg searched the large room.

"Have ye seen Ronan since we've arrived?"

Sean snorted in disgust. "Methinks that man is wise enough to stay clear of us."

Tadhg agreed wholeheartedly.

The MacNaughton men were sitting together. They seemed none the worse for wear although they'd only been allowed a limited amount of carousing. Indulging themselves the way Aodh and his clan did wore men down. That was not the way battles were won.

Tadhg glanced over his men. All present but Cormac. He waited patiently with his horse at the forest's edge ready to ride south and get word to Peter across the sea. This may be the only time for his escape to go unnoticed.

"In no time, we'll be facing strong opposition of trained men. We need to continue our practice until the call comes and we make our way into England," Aodh said. "When the boats arrive, nigh on two thousand me—"

The back door busted open. All eyes turned toward it. Darragh came in, pushing between men packed tight together, and moved up beside his father and to take his seat.

Aodh continued. "Nigh on two thousand men..."

The general lack of details caused Tadhg's mind to wander. The men around him seemed more interested in doing than sitting and listening as well. Some men were meant to plan while other men were meant for the fight.

O'Brien's man, Breandan, came in from outside and leaned beside the door. Tadhg had no idea Breandan had left the O'Brien and come up here. He was certainly not here as a soldier, the kitchen was more his area yet he seemed intent on Aodh as he discussed the plans.

Darragh fiddled with something on the table. The captain sat right in front, facing him. He didn't look like a very strong warrior either but he could be a good strategist. Breandan shifted, attracting Tadhg's attention again. The young man had moved. He stood apart, his hands fisted and a tight scowl on his face. Tadhg saw nothing that could have happened to result in his reaction. He could only follow his gaze to Darragh.

"Captain, give us an accounting of what we'll have for additional weapons," Aodh said.

The young captain came to stand close alongside Darragh, a hand resting on the table in front of him. Darragh leaned back but kept his eyes down, mayhap on the man's hand. Breandan slammed out of the room. All eyes went to the door. The captain stopped speaking to look as well but then continued.

"'Tis a hard coast to land on but no worse than our own."

Tadhg would have to agree.

"Not all of the coast," Sean whispered to Tadhg while the captain continued his talk.

Tadhg recounted the details of Sean's encounter with the local authority. The Earl of Essex had sent his most trusted man, Mort, to offer protection. That had been while he and Peter were busy with the siege at York. Mort spoke more than was necessary and tried most men's patience. Tadhg didn't believe half of what the man said which was why he'd not believed him about Sean having a wife.

Tadhg had to admit marriage seemed to sit well with Sean. There was a peacefulness about him now. Less angst and worry. Thomasina helped him to settle himself.

"He's not telling us anything we dunna ken," Sean said through tight lips.

"Aye. They're keeping their plans to themselves." He rose. "Methinks I need a rest from all this."

Tadhg went through the back door, choosing not to acknowledge the scowl from Aodh or his son. He needed to meet Cormac with news of the impending attack on the western coast and the number of warriors. If Tadhg or Cormac were discovered, they would be killed without any qualms. Tadhg had no choice. A threat to the Normans was a threat to his sister. He could never allow anyone to jeopardize Brighit, not again.

Since the Meic Lochlainn cared nothing for their hired thugs, they had no reason to doubt Tadhg's own willingness to follow orders. Had they cared enough to speak to his men, someone might have mentioned his treasured sister. They might have mentioned her whereabouts and even that she was married to a Norman knight. Their own arrogance was Tadhg's best protection and he would use it to full advantage.

Chapter Twenty-Eight

Tisa pulled the hood tight around her face. The odor of fresh horse manure surrounded her. She stomped through the woods as she'd seen men do, intent on the cave. The time away seemed forever and she needed to see how her little patient progressed. Malcolm was, no doubt, off with Caireann somewhere.

Approaching the hillside, she saw the entrance to the cave at the last moment. There was just enough light inside this small area to continue toward the back wall. Turning sideways, she slipped through the narrow passage barely visible on the left. It opened up to a wider space with high ceilings. A small fire glowed in the center, creating a warm space of refuge.

"Tisa!" Aednat hobbled toward her, her arm held motionless in a sling.

Tisa held her tight, careful of her injury. "Oh, sweetling, I have missed ye so."

The tears welling in her eyes threatened to fall and she pulled back, smiling at Will and Cad who came to see her.

"Greetings, lads. Have ye taken good care of my patient?"

Aoife moved in closer as well.

"We have tried but she is a terrible pain to care for." Cad made a face.

Aednat's expression changed to irritation. "I am not! Grandmother says I am a good patient." She looked up at Tisa. "And I am healing remarkably well."

"Welcome again, Tisa. Does Malcolm ken ye are here among us yet again?"

Tisa felt the heat in her face but the room was too dim for anyone else to notice. "I have come disguised and no one has followed me."

Aoife nodded, that wise smile on her face. Without a word, she conveyed her disapproval at Tisa's being there. The woman didn't understand. Tisa needed to feel wanted.

Aednat pulled on Tisa's arm. "Come, sit. I am feeding my baby."

Tisa did as she was bid, sitting alongside the little girl's small bed. Aednat put her threadbare doll on her lap and held some hard, stale bread to its berry-stained mouth.

"Oh, she is a good eater, I see. Just like ye," Tisa said.

Aednat took a bite, nodding as she chewed.

"Would ye like to see my new carving?" Will asked.

"I would."

Will and Cad disappeared through the small passage but quickly reappeared. Their faces stricken with fear.

Tisa stood "What is wrong"

"There's a man outside the cave. He's on horseback."

"He's followed ye," Aoife said. She lifted Aednat into her arms.

"Nae." Tisa was overwhelmed with guilt. "There was no one."

Aoife held a finger to her lips.

Will threw sand over the fire and they were in complete darkness. Tisa could hear them as they moved further to the back of the cave.

Tisa waited until she could no longer hear them moving. She pulled her fur up tight and over her head. With her hand guiding her along the wall, she found the passageway and slipped through.

A tall, broad man stood at the entrance, facing out into the forest. He indicated no knowledge that she was there. Hunkering down, he settled himself. That was when she noticed the hail outside. It came down in merciless, pounding sheets. The man pulled his hood off. It was Tadhg.

Her heart lurched. Butterflies fluttered in her belly.

No! She needed to back away unseen.

Tadhg stiffened. "No doubt, ye've come out of the weather as well. I'm not here to cause trouble."

Her breath in her throat, she fought to control her trembling. "I have."

She nearly sighed aloud at how low her voice sounded. Just the way Sean had kept reminding Thomasina to speak.

Tadhg continued facing outside.

"A short reprieve is all I need." He said it as if to himself so Tisa did not reply.

Adjusting himself, he leaned against the curved entrance. He bent one knee and rested his arm there. His silhouette visible, Tisa felt an overwhelming calm. She sat where she was and watched him. Let her have this moment to look on the man she loved.

"Methinks it may be getting worse."

Lightning flashed beyond him.

"A fire for warmth is needed in here." He finally turned to her.

She gasped, an inaudible sound. He showed no recognition and paid her even less attention when he stood to walk around the small area. Picking up a twig here and there, he made a small pile and added dried leaves that had blown inside.

The flame licked hungrily at the wood.

"Any bigger pieces?" He spoke but it wasn't directly at her and he continued his search, kicking at the acorns littering the ground. "Damn, never anything when you need it. No water when ye thirst. No food when ye hunger. No wood when ye're cold."

Tadhg stopped and faced her, as if just remembering she was there. "Have ye been in here before? Is there wood anywhere about?"

She noticed the bigger pieces of wood tucked into the narrow gap where the ceiling dipped low. It was very close to the passage and she yanked them away, carrying them to him.

He smiled at her. "Good man."

Adding the wood to the hungry flame, he glanced around. "Quite a nice place to hide from the elements."

He settled himself again, leaning his head back against the cave wall and closing his eyes.

Tisa sat down as well, hidden by darker shadows.

"Is this where ye live?" Tadhg didn't open his eyes.

"Sometimes." Her voice low and deep.

He looked at her. "And when is sometimes? When it's hailing outside?"

Tisa laughed at his sarcasm. "Aye."

He continued to watch her a few more minutes before closing his eyes again.

She pulled the fur close despite the warmth that flooded her. Unlike on the road or when others were around, she could take in her fill of him. They were alone. His hair had grown quite long as if he'd not the inclination to see to such things. Where he'd had shorter curls, he now had longer waves making his chiseled features even more pronounced. More handsome. His legs were firm and dark with hair. The brat he still wore was held at the neck by a circular pin and his broad shoulders rose with each breath. She could almost feel his breath on her face.

He opened his eyes, piercing her with his look. "Save me from my own dark thoughts. Tell me of yerself."

Her breath caught, recognizing that familiar quality in his voice from when they were young, the bitterness gone.

"I am an outcast." She decided to tell the story of the people she had come to meet. "The chieftain finds a reason to throw us away and we live out here, in the wilds."

"We?"

Damn, she hadn't thought about hiding that fact. She should have spoken of only herself. "Aye, my brother and I."

"Oh, ye've a brother? And where is he?"

Tisa looked around, trying to come up with some plausible reason they were separated. "He must have been caught in the storm as well."

"Ye needn't lie on my account. Ye are safe with me even if ye are alone. I will not harm ye."

"I dunna lie."

"Then where is this brother? Why would ye not stay together?"

Tisa shrugged. Tadhg snorted and unhooked his brat. He stood and spread it out on the ground. Lying on his back, he used his arms to pillow his head and looked up at the ceiling. She licked her dry lips and thought of going to him, laying her head on his solid shoulder, his strong arms closing around her. Just like in her dreams.

"Strange how the storm just comes upon ye suddenly here. I suppose it is the sea that hides the oncoming storm."

Tisa laughed then covered her mouth. He tipped his head back, lines on his forehead, to see her.

"Why do ye laugh?"

"The storm canna hide."

"Aye."

She'd always found him very entertaining. He often laughed at things that would cause another consternation. "'Tis important to be able to laugh."

He closed his eyes. "I've not much to laugh at of late."

The voice of a sad man and it tugged at her heart. "No doubt 'twill get better."

"Nae. Despite what I wish to have happen, I will not spend my days laughing. Instead, I will pine over what can never be and dream of a woman I can never have."

Tisa's breath caught. She waited for him to say more but he did not. To whom did he refer? Certainly it wasn't her. He could barely stand to be in her presence. He must have met another. Her heart squeezed. She should be happy for him but she would never stop loving him. His foot slid. He cleared his throat.

"Why do ye think we have a heart? To have a deep love for people who will never accept what ye offer?"

He deserved to be happy. She wanted that for him.

"Mayhap if ye go to her again and tell her how ye feel," she said.

"Ah, ye are a romantic, my friend. 'Twould be a wasted gesture. She cares not for me or my feelings."

How could anyone not love this man? "Have ye told her how ye feel?"

"I have. And she swore she felt the same. Then she went to be with another and left me alone."

Tisa would never have chosen another over Tadhg. She'd fought in the only way she knew how to keep him hers. Even now. He was the husband of her heart. Her one true love.

"Mayhap she had no choice. Women have little choice. They are married off by their fathers and uncles," she said.

"That was the way of it."

She stilled herself, forcing her breathing to remain steady. In. Out. In. Out. "She was married to another?"

"Aye. Betrothed to me but her father gave her to another."

Tears blurred her vision. "And ye love her still?"

"It matters not. She warms his bed." He took a shaky breath. "She'll bear his children."

Never! "Mayhap she would choose to be with ye if she had a choice."

"Nae. Women are vile creatures," his tone hardened, "they feign adoration, and love, and faithfulness but when 'tis cold at night? They seek the arms of another and worry not about the consequences."

Tisa had never done that. What was he talking about?

Tadhg sat up and leaned against the cold wall. He blew out a breath as if to push away his sad reminiscences. "What of ye? Has love served ye well?"

"Nae. I was taken from the one I loved and now can find no way back."

"There is no way back. Ye must live the life ye have until, God willing, it ends quickly."

"That is no way to live."

"A life without love is no way to live."

"No way to live," she repeated his words as if they had sworn a solemn vow.

Tadhg stood suddenly, grabbed up his brat to wrap around himself. The hail had stopped.

"I've enjoyed our talk." He turned to her and said, "Safe travels."

"And to ye."

And he was gone. She stood looking out for a long while, long past the time she could hear his horse. The little space was empty and cold despite the fire that still burned. Tadhg turned angry scowls on her and showed her little patience but he'd professed his continued love for her. Her chest hurt from the loss of what might have been. Surely theirs would have been a deep, abiding love if they'd only had the chance to be together.

"Tisa?" Will spoke to her from the passage.

Turning, she tried to smile at him. "All is well. The man has left. He came in to be out of the storm not to follow me. Please let Aoife ken that. Ye are safe. He dunna ken ye are here. I need to get back before I am missed."

With a heavy heart, she walked back to the village, her face awash with tears. It would be even more difficult to face Tadhg now. She needed to tuck away what she knew, what she felt, the deep loss for the husband of her heart.

Sean stood at the entrance to the longhouse, a mug of mead in his hand. Aodh, Darragh and Godwin sat at the head table.

"Where have ye been?" he asked.

"I saw our friend off with my missive. Mayhap he will not be missed with so many more here now. Were there any details forthcoming?"

"We are to remain at the ready and continue our practicing." Sean tipped his head at Tadhg, a crooked grin tucked in the corners of his mouth. "And we will have a celebration."

"For what purpose now?"

"A wedding. The arrival of more forces. The sun coming up in the morning." Sean's tone was flat.

"More forces than those here?"

"Many more. It appears there are clans from across Eire that come to support Leofrid Godwin as King of England." Sean drank from his cup. "I heard Gerrit and his men battled the western clans into submission, the ones with the ships."

"Ah. And they do enjoy their celebrating." Tadhg retrieved his own libations, nodded to Darragh when he noticed his eyes following him, and returned to Sean. His back to the head table.

"Darragh is a strange man."

Sean's face showed no expression. He remained silent.

"Ye can agree with me, Sean. 'Tis not the same as speaking of his wife."

Sean nodded his head, a slow, deliberate movement.

Tadhg narrowed his eyes at his friend then turned about and settled at a table not far from the back door, situating himself so that he could see all comings and goings. Tisa came in the back, her cheeks pink, breathing hard.

The sight of her set his heart to beating faster. A lock of hair tucked into the corner of her mouth. Her lips a dark red. He glanced at Darragh and was surprised to find him not looking at Tisa but still watching him. When their eyes met, Darragh compressed his lips into a thin line. Tadhg preferred to watch Tisa. He followed her with his eyes as she went to her husband's side, pulling out the hair as she spoke to him. Her backside as comely a sight as any other part of her.

He forced his face away but could still feel Darragh's eyes piercing him.

Aodh stood, his embellished gold chalice in hand. "Tonight we celebrate for tomorrow my man, Malcolm, takes a wife!"

Cheers went up although Malcolm was not present. The men glanced around but did not seem overly concerned at his absence and drank as enthusiastically as if he were there.

Aodh continued. "And in a fortnight we sail for England with the best warriors in all of Eire. Victory will be ours. Huzzah."

"Huzzah!"

Aodh drank deeply from his cup. Tadhg held his mug to his mouth but searched over the rim to lock eyes with Sean. Even riding like the wind, Cormac did not leave in time to get any word to the Normans of the impending attack. If they were to get the information to England, they would have to think of a new way.

Chapter Twenty-Nine

The sun was bright but did little to ward off the chill in the air. A priest had been notified of the impending nuptials of Malcolm and Caireann. He arrived in time to break his fast before the ceremony. Although not considered a religious event, a blessing was always considered a good omen. Tisa sat at the high table beside her husband and considered there was definitely something to say about that, not having had a blessing herself.

Darragh seemed in good spirits although totally ignoring the priest who sat at his elbow. His interest in Ian had not waned even with Breandan's return. That one was not taking it well and Tisa worried for him. He seemed so lost without Darragh's attention. After his sister had delivered a healthy son with no complications, he returned, no doubt expecting to pick up where he and Darragh had left off. Mayhap it would have been best for him to stay with his family.

"Do ye come by for mass often?" Tisa spoke to the priest before spooning warm oats into her mouth.

"I come by when I am asked. There has never been a regular time for my visits."

The man had a full head of short, gray hair. He glanced toward Darragh who sat between them. Her husband merely looked off over the men in the room as if searching someone out. Ian had not yet arrived.

She smiled her encouragement at the priest and he continued.

"Was it not so where ye come from?" he asked.

"Nae," Tisa said. "We had a chapel and a priest always at hand. He saw to the needs of the surrounding villages as well. We offered our protection and saw to his well-being when 'twas necessary."

211

"Ah, not quite the way of it here." The priest darted his eyes toward Darragh who again showed little interest in conversing with him.

The priest turned his attention to his food. Tisa sighed. It had already been a trying morning. Caireann was certainly happy but her jumpiness was contagious. Tisa had helped with her gown, fixed her hair with a ring of new spring flowers, and tried to reassure her friend.

"Malcolm loves ye! He will be kind. Thoughtful. Patient. Ye have no need to be concerned."

Tisa's words had little effect. Nothing was beyond Caireann's worry. The ceremony. The crowds of well-wishers. The fact that Malcolm had decided to accept his right for a honeyed-moon, even taking her south so that she could meet his mother. Caireann focused only on what could go wrong.

"I'm afeard I will have no one to talk to. He's taking me away even from ye."

"Not forever. And ye'll have him to talk to! That is the way it should be. Ye'll not need to have me to speak to."

Caireann had broken into a fresh flood of tears which nudged Tisa out the door. She was not helping her friend feel any better. On her way to the longhouse, she'd passed Malcolm. Unlike his bride to be, he seemed to be walking on clouds, greeting her with a wide smile.

"Caireann is within. Methinks 'twould be well for ye to spend time with her."

"I want nothing more than to do just that."

Tisa nibbled at her lower lip. "No one should bother ye if ye need some time."

Malcolm bowed. "My thanks, sweet lady. I will see to her."

Mayhap if the joining were seen to—no, Malcolm was not that sort of man. He'd wait for years if need be for her to be comfortable with him. He loved her most deeply. Her needs would always come first.

"Tisa?"

Darragh's annoyed expression brought her out of her own thoughts. "Aye?"

He rolled his eyes.

She glanced around and saw Ian standing by the side door. "Ye are saying goodbye?"

"Nae! I was asking if I needed to stay with ye for the joining ceremony."

Tisa didn't miss the priest's wide-eyed expression of surprise. The ceremony was not very long. Caireann and Malcolm would pledge themselves to each other before God and receive a blessing. The warriors were given the morning off to partake, no doubt since it was one of their own taking a wife.

"Whatever ye think best," she said.

He smiled, walked toward Ian, and they left by the same door. The priest kept his eyes on her.

"Is there something ye need?" she asked.

"Ye are from the O'Brien Clan?"

"I am Roland O'Brien's youngest daughter."

"Ah, I remember Roland. He was very close with the MacNaughton?" She nodded.

"I was the priest for the MacNaughton for many years."

"I dunna remember ye."

The man looked down into his food. "'Twas very unsettling times when ye were young. There was much fighting. Many dying. Life itself so momentary."

"I have heard some of the stories."

"The MacNaughton had many sons, some who went with him to battle."

"But none were lost."

The priest jerked his head up. "Aye! The eldest son was lost. 'Twas a terrible blow to Padraig. A son from the bride of his youth."

"He'd been married to someone before Moira?"

"Not for very long. She died right after the birth. A high fever."

"What was his name?"

The man frowned. "I dunna remember. He was raised by his mother's clan. Only coming to the MacNaughton when the battles started. His own mother's clan had been destroyed. He was a young man by then. That is how he came to fight beside Padraig."

"I have heard nothing about him."

"Mayhap I am speaking of what I should not. Beg pardon. Ancient history now."

Tisa smiled. She enjoyed the stories told at their gatherings with the MacNaughton and would have remembered one so intriguing as that. "Tadhg is here."

"Tadhg? I remember him very well. I hope to talk with him before I am sent away."

He reddened.

"Sent away? They dunna like yer presence here?"

"This clan has been close to the Norsemen who remain outside of the Christian faith. I am a reminder of things they would rather not be reminded of."

"How did ye come to be here today?"

"Malcolm has been part of this clan since before Darragh's father, when Eirnin was chieftain. He asked for me."

Tisa frowned. Malcolm's loyalty to Aodh was so strong. It was surprising to hear he was not always his man.

"Was Aodh not from this clan?"

The priest looked around before answering. "He may have come from a more southern clan, near the Liffey."

"I believed there were Christians to the south."

"Not all. The ones who kept to the pagan ways found themselves alone. Aodh came here with his young wife and son. Outcasts. When he put her aside to wed the chieftain's daughter, Lilith, the church objected. That priest has since passed on but Aodh still prefers to not have me nearby, a reminder that he lives in sin."

Aodh chose that moment to swagger in. "Priest, yer talents are required."

The priest extended his hand to Tisa as he rose. "My name is Matthew. If ye ask for me to come, I will be here without hesitation."

"My thanks."

Matthew went to Aodh who kept his distance, indicating the man precede him out the door. Tisa followed behind to where the crowd had gathered. Caireann looked lovely wearing her best dress and the flowers in her hair. Malcolm's hair was combed and his clothes were cleaned. He held his hand up and the crowd grew silent.

"When I was a boy and came to learn my warrior skills from Eirnin, we had a building on the hill that served for our services. With Aodh's permission, I would like to pledge to my wife and receive God's blessing at that place."

Aodh shrugged his shoulder as if it mattered not at all to him. Tadhg stood outside the crowd, his back to her. Did he recognize Matthew? She should have asked how much time had passed since the priest left the MacNaughton Clan.

The large group followed the path that circled up to the building Malcolm had shown her that first day when he told her she needed to learn the lay of the land. Tears welled. It seemed like such a long time ago now. Malcolm had been her very first friend here even if she hadn't recognized it at the time. Now he seemed like a different man. A man fulfilled. His total focus on his love and seeing to her. When a few crude comments were made regarding their wedding night, Malcolm's expression shut them down. No one dared go against the man. No doubt he'd noticed how upset it had made Caireann.

By the time they reached the little building, it looked quite a bit different from her earlier visit. The entrance had been cleaned and set right. The interior was bright and welcoming with candles burning within. Caireann's face broke into a huge smile and she reached up to kiss her husband. Malcolm bent to accept her thanks, hugging her gently to him.

"My thanks."

"Anything for ye, my love."

He took her hand in his and they stood at the door.

"Accept my life as I offer it to ye. I promise to see to yer needs, protect ye always, and love ye. I'll take no other unto me and my words of faithfulness will never falter," Malcolm said.

"I accept yer protection and yer love and offer ye my respect and love, and I will cleave unto ye alone, my husband."

Matthew smiled at each of them in turn then raised his hand, his eyes dropping to the opened book.

"May God add His blessing to this pledge and that Caireann being flesh of his flesh and bone of his bone, Malcolm will always care for her even as his own body. And let marriage be held in honor among all, and let the marriage bed be undefiled—"

"Enough, priest! Let us see them married, not cast into hell," Aodh bellowed.

Malcolm and Caireann did not turn away from the other.

Matthew coughed. "Ye may kiss yer bride, Malcolm."

Malcolm bent slightly to hold her against his large frame. Caireann went up on tiptoe to press herself to him. Their sweet kiss was met with loud applause. They turned to the priest who offered a kiss of blessing to each of them.

Tisa wiped her cheeks, her own face hot with emotion. Struggling to take a steady breath, she gathered her composure. She wanted no less than this for her dear friend but had hoped the same for herself. When she turned toward Tadhg, his sad eyes were on her before he turned away to blend in with the rest of the people headed back down the hill.

"Mistress." Malcolm held Caireann's hand. She stood beside him. "I wanted ye to ken we will be back on the first new moon. Dunna fear. Ye are well protected."

Tisa cleared her throat. "Ye two spend time together, learn to love each other, and dunna think of things here. We will all be fine."

Caireann squeezed her tight, her eyes filled when she withdrew. "Thank ye, Tisa."

Malcolm nodded and led his bride down the hill. Tisa was left alone at the top of the hill. Darragh had not been present. There was no doubt that he was with Ian even now. She did not feel much like being with others right now. Her eyes continued to tear up despite her best attempt to stop crying.

The priest came up beside her.

"Are they tears of joy for yer friend?" Matthew asked.

"I do wish her great happiness."

He nodded and smiled. That knowing smile that told her he knew she had not answered his actual question but he didn't press her. When he started to turn, she grabbed at his arm. His glance toward her hand made her aware of how desperately she clutched at him. She loosened her hold.

"Will ye be allowed to stay on if I ask ye to do so?"

"I dunna believe Aodh will order me to leave and if ye have need of me, I will certainly stay."

"Can we have Vespers this evening?"

"I will be happy to do that."

"My thanks. I will be back before the evening meal."

Chapter Thirty

An early spring snow impeded Aodh's plans for yard practice the next morning. Tadhg prayed that Cormac had missed the brunt of the bad weather since leaving. The washer woman's home was a busy place even while the other homes were sealed up tight, no one coming and going. That included Darragh's house.

"Settle down, Nell." The little girl fussed for her mother even as the stiff garment was yanked over her head.

Tadhg waved when her little head popped through the top of the gown. Nell's face screwed up just before she let loose a loud wail. He gave her his back and she ceased the sound.

Five of her siblings made mischief as they waited, pulling at this and playing with that. Barely halfway through the morn and Tadhg again needed a reprieve from the place. He slipped out the door unnoticed.

The snow fell in thick, wet flakes making any travel extremely difficult. Tadhg breathed in the salt sea air. No doubt the water was covered with frozen whitecaps. He'd heard the waves crashing all night long with a mighty force as he lay awake, thinking over the conversation he'd had with the man in the cave. Probably a bit younger than Tadhg, he had great wisdom. Wishing for the end of his life was no way to live and it offered no honor to the God he believed gave him that life. Mayhap the man knew a way to overcome the eternal bitterness eating away at him.

Tadhg sloshed his way through the snow, against the driving onslaught, secluding himself in the stable. Enveloped in the warmth, the smell of horses surrounding him, he paused before untying his mount.

"Easy, now." He guided it toward the meadow's edge, waiting until then to jump on top.

Within the primeval forest, the heavy canopy above held much of the snow at bay. The travel was easy despite occasional plops of heavy snow dropping down on him. Only an eerie silence met him as he plodded back to the hidden entrance of the cave. There was no guarantee the man would be there but with his horse, Tadhg could continue on to wherever he might choose. Mayhap to get some time to himself, think things through on his own if he must.

"Hello?" His call echoed back to him, the darkness within all encompassing.

The embers from the day before remained undisturbed, a sure sign that no one else had been there. He paced the small area, turning back toward the opening repeatedly as if he could will the man to return by his own insistence. Leaning against the far wall, he sat to face the opening. The bush hiding the entrance shivered in the wind. A breeze tickled the hair on his hands. This far from the entrance, it couldn't be wind from outside that he'd felt. He went to all fours and moved closer to the side wall where the other man had found the wood.

"Hah!" Tadhg stood along the narrow opening that led further into the cave.

Looking as far as he could, there was no light, no sound but the wind whistled through. It must lead to the outside. He turned sideways to slide along the cold wall and was rewarded by a greater opening with high ceilings and low sloping walls all around.

"Hello?"

He found a small pile of smoldering embers in the center. Someone had been there just a short time before. Mayhap they would return.

The darkness here was complete with no light source beyond the glow of the dying embers. The warmth from the fire hung on and he removed his brat, shaking off the melting snow before settling on top of it.

A strange little place of refuge yet he felt peaceful here. Mayhap it was unburdening himself to the stranger. Mayhap it was finally speaking from his heart of his anguish. The peace wrapped around him and he was in no hurry to return.

"Oh!" The stranger passed through, startling Tadhg and he stood.

"I dinna think ye stayed here," Tadhg said.

The white of the stranger's teeth indicated he smiled and it warmed Tadhg's heart.

"Aye. Only when it hails. Did I not mention when it snows as well?"

Tadhg nodded and sat again. "Oh, I see. And I as well."

He indicated the man sit with him on his brat. After a moment's hesitation, the stranger did sit on the very edge of his overlong covering.

"I realized although we had spoken to each from our heart, we had not even exchanged names."

The other man looked around as if for something in particular.

"Did ye lose something?" Tadhg asked.

He cleared his throat. "I am called Ultan."

"Ah 'the saint of orphans and children.' Pleased I am to meet ye, Ultan. I am called Tadhg."

"And what brings ye back here this day, Tadhg? Surely ye were not caught out in the storm again. 'Tis been coming down all night."

"I sought ye out. I'd hoped we could speak again."

Ultan did not respond. Tadhg could swear the room was suddenly more quiet. He made to get up. "Mayhap we need a fire."

"Nae!" Ultan reached a hand toward him. "'Twill get too warm methinks."

"Ye ken best, living here sometimes as ye do."

The other man laughed again. The tinkling sound soothing and he settled back down on the brat. He seemed an easy sort. Mayhap that was why Tadhg spoke so forthrightly with him. It really wasn't like him at all.

"I thought of what ye said to me," Tadhg said rather quickly, suddenly afraid he might change his mind.

Ultan had to turn back to him to answer. "And what was that?"

Tadhg's eyes had adjusted to the darkness. He tried to make out the man's face but with him still wearing his hooded fur covering, it was impossible. "No way to live—without love I mean."

Ultan nodded but remained silent, his face toward him as if he could make out Tadhg's features just fine.

"I dunna ken how to move beyond the loss. My heart cries out in agony at the pain I canna show."

"Pain ye canna show?"

Tadhg could see the whites of Ultan's eyes now and he focused there. "She is the wife of another—the woman I love. I would not take her from the man." He closed his eyes, battling the anger that felt like a hefty stone lodged where his heart once beat. "She seems quite contented with her lot but her betrayal—taking another unto herself—it burns like fire against my flesh."

"'Tis not betrayal if she was forced by her father to marry another." Ultan's voice sharpened as if in anger.

Had Tadhg explained in such detail? He turned toward the fire where a few embers still glowed. "Women feign their feelings so easily."

"When has she shown herself so vile as to do such a thing? If ye loved her once—"

"I love her still."

The quick intake of air pulled Tadhg's eyes back to the man. No other response. Almost as if the man held his breath, waiting for more information.

Something stirred in Tadhg's memory but he pushed it aside. "Nae, she has never been caught in such a lie."

"Then why would ye believe her capable of such deceit?"

Ultan's tone caused Tadhg's own defenses to rise. "*All* women are capable of such deceit."

"Capable but not something *all* women would choose to do," Ultan replied rather quickly.

This seemed a moot point to Tadhg. "I disagree."

"Why do ye disagree? To say all women will practice deceit is the same as saying all men will practice rape."

"Rape? How are they the same?" Tadhg had said nothing about rape.

"*All* men are capable of it, are they not?"

"I suppose," Tadhg struggled to follow wherever these thoughts were leading.

"So will *all* men rape?"

"Nae! That is a ridiculous thing to say."

Ultan turned his small palm up as he spoke. "An example of ill treatment by a man. Deceit is surely as deplorable as rape. The one is bodily forcing another, an intentional act; the other, mentally misleading another, also intentional."

Tadhg realized for the first time that the man was not very big at all and wondered at his age.

"Deceit requires planning and forethought," Ultan continued. "Not even dismissible by bodily functions that overtook yer mind, as deplorable as that sounds. Deceit requires yer mind. Ye must *think* about what ye will do. Not *all* women will deceive."

"Ye are correct." Tadhg looked toward the passageway not even visible from where he sat. "My mother was the sweetest, loving woman. A wonderful woman. She deceived my father and lay with another. A man as close as kinsman. My father's most favored friend."

Ultan gave a melodious gasp.

Memory stirred and Tadhg heard the sound again and again in his head. Tadhg wiped at his face. Surely he was overwrought from lack of sleep.

"A child was conceived from their union and my mother passed it off as my father's own daughter. It wasn't until my mother died that the truth was uncovered." Tadhg faced the stranger. "A bad story. One I have not shared with another."

The other man remained silent, until he stood so quickly he nearly tripped on the material beneath his feet. "Beg pardon, I must leave."

Tadhg stood as well, following Ultan who continued through the passage in great haste. "I dinna mean to offend. Please! Stay!"

Ultan finally faced him, shook his head but did not speak.

"I wished only to share the story with another person not to cause ye to quit my presence. Please stay."

"I—I canna—stay."

Ultan ducked out and was gone. Tadhg stood staring at the entrance for quite a while. Had his story been so devastating to a total stranger that he could no longer remain in Tadhg's presence?

"'Twas devastating because of the kind, loving nature of my mother. Her soft heart. Her gentle ways. It does not make sense even now. She loved my father."

Tisa ducked into her house, her heart beating against her ribs. Where had the outcasts gone to? She yanked the little doll out from inside her tunic. She'd made it for Aednat. Had something happened to them? Surely Malcolm would have told her.

The telltale sound of Darragh's piqued passion met her ears. Her hands closed into tight fists, her grip on the doll causing its berry lips to smoosh into her thickly twined hair. Tisa dove behind the curtain, kicking off her shoes as she went. Tadhg's mother had slept with another? Tisa needed time to think. The sound ceased and she held her breath.

"Who is here?" Darragh called.

Tisa tossed the doll into the corner, took a shaky breath, and swallowed.

"Only me, Darragh. I am sorry to interrupt. I am not—" she yanked down the trews "feeling well. I need only to lie down—" she threw the leine on top of the growing pile behind the chest "for a few moments."

"Ugh!" Darragh's disgruntled outburst said it all.

Tisa yanked on her chemise and climbed under the covers, turning away from the entrance just before the irritating man yanked back the hanging.

"Tisa! Ye are interrupting me! Is there nowhere else ye can rest?"

Anger ripped through her innards. She bolted up and let her expression speak for itself.

Darragh stood there naked with his hardened rod bobbing in front of him. She wanted to scream. Loud. By the way he stepped back, she assumed it showed on her face. She didn't pause to think but let loose her mouth.

"I wish to lay down in peace but dinna request ye leave or find another place to meet with yer lover, did I? I asked only to be allowed to rest my head until this passes."

"Mayhap she's with child!" Ian called from Darragh's room then laughed at his own joke. A crass sound.

Darragh started to laugh as well but then a frown lined his brow. He moved closer. "What is it that ails ye, wife?"

"My head."

"And yer courses are fine?"

Tisa rolled he eyes. "What care have ye about my womanly time? Ye are my husband and ye ken well enough there is no chance they are less than fine."

Ian again laughed but Darragh's expression changed into a dark scowl. His eyes narrowed. Fear gripped her and she wished she could call back her outburst. She knew better than to let loose her anger on him. The man was dangerous. He held her fate in his hand. He had a cruel streak.

"Ian, I need ye to leave," Darragh said in a loud voice, his eyes on her.

Tisa's breath accelerated. She dared not move.

"But we're not—"

"Now!" Darragh bellowed.

Rustling could be heard as he dressed, then the curtain being lifted and the door finally closed. Darragh settled beside her, naked but no longer aroused, and stretched the full length of the pallet. She was not fooled by his languorous movements.

"So tell me of yer discomfort, wife."

"Please, Darragh." Tisa worked to even her tone. "I dinna wish to disrupt yer... time alone with Ian."

His face tight, the heat poured off of him. His anger. She remembered it well. Their wedding night. Their first night here. The inn just a few days earlier. This man was easily enraged but she had been able to disarm him.

She reached toward him. He clutched her hand with tight fingers. A gasp froze halfway up her throat.

"Are ye cuckolding me?" He asked the question but his tone condemned.

"*I* am not, Darragh."

She hadn't meant to stress the word.

He released his grip, his tight features softening. "I search for my pleasure elsewhere as sure as if ye denied me yer body. And I am denying mine to ye, am I not?"

"I care not, Darragh. We have found a way to be content."

"Are ye content?"

"I have no needs ye dunna see to."

"Truly?"

"Aye."

"There is no one ye long for? Whose hands ye would have on ye? Who ye would have unleashing yer passion?"

Something in his expression—Gerrit! That whoreson.

"Has someone been spreading tales?" she asked.

Darragh's frown deepened. "I dunna need to learn from others what I can see with my own eyes."

"Nae!" Her voice rose. "There is naught to see."

"Dunna forget, sweet little Tisa, that I was the one ye clung to when ye longed for Tadhg, when ye imagined him taking ye. I was the one ye would not even allow to touch ye."

She shook her head. "Nae. 'Twas a mistake for me to pretend and ye encouraged it. Ye wanted me to... feel those feelings. I have no use for such feelings."

Giving him her back, she closed her eyes against the tears. They slipped down her hot cheeks. Darragh stroked her side as he settled close behind her.

"But they are there. Just below yer calm demeanor." His lips beside her ear sent a shiver down her spine. "Ye're a passionate woman. I have said as much."

"Please, Darragh. Dunna cause me... more humiliation."

"Show me yer passion again."

He whispered the words, as if to entice her.

"Nae! There is no one here."

He snaked his arm around to cup her breasts. It could have been a sword hilt, the way he gripped her. "Because ye're a woman and if ye have needs, I will see to them as yer husband."

Tisa tensed against his assault. "Even though ye dunna desire me?"

"There are ways I can ease yer needs."

"I have no needs, Darragh. Leave me that way."

He kissed her neck and pulled her tight against him. "Methinks ye do have needs."

She turned to face him. "Am I not a good wife to ye?"

Darragh glanced at her lips. "Ye are. Too good. I can play the part for ye."

"There is no need when we are alone."

"I've seen this many times and I'll be very good at it... at setting ye on fire."

Brushing his lips over hers, his insistent tongue slid along the seam of her mouth. Surely he would lose interest. She opened her mouth to him but he deepened the kiss, surprising her. Pressing her back, he leaned over her a little too heavily.

His mouth dropped to her neck, nibbling and stroking with his strong tongue, as his hand rubbed across her breasts. Except for the fierceness of his touch, he was quite adept but it did not stir her.

He yanked his head back, a scowl on his face. "What is that stench?"

Darragh looked past her to the pile beyond the chest. Her disguise.

She used the interruption as an excuse to sit up but he held her with a firm arm. "I slipped by the horses. I need to see to that."

"Is that not men's clothing?"

"Nae!"

Darragh sat up with her, pulling her into his arms and again covered her mouth with his hard kisses.

He pulled back. "If ye have needs, Tisa, ye need to allow me to see to them."

"To what purpose? Ye have no need for my passion. Ye seek passion and fulfillment that I canna give ye."

"I will not have ye go to another." His tone was reprimanding.

"I will not go to another, husband."

He searched her face then lay down again, keeping her in a tight grip. "Then rest against me until the pain in yer head has gone."

She needed him to leave her to her thoughts. "Ian will be angry with ye."

"He kens he is lucky to have my attention."

Tisa closed her eyes and tried to settle her inner turmoil. Her father could not have lain with Tadhg's mother.

"When my father told me I was to marry, I expected a spoiled girl that I could never satisfy. A girl who would belittle me as I'd always been belittled. My father said my marrying ye was best for the clan that I would one day lead. I ken he never expected me to lead. I was not my brother."

Tisa heard the sadness in his voice. Was it for the loss of a brother or for his father's disappointment in him?

"Yer father believes ye are capable of leading now, does he not?"

Darragh's arm tightened around her. "I believe he does and 'tis ye I have to thank."

"I have done nothing."

"Ye accepted me. Ye sought to protect me."

"And myself."

"I ken but ye could easily have come here and chosen one of my father's many warriors to take to yer bed."

"I would never do that, Darragh."

"Well I ken it. Ye have stood up to any who would degrade me—even Gerrit. Because of ye, I have the desire to no longer cower in the path of others' judgments. I will become who I was intended to be."

He was quiet for a long while and Tisa wondered if he'd dozed off. Her thoughts returned to Aednat and Aoife and the rest of the outcasts. She was tempted to awaken him and encourage him to leave.

"I have very few memories of Malachi—my brother," he said, his voice quiet. "I was very small when he died. I remember him throwing me into the air and catching me, and his smiling face looking up at me. He was a formidable warrior. Strong. I believe I am strong as well."

He kissed the top of her head. "Are ye feeling any better?"

"A bit."

"Good, then I must quit this place for that disgusting odor is overwhelming my gut."

Leaving the bed, he went back to his room then left without another word.

Tisa lay on her back. When Darragh's brother died, he was probably about the same age as she was when her mother died. A long while now. And yet, her father never sought comfort in another's arms that she knew of.

Was it her father Tadhg spoke of?

My father's most favored friend.

It could be none other.

Brighit was the only female in his family. Could Brighit be her half-sister?

The questions that Tadhg had ignited with his words made it impossible for her to remain with him in the cave. Not without revealing her true identity. She would have badgered him with questions. Questions she needed the answers to even now.

Was this past transgression the reason Padraig had broken from them? The reason the betrothal was broken? The reason she lost her one chance for happiness?

The pain increased at her temples. She covered herself with the blanket. Either she would doze off and feel better or she would throw up. With the stench of manure wafting up to her, she was almost certain it would be the latter.

Chapter Thirty-One

On the first clear day, the sun high in the sky revealed the damage to the coast from the unrelenting storms. It also gave the men an opportunity to get out of their houses. Tempers were flaring despite attempts at fighting practice held within. Even with the slippery ground, a chance for unrestrained fighting was a godsend. It was the Godwin's idea to make a competition out of it.

"We've many fine warriors here. Which clan offers the best? How about a wager on it?" Aodh held up a heavy sack of coins. "Or a great purse?"

The others cheered and nodded, slapping each other on the back, encouraging one another at the chance to take home such a prize.

Tadhg, unlike the other men, had not chosen to remain inside. His need for solitude had carried him out even in the fiercest snows. That he had not met again with his own outcast was not for lack of trying. To have to stay here now to appease the other men's need for sport did not sit well with him. Besides, good-natured sport could so easily become a battle to the death.

"What say ye, Tadhg?" Lughaidh asked. He had made friends with some of the Meic Lochlainn men despite Aodh's attempt to keep them separated. "Could be entertaining. I could use the coins he offers."

"Ye have my leave to compete. I dunna choose to."

The man nodded. "Then I think I will put my name in."

Tadhg watched his retreating back.

"Not participating, Tadhg?" It was Gerrit who came up to stand beside him.

The man had not spoken to Tadhg since the night he had rescued Tisa.

The leathered man seemed to look right through him on all other occasions. That Gerrit chose to speak to Tadhg at this moment gave him pause.

"Now why would ye suddenly have an interest in who participates? Could it have been at yer urging that Aodh offered this entertainment? Mayhap even yer own purse?"

"A good way for the men to work off their tempers."

"Ah! Concern for the men? Or easy targets for ye to use for yer own sport?" Many of the warriors collected had far less experience in battle than Tadhg or Sean. Or Gerrit.

Gerrit's lips curved up but it could not be described as a smile. "Are ye not willing to show yer mettle?"

"I show my mettle in battle," Tadhg answered, crossing his arms. "Not for entertainment and not for wealth."

Gerrit tipped his head back to let out a hearty laugh. The sound carried and many of the curious warriors looked their way.

"Ah, ye speak nobly and yet..." his smile vanished, his face leveled to Tadhg's, "I ken ye are less than that in truth."

Kicking this man's arse was quickly becoming a worthwhile endeavor. "An opportunity to see ye flat on yer backside would give me great pleasure."

Gerrit's blue eyes twinkled. "I dunna believe that will be the case."

"Of course ye dunna. Bullies rarely recognize their own weaknesses."

The man's face darkened, all pretense of humor gone. "I will enjoy showing ye the error of yer ways." He stepped in close, his nostrils flaring. "And teaching ye to keep yerself out of things that are not yer concern."

"Who else will partake?" Leofrid asked from where he stood beside the ice-covered yard. Several men were assembling a raised seating area where he and Aodh could watch the entertainment.

"Here!" Gerrit raised his hand, never taking his eyes from Tadhg. "And Tadhg will do the same."

Aodh's eyes widened. "Aye. Tadhg! Entertaining, indeed."

"Piss and wind," Gerrit growled before approaching his leader.

"What say ye, Gerrit? Shall we work ye up to the O'Brien or start ye there?" Leofrid asked.

"I believe ye should let them go first." Darragh spoke in a loud voice. He moved closer to his father whose surprised expression quickly vanished. "Then I will kick the winner's arse."

Gerrit faced him but Darragh showed no signs of cowering this time.

"Are ye certain, Darragh?" Gerrit's voice softened. "It may be myself ye will be fighting."

The crowd of men grew silent, all watching this encounter between

Darragh and Gerrit. Even Aodh looked on with interest, stroking his beard. Darragh remained stoic.

'Twas a strange relationship between these two—Darragh and Gerrit. Every time Tadhg approached Sean for information, the man refused to comment.

Darragh worked himself harder than the rest at practice as if he had something to prove. His work was paying off. The man had become quite adept at hand-to-hand fighting as well as with the mace and broadsword. He, indeed, showed himself a fine protector for Tisa. Tadhg's gut tightened.

Darragh turned to Leofrid, continuing in the same loud voice. "I take the right to fight Tadhg first." Then he turned back to Gerrit. "And then I will fight ye."

"Sword-to-sword here." Leofrid smiled, indicating each area. "Hand-to-hand here."

Aodh offered a different course of action. "Let a tournament begin first. Tadhg, Gerrit and Darragh can fight it out after we watch the entertainment."

Tadhg and Gerrit agreed to Aodh's suggestion on the way the day would progress. Darragh, growing more confident with each passing moment, did not. "I will enter the tournament, then I will deal with the other two!" Aodh simply smiled at his son and nodded.

The frozen ground gave way to thick mud as the day progressed, the best warriors from each clan stepping up to fight. One by one, no clear winner stood out among the men as they moved up the ranks. When it was time to compete with Darragh, he easily became the champion in both sword and hand-to-hand competitions.

Darragh bent at the waist to catch his breath, his hands resting on his knees.

Aodh beamed at the man. "Ye show yerself a warrior unmatched."

The blond quickly stood upright, his chest swelling at the compliment. "My thanks, Father."

Leofrid also looked pleased. He had accomplished his goal. No doubt he needed to see these men and judge their ability in order to discern who would lead and how best to divide the ranks.

"We wish to see yer son against the great MacNaughton," a man from one of the western clans answered.

"Yer son we've not heard of before," another said. "Not like we've heard about the MacNaughton."

Tadhg couldn't be sure if he'd heard about Sean or himself. It didn't matter. A glance toward the longhouse confirmed that the man remained in a mire of discontent. Sean sat on a bench, leaning back with his elbows resting on the table set out with food and drink. His face was the face of a truly unhappy man.

Keeping a man as active as Sean within for this many days was asking for trouble. That he didn't seek immediate release by participating in fighting practice, whatever the reason for it, assured Tadhg that the man was missing his wife. There was nothing Tadhg could do for that.

"Sean!" Tadhg called to him, walking toward him with long strides. "They're hoping for some entertainment from the MacNaughton men. Can ye give yer assistance?"

Sean scowled and looked away, crossing his arms about his chest.

"Darragh is looking to get his arse kicked but I've my sights on Gerrit."

Sean's scowl quickly turned to a tight smile and he strode toward the other warriors. "*That* man I've a bone to pick."

"Darragh? What are ye about? Ye said nothing to me."

Sean shoved him off his arm when he pulled on him to stop. "Ye dinna want to ken. I respected yer wishes."

Sean pulled off his leine and crossed to the man in nothing but his braies. The other men quickly circled around him as he approached Darragh. The muttering came to an abrupt stop.

"Are ye looking to get yer arse kicked by a MacNaughton?" Sean asked.

Darragh smirked. His recent accomplishments no doubt fresh in his minds.

"I dunna mind setting ye on yer arse." Darragh moved in closer to say something and Sean shoved him away.

Tadhg felt like he'd missed something important. "Wait. Dunna start yet."

"Step away, Tadhg," Aodh said, holding his hand up to halt Tadhg from getting any closer.

Darragh threw a firm right to Sean's torso with enough force to double the man over. Tadhg froze at the sight. Surely it was a ploy but Sean didn't immediately straighten himself. For the first time in his life, Tadhg had deep concern for his friend.

After a moment, Sean did right himself but he still seemed shaky. He wrapped an arm around Darragh's middle, driving him back against the wooden post. No doubt, it was the man's extremely satisfied grin that set Sean off and put the spark back into him.

Fists flew as the two shoved off each other again and again, neither demonstrating any perceptible leverage over the other. One would fall and the other would grab him back up to punch him again.

A glance toward Gerrit showed a man mesmerized by the sight.

Tadhg did a double take. A bit too mesmerized. His body rigid. His breathing shallow. When he took a slow, deep breath and blew it out through open lips, Tadhg would swear the man was sexually aroused by the sight.

Gerrit did not blink. His eyes remained fixed on the two. No, not the two of them but on Darragh. It became obvious. Each time Darragh fell, the man held his breath and when he came back up, he relaxed his shoulders. His jaw loose, closing with every punch received, wetting his lips when Darragh had the upper hand. How could Tadhg not have noticed this before now?

A melodious gasp sounded behind him and Tadhg closed his eyes. He listened again to the sound in his mind. And again. Each time more distinct. More recognizable. He knew who made the sound before he even turned to see Tisa. The same sound as the man had made in the cave. Tadhg paused before he opened his eyes. His body was taut and when he turned, Tisa stood there. Her wide eyes were on Darragh and Sean as they flew past. Sean grabbed the other man by the head and ran him into the post. Darragh dropped at Sean's feet. All around cheered.

Ultan was not a man. Ultan was Tisa. The reason Tadhg felt so at peace talking to him. The reason Tadhg wanted to seek the man out. The reason Tadhg felt safe baring his soul to him. The reason he shared his deepest concerns as he'd always done with his own lovely Tisa. The love of his heart. The only woman he could ever love.

When Tisa finally turned to Tadhg, he recognized her look of alarm.

"Tadhg!" She dragged on him. "Tell Sean not to kill Darragh."

Her concern was for her husband. Of course. Tadhg strode over to assist Sean in lifting the unconscious man. Leofrid beamed, slapping Sean on the back.

"Well done, Sean. Well done indeed."

Aodh was just as quick to congratulate Sean although his concerned glances toward his son were understood. When Darragh began to shake his head and mumble, the older man visibly relaxed.

Tadhg turned to Tisa and said, "Yer husband will be fine."

Tisa did not go to Darragh but her relief was genuine. Tadhg wanted to ask if she loved the man. He wanted to confront her with her deception. He wanted to find out why she had deceived him not once, but twice. Instead, he stepped toward Leofrid.

"I believe there is another match."

Leofrid's pleasure gushed forth with his wide smile. "Tadhg and Gerrit! Aye, what a match."

Tadhg turned to find the man beside him back under control although his eyes darted toward Darragh who now stood between his father and his wife.

Tadhg smirked at him. "Or would ye prefer to see to yer lover?"

Gerrit turned dark eyes on him. A low growl that didn't sound human was the only warning before Gerrit attacked him full force and his body slammed into Tadhg.

Tisa was not so naive as to think her husband needed her attention. His own mother had said even as a child, he'd never sought comfort from her. So she watched from the longhouse. Darragh looked like he'd been through hell but Sean looked hale and hearty. He swaggered toward her, a huge bruise across the side of his smirking face.

"Tisa." He nodded and opened the door to go inside the longhouse.

"Halt!" Tisa fumed. "What are ye thinking?"

Sean made an elaborate show of looking to see if she was, indeed, talking to him, even looking around him to see if someone else was nearby before pointing to his own chest with a questioning look.

"Ye're quite the entertainment. Both here and with my husband."

"Tisa, yer husband had it coming to him."

"How so?"

Sean's shoulders raised then dropped with his deep breath. The painful expression that shot across his face indicated he did have some pain. That knowledge gave Tisa more satisfaction than it should have.

"Sit with me," Sean said.

Tisa settled beside him on the bench, the men still a distance away. The sun was high in the sky now. It should have been a boon to her spirits after the cloudy days, but she was too afeared of what Sean may say.

"Why have ye allowed Tadhg to believe ye're married to yer husband in truth?"

Her jaw dropped but no words came out.

He placed his large hand on her arm. "I am not blind. Nor is my wife. And the fact that Darragh was quite taken with my size when I first met him, even showing an unnatural interest in me, confirms his desire is not for women but for men."

Tisa's face reddened, tears threatened and she turned away. "I canna speak to ye of this."

With a gentle grasp of her chin, Sean turned her to face him. "'Tis not yer blame. He's been like that since before ye. I'm just saying ye should let Tadhg ken."

"Why?" The damn tears spilled down her cheeks. "What can he do? It matters not at all. Darragh's my husband."

"He is not!" Sean showed his anger which he was no longer so quick to do revealing his deep concern for her. "A wife is to cleave unto her husband. Ye've done no such thing."

Turning away, she brushed her cheeks with an angry swipe of her hand. "And I am glad!"

The ongoing silence finally drew her eyes back to Sean. He had a peculiar expression as he watched her. As if seeing her for the first time.

"Ye're still in love with Tadhg."

"I will *always* be in love with Tadhg. He is the husband of my heart that I could never forsake. I am glad to not have to be touched by another when 'tis Tadhg alone that I want."

"Sweet Tisa." Sean pulled her into his arms and she allowed him to comfort her. She cried until no more tears would come. He brushed her hair back, stroking her head with long, comforting motions.

"Ah, Sean, whatever did I do to deserve a life without my Tadhg?"

"I dunna ken."

The shouting from the men tore them apart and they both stood to see what was going on. Sean ran toward the sound but Tisa did not. She walked. She couldn't understand what they were shouting. Not until she came closer.

"He's no breath left in him!"

Tisa's chest constricted with pain at the same time her brain was convincing herself they were speaking of Gerrit.

"Quite a knot on his head."

"A dent, I'd call it."

"Mayhap just the wind knocked out of him."

The crowd of men blocked her from seeing what they referred to. She glanced at the tall, leathered man who stood to the side now. Gerrit wiped at the blood coming from his nose and mouth, his labored breathing loud in the sudden silence. Some of the men had dropped down to their knees in the mud. Sean was there. He kneeled beside the length of a man, only his legs visible. One spectator moved aside and she could make out Tadhg. Blood was matted along the side of his head to puddle beneath him, turning the mud a strange brown. Sean glanced up at her. She read the concern on his face.

"Tisa, go get yer herbs."

The men turned to her. Most of their faces smeared dark with mud from fighting. Their eyes looked unnaturally white and wide. She couldn't get her feet to move or her body to turn away.

"Tisa!" Sean shouted her name. When she looked at him, she saw his mouth move and then Darragh was pulling on her arm, drawing her away.

"Tisa! Ye need to get yer herbs." Darragh's voice sounded muffled. "Hear me! Yer herbs, Tisa. Tadhg is hurt. He needs yer help."

Her eyes began to close, the world darkening around her. Strong arms caught her as she dropped to the ground. But she couldn't feel the ground beneath her. She could only hear the voices.

"I'll carry my own wife."

"Dunna be an arse!"

Gerrit's voice was very close. Too close. Tisa struggled to open her eyes. The man was devil spawn.

She moved above the ground. When her eyes finally opened, she was in Darragh's home and being laid across his bed.

"Here are her herbs." Darragh's voice came from a great distance although he stood beside her.

She needed to protect him from Gerrit. She struggled to sit up. The memory of Tadhg covered with blood came to her and she bolted up with a gasp.

"Lay back down, damn it. Ye've had a fright," Gerrit scowled at her.

Darragh shuffled through the dried herbs in her basket. His large hands pushing some of the more delicate flowers onto the floor. He gave a heavy sigh. "We'll get these to him. Mayhap someone will ken which one to give him."

"Nae," Tisa sat up and grabbed at her stomach that suddenly felt queasy. "I'll help him. I'm sorry. I will come with—"

"Tisa," Darragh's demanding tone indicated his patience with her was at an end, "are ye with child?"

Gerrit could not have whipped his head to look at her any faster than he did. His eyes were huge.

Her concern for Tadhg was overpowering but the opportunity to take this man down could not be missed. Satisfaction purred inside Tisa's chest at this perfect opportunity to slam Gerrit's mouth shut for good. This whoreson who dared to hurt her Tadhg.

Tisa stood on shaky legs but placed a hand affectionately to her husband's chest. She smiled up at him, "I may be, Darragh. Would that not be wonderful?"

Darragh's breath stilled beneath her hand. He studied her. With the slightest lowering of his brows, she knew he understood. He smiled, his eyes creasing at the corners and pulled her into a tight embrace.

"It would, indeed."

She reached up to receive the kiss he offered. He jerked away, touching his lip. "A bit painful still." He smiled again. "Ye are a wonderful wife."

Darragh caressed the side of her face, a sincere expression of gratitude on his face. "Let us see to Tadhg. Get a heavier covering, 'tis getting colder out."

Darragh headed to the door without so much as a glance at Gerrit.

The doubt she read on Gerrit's face as he followed Darragh out the door gave her extreme satisfaction. She rummaged through a pile of Caireann's clothing alongside the fire and grabbed the heavy, woven shawl before heading back out.

The crowd of men was smaller and that gave Tisa hope that Tadhg's injuries were not as serious as they first appeared. Sean still sat beside Tadhg, supporting his head as he offered him water.

"How fares he?" Tisa asked.

Tadhg's eyes opened and he smiled weakly at her. "Methinks I'll live. Sorry for the scare. Ye're white as a ghost."

Gerrit shuffled beside her then huffed off without saying a word. She bit her lips to keep the smile from her face. That was the perfect thing for Tadhg to say.

"I'll get him to his bed. Rest is all he needs," Sean said.

"I have something to help him rest." Tisa pulled out a few twigs, the leaves still intact. "I can make a tea for him."

Sean kept his eyes on Darragh and Gerrit walking toward the longhouse before responding. "Is it a good thing for him to sleep so deeply with those two nearby?"

Tadhg began to stand and Sean caught him when he stumbled. Wrapping Tadhg's arm around his shoulders, Sean began to lead him back down the road. "Gerrit could never have laid Tadhg low without the aid of something else."

"The man cheated?" Tisa asked, her voice betraying her astonishment.

"With a dent in his scull? No fist, no matter how hard, could leave a mark like that."

Tisa saw only the matted hair and that sight made her want to rip the man's heart out. She turned to do just that but Tadhg stopped her.

"Dunna!" Tadhg's voice was so weak. "I will see to this."

She struggled against the need to avenge her Tadhg but calmed herself.

"Of course." She had no right to confront Gerrit. Tadhg was not her husband. He was no one to her. The heaviness in her chest made it hard to take a breath. She stopped. The two continued a few more feet before Sean turned back to look at her.

"Ye need to come, Tisa. There are things that need to be said."

"There are not, Sean." She leveled her gaze at him. There was no reason for her to go with them except to torture herself with things that could never be. "See to him. Find me if the pain becomes too much for him."

Chapter Thirty-Two

Tisa turned away from Tadhg and Sean, forcing her feet to carry her back toward the longhouse. With every step, her heart pained her, the breath trapped in her chest. Then she stopped. She could not go in and pretend. Her strength was gone. Her will depleted. To hear Gerrit speak of what a great warrior he was for felling Tadhg would push her over the edge. If Sean said the man cheated, she believed him.

The thought of Tadhg possibly dying brought everything crashing in on her. He could die and she would never be told. No one would think to inform her. And if she did find out he'd died? She could not continue on as she had. Even if she could never have him in truth, she needed to know he still lived. Somewhere. That he breathed the same air. That he saw the same stars overhead. That he felt the same sun on his face.

Turning to the forest, she thought about what she would do when all the men left to fight. Many would die, as they'd said. Maybe even Darragh. And if her husband died, what would become of her? Would she be exiled? Sent off to go live with the outcasts? Would his father take her and treat her as the other women? Passing her around if she pleased him enough?

She scanned the darkness of the trees for any sign of the children. Would they have moved out of the cave on their own? Had they been attacked? Glancing around, she saw no one. Mayhap just to check the cave again. With Malcolm away, no one was looking out for them.

Tisa ran to her house and changed into her disguise. Wrapping herself again in Caireann's shawl, she used the fur as her final covering. At the last minute, she grabbed the little doll. She prayed they had returned and that they were all safe.

The moon was rising and the chill in the air spoke of spring. With the days longer, she would have enough time to go and come back before she was missed. The men would be celebrating for hours. It took very little time for her to find the cave and she slipped through the passage to the back opening. There had been a fire but she saw no sure sign that it had been her outcasts and Aoife.

She sifted through the embers, heaping dry needles and leaves on top until the flame caught. The smoke rose to the opening in the ceiling. The children loved to point out their escape passage. She never had the heart to ask them how they would get up to it.

"In case we're attacked," Will had said, his eyes wide.

Children could find adventure in the scariest ordeal. Were they well? Or had some evil befallen them?

The last bit of wood quickly caught and the smokiness was clearing. She prayed that wherever they were this night, they were safe.

"Ultan!"

Tisa jumped up and turned around. Tadhg stood beside the passage.

"Tadhg. What are ye—"

"I was hoping I would find ye here."

Tisa clamped her mouth shut, glad he had interrupted what she was about to say. Ultan demanding to know why he wasn't abed would definitely have roused his suspicions. He looked terrible.

"Please, sit." Tadhg spoke quickly then dropped to his knees close beside her. He unhooked his brat, letting it drop behind him. He stretched it out and sat on it.

"Please?" He looked up at her with those wide, brown eyes, his hands stretched toward the material placed alongside the fire.

His hair had been cleaned and brushed back, revealing a large bruise on the side of his face. She realized she could make out his features quite well this close to the fire. She could not allow him to do the same.

"Nae, I should—"

Tadhg took her hand. His hand was unnaturally warm. "Please. Sit with me."

His eyes shimmered in the light. He could have a fever and should be resting. What was wrong with Sean to let him out after such a bad injury? The steady tug of Tadhg's hand finally broke her resistance and she sat beside him. She turned away from the fire, pulling the fur forward to hide in the shadow. That made it so she had to look directly at Tadhg and every nuance of his expression showed in the glow of the firelight.

Tadhg smiled, releasing her hand but only moving a few inches away as she sat. "I've missed our talks."

"We barely ken each other."

He looked at her, his eyes dropping to her lips. She fought against the wild beating of her own heart. Surely he couldn't see her face let alone make out where her lips were.

"Mayhap at some distant time? Surely we were friends. Close friends."

His sad smile tugged at her heart. He also seemed pale. "Are ye not well?"

Tisa prayed he didn't become suspicious with the question.

He glanced toward the fire before facing her again. "I have been better."

"Mayhap ye need... to go... home?" She chose her words carefully.

"Nae. I need to speak to ye." His smile widened. "I've learned something—I—I want to share with ye."

Tisa's gut tightened. She could not listen to him talk of her father again. More turmoil she did not need. When she started to stand, he grabbed her hand. Tight.

"I need ye to hear me."

He did not stand. Nor did he release her hand. Something in his expression heightened her already sharpened senses. The fire shot off sparks beside them. She needed to get out of this cave.

She only partly feigned her irritated tone. "Hurry then. I canna stay long."

"Nae?" Tadhg's fingers intertwined with her own and he pulled her hand toward his face. His eyes remained on hers even when his lips touched the back of her hand. "Are ye sure ye canna stay with me?"

She stared, mesmerized, struggling with how to make his kiss make sense. She could not and yet she sat, far too close, beside him. He released her hand only to reach toward the brooch holding her fur together at her neck. It was fine. It didn't mean anything. Not the kiss. Not his hands on her.

"'Tis warm enough in here now."

She couldn't move away.

He undid the fastening. Slipping his strong, warm hands beneath the heavy fur, he rested his hands on her shoulder before running them down, along her arms. The garment sliding down with the movement. "I want ye comfortable."

Her eyes stayed fixed on his mouth. The touch of his lips on her hand still tingled along her skin. The feel of his hands stroking her arms making it hard to catch her breath. He shifted closer and made to push a strand of hair from her face. He tucked it behind her ear but didn't withdraw his hand right away. Instead, he stroked her hair back to reach behind and pull out her long braid tucked inside her leine.

"I have not been able to speak of my feelings to another," he said. His eyes remained on hers and she couldn't turn away. The gentle tug of his hand unraveling the braid sent shivers over her heated skin.

He leaned closer still and she closed her eyes.

"I am deeply in love." His voice was quiet beside her ear. "A woman I've loved since she was a girl."

The gentle kiss came at the same time his fingers worked their way beneath her hair, touching the sensitive skin at her neck. Her hair fell around her shoulders.

"She had lovely hair that I longed to feel between my fingers."

Sensations washed over her, her defenses down, she leaned toward him, wanting to feel more of him. He rubbed his thumbs in tiny circles against her scalp. When his lips touched hers, she accepted his kiss. She longed for his kiss.

Tadhg increased the pressure against her mouth, leaning her head back, and ran his tongue along her lips, tasting her. She opened her mouth to him and welcomed the invasion of his tongue. The feel of him was just as she'd imagined. He moved closer, deepening the kiss, his hand supporting her head. She ardently kissed him back, enraptured by his touch, his scent, his urgency.

He pulled back, "I have longed to touch all of her."

He slipped his hands down her length, kneading her body as he went. Reaching for her feet, he removed one shoe and then the other. His hand slid along the sensitive arch of her naked foot then up along her calf, raising goose bumps along her skin, before returning to slide his hands down her back. Grasping as he went, he set her on fire wherever he touched. Shifting when he pulled the leine out from under her, it seemed right for him to grasp her bottom in his hands. The heat from his skin singeing through the thin material of her trews.

And his lips were on hers again. She gasped at the pleasurable sensations and smiled against his lips before kissing him again. A wonderful place to be with Tadhg's hands spreading across her body. His lips on hers.

He dragged the leine up, his palms sliding along her bare skin beneath, pressing into her, drawing her closer. The wetness was there. The longing to be his. She didn't want to speak. She wanted to feel. With little encouragement, her arms rose over her head, he removed the leine, and her chest was bared to him. Overwhelmed by sudden shyness, she leaned her face in closer to bury her head against his shoulder. His heavy breathing fanned her face while his fingers spread around one plump breast. He fondled her with a gentle touch, pulling and stretching the sensitive skin of her nipple, heightening her awareness. Smattering kisses along her cheek, he stopped at the corner of her mouth. "I want to make love to her."

She turned into him. His tongue delving into her mouth, his sound of deep longing blew like a breeze against the embers in her core, igniting her into a fire. Heat spread across her bosom with his unhurried stroking. Wrapping his arms about her hips, he drew her to sitting on his lap, straddling him. His stiffness pushing against her softness. Overwhelming need coursed through her. The need to feel his mouth on her breast, suckling her. She arched into him, stroking her sensitive mounds against his firm chest. He cupped each breast with his large, hot hands. His breathing ragged, he eagerly dropped his mouth to suckle a hardened nipple. His sweet tongue stroking her, increasing her desire.

His knuckles brushed against her sensitive skin as he loosened the ties of her trews. His tongue worked around her nipple. Stroking. Suckling. Need shot straight down to her most intimate place.

"Aye I need my love, more than my next breath." His breath hot against her exposed skin dampened from his kisses.

The loose material fell away. His large hand on her bare hips, he worked the material down, wiggling it under her bottom.

"Will ye give me what has always been mine?"

"Aye."

Her dreams were real. Her husband. Her Tadhg had come to make her his. He held her against him, stretched out, and she was beneath him. His lips on her neck, she couldn't sit still. The fire burned hot within her. When his hand slipped between her legs, he moaned again then stilled. His breathing labored. She waited. Worrying her lip, she was overwhelmed by how much she wanted him. Needed him.

Ever so gently, he worked his fingers over her slick passage. Slipping a finger inside, his breath hitched.

Her loins were on fire, needing him, needing this.

"My body longs to be yers," she whispered.

The trews were being shoved away. His mouth on her breast and his finger moving in and out of her wetness. She cantered her hips up against his hand. And he filled her even more. Pleasure washed over her like a storm's tide, pushing aside any other thoughts.

She dared not open her eyes even when the cold moved over her skin but then he was back, his solid chest covering her. Naked now, she spread her legs for him. He fit perfectly. Supporting himself, he touched her wetness with the tip of his tarse before sliding its length along her folds, heightening her desire for the feel of him inside.

He moaned. "I am aching with love for ye."

"Come into me."

With one firm thrust, he filled her. She gasped at the sensation. He stilled. His broad back tight under her hand. He nuzzled his face into her hair, dropping kisses along her shoulder. One long sweep of his tongue along her neck. She sighed and he relaxed again, shifting his hips to move ever so slightly within her as his tongue continued its delicious assault.

Entering her more fully, there was no more pain. His warm lips brushing over hers, he took her mouth in an exquisitely gentle kiss. She nearly cried out when he withdrew but then he was pressing into her again. And then again. Stretching her. Little by little. He flamed her burgeoning need with slow, deliberate movements. Each time pressing further into her until he was fully sheathed.

"Look my way, my love."

She opened her eyes. It was like her dream but so much more. Him inside of her. The look of love on his face. His endearing smile of unsurpassable pleasure.

He thrust into her. His tempo slow at first, began to increase. Controlled. She slid her hands down his back, savoring the feel of him, his firm buttocks. The tension in his body seemed unbearable. Her eyes closed, she savored the intensity. Building with her heightened awareness of him. His heavy breathing. His strong hands on her, gripping her, grasping her bottom as if he would die if he couldn't have her like this. He gave in to his own need for her, plunging harder and deeper, touching her womb and his heart pounding against hers.

Overwhelming sensations forced a groan of longing that wasn't even recognizable as hers.

An answer. A low sound rumbled through his chest, vibrating into her, and she was over the edge, the waves spreading out from her core, cascading throughout her body.

She cried out his name and it echoed back. A slow, hard thrust. And again. And he stilled within her, spilling his seed. She squeezed him tight inside her. She would never be satisfied again.

He covered her face with gentle kisses, trailing along her cheek. His unsteady breath in her he ear, he whispered, "I love ye, Tisa." Taking her face in his hands, he gazed into her eyes. "I canna be without ye anymore."

Tisa shook her head. She did not want to think. Not now. Not when she could still feel him inside of her. Not when total contentment filled her. Not when she was enveloped in such a great peace, a knowledge of being right where she belonged.

"My love," he said.

Lowering his lips, he kissed her with great care as if showing his love to her. His need for her. Showing he could never have a life without her. The tears slipped down into her hair.

He pulled the long brat over them. She snuggled tight against his solid length, still overwhelmed by sensations. Her body satiated, she drifted off. Contented. Fulfilled.

Sometime later the cold awakened them. With no light, Tisa couldn't guess what time it was. She tipped her head up to watch Tadhg as he slept, startled when she found him watching her.

"Ye look like an angel when ye sleep."

She scoffed. "And how do ye ken what angels look like when they sleep?"

"I have one in my arms." He kissed her lightly.

When she would have wiggled up closer to kiss him again, he stayed her with his hand. "What are we to do now, Tisa?"

"Nae, Tadhg. I canna speak of this now. Make love to me again."

He sat up beside her, his eyes all but caressing her skin where he searched every bit of her as if he couldn't get his fill of her. "God kens how much I wanted ye for my wife. Things can never be right for me without ye."

His pained tone cut through her like a knife. She had no words of comfort.

"Do ye believe we have sinned here?" she asked.

Tadhg's expression changed into one of confidence. "There is no sin when a husband takes his wife."

"But I have another who calls himself my husband."

"He is not yer husband in truth. He married ye not to take ye as his wife but as ordered and with no thought of ever fulfilling his duty."

"There was no pledge made between us. No blessing."

"Darragh does not seem to care about such things," Tadhg said.

"He believed there was no need, no doubt, since he would not be consummating our union."

"Now ye are bedded." Tadhg stood. "And I will see to ye in all things."

Tisa glanced down to the blood smeared between her legs and on his brat beneath her. He gently cleaned her with water from the spring, his tenderness bringing tears to her eyes.

"Ye have me as yer wife, Tadhg. Ye are my husband in truth. I will never go willingly to another."

Standing, he rubbed his head in frustration until he happened against the sore spot and winced. Even with such a grimace, her Tadhg was a handsome man. She allowed herself to look over his nakedness. His broad shoulders and bared torso, lightly covered with dark hair, down to his well-honed legs. She paused at his tarse, surprised when it changed under her perusal, growing in length and thickness. Tisa looked up at Tadhg in astonishment.

He snorted, a lopsided grin on his lips. "Ye canna look on me like that and expect no reaction from me. I burn for ye even now."

She opened her arms to him. "Then dunna wait. Take me again, husband."

He dropped beside her and again made love to her. And she again cried in his arms, wishing things could be different. She rested her head on his shoulder, his arm holding her there, tight against him. It was a long while before either of them spoke.

"Tadhg?"

"Aye?"

She dreaded bringing up the unpleasant subject but she needed to know. "Please tell me about your mother. Did she lay with my father?"

"I should not have shared that with ye."

She leaned up on her elbow to look into his face. "How do ye ken? Mayhap ye're wrong."

He shook his head. "I am not wrong. 'Twas in her own hand. My mother named yer father as Brighit's father."

"How can that be?"

He shrugged. "My mother was deceitful."

"And she is not here to defend herself."

Tadhg pierced her with his look. "There is no defense."

Tisa shivered, his harsh tone washing over her. His anger so very deep.

"We canna ken what happened. We need to let it go."

He looked toward the wall, a hard expression. "I am having a hard time with that. Especially since it made me lose ye."

If that was the reason Padraig broke off their betrothal, then his mother's betrayal did cost them their chance for happiness. There was nothing Tisa could say to him.

"Methinks we need to get ye back," Tadhg said.

Tisa sat up, tucking her knees up under her chin. "I dunna want to return. I want to remain with ye."

Wrapping his arms around her, she welcomed his strength, him holding her close. "I want to make ye mine."

"I *am* yers."

With a gentle hand, he lifted her chin and placed a kiss on her lips. "I take ye as my wife, to love ye, to protect ye."

A small breath lay trapped in her chest as she responded. "I take ye as my husband, to respect ye, to honor ye."

"I'll take no other unto myself."

"I will take no other unto myself. I will cleave unto ye and accept yer protection."

"And I will love ye all the days of my life, holding ye deep in my heart, cherishing ye as my most my precious gift, more precious than my own life." He pushed the hair from her face. "But how can I protect ye when another calls ye wife?"

"I am not his wife."

"Ye are not. Ye belong to me." Tadhg scanned the area. "Can I stay with ye here? Have a life with ye here, hidden away?" He picked up the small rag doll that lay with the rest of their clothing. "Is this yers?"

Tadhg settled down beside Tisa and she took the doll.

"There *were* people here. People Aodh would not allow to live amongst us. He claims they will weaken the group. Some are sick. Some are mangled. His own granddaughter lives as an outcast. Aednat."

"Does Aednat have a malady?"

"Her foot is not right so she limps but she is a charming lass. I brought that for her." She looked around the area. "I dunna ken where they've gone now. Malcolm will ken. Until his return, I will pray they are still safe."

"He has returned. I came upon him three nights ago when I was out looking for Ultan—ye."

Tisa shook her head. "It could not have been him. They traveled south along the coast."

"I spoke to him."

"Was Caireann with him?"

"She was not. He had an older woman with him that I dinna ken. He kept her behind him as if to keep her from my view so I dinna press the matter."

"How did she look?"

"She had long, dark hair with gray sprinkled throughout. A noble bearing."

Tis gasped, covering her mouth. She shook her head before facing him. "Methinks ye saw him with Aoife, Darragh's mother."

"Darragh's mother? Aodh's wife?"

"His first wife. She is one of the outcasts. He set her aside when he married the chieftain's daughter, Lilith. Aoife told me Aodh poisoned the old chieftain, Eirnin, when he refused to fight him for leadership."

"Eirnin? I remember that man from my youth. He visited my father every summer. A proud man."

"Eirnin refused to fight Aodh because his young son, Brian, was tanist. He had been named after the great Brian Boru and held great promise as a warrior and leader. Aodh poisoned Eirnin but no one could prove it. Darragh's mother was the only one that knew the truth and she was put with the other outcasts. Brian was too young to take over as leader so the clan accepted Aodh once he proved his mettle. Aodh allows

Brian to remain at a place of honor but not to fight beside him. He does not trust him."

"If Brian kens that Aodh poisoned his father, no doubt Aodh fears Brian will do the same. Brian is brother-in-law to Aodh. He would not put his sister in jeopardy by challenging her husband. And who are Aednat's parents?"

"Darragh's brother."

"I dunna ken any brother."

"Aoife told me of him. Malachi. He and his wife died in some tragic accident she would not speak to me of, leaving Aednat. Aoife said the loss nearly broke Aodh. That was when they traveled north with Darragh."

"Aodh is ruthless. I am afeared for ye if they notice ye're missing. Mayhap we should prepare to return."

Tisa did not protest and dressed herself. Tadhg did the same. When he picked up the well-worn shawl, shaking it before handing it to Tisa, she frowned and shook it out again.

"Sorry I am that ye dunna have something less worn than this. Ye deserve better, my fine lady."

Tisa held the material in front of her, squinting. "'Tis Caireann's, not mine. She is very careful of her things."

Tadhg leaned beside her. "What do ye see?"

"'Tis strange." She shook her head and grabbed a section of the material. "These holes dunna look as if from wear."

"Nae. Mayhap it became stuck on something? Or something poked her?"

She ran her hand along the material, counting out three very prominent holes. When she grabbed at her shoulder, her eyes widened.

"What is wrong?"

"I had the same mark on my shoulder. 'Tis from Gerrit's brooch, the one that holds his brat. See the circular pattern? Very ornate with large stones that jabbed into me, breaking my skin."

Tadhg's face tightened. "Was that at the inn?"

"Nae. 'Twas here. He came upon me in the woods."

Her jaw tightened and it was difficult to swallow.

Tadhg took her hands in his warm ones. "What? What did he do?"

"He almost ran me down... he wanted to take me. He said he would do to me what Darragh could not."

"He kens Darragh has no desire for women? Ah, because they had been lovers."

She searched the material, barely able to voice the words. "And then that devil spawn went and raped Caireann."

"Caireann was raped? Sweet Caireann?" Tadhg's upset matched her own. "How did I not hear of it?'

Tisa's heart thudded in her chest as if simply sitting there was unacceptable. She would confront Gerrit.

"These people are not like us. They take what they want. They share women who are unwilling. The men—"

"—are reprehensible! And I will be yer champion. Sean and I have spoken of this. Forgive me that I could not bear to think of ye with another and refused to listen to him afore now. What ye've had to endure? But no longer."

She placed a small hand to his cheek, a sad expression. "That ye ken does not change anything."

"It does! I canna allow it to continue. I will not allow ye to be treated so! These men act more like animals and if Gerrit raped Caireann, it will not go unpunished."

"He prides himself on having willing lovers. Men and women. But Caireann had not been willing. He came up from behind." She held up the material. "And took her, forcibly, tearing her with his brutality, ruining her."

"Did Malcolm ken?"

"Malcolm had loved her from the very first. When we found her after the rape, he berated himself that he had not taken her to wife afore. He believed he would have been able to protect her. We had no thought of it being Gerrit." She glanced again at the material. "This will be seen to but we need to return."

Chapter Thirty-Three

Once inside the longhouse, Sean took but a moment to locate his target.

"Gerrit! Ye whoreson!" Sean strode toward the man who now stood beside the table where he'd been ensconced with men offering their congratulations for taking down the great MacNaughton warrior.

"Sore loser?" Gerrit rubbed at the stubble on his chin, inspecting Sean as he approached.

"Ye're a cheat because ye haven't the bollocks to fight the man fairly."

Despite having given him a considerable amount of warning, Sean's fist easily slammed into Gerrit's jaw. The contact sent him back a good three feet before landing him on his arse.

Sean looked down into the very bewildered face of the leathered man.

"Have a fair fight with me now and we'll see who is, indeed, the greater warrior—the MacNaughton—or the sodomite."

A few of the men bent to help Gerrit to his feet but the rest dispersed, exceedingly careful to do nothing that could be misinterpreted as aggression. His jaw tight, Sean was barely able to contain his rage.

A safe distance from Sean, Gerrit brushed off his clothing with casual hands. "I'd say ye are, indeed, no more than a sore loser. What proof do ye have that I cheated?"

"This!" A loud voice came from the doorway. As one, they all turned to see Darragh standing there. In one hand, Gerrit's leather glove; in the other, a large rock, flat on one side.

"Yer weapon of choice? Fear not, Sean, yer friend will be avenged. I have yet to make my own impression on this man."

Gerrit's expression quickly shifted from one of guilt to one of seduction.

His lips curling into a smile before he spoke. "Ah, my dear Darragh."

"Dunna call me that ever again." Darragh barked the words, his composure slipping a bit. Gerrit would have seen it as well. A trained warrior watched for any show of emotion and that man thrived on manipulation, exploitation, and bullying. Darragh standing up to this man was obviously personal which would give the advantage to Gerrit.

"He's devil spawn for certain, Darragh. Are ye certain ye wish to lower yerself to deal with the likes of this man?" Sean paused long enough to offer a contemptuous scowl at Gerrit. "Ye're the chieftain's son, after all. And ye've proven yerself today in front of all of us. Ye're a man to be reckoned with, Darragh, and make no doubt about that. Ye have earned the right to have another see to someone so far beneath ye. Ye only need say the word and I will gladly take this caitiff down."

Darragh turned his hardened expression on Sean. His eyes rounding once he realized Sean was supporting him, he clipped a nod of acknowledgement. "My thanks, Sean. I will see to this one myself."

Darragh stiffened his face, wiping away any sentimentality, and headed to the door. The men cheered as they filed out of the longhouse behind Darragh, followed by Gerrit, and back toward the well-worn fighting area. The sun was lower in the sky. The night promising to be a cool one.

Sean picked up the rock as he passed the table Darragh had dropped it on. One side was flat just like the dent in Tadhg's head, his blood and hair still visible. Sean's blood boiled and he marched toward the makeshift viewing box. He would be nearby and ready to assist if Gerrit was somehow able to get the upper hand on Darragh. It was no longer about being a fair fight, not when the man had violated all rules of fairness himself.

Leofrid and Aodh were deep in conversation, standing alongside their seats. They relaxed with refreshments of their own but both turned toward the throng of men coming their way. Sean took a second look when he noticed Godwin paling as the men came toward him. He appeared truly frightened. Hard to lead men into battle when ye are afraid by the mere sight of them.

"What is this?" Aodh asked.

"My fight with Gerrit," Darragh said.

Aodh put his hand on Darragh's arm when his son stopped in front of him. "Son, ye dunna need to do this for me. I am proud of ye. Ye've nothing to prove to me. I swear it."

Darragh's expression never changed but he bent his head in a show of respect before facing his father. "My thanks for that. I wish to make ye as proud of me as ye were of Malachi. He and I may be different in some ways but we are of the same blood, after all. Yer blood."

Sean couldn't miss the shimmer of tears in Aodh's eyes. The man struggled for composure before he wrapped his arms about his son in an awkward hug. He resumed his seat next to Leofrid.

Darragh picked up a long sword and looked it over, a small smile on his lips. He had done quite well with it. A good choice of weapon but he tossed it to the side.

"Methinks since ye find it necessary to deal unfairly with someone ye fear ye canna beat, I would choose maces for our weapons."

Gerrit burst into a smile. "How quickly my young lad forgets. I am a master at the mace and will gladly see ye on yer knees at my feet..." He accepted the mace offered him, a short-handled pike with a spiked iron ball at the end. "...and looking up at me. My favored position for ye if I remember correctly."

Darragh shoved his hand through the back of the round shield to secure it to his arm and advanced on Gerrit before he could prepare. The man's smile surely fanned Darragh's rage. The well swung mace barely missed Gerrit's shoulder, the shield coming up at the last minute.

"Oh, ye've learned some new techniques." Gerrit's tone indicated his enjoyment.

Darragh moved back from Gerrit's swinging mace. The spikes just shy of making contact with his face before the shield went up. Gerrit laughed. Darragh shoved back against him with the stiff wood. Gerrit had a few inches on the blond, but Darragh had passion for the fight. He wanted to see this man defeated. Gerrit's taunting was only deepening his need to make it happen. Sean was impressed by Darragh's ability to channel his rage.

"Mayhap ye can demonstrate what else ye've learned when we're done here."

Darragh lunged, feigning left with his shield. Gerrit protected himself, giving Darragh the perfect opening with a swing at the man's arm. The spikes smacking soundly against his upper arm but his leather protection held firm. Gerrit laughed again.

Sean had not been convinced Darragh's attack could be effective if he allowed himself to be distracted by the taunts. Instead, Darragh quickly adjusted the weight to his back foot before charging ahead, pushing Gerrit back again.

"Oh, ye've still more bollocks than brains. Not that I ever complained." Gerrit was playing him. Allowing him to push him back but his stance was firmly planted. He still held the upper hand.

"Nae, ye never complain. An arse, human or beast, would do for ye."

Gerrit's face reddened. He charged forward with enough momentum that Darragh stumbled back, barely able to stop himself from falling. Their shields slammed together. The sound of wood on wood splitting the air.

The men shifted around him but Sean didn't hear anything that was said. He was intent on Darragh's skill and realized he truly wanted the man to win. Gerrit deserved to be taken down by him.

"Ye've got him, Darragh." Sean's low voice carried. He hoped it would encourage him.

"Oh, have ye a new lover? He's a big one!"

Sean growled. A light touch on his arm and he swung around, ready to land a fist on whoever it was.

"What is amiss?" Tisa's face was lined with concern.

Sean blew out a breath, just noticing Tadhg standing a bit closer to her than usual. Their new intimacy evident in his peaceful expression. "How fare ye?"

Tadhg smiled. "I'm hopeful."

Tisa glanced toward him, so close that he all but surrounded her. Her love for the man no longer hidden before she again faced Sean.

"Why is Darragh fighting Gerrit?" she asked.

Tadhg moved in for a better view, past the others circling around, close to Aodh and Leofrid.

"Darragh had wanted to fight the man from the first. He is just now getting a chance to do that."

She nodded, a thoughtful nod, before she turned on him. "He seems quite furious. Are ye certain there is nothing else happening here?"

Tisa was right, Darragh's anger was now very apparent on his face. His mask of indifference slipping with his tiredness. Gerrit was pressing him hard, his momentum never letting up. In all fairness, Gerrit had fought far less than Darragh had this afternoon. The man was still fresh.

"He found the rock Gerrit had used on Tadhg. Darragh wanted to see the wrong righted."

Tisa looked into his face but Sean couldn't guess what she was thinking. He was her husband in word alone. They lived in the same house. Was there some unseen tie between the two of them? Could her husband know of her love for Tadhg?

Darragh knew of her love for Tadhg and fear tightened Tisa's chest. Fear that Darragh could be mortally wounded or he could kill this vile man. The latter suited her fine. Gerrit's arrogance was all consuming. Men stepped aside when he approached, women and men fell at his feet for the smallest amount of attention paid them. What was the attraction this man held? He truly was the devil's spawn.

Darragh's strength was waning. One glance at Aodh convinced her he saw it, too. The man had been battling for hours now, giving his best to every encounter. She hadn't lied when she told him he was formidable. But there was a limit to how long someone could continue without resting.

Tisa crossed to stand alongside her father-in-law. He never took his eyes off of his son. Aodh's body strained with every advance, every lunge, every shove against his son. When Darragh's shield was ripped from his grasp and he fell to one knee, Aodh stood as if ready to intervene. She prayed he would do so before it was too late. Gerrit backed away, giving Darragh a moment to regain his footing. He bent over his knees trying to catch his breath. Gerrit appeared barely winded. He cocked a brow, his blue eyes bright, and threw his shield to the side as well.

"Come, my dear Darragh. Do yer best," Gerrit said, his voice sounding very much like it had in the woods when he'd tried to entice Tisa.

"Ye impudent dog." Tisa hissed the words.

Darragh lunged forward, fisting the mace in both hands, to run the unsuspecting Gerrit back against the post. The wood pressed against his neck, Gerrit's eyes bulged. Gurgling sounds were the only thing breaking the silence. It was as if the onlookers were afraid to even breathe.

Tisa's eyes widened, preparing herself to witness the murder of this man before her very eyes. He was more than deserving. He'd raped her innocent friend. He'd treated her husband cruelly. His own pleasure was all he ever sought and he cared not who got in his way.

Gerrit's eyes were closing, his face turning red.

"I am going to end ye." Darragh shoved harder, his feet sinking deeper into the mud. No one dared stop him. Even Leofrid refused to announce Darragh the winner and cease this.

Darragh wanted this man dead and dead he would be.

A movement beneath Gerrit's brat and Darragh's hands went slack. He gasped and fell back, his feet sucked into the mud giving him no chance to escape. The dagger wound opened his side, just below his ribs. Blood flooded his leine and down the hose Tisa had made him.

She gasped, her heart slamming into her throat, and ran to throw herself alongside her husband. Pulling at his arm, the mace still clutched in his grip. His mouth opening and closing, a rasping sound was all she could hear.

"Darragh!"

He turned his wide eyes to her. There were tears there and her own eyes filled. Poor, poor Darragh.

"Nae, Darragh!"

He closed his mouth to swallow then took a shaky breath. "Forgive me, Tisa. I tried to defend yer honor but have failed."

"Nae. Ye dinna fail. Ye show me great honor."

He reached a hand toward her and she grabbed it, holding it tight against her bosom where her breath was trapped.

"Love yer Tadhg with yer great passion, sweet little Tisa."

His eyes closed. His hand went limp.

Tisa opened her mouth but no sound came out.

Aodh kneeled beside her. "Son?"

He swallowed in great gasps of air in his pain. "Darragh?"

Tisa heard the deep anguish in that one word and her own heart squeezed. Through blurry eyes, she watched as Aodh snatched up the mace lying uselessly beside his dead son. Swinging it over his head, he stood and approached Gerrit with such speed she would never have thought him capable of. The wide-eyed look of surprise on Gerrit's face shifted to fear. He clutched at the knife, turning it out toward Aodh who was quickly impaled. He dropped at Gerrit's feet.

No one moved.

No one spoke.

Tisa broke through her miasma and went to Aodh. She turned him over onto his back, his sightless eyes still wet with his tears for his son. He was dead.

Gerrit had a death grip on his weapon, his shoulders hunched forward, and his eyes darting back and forth. No longer the smooth seductress, his face was frozen with fear. Leofrid stood but did not speak. Tadhg came forward, standing out of harm's way.

"Gerrit, drop the blade."

Tisa sat back on her haunches and looked up at the evil man. "Ye've done enough, Gerrit. Drop it."

"I dinna... I meant..." He rounded his eyes. "I dinna mean to kill anyone."

"Then ye've failed because ye've killed two men." Tadhg stepped closer. "And one of them is the chieftain here."

Leofrid cleared his throat from behind them. "Gerrit, drop the blade and we will decide what to do about this."

Tisa rounded on the man, her mouth gaping open. Tadhg was at her side. He touched her arm. "Dunna, Tisa."

Gerrit dropped the blade in the mud and kneeled, lowering his head in a show of respect. "My lord, I dinna mean to kill these men."

Tadhg grabbed the knife and helped Tisa to stand, backing her away from the groveling man.

"I ken that, Gerrit. Come forth." Leofrid had found his voice finally, his commanding tone undeniable. Gerrit did as he was bid.

Tisa waited between Sean and Tadhg. All eyes were on the leathered man as he approached Leofrid Godwin. He dropped to a knee again. A quiet mumbling started from the back but quickly expanded across the throng of onlookers. The bulging-eyed woman came forward and walked to where Aodh's body lay. She did not bend down. She did not touch the dead man. She did not cry. She merely looked down.

"Lilith?" Leofrid spoke to the woman.

The unreality of the scene pricked Tisa's mind. The woman who came in for the bedding cloth? The one who held her "virginal blood" in front of all present? That was Aodh's wife?

Lilith turned to the man now seated alone in the viewing stand. There were tears sliding down her cheeks but no other visible sign of any feelings at all.

"What say ye?" Leofrid asked.

Lilith scanned the onlookers, not stopping until she had looked each one of them in the eye. She barely paused over Tisa but surely she saw Darragh was dead as well. Tisa's breath hitched.

"Brian?" Lilith called, her voice strong and clear.

The man who had sat at the far end of the head table at every meal came forward. He was a good sized man carrying himself as a warrior; his shoulders back, his chest forward, his legs firmly planted. He'd never offered a single word to Tisa. Not in greeting. Not in welcome. When Leofrid arrived, he'd been displaced, sitting with Lilith. The same man Darragh had referred to simply as his father's brother-in-law. Aodh's brother-in-law. His wife's brother. The son of the man Aodh had poisoned.

Brian went to his sister and took her into his arms. The sound of weeping carried to them and Tisa's heart lurched with compassion. Darragh lay there on the ground. She wanted to go to him to cover him up but she didn't move.

Sean put a gentle arm around Tisa's shoulders, pulling her tight against his side, and kissed the top of her head. "I ken yer loss, Tisa. I am sorry."

She turned her head into him and cried. *Never* would she have believed she would feel this immense loss. Darragh was dead. Her husband? No. Her friend? Mayhap.

Brian turned to the onlookers, his sister still clinging to him and crying. "This is the widow of our chieftain, my sister. I choose to take over as rightful chieftain if ye will be behind me."

A moment of time, imperceptible beyond the sudden silence, passed and the men were dropping to their knees in a show of acceptance of Brian's declaration. The many warriors from surrounding clans remained standing, shifting as if unsure what to do. Their allegiance would not be to this clan leader but to their own, most of whom were present.

Brian bowed his head. "My thanks."

Lilith pulled away, wiping her face, to look on those who remained kneeling.

"Those of ye that have come from other clans," Brian said, "I ask ye to please leave us in this time of great loss. We will need a time of mourning for our own—"

"Nae!" Leofrid bellowed. "They are here at my behest! They will remain until I give them leave to go."

Chapter Thirty-Four

Tadhg could feel Sean's eyes on him as he waited in expectation. He wanted him to step out and Tadhg agreed. He nodded and approached Brian.

"Brian, my heart goes out to ye at yer loss but I fear Gerrit will go unpunished if the crimes committed here are not seen to without delay."

Brian tore his eyes from Leofrid who still stood at his chair, a look of indignation on his face. "Ye are right."

Tadhg lowered his voice. "The man has moved closer to Leofrid even now as if to offer a defense."

Brian's eyes darted toward the man to confirm the truth of his words. "And what do ye have in mind?"

"Gerrit needs to be taken in and treated as any prisoner."

Brian looked around as if assessing his clan's feelings on the subject.

Tadhg smiled. "Methinks ye will have little discontent among yer own. The man is a miscreant and well they ken it."

The man's chest rose as if breathing for the first time since he'd stepped into the arena, his eyes warm on Tadhg's face. "And I can count on Clan O'Brien and the great MacNaughton warriors to aid me if trouble results?"

"In this, ye have my word."

Brian squared his shoulders, stepped away from his sister, and turned to face Leofrid full on.

"Lord Leofrid, I have said my peace. These clans are free to go back to their homes. Support for ye and yer cause have died with Aodh. At the hands of yer own man. And now I will take Gerrit into my keeping until his offenses against our clan can be seen to. Do ye yield?" Brian waited, his face stoic.

The man was impressive. He surely could have led as his father had always planned.

Leofrid was just the opposite. His frown spoke of his own lack of skills as he tried to determine the best course. Mayhap he needed a little push in the right direction.

"Leofrid," Tadhg said. "Brian is being forthright in his dealing with the situation. Surely yer support here in Eire, if there is any aside from Aodh, will not disappear. This tragedy requires immediate attention. 'Twould be best for ye to allow Gerrit to be taken—"

"NAE!" Gerrit bellowed his objection, his eyes remaining on his lord.

"Silence, Gerrit!" Leofrid said.

Gerrit quickly lowered his eyes.

"'Twas *ye* who saw fit to murder two men from this clan. Two important men. And this clan, our closest ally, is a clan which I hold in the highest regard."

Leofrid's eyes darted toward Brian, convincing Tadhg of the insincerity of his words. A ploy to win over the new chieftain, nothing more.

Brian's expression never altered but he crossed his arms, his feet in a warrior's stance.

The outcome mattered not at all to Tadhg. He just needed to see Gerrit arrested and be assured that justice would be done for both the murders and the raping of Caireann.

Tisa appeared stricken and Tadhg longed to take her in his arms, hold her close while she cried, to help her with this loss. She and Darragh had a special bond. Not one that threatened Tadhg or his love for Tisa, but a bond that Tisa felt the loss of. That was all he needed to know.

Sean's expression told Tadhg the man was feeling quite calm. His angst was gone, replaced by absolute peace. Tadhg glanced away to hide his smirk. In Sean's mind, he must be nearly packed up and headed home to his wife! The rules for their engagement here had been clearly outlined by the O'Brien. They were to do as Aodh commanded. With the death of Aodh, their time here was at an end.

When Sean turned to Tadhg, he struggled not to smile at Sean's joyful expression. Murder was a serious business. But a clan being released from any sort of involvement in a scheme they did not agree with was a relief for certain.

"However ye see fit to deal with the criminal," Leofrid assured Brian.

Gerrit remained in his spot even when Brian signaled three men to come forth. "Take him to the prisoner's hole."

And when they tied his hands behind his back and shoved him forward,

Gerrit gave no resistance. He accepted the yoke of prisoner better than Tadhg would have expected. The pained expression the man wore when he glanced at the bodies indicated his remorse may be sincere. Regardless, the price for the crimes would be paid.

The surrounding men were dispersing, picking up their weapons as they went. Tadhg had always assumed that just as his warriors were forced to be here, the others were as well although it was never discussed. That they were being coerced directly by Aodh was becoming apparent. Leofrid's support for invading England and overtaking the Normans died with Aodh, the man who shared that same lust for power.

As soon as Gerrit was taken away, Brian and another man gently lifted Aodh's body. His widow looked on as they walked as one up the hill. Tisa was overwhelmed with guilt and pulled out of Sean's warm embrace. Dropping to her knees beside Darragh, she placed a hand on his motionless chest, already chilling to her touch. Her tears began anew.

Someone came to stand beside her. Ian, his face tight with emotions he dared not show, looked down at her. He was giving her a chance to accept his presence beside his dead lover. She nodded to him. Darragh had spent time with this man. She must assume he cared for Ian.

"What would ye—" He cleared his throat. "What would ye have us do with him?"

Tisa took a shaky breath. Surely 'twas worse for this man who could not show the depth of his own emotions at this great loss. She smiled at him, motioning him to come beside her. At his nearness, his unshed tears that clung to his lashes were no longer hidden. Ian's hand rested on his knee, very close to Darragh's own. His fingers stroked as if caressing his leg. She took his hand in both of hers.

"I dunna ken for certain what Darragh would want. What say ye, Ian? Ye were friends."

The redhead turned wide eyes on her. "Mistress, I ken he cared for ye. I believe he would be grateful for any decision ye made on his behalf."

"Then I will see him have a Christian burial. The priest. Is he still here?"

Ian searched the crowd before speaking. "Does anyone ken where the priest is?"

"Here." A quiet voice called out from the crowd that parted for the man to approach. "I am here."

Tisa stood. "Please! Come and offer prayers for my husband."

Her face tight with emotion, she clung to Ian's hand as the priest spoke in perfect Latin. Many from the crowd moved closer, joining in with the expected responses. Tadhg stood behind her, his deep voice soothing her.

Ian suddenly faced her, struggling to hold back his own tears. She took him in her arms to comfort him, hoping onlookers saw the warrior comforting her.

"We shall grieve together," Tisa whispered the words.

Ian may be maintaining his outward composure, but Tisa felt his body shaking gently against her. His heartfelt loss was quite great. Tisa closed her eyes against the sight of the men who came forward to carry Darragh's body away. The deep respect they had for her husband was evident in the sheer number of men who accompanied them.

They all hold ye in very high regard, Darragh. Ye will be missed.

Chapter Thirty-Five

Tisa sat on the immaculately clean pallet where Darragh had slept. Everything was in its place as usual. His chest held some strange items she could not begin to understand. A pair of braies that would hang off of Darragh. A wood carving of a puffin that was very well done. More of the balsam soap he used on special occasions. An infant's night shirt.

She had rummaged in the chest many times, always assuming there'd be a time when she could ask about the objects. Now there was no more time. Standing in front of the closed curtain, she viewed the scene she had stitched of the birds and the trees with a critical eye. Darragh had often remarked on her ability, praising her. She glanced at the bed. He had done what he could to protect her from his father and he'd been successful, making it his goal to keep up the pretense. He had been good to her. The stool leg being dragged through the rushes brought him to her mind even before she lifted the hanging.

Tadhg's eyes were bright with his smile as he sat. "I dinna mean to disrupt ye."

"Ye've come at a good time." She took a deep breath. "I'm sad being here alone."

"'Tis as I thought, Tisa. Darragh was part of yer life." He did not move to take her into his arms but remained seated, his eyes locked on to hers. "He has been yer life. A great loss."

She hugged herself tight.

"Aodh expected to share me—or rather take me for himself. 'Twas his decision that Darragh take me to wife, not Darragh's. *Darragh* resented everything about me and all he had to do for me as his wife. Once he learned I truly dinna want him or anyone else in my bed, we

258

came to an understanding."

Tadhg's eyes never wavered.

"I dinna stop him from having his lovers. Breandan. Ian. I still acted the besotted bride, totally satisfied with my husband. And I was satisfied."

His expression did not change.

"Just not the way everyone else assumed." She walked to the intricately carved chest in the other alcove, carried it to the table, and placed it in front of Tadhg.

"There was no one I wanted but ye, Tadhg, and Darragh understood that." She cleared her throat before she continued. "Do ye ken what he said to me right before he passed?"

Tadhg shook his head, his eyes dark.

"He told me to love ye with my great passion."

She opened the chest and took out the little carving Cad and Will had made for her, setting it on the table in front of Tadhg.

"This is all I need to take with me when we return home. I will leave with ye when ye say 'tis time to go."

Tadhg stood then, drawing in a deep breath and turning away as he shook his head. When he finally faced her, she recognized that look of love. He opened his arms and she fell against his chest.

"My love, I needed to ken ye want that," he said. "I would not take ye away if ye wished to remain."

"Nae. I dunna wish to remain. I dunna belong here. I belong with ye."

"Glad I am to hear ye say as much. Ye seemed so upset at the deaths. I dinna ken for certain if yer feelings ran deeper than I understood."

Tisa looked up at him. "Darragh was a man of honor and he did his best to protect me. Now I ken he protected me so that he could give me to ye."

"Sean told me he had acquired a new respect for the man as well. He believes ye changed him, helped him to become a better man."

"Nae. I helped him to be the man he was meant to be."

Tadhg kissed her lightly. "Then we should do as he asked."

"Let me love ye with my great passion?"

"Aye! And to have our joining blessed. Sean has gone to find the priest for me but we dunna want to disrespect Darragh so 'twill be in secret. Is that acceptable to ye?"

Her hands on either side of his face, Tisa kissed him with as much passion as she'd seen Darragh display with Breandan. Tadhg drew her in close, flattening her up against him so that his heavy need pressed against her. Heat spread like a wildfire through her body. Their tongues quickly sparring and stroking. A knock at the door broke them apart, both breathing heavy. Tisa wiped her mouth, she did not want to stop.

"I should… I should open… the door?"

"Aye." He took a deep, slow breath. "Mayhap 'tis Sean."

"And the priest?"

Tadhg nodded. Tisa blew out a loud breath and walked to the door. Sean leaned a shoulder against the frame. His eyes scanned her then he looked beyond her to Tadhg. "Is this a bad time?"

The sincerity of his expression made Tisa giggle. "Nae. 'Tis fine, Sean. Come in with the priest."

Sean led Matthew into the area, his eyes taking in everything around them.

"Have ye never been in here afore now?" Tisa asked.

"I have not. Darragh and his father saw no use for having me around."

Tadhg extended his hand. "Pleased I am to meet ye."

"Oh, we've met before. I was yer priest when ye were but a small child. I dunna suppose ye remember me though. I was quite a bit younger then."

Tadhg tilted his head. "Did ye have red hair?"

"I did!"

"Methinks I do remember ye."

"I spent much time with yer mother back when there was all that trouble."

Tisa saw Tadhg's expression closing off and she took his hand before addressing Matthew. "What was the trouble?"

"Oh, there were many battles. Padraig MacNaughton was sought out by all for his leadership and wisdom. Every time he was called away, he would have me come and pray with him and Moira. The prayers always worked… except for that one time."

"Every time the prayers were effective." Tadhg's voice held a correcting tone. "My father lived to become an old man."

"Yer mother and I believed him lost during the troubles. He had been gone for three years and no word. What else could she think? A blessing 'twas when he came home hale and hearty though a bit thinner for wear."

Tadhg did not respond, his face stricken.

"What is amiss?" Sean asked. He had been listening quietly but Tisa knew his concern. Tadhg's expression was fearsome.

"My father was believed dead?"

Something in Tadhg's tone sparked the memory of what he had told her in the cave. If his mother believed her husband dead, she would not be an adulteress by laying with another.

"She dinna want to believe it. 'Twas yer father," Matthew pointed at Tisa, "who came and tried to help her as best he could. They always prepared for Padraig's return. The last winter was the worst. Miserably cold. Wind that would not let up. Even our food ran out. Many perished."

"Ye were still young, Tadhg." Matthew turned to Tisa. "Yer own mother had just died. Yer father was beside himself but he set his grief aside to care for Moira and keep her hope alive. We often prayed together that Padraig would return, never a word that he may not."

"There must have been at least one time that they believed he would not return."

Tadhg's quiet tone was ominous.

Matthew's face reddened and he averted his gaze. It was suddenly difficult for Tisa to breathe but she couldn't take her eyes off of the priest, as if he were a snake ready to attack.

"Is that not so?" Tadhg prompted him.

"The winter was brutal, Tadhg. We all expected to perish. Yer mother... she was overcome with anguish." Matthew turned to include Tisa. "Yer father was a good man. He loved Padraig with all his heart. He would never betray his dearest friend."

Matthew quieted. After a moment, he swallowed, squared his shoulders, and sat up straight as if about to deliver a eulogy.

"Padraig returned that spring and he brought food stuffs. He had traveled through the harshest conditions to get home so that he could provide for ye and yer mother and yer family. A miracle. A true miracle but ye have the right of it, Tadhg. Yer mother came to me that spring. She told me she was with child and that 'twas Roland O'Brien's baby."

"Brighit." Tisa murmured her dear friend's name.

Tadhg did not move.

"Did she tell Padraig she carried Roland's child?" Sean asked.

"She did not." Matthew glanced at Tadhg. "But we were in agreement, Moira and I, that Brighit's true father needed to be listed within the records. We could not allow her to be married to her half-brother."

Tisa gasped.

"That was why Padraig broke with the O'Brien?" Sean asked but he knew the answer. "He must have seen the records... just as ye saw the records, Tadhg?"

Tadhg glanced away, clearly struggling with all that they had just heard. Tisa's father and Moira had lain together but they were not adulterers. The conditions they must have endured! That they survived at all was a miracle, just as Padraig returning home was a miracle.

"Father, ye have given me great peace of mind." Tadhg offered a sad smile. "I have taken the yoke of betrayal upon me without cause. I have cursed my mother her unfaithfulness and require forgiveness."

"God forgives all who come to Him in sincere repentance and so He does the same for ye now."

The joy on Tadhg's face caused Tisa's breath to catch. It seemed as if she were looking on the Tadhg of old, the Tadhg of her youth.

"I understand yer foul mood now," Sean said. "I knew 'twas a heavy burden ye carried but had no understanding of exactly how heavy."

"I made it much worse, condemning another out of hand, just as my father had condemned her and Roland." Tadhg looked at Matthew. "I wish my father had received peace before he died."

Matthew nodded, a sage expression on his face. "We ken nothing about the moments before death. Mayhap he did have that peace. I wish to believe that he did."

Tadhg smiled again, a peaceful smile. "I will believe it as well."

He turned toward Tisa, taking her hand and kissing her palm. "A load off of me for certain but now I want nothing more than to take ye as my wife."

Sean stepped closer. "I explained to Matthew about Darragh's inability to consummate the marriage and that ye dunna wish to tarnish his memory by publicly declaring but that ye dunna wish to wait."

He winked at Tadhg before kissing Tisa's cheek. "Blessings to ye and yer husband."

Matthew raised his hand.

"And may the blessings of God the Almighty, Creator of heaven and earth, our Lord and Savior, Jesus Christ, and the Holy Ghost, our greatest help in times of trouble, be with ye now and on this binding, Tisa and Tadhg."

The priest kissed Tadhg's cheek and then Tisa's before pulling away. "Ye may kiss yer bride, Tadhg."

Tadhg's serious expression when he turned to her made her heart leap with happiness. This was the day Tisa had dreamed of since she was very small. Tadhg would take her as his wife and she would be his. She'd had no idea of her own strength and that was certainly put to trial but now her trials were over and she was blessed with her deepest desire.

Her eyes closed as he lowered his lips to hers. The feel of his warm mouth pressed against hers set her heart to fluttering. He wrapped a gentle arm around her, pulling her in close. When he broke the kiss, Tisa looked up into the eyes of love.

"I take ye as my wife until time is no more, until the sun no longer shines and the moon no longer rises. Even then, I will hold ye close and cherish ye. For eternity."

Chapter Thirty-Six

Their wedding night was spent ensconced in Tisa's bed. Where she had spent so many nights dreaming of Tadhg, being with him was most enjoyable. The knock at the door the next morning was not.

"Mayhap 'tis just Sean." Tisa tried to slow her rapid heart and donned her gown. She could feel Tadhg's eyes on her still.

"Ye're a lovely lass, wife. Shall I wait here for yer return?"

Tisa exhaled a slow steadying breath. "Yea."

The curtain dropped behind her and she fed more wood to the fire. The knock sounded again, hurrying her to the door. Malcolm and Caireann, a huge smile on both of their faces, stood there.

"Good morning, Tisa!"

Taking her friend into a tight embrace, Tisa stretched her hand toward Malcolm to squeeze it, including him. "Ye've returned. Come in. Have ye only just arrived? A nice honeyed moon?"

Caireann blushed prettily from where she sat beside her husband. Malcolm pulled her closer. "Ye show yer satisfaction with yer husband. That gives me great pleasure. We came here first, mistress. Caireann insisted."

"I am very happy for ye." Tisa hesitated, not certain what to say next. "I hate to ruin that happiness but there has been trouble here. The warriors were competing—a friendly competition and Darragh... Darragh was killed."

Caireann's jaw dropped.

"Darragh was killed? Surely there are few that could best him. The MacNaughtons alone. Tadhg or Sean but surely they would never do that. He is—was yer husband." Malcolm asked, his amazement visible as well. "How did he die, mistress?"

"Gerrit." Tisa's tone conveyed her bitterness. "Though they fought with the mace, Gerrit stuck him with a knife, concealed beneath his cloak."

She shook her head, reliving the scene again. "Aodh was beside himself. His anguish at losing Darragh. He charged at Gerrit, mad as a bull and ready to kill him. That whoreson did the same to Aodh, gutting him in front of everyone."

"Aodh is dead?" Malcolm's tone of disbelief drew his wife's concern.

"Were ye close to him, love?" Caireann asked, though she sounded quite surprised at the revelation.

"He is—was chieftain. He was the head of this clan." Malcolm shook his head. "I did what I was told but no one was close to that man. His word was law. Chaos can easily overwhelm us. Sorry I am that they are dead and that whoreson Gerrit—"

"There's more." Tisa retrieved Caireann's shawl and shook it out across her lap. "Do ye ken how these holes came to be at the back of yer shawl here?"

Caireann peered at the punctures. "I dunna. That is what I was wearing when I was raped. I dunna want it. I dunna even want to look on it. Burn it."

Gripping her friend's hand, Tisa stared into her eyes. "Methinks these holes were left by the man who forced himself on ye. Can ye think of anything else that could have left this round pattern of holes?"

Caireann shook her head.

Tisa included Malcolm before continuing, "I had these same marks after ye found me in the woods. Do ye remember?"

Malcolm's expression went from bewilderment to understanding in a flash as quick as lightning. Tisa yanked at his arm before he could pull it away and stomp out the door. "Nae! Malcolm! Ye canna go now. Gerrit is in the prisoner's hole until they decide what fate awaits him. He's murdered two men, one the chieftain!"

"Malcolm? What is she saying?" Caireann searched his face. "What does Gerri—" she gasped, "Gerrit raped me?"

Tisa watched her, experiencing the trepidation in her own heart, waiting for the onslaught of tears when the truth hit. But Caireann tightened her jaw, her lips flattening into an angry line.

"That foul dog!" Her tone was incensed. "Why? Why would he need to touch me? So many fall all over him."

Caireann's controlled rage was quite a change from the helpless victim. Tisa swelled with pride at this change in her dearest friend. Marriage was making her stronger.

"That foul dog will pay for raping me as well." Caireann turned to Tisa, her appearance intent. "In yer father's household, such an act was never be allowed to go unpunished. No woman was allowed to be mistreated so. They hunted down the man who forced himself upon the woman and gelded him. I expect no less!"

Malcolm smiled, a satisfied smile. Clearly he was in agreement with his wife over Gerrit's punishment. "Aye. 'Twill be so here as well. When will a new chieftain be named?"

"He has been named."

"By whom?"

"Aodh's widow and the clan accepted her will. Lilith's brother, Br—"

"Brian! Ah, a good and fair man." Malcolm placed an arm around his wife. "He will see that all crimes are punished."

"And that way, chaos will not ensue," Caireann said, her grasp of the situation was a good one.

Malcolm gave a heavy sigh. "But I have a sad message that I must bring to Aoife."

"Oh!" Caireann's eyes did fill this time. "Ye must tell Aoife that her son is dead?"

"Ye ken Aoife?" Tisa asked.

"I do now." Caireann's lips curled into a mischievous grin that Tisa had never witnessed on her friend before. "I have met all the outcasts."

In the next moment, Caireann's face lit up, her mouth rounding with a small gasp. "Malcolm! Mayhap they will no longer be outcasts? Was it not Aodh himself that wanted them separate from the rest? And he is dead."

"Did Brian believe the same as Aodh?" Tisa asked.

"He does not." Malcolm's chest expanded. "Brian and his father were kind, generous men. Lilith as well. It was not until Aodh became chieftain that the clan became so brutal."

"Will there be some who wish to remain brutal? Or will they willingly change their ways?" Tisa feared his answer.

"Those who dunna wish to change their ways will become the outcasts."

"As it should be!" Caireann announced in a loud voice.

Sounds of Tadhg moving within the alcove drew both Caireann and Malcolm's eyes to her room then back to Tisa.

"Tadhg," Tisa said.

"Tadhg?" Caireann's jaw dropped. "Tadhg? Is that ye?"

Tisa's husband joined them. "'Tis none other, Caireann."

Caireann fell into his arms. Malcolm's face remained stoic. Tisa knew the man well enough to know he would never ask for an explanation.

265

It was Caireann who turned to Malcolm to explain. "Tadhg is Tisa's betrothed."

"Husband," Tadhg corrected her.

"Husband? Oh, Tisa!" Caireann took Tisa into a tight embrace. "As it should be!"

"Tisa's betrothed? How can he be her betrothed when she was wed to Darragh?" Malcolm appeared to be losing his patience, being completely in the dark as he was. He needed more facts.

"We were betrothed since we were very young. My father broke off the betrothal with no explanation. A misunderstanding," Tadhg said, his eyes on Tisa.

She tipped her head in agreement.

Tadhg continued, "But that left her family open to attack. The Meic Lochlainn offered protection and that was when Tisa was wed to Darragh."

Malcolm frowned and said, "We have not been gone so long but much has happened!"

"Oh, Malcolm, Darragh was a good husband to me. Ye must think me terrible to marry another so quickly."

"It does seem quick to me."

Tears gathered as soon as she started to speak. "Darragh lingered but a short time after he was stabbed. He feared for me being alone. He told me to marry Tadhg and love him, love him as deeply as I could. I honored his wish for me."

Malcolm's intense gaze caused Tisa's breath to cease. She realized this man's opinion of her actions mattered greatly. If Malcolm saw her as anything less than honorable, she would be devastated.

"Mistress, yer husband was a good man. Beg pardon for thinking ye would not respect him in all things. Ye have, again, shown him great respect by following his dictates even at this difficult time for ye. Come, wife, I wish to go to Brian and offer our support."

Caireann pulled her few things together before heading for the door.

"Are the outcasts safe?" Tisa asked.

"They are, mistress. I moved them to a spot closer to the sea. They have always gone there come spring." His eyes rounded in understanding. "Forgive me for not telling ye." He glanced at his bride. "I was a bit distracted."

Relief flooded her, like a weight lifting from her shoulders. "I was much afeared for them but rightly trusted that ye had seen to them."

"My thanks for yer trust. Oh—" Malcolm turned from the door, reached inside his leine and presented a rolled up parchment to Tadhg. "For ye. We came upon yer brother-in-law, Peter, during our travels. He bid me give ye this."

Tadhg took the missive, struggling to appear unaffected. "My thanks, Malcolm."

After Malcolm and Caireann left, Tisa turned on Tadhg with that all-knowing expression. "Yer brother-in-law? That would be Brighit's husband? The Norman knight?"

"Peter." Tadhg lifted the missive. "No doubt he sends his greetings."

"No doubt." Her eyes narrowed. "Here at yer behest? Did ye get word to him of Leofrid's plans?"

Why would he think she would not be aware of all going on around her? An intelligent lass as well as lovely.

"I would not have my sister put in harm's way by a surprise attack on England."

"Agreed! Well? Open it!"

Tadhg,

We bid you greetings, brother, and pray you fare well. Brighit is with me and anxious to show off your nephew to the rest of the MacNaughton Clan. Even Sean. The bearer of this missive tells us you are nearby. At your word we will come before heading south.

Peace be with you.

Peter

Tadhg couldn't hide his joy at this turn of events. "Brighit is here! They have a healthy son!"

"'Tis wonderful news! Can we go to them?"

Tadhg glanced again at the missive. It was simply a message saying they had come for a visit. No more. "I will send word for them to come here forthwith."

"Tell me of Peter. Is he a handsome man?"

Tadhg frowned at her and she smiled in response.

"I ken that he is. He is wonderful and handsome and everything my sweet little sister deserves."

"He loves her greatly."

"Will ye tell Brighit that she and I are sisters?"

"We are wed so ye are sisters."

"Will ye tell her of her true father? Of our father?"

He shrugged. A long, thoughtful movement. "I need to think on it. It may not be worth the upheaval she is bound to feel. Mayhap it no longer matters since she is married to Peter."

"'Twill be wonderful to see Brighit. And a son?" Tisa said, her hands worrying in her lap. "It must be wonderful to have a son."

His heart went out to her. "We have only just begun, Tisa, and ye could be with child even now."

Her face brightened and she closed the distance between them. "True. Mayhap we should set about trying again?"

A wise lass, as well.

"Come," Tadhg lifted the curtain and directed her to their pallet.

He lay down beside her, one leg draped over hers, partially covering her. He kissed just to the side of her lips. "Sweet."

Then the other side. "Very sweet."

Pressing a kiss to each of her brows, then her nose. He glided his hand across her breasts, her nipples stiffening against his palm. "Very nice."

Tisa shifted to wrap her arm about his waist but he resisted her tugging him closer. He took her small hand, kissing the sweetness of her warm palm, before covering his hardened shaft with her hand.

He urged her to fondle him. Stroking, squeezing, and pulling his hard length.

"Very nice."

She was quite eager and he withdrew his hand, again returning to her lovely breasts. He opened her gown to his needy gaze. Each rose-colored peak begged for his attention. Her round globes heavy in his hand when he cupped them. He gasped as she fondled him, grasping him in a firm hand.

Drawing her deep inside his mouth, his tongue traced her hardened peaks before suckling her. Her hand moved more insistently. When she leaned up to reach beneath his leine, her breast pressed further into his mouth. He couldn't hold back the moan, her hands hot and persistent. He traced the flat of his palm along the soft planes of her belly to the juncture of her legs, meeting blessed dampness. His finger prodded her gently and when her stroking began to match his rhythm, he became more enthusiastic, her wetness slicking his hand.

Tadhg moaned and had to still her hand. She was far too adept. He pressed her flat on the bed and covered her. Looking down into those expressive eyes, her lips slightly parted, he knew he was where he belonged. Overwhelming peace filled him.

He licked her lips, teasing her, until she smiled. His tongue plundered her mouth and his tarse slipped deep inside her. He had found heaven. Her skin like velvet, he slid his hand along her scrumptiously tight arse, gripping each cheek. He drove into her softness, knowing he had always belonged right here. She opened to him, encouraging him, small noises emanating from the back of her throat.

"Let me hear ye." He sounded winded but she nodded, her eyes remaining closed, a definite look of pleasure on her face.

Her moans grew louder and her breathing more labored as he loved her. The smell of her was as sweet as an ocean breeze. When she pulsed around him, her passionate cry surrounding them, he pressed into her. Nothing in this world felt as good as this and her moans assured him she felt the same. Fitting tighter than a glove, her body pulled on him with each withdrawal, dragging against him, threatening his staying power. He shoved into her again, lifting her legs to deepen his entry. Her deep-throated moan pushed him over the edge. He was letting go, allowing his release, pumping into her still until at last, he dropped beside her. Exhausted. She snuggled close to his side.

"I have sorely missed something quite enjoyable," Tisa said, licking her lips, but her eyes remained closed.

"I promise to make up to ye all the time we've lost."

She smiled and he kissed the tip of her nose before falling into a deep sleep.

Chapter Thirty-Seven

Sean faced the ocean, listening for the sound of the fog-shrouded waves. Strange sounds carried to him. He imagined he heard men and the creaking of boats. He laughed at his own imagination. Surely the excitement of preparation coursing through his veins was the cause. This time his excitement was not from preparation for battle but from preparation for his return home and to his wife. Lovely Thomasina. His heart ached. He missed her immensely. Talking to her. Listening to her. Helping her with chores. Bedding her. He felt lost without her by his side.

"Sean!"

He whirled around at the familiar voice, never truly expecting to see Peter, but there he was, standing right behind him. He was dressed not as a Norman knight but as a simple traveler. And Brighit stood at his side.

"Peter?" Sean shook his head, his mind confused. "How are ye here?"

"We sent Tadhg word through Malcolm telling him we had come to Eire and were headed to MacNaughton land."

"We met Malcolm and Caireann at the inn," Brighit said.

"Tadhg bid us come here so here we are."

Sean burst into a wide grin and closed the distance to Brighit, taking her into his arms.

"Brighit!" He lifted her up into the air and twirled her around before placing her feet on the ground again. Sean stepped back, hands on his hips. Her face bright, she looked truly happy.

"But look at ye! Ye're no longer with child," Sean said. "Where is the babe?"

"Asleep with Tisa and Tadhg."

"You appear a little homesick standing there, Sean," Peter said, pulling his wife close to his side.

Sean resisted the urge to comment at the protective gesture. "I am missing Thomasina greatly."

"She is well and missing ye, of that I am certain." Brighit cocked a brow, giving him her I-told-you-so expression. "Is it not just as I told ye? Ye needed only to open yer heart to find yer love."

Sean nodded, rubbing his chin. "Ye were correct."

"As you so often are." Peter dropped a kiss to the top of her head. "And you do find great pleasure in saying as much." Peter's words were casual but his eyes remained steady on Sean. "We cannot stay long. Brighit wanted to see her brother."

Despite Brighit's contented expression, there were dark circles under her eyes. A visit to the clan could easily have waited. No, this was definitely connected to Leofrid's plans against the Normans.

"Brighit is eager to get Padraig hom—"

"Padraig? Ye named the child after yer d—da?" The word stuck in his throat. Padraig was not her father. "He would be very proud, Brighit."

Sean's face heated and he hoped they hadn't noticed.

Brighit glanced at her husband, an undeniable look of love. "Peter named him. He said it was a good, strong name."

"Padraig loved Tisa from the first and fell asleep in her arms." Peter glanced around the area. "We decided to take a walk around to see the place."

And get a lay of the land. Any trained knight that journeyed as a simple traveler was wearing a disguise.

"Malcolm is going to show us the caves hidden in the cliffs. People live there."

Peter turned to her, a frown on his face. "You and Caireann go with Malcolm. I will remain behind. I wish to visit with Tadhg."

She turned to Sean. "Is it not wonderful that Tisa and Tadhg are together?"

"They were always meant to be together."

"Surely all will be worked out between the clans."

Sean believed Brighit was correct yet again.

Sean's admiration for Peter increased the more he watched his gentle and caring ways with Brighit. He treated his wife with the utmost care, like a precious treasure. He treated their babe the same. A man of great honor and duty. Sean would be proud to fight alongside him if need be.

Malcolm's long strides made the walk to the caves more of a run but he seemed to be a man on a mission. He noticed Brighit's struggles not at all and his own bride's even less. Sean was glad he'd been asked to accompany them and followed up behind the single line.

"Malcolm?" Caireann called to him even while she tried to keep up with him. "Is aught amiss, my love? Ye're all but making us run."

The huge man stopped and glanced back at them.

"Please. Is there something ye have not shared with us?" His wife placed her small hand on his arm. "Ye are in a great hurry."

Malcolm's feelings were well-hidden beneath a full beard but Sean did not miss the intensity of his gaze. "Beg pardon. I wish to get there before the rain."

Caireann looked up through the canopy of trees overhead. "It does not look like rain to me."

Sean held little Padraig tightly in his arms. The babe slept, totally unaffected by the speed or the weather. "Mayhap we are close?"

"We are. Take my arm, love." Malcolm offered an arm to his wife, returning to a much slower pace. "Just a bit further."

The babe started making a quiet sucking noise. Sean was surprised when Brighit turned around to look at the child. Could she have heard the quiet sound? She nodded at Sean but kept up her steady pace behind Malcolm.

A short walk along the cliff and they were tucked safely inside the cave. Coming up last, Sean took a moment to look out over the sea. As he had begun to suspect, several Norman vessels lay in wait just beyond the bay. Most of the clans Aodh had gathered to support Leofrid against the king had left, despite the Godwin's attempts to coerce them to stay. Even the great Ronan had sent word he was no longer able to come. A battle would not ensue.

The babe made a noise in his arms and he hurried in behind the others.

There were about ten people within. Three children, a few old men and women, and one striking woman with long hair who hugged Malcolm.

Brighit scooped Padraig from Sean's arms.

She smiled her thanks. "He must be hungry."

As if on a signal, the small face screwed up to let out a large wail. It called the others to them like a siren.

"Oh, a real baby." A pretty little girl started toward them, a limp barely slowing her down. She had long hair and big eyes. She stopped suddenly, ran back, but quickly returned, a doll in her arms. "Just like mine."

Watching Brighit intently, she mimicked the way she rocked the baby and bared her breast for the feeding.

"Ye've a lovely baby, too," Brighit said.

Padraig locked his tiny mouth on to her dark nipple with great eagerness. The suckling noise filling the small space.

"And what is yer name?" Brighit asked.

"I am Aednat. This is Tisa." Aednat indicated the doll she now held to her breast.

Sean went back to the entrance. He could make out seven vessels. Malcolm came to stand beside him. "Peter asked me to get these three to safety. I dinna want them to be alarmed."

"And what of Tisa?"

"Tadhg did not worry for her. She kens how to get to the other cave if need be but he does not believe there will be any need."

The woman with the long hair came forward, surprising Sean when she hugged him. "Do ye remember me?"

Sean was certain he had never met this woman before. "I dunna."

Malcolm went out along the path they'd just come up, leaving them alone.

"I have not seen ye since ye were very small. Mayhap ye remember my son? Malachi?"

The image of a skinny, blond boy with a huge lock of hair that constantly fell in his eyes came to Sean's mind. Malachi. He'd had his own bow and arrow and a broadsword made just for him.

"I do remember a young'un by that name."

The woman smiled. "That surprises me not. Ye two were very close."

"He had his own weapons." Sean frowned his dislike. "I was never allowed to touch."

"True! But *I* would let ye touch them. Do ye remember that?

He smiled. "I do remember that."

"I am Aoife."

"How do I ken ye?"

"We were of the same clan, Sean."

"Ye are a MacNaughton?"

"I am not."

This same woman, but younger, alongside his own mother hard at work flashed through his mind. "Did ye ken my mother?"

"Very well. We are sisters."

More memories flooded him. His mother smiling. Singing with Aoife. A huge fire burning before them. Sean and other children dancing. Music surrounding them.

"Figs!" Sean's face heated at his outburst. The memory of this woman giving him the sweet fruit any time he asked her came to him. He remembered he liked this woman. More memories flooded him. Her helping him don his leine. Washing his face at the stream. Helping him to play a wooden flute. "Methinks I do remember ye."

"A long time ago now." Aoife sighed and looked over at the little girl who was propping her doll on her shoulder just as Brighit was doing with Padraig. "So long ago."

"Where is Malachi?" Sean glanced over the others but there were no men young enough here.

She kept her eyes on Aednat. "Long dead now. So many dead. Now Darragh."

"Darragh was yer son as well?" Sean stilled. Darragh and Malachi were brothers. Both were his cousins. He shook his head before continuing. "I feel yer loss, Aoife. To lose two sons is a terrible blow."

She turned a sad smile to him. "And how fares my sister?"

"She has passed as well." Sean swallowed, again feeling his own sadness when she died. "I am all that remains from my family."

Aoife's brows lowered into an angry scowl. "That is not so, Sean. Ye have many who are kin to ye."

Sean sifted through his mind for any information to confirm what she was saying. He had a great amount of money and land from his mother but he never understood from where it came. His childhood memories, until now, were of being in the MacNaughton Clan and that his wealth was not spoken of.

"I dunna ken them and my mother never spoke of them that I remember. Why would that be? Surely there was some trouble that would make my mother leave?"

Aoife shrugged. "Yer mother left to be with yer father. Our clan, your mother's and mine, is from south of the Liffey. There *were* troubles. The Christian beliefs battled the pagan way. It caused much strife. My own Aodh had been baptized a Christian but followed the pagans after Malachi died. He was angry with God for taking him. I had hoped to turn him back." She shrugged, seeming to age before his eyes. "When he set me aside, I had no choice but to remain here with my granddaughter and care for her."

"The little girl is Malachi's daughter?"

"She is. Both Malachi and his wife are dead. She is all that I have left of him. Aednat?"

The little girl turned, her expression of pure joy caused Sean to smile.

"Come here. Meet yer cousin, Sean."

Sean could not have believed the little girl could appear any happier but when she came toward him, her intense gaze of pure love overwhelmed him and his breath hitched. He cleared his throat.

"We are family? Ye are so big!" She turned to Aoife. "Will I become this big?"

"I dunna believe so."

Sean pulled Aednat up onto his lap and she immediately wrapped a tiny arm around his shoulder.

"Would ye ever want to be this big?" he asked.

"Ye must be able to see so much at such a great height."

Nodding slowly, Sean struggled to remain composed at the awe in her voice. "True, but I am always the one called when something is too high to reach."

She frowned suddenly, thinking hard. "And that is a problem for ye?"

A quick mind. "Sometimes. When I am very busy, I dunna always want to come and help."

"Will ye stay with us? We dunna have many things up high but I would like ye to be here."

The sincerity on her face, the intensity of her gaze, made Sean realize he did want to stay with her. He was enamored with her. "Mayhap ye can come with me."

Aoife offered him a shy smile. "Mayhap that is what we should do."

"Ye are family. Mayhap ye would come and meet my wife, Thomasina. She will soon have a baby as well."

"Oh! Like that one?" Aednat pointed to Brighit who had moved closer. Padraig once again asleep in her arms.

"Just like that one."

Malcolm came in, his face lined with worry. "Can ye stay here with them, Sean?"

"What is amiss?" Sean felt his angst and stood.

"I was told to remain here and send ye back," Malcolm said. "I need to return. I have something I must see to myself."

Malcolm's angst and his urgency unsettled him, making him anxious. Malcolm was a man who did not deviate from his orders. He glanced at Caireann who sat talking with two young boys. Something was bothering the man that he did not wish to share with Sean. Malcolm needed to return, for whatever reason. Sean would respect his decision.

"I will remain here." Sean glanced toward his aunt. "Tell Tadhg that I have met my mother's sister and wish to remain here a bit longer."

Malcolm blew a sigh of relief. "I will."

The big man took Caireann into his arms and kissed her goodbye. Sean avoided Brighit's questioning glance.

"I will return anon," Malcolm said.

Brighit nodded, her concern gone. "Thank ye for bringing us here, Malcolm."

Aednat jumped up and grabbed Malcolm around the legs before bending her head back to look up at him. "I love ye, Malcolm. Thank ye for bringing me my family."

Malcolm caressed her head. "My pleasure, little one. Be good."

Chapter Thirty-Eight

The group of five older men sat at the head table. Brian, much younger, sat between them in Aodh's former place of honor. The council. Benches were lined up opposite to watch the event. The area between the onlookers and the head table allowed a small place for both the accused, seated on a stool, and the witnesses as they were brought forward. Tadhg sat to the side so that he could watch their faces.

Leofrid was not among the six. He sat on a stool to their left, his face tight and body stiff, separated as if he did not belong at all. Tadhg had to agree. He was not a part of this clan and deserved no say in how they handled things. To say Leofrid appeared uneasy over the proceedings fell far short. If the man were given a broadsword, he would probably slice off the heads of the six men and Gerrit without pausing for a breath.

One by one the witnesses spoke. All who saw what had transpired, which included all the warriors who had not yet returned home, came forward. Sean was not needed so Tadhg had thought it best for him to see to Brighit and the baby. Peter worried less knowing she was away from all that was going on. He'd kept his plans to himself which suited Tadhg just fine since he trusted the man. The MacNaughton warriors were ready in case trouble erupted.

The recounting of events were the same. There were no deviations. Gerrit wielded the blade that had killed both Darragh and his father.

"What say ye, Gerrit?" Brian spoke in a loud, confident voice.

Brian's eyes never wavered from Gerrit who slowly stood before them, dressed in his full leather attire and even his cloak. Arrogant was the best way to describe him. His shoulders back. His face empty of any feeling. He looked more as if he were about to be dispatched for a battle than to defend himself against murder charges.

"I dunna deny what has been spoken of me. I took the life of both Darragh and Aodh. I did so only as a last attempt to spare my own life." His eyes darted toward Leofrid. "Darragh had decided to murder me even though it was a friendly competition we were engaged in. I ken not why he chose to do so."

Mumbling rippled through the people in the longhouse behind Tadhg. The fire had been allowed to die out due to the overwhelming heat of the tightly packed bodies.

"Or why he was not halted." Gerrit's tone indicated his indignation. "I acted to defend myself."

A door opened but Tadhg kept his eyes on Brian. The man was impressive, handling this trial with the strength of a true leader.

"And what of Aodh?" Brian asked.

Gerrit's nostrils flared and he paused before answering, as if for control. "The man came at me in a rage. All were witnesses. He sought to end me. I was defending myself. "

Movement behind Tadhg called for his attention but he ignored it.

Brian tipped his ear toward the man on his left, faced him, and then nodded before continuing with his questions.

"So yer claim is that ye murdered both our chieftain and his son in defense. ?"

"It was defense." Gerrit crossed his arms in a stubborn stance. "I will say no more."

Brian nodded, the men on either side gathering close to him. Their words were few and they did not carry. They separated, each leaning back now.

Brian glanced toward Leofrid. "Leofrid, I ken that Gerrit is yer man but he has come before me as we are the ones who have been wronged by his actions. Will ye accept the ruling of this council?"

Leofrid's eyes widened and he sat up a little straighter as if happy to again be shown any type of consideration. Since Aodh's death, many began to demonstrate a lack of respect toward him and his cause. It seems Tadhg and Sean's opinion that what happened outside of Eire was of little concern to them was shared by most.

Godwin tipped his head, momentarily closing his eyes. "I will accept yer decision as fair and right."

Brian took a deep breath. "Then Gerrit, I must say ye have the right of it. Darragh was trying to end ye. The why of it we will never ken."

The murmuring again. Rumors. There had been a lot of talk. Always in defense of Darragh. He'd been taken advantage of by the man. Nothing specific, only that it had been unusually cruel and may have included sodomy. These events were now considered the very reason Aodh had handed Gerrit off to Leofrid. Darragh's father had been trying to protect his son. The offenses were considered justification for Darragh wanting Gerrit dead. The reason Darragh was not stopped.

"Aodh's action as an aggrieved father is understandable. He sought to avenge the murder of his son. For this, ye will be banned from our clan and if anyone encounters ye, they have the right to end ye."

"And what of rape? What punishment will he have for that?"

Tadhg whipped around to see Malcolm just behind him. Caireann's shawl hung from his hand.

Gasps and whispers rippled through the crowd.

"What have ye there?" Brian asked. "Come forth, Malcolm."

Malcolm glared at the man seated on the stool, stopping just a few feet in front of the trestle. He shook out the material.

"This is what my Caireann was wearing when she was knocked down and forcibly taken from behind by this animal."

Brian pointed to the shawl. "And that is the proof?"

"It is."

Malcolm turned and took the few steps that brought him directly in front of Gerrit. With tight lips and a locked jaw, Malcolm put his hand to the brooch holding Gerrit's cloak. Before the man knew what Malcolm was about, he ripped it from Gerrit's shoulder.

Gerrit pulled back, aghast at this maltreatment. He turned wide eyes on Leofrid. "My lord!"

Leofrid could no doubt read the same fear as Tadhg saw on Gerrit's face. After a moment's hesitation, Leofrid turned away from the prisoner in a definite show of abandonment. For the first time, Gerrit's shoulders slumped.

Malcolm returned to Brian with the brooch, placing it on the table before him. Malcolm put the material over the bejeweled item, each prominent stone matching up with the unusual holes. The men all nodded their heads in agreement. Brian's grave expression said he was convinced. He motioned for Malcolm to step aside. The large man moved exceedingly close to Gerrit as if to guard him, even ensuring his punishment if need be.

"Gerrit. Did ye force yerself on Caireann?"

"I dinna."

"We have evidence here that ye did, indeed, rape the girl."

"I dinna."

Brian glanced to both sides, being met by nods of approval from all. "The council agrees this is sufficient proof that ye did."

"I dinna."

"The punishment for rape in this clan is gelding."

Gerrit's jaw dropped in objection. "She wanted me—"

The loud sound of Malcolm's fist solidly connecting with Gerrit's jaw echoed throughout the room. The man was knocked off his stool, falling flat on his back. After a stunned silence, the crowd erupted with laughter.

Malcolm glared down at the man. "Watch yer mouth."

Brian sat at the table, his hand in front of his own mouth and waited for the laughter to die down. Gerrit only pulled himself back onto the stool once Malcolm moved away. He remained close, his arms about his chest.

When the attention was back on Brian, he stood. "Gerrit we find ye guilty of rape and a gelding will take place immediately." His eyes fell on Malcolm. "Malcolm, will ye administer the punishment?"

Over Gerrit's loud objections, Malcolm smiled and announced. "Without hesitation."

Stiff lipped, Leofrid kept his eyes averted as Gerrit's hands were tied behind his back and he was forcibly taken from the longhouse. Several men followed behind, although it certainly looked like Malcolm had the man under control. Brian and his advisors stepped out from around the table, relief on their faces. The older men sauntered off.

Tadhg approached him.

"Well done, Brian." He meant the compliment but he was also wary of Leofrid. Brian should not be left alone with the man.

"My thanks for yer support, Tadhg. It means much to me."

Leofrid came up close to them, as if they were all well acquainted. Brian's open expression shut down. A wise leader.

"Well done, Brian. Beg pardon for my man's behavior. Some bad blood between the two. Awful about Aodh. Terrible loss for the cause."

Brian offered a noncommittal grunt.

"And have ye been practicing with yer men, Tadhg?" Leofrid asked.

Tadhg's breath quickened. "My men are always ready."

"Good to hear. Very good." Leofrid scanned the room. "Enough have remained. Enough indeed."

"Despite my request for a time of mourning, ye and yer men have remained." Brian's clipped reply spoke of his own irritation with the situation. "Methinks ye taking yer soldiers and leaving this place is best for all."

Clearly shocked, Leofrid glanced between them as if not certain of what he'd heard. "Why ever would I leave this place?"

Tadhg's hands grew slick. He hadn't anticipated open defiance from this man.

"Because I tell ye to."

"There is an agreement."

"There is not." Brian's louder tone was calling attention. A quick glance around told Tadhg they were not just his own men that remained. "Any agreement ye had was with Aodh. He is dead as is any agreement ye had with him. 'Tis not a difficult concept to grasp, Leofrid. We dunna choose to side with ye against the Normans."

"And who exactly is we?" Leofrid looked around, catching the eye of many of the more belligerent warriors who now moved in their direction, surrounding them.

MacNaughton men shifted as well, one for nearly every one of Leofrid's. Tadhg wanted to kick himself for his own stupidity. How could he have believed Leofrid would step down and just go away? The man had the most to lose. It was his family's kingdom that he fought for when he went up against the Normans. A kingdom already taken from him. The truth was this man would fight until the death.

A loud commotion outside that sounded like a cry of alarm tightened Tadhg's gut. He prayed Leofrid had not managed to rile even more men to his cause. The flash of surprise he glimpsed on the man's face gave him hope. All within the longhouse flooded out the door and into the yard.

The fog had lifted and seven large Norman ships could now be seen coming into the bay. One boat was already sending men ashore who were walking up the rocks. All the men wore shields, sidearms, and helms. The weapons pointed down indicated they did not come for battle but could easily be made ready.

One man stood out although he was fully mailed, the same as the twenty or so men coming up around him. Lord John of Essex from Brighit's wedding to Peter. Even without seeing his face, the knight was easily recognizable by his swagger.

Brian shot a glance at Tadhg before they both turned to see Leofrid's stricken expression.

"Normans!" Leofrid announced. He turned around in a circle, his eyes searching out his warriors. "Men!"

Even the men that had followed the Godwin out of the longhouse were now keeping their distance. These Normans were well armed and well protected. They appeared to be coming casually up the shore but any seasoned warrior could see they were in a formation that could easily be closed into a wall of defense.

"Men!" Leofrid's voice cracked. "Where are my men?"

Brian shrugged. Peter came up to stand on the far side of Leofrid, never taking his eyes off the men coming toward them. Tadhg didn't miss the slight nod Peter gave to John.

Once Brian stepped forward, signaling he was leader here, John approached him.

"Hail," John said.

Tadhg would swear he felt Leofrid take a step back.

"Welcome." Brian reached out a hand toward John.

The men behind were grouping in twos and threes, perhaps in a sign of solidarity against the daggers Leofrid was shooting at them. The man's stench wafted to him. He must be sweating torrents.

"Normans?" Tadhg couldn't resist asking the man. He was rewarded by a wide-eyed stare followed by a short nod. "These are the soldiers you would have us fight?"

Leofrid sighed in relief, misunderstanding the question.

"Why would you need to fight these men?" Peter had stepped closer to Leofrid and now looked past him to Tadhg. "Have they done anything to you?"

Tadhg stepped closer as well. "They have not."

Brian and John, his face still hidden, came to stand before Leofrid. The panic of the man between them could be measured by his breathing but still no one said anything.

"How have you been, Leofrid?" John asked.

"Do I ken ye, man?" Leofrid's accent had become a bit stronger. "I dunna ken ye. Show me yer face."

"Oh, you do know me, Leofrid. And my wife sends her regards." John shook off his helmet.

Leofrid jerked away but not fast enough. Tadhg and Peter each clasped a hand on his arm. Tadhg held tight against the jerking motion Leofrid made in an attempt to free himself.

John raised both brows. "No words for your dear cousin's husband? The dear cousin who begged your life be spared?"

"Oh, John! I dinna recognize ye. How fare ye?"

Peter turned to face the man. "Not well, since the man whose life he spared now plans an attack on the very soil he was told not to return to. Ever."

"Hello, Peter." John smiled, looking at Peter and then Tadhg. "Tadhg."

Leofrid glanced at the men on either side of him as if he'd never seen them before. "Ye ken this Norman?"

"Very well," Peter said. "I am a Norman as well."

"Married to my only sister," Tadhg added, not holding back his own smile.

"Unhand me. I have done nothing wrong." Leofrid's blustering seemed so sincere.

"So that you can get away and start more trouble for me?" John's even tone did not match the fearsome anger etched in his face. "I prefer to be with my wife now, yet here I am. With you. I do not wish to have to do this again."

"Ye will not, my lord." Leofrid bowed his head, trying to kneel but they would not release his arms. "Beg pardon. I had forgotten myself. I am forever in yer debt for sparing my life—"

"Silence! You beg pardon only for being caught." John glanced around the camp. "And where is that she-devil Abigail?"

"I dunna—"

"John!" The blur of a woman running past and throwing herself at John startled Tadhg. "My John! You've come to take me back."

Abigail gripped John's face and kissed him. He shoved her off.

"Enough, Abigail. I have come to arrest you—you and your lover."

"Arrest me? Whatever for?" Abigail's innocent expression was well played. "I have done nothing but love you and wait patiently for you to come back to me."

John took a step away, his eyes studying her intently. "Do you think me the fool?"

She took a timid step forward. "Of course not, my love." Abigail placed a hand on John's chest. "I wish only to be with you again. Our son—"

"Ah, yes. The lie you told my wife."

"Ye have a son?" Leofrid asked.

"There is no son!" John barked the statement as he jerked back, his eyes never leaving her face. "There will be no son. I am married to the woman I love. You are not that woman. You have never been that woman."

Fat tears slid down her cheeks, her eyes rounding in pain. Tadhg noticed her hands clenching at her side. If not for that, he would have believed this entire act. He moved his hand to his sword. Leofrid had stopped struggling, seemingly as mesmerized by the black-haired woman as everyone else. Her long, flowing gown did little to mask the sensual body beneath. She slid her hand down her side as if to call attention to it as well.

"You have hurt me to the core, my love. That woman has bewitched you."

John finally looked at Leofrid again. "You have accepted this woman into your bed, have you not?"

"Isn't that what ye had hoped for when ye sent her away with me?"

Abigail spit on the ground at Leofrid's feet. "I never wanted this man to touch me. Ever."

"I would not wish this woman on anyone," John said.

"You do not mean what you are saying. That witch—she has cast her spell on you."

John kept his eyes on Leofrid. "And you allow her to speak of your cousin in that manner? Intimating she is a witch?"

Her jaw dropped when she turned her face to Leofrid. "Your cousin? My John is married to *your* cousin?"

Abigail screeched her outrage, the ungodly sound piercing the air. In one swift motion, she pulled the dagger from John's belt and buried the blade into Leofrid's gut. "You foul pig!"

Leofrid collapsed, his body heavy between Tadhg and Peter. Dark red blood dripped from Abigail's hand where she still gripped the weapon. John shoved her down, face first, his knee in her back, and ripped the dagger from her tight grasp.

"Let me up, John." She wiggled beneath him, throwing the words over her shoulder. "I won't hurt you. I would never hurt you."

"Phillip!" John called and a man came forward from the ranks. He tied her arms behind her back but left her on the ground. Her wriggling working her deeper into the mud.

John was breathing heavy when he dropped to his knees beside Leofrid. The man's unseeing eyes were wide with surprise.

"He's dead," Peter said.

They exchanged glances. Tadhg searched the crowds that were closing in, looking for any sign of a threat. But there was no malice on any of the faces, just a morbid curiosity.

"Well, you will not have to worry about what to tell Rowena."

"Rowena. Rowena." Abigail had managed to get to her feet, her gown caked with mud. She spit again. "That whore."

Rage covered John's face. Tadhg wasn't sure whether he hoped John would slap her or if Tadhg needed to defend her from him. But John merely gripped her chin tight, piercing her with his eyes. "I am sorry I ever laid eyes on you, Abigail."

"NO! You don't mean that, John."

But John had turned away from her.

"Brian, have you any use for her? If not, I will bring her to King William and he can do with her as he likes."

"No! No, John!"

Brian glanced at her, a grave expression. "My sister has need of help. I could present her as a gift, see if it is something Lilith would appreciate."

John nodded.

"We will need to brand her first in case she believes she can escape," Brian said.

"John! I do not belong here. Take me back with you."

"And keep her well secured."

John agreed. "Do with her what you will. I have no objection."

Brian signaled to one of his men who came forward. "Where would ye have me bring her?"

"Give her some time in the prisoner's hole. Methinks she'll be a much better help after that."

Kicking and screaming, Abigail was dragged up the hill and away from the longhouse.

All eyes remained on the beautiful woman whose continued screams carried to them until she could no longer be seen or heard.

The men exchanged glances.

"We need to have Leofrid buried," Peter stated the obvious. "Is there a priest who can help us with that?"

Brian nodded. "At least for now we have a priest."

"Is he going somewhere?" John asked.

"I believe he wishes to travel south with Tadhg," Brian replied. "Something about wishing to spend his last days in a warmer clime and among people from his past."

"Bah, he has many days left. A ploy for us to take him with us." Tadhg laughed quietly. "We will be happy to have him return with us to MacNaughton land."

"And Tisa?" Brian asked.

"Aye. She will return to where she belongs."

"I have heard enough of yer story to ken that is true, Tadhg. But for now," Brian wrapped an arm around both Tadhg and John's shoulders, "Come! Finally we have real cause for celebration."

As they headed toward the longhouse, John stopped to look back at Peter. "Are you not coming?"

"I would prefer to find Brighit. I can let them know all is well and bring them back down. Besides," Peter tipped his chin towards the other soldiers just coming up the beach. "You will have your hands full explaining to the men there'll be no more excitement here."

"That is the way of it," John said. "And I would choose that for this night. Tomorrow? Well, tomorrow I return to my Rowena whom I hope to not leave again anytime soon... if at all."

Chapter Thirty-Nine

After seeing Peter and Brighit back to York, John had returned to Rowena as quickly as he was able. If not for the added protection of guards required for all earls, he'd have made much better time. All he wanted was to be home and have some time with his wife and new born. To instead be met by a missive from the king demanding not only his immediate presence but his wife's as well, had pushed his patience beyond endurance. It was Rowena alone that soothed his ire and kept him focused on the truly important things.

Rowena pulled at her bodice, the babe crying across the Great Hall at Westminster Abbey no doubt causing havoc to her own need to feed her child. Ruth, however, was tucked safely away in the upper chamber, sleeping. The trip here had been difficult for both of John's ladies. He wrapped an arm around his wife's shoulder holding her tight against him.

"My thanks for attending me in this as well," he said.

Rowena shook her head, "Even if I had been given a choice, which I was not, I would not have you come to this man unprotected."

"Ah, you are my protection?"

Her eyes widened in one of her do-you-really-need-to-ask looks. "I am. I have no fear of this man. He is nothing more than a bully."

John kissed the top of her head and took a quick look around to ensure no one heard her comment against the king. "I see. Being wed to me has made you fearless."

She dipped her head, as if trying to hide her smile from him. "It has indeed."

Rowena wiggled closer to him. The dampness of her dress made him sorry he'd not left her home, accepting the wrath of the king for not bringing her. As it was, he was most certain the king had heard about Leofrid, hence the summons.

"Would you prefer I return you to see to Ruth?"

"I thought you preferred my company to standing here and waiting for William alone."

He indicated the crowd of people in the large room with a sweep of his hand. "Verily I am not alone!"

Tipping her head back, she smiled. "None as desirable as me!"

"Not even close." He dropped a chaste kiss on her mouth.

She darted a glance around herself and put her lips closer to his ear. "I had been raised a genteel lady, my lord, having to fight was not in my training but I have learned. Have I not?"

Pulling away, her frown deepened when he didn't answer immediately.

"My love, you know I would not have you fight on my behalf."

"I will not allow the slander against you to continue. Any who would speak ill of you will have a piece of my mind."

"Truly it is not necessary. It concerns me that you have not made up with your handmaiden. Are you certain that is how you want things to be? Even now with Ruth? Would you not trust Joan more with our daughter than Helen?"

Helen was matronly but not doting. Rowena spent very little time apart from their daughter. John was just not convinced it was totally her choice.

"You are wrong." Rowena shook her head. "It is not the way *I* would have things. It is just the way things are. Joan would have had me choose Arthur over you. I would not. She did not acquiesce even after my choice was made so I set her aside. Her choice."

"I've seen her attempts at making amends, my lady. Mayhap when we return home, you can sit with her and assess her feelings again?"

Rowena rolled her eyes and sighed. "Yes, my lord."

John lowered his face to her. "I would prefer you willingly agree with your husband than to merely give in."

"John!" King William's loud voice caused all other chatter in the room to stop abruptly.

John and Rowena glanced around the twenty or so people in front of them in line to search out the king. He sat in his large chair, great furs about his shoulders, and a large, gold chain around his neck. With beckoning fingers, he motioned them both closer. No one dared object as they passed by the others who had been waiting much longer than them.

King William was much more imposing than her Uncle Harold had ever been. Harold was kind and loving. William never smiled, not a real smile. His eyes were never kind. He was a brute.

Rowena curtseyed deeply, pulling her shawl tight around her milk-stained gown while John bowed at the waist. King William's eyes held that condescending look she remembered far too well from his many visits during John's absence from the castle. John had returned to Normandy in the hopes of never having to consummate his marriage to her since he believed her some wild creature that would murder him in his sleep. That was until he found her no longer being threatened by the king's guard. He found her quite fetching and desirable then. Rowena smiled at the memory of his eagerness to get in her bed.

"Rowena. Your smiling face assures me, as does your untouched figure, that motherhood becomes you."

"My thanks, my lord."

William looked at John. "And you! You look no worse for wear and mayhap in need of a few more hours of sleep."

"Indeed, my lord."

"Leave us!" King William made the announcement with a clap of his hand. None hesitated to follow his orders, quickly exiting the room. He motioned for food, drink and a seat to be brought forward.

The cushioned seat was wide enough that both John and Rowena could sit before him, like good little puppies. She struggled to maintain her composure when her nerves were making everything seem extremely funny. If John were to find out she was pregnant yet again, she wondered if he would radiate as happily as he was now. His smile was quite genuine.

"I will not make you stay overlong here. I just wish to see how you two fare."

William's eyes stayed on Rowena's a bit too long. She focused on keeping her hands still in her lap.

"We are well, my lord. The villagers have accepted me as lord and sworn their allegiance to you as requested. They prosper in the fields under your generosity."

"And how do you see the villagers, Rowena?"

"They have great respect for their lord." She turned a genuine smile of appreciation toward John. "They know him to be a kind man. They do not hesitate to bring to him their many concerns and he deals fairly with them."

"These are the Saxons you speak of?"

John's sharp gaze turned on the king.

Her pulse quickened. "There are both Saxons and Normans on our lands."

"We have a great mix of Gaels and Celts as well, my lord. Did you wish to have an exact accounting of those living on our land? It would take me time but—"

William waved his hand. "No. No."

Moving his jaw side to side, William kept his gaze fixed to Rowena's face. Her hands grew slick. A slow nod followed by a harrumph, Rowena swallowed with a loud gulp. John cleared his throat.

"My lord, is there anything in particular you need to speak with us of?"

King William finally faced John, his back stiffening as he adjusted himself, his shoulders pushing back against the fine cushion covered in silk, the color of robin's eggs.

"Tell me why you were in Eire."

Rowena pressed her lips together to keep her gasp from escaping. John had told her the king would know. They were his ships, his knights, his earl.

"My lord, I had heard a rumor that supporters hoping to overthrow you were gathering in the north. I had two choices. I could send you word, wait for your reply, and then act or I could immediately see to the rumors and report back to you after the fact."

"Hmm, and is that what you are doing now? Reporting after the fact?"

"I have nothing to report. I found no reason to bring it up. Rumors, nothing more. The adventure cost you nothing as I saw to all expenses including the refitting of your ships. They are in better repair now than before we went."

"Mmm, a loyal knight you are, John. Always following my dictates, yes?" His words were wrapped in sarcasm.

Rowena's heart pounded loudly in her chest. She wouldn't be surprised if they both turned to her and asked, "Is that *your* heart I can hear?"

A giggle threatened to erupt and she coughed into her hand.

"My lord, I cannot possibly report everything that I do. You must trust that I act in your best interest as I always have. Do you question my loyalty? You have only to say so. If you wish me to step down as earl, I will do that as well."

John's humbling tone riled Rowena. Her husband was the better man here and she resented vehemently the king implying anything else.

King William settled back again, his lips puckering in that thoughtful way. A door opened behind them. The king barked his command to leave.

She gulped again, torn between throwing herself at this man's feet and begging for mercy or obeying John's suggestion that she stay calm, sit still, and only answer what was asked. The moments dragged by. The king glanced down and sighed quietly before facing John. Trepidation flooded her until she noticed the softening of his features, the brighter blue of his eyes.

"John. I have never spoken of your father to you."

Rowena's throat clenched. She was certain John was no longer breathing. The black cloud that had always hung over him came from the fact that he could not name his father. No claim made on him. To John, that spoke of his own worthlessness as a man. A difficult thing to overcome.

"You know who my father is?" His words were tight as if they'd been squeezed out between clenched teeth.

She dare not look at him and see his pain.

"I do."

Silence ensued. Complete, utter silence. She imagined John running over his miserable life in his mind. All this time, William could have named his father, given John rest from the constant uncertainty that hung around his neck like a stone.

"How long have you known?"

The words hung in the air. Heavy and thick.

"Since the first. I kept watch over you. Kept you safe."

A childhood spent in abject poverty, beaten by a couple that cared nothing for him.

"I was not always successful. I thought the monastery might be better for you. When I heard you had your father's propensity for... adventure, I realized I was wrong."

A monastery where he dared not show any "passions" of the flesh or he would be condemned to the fires of hell.

"My father was a knight?" John's voice cracked.

He'd shared with Rowena that he would pretend William was his father, working especially hard to please him and receive his approval.

"My dearest, most loyal friend."

Names ran through Rowena's mind. De Boer, Mortimer, FitzOsbern, De Noer. She had heard so many but no faces to put to them.

Rowena turned to John. His stoic expression ready to crack. Just as she was convinced he was not going to ask for the name, his mouth curved into a sad smile.

"I have never hidden the fact that I wished to know who my father was. A bastard yourself, you were raised always knowing who your father was. Always knowing you would take over your father's dukedom. I had no such inheritance. I was thrown away. Discarded. Unwanted."

"He did not know of your existence." William's tone implied that explained everything. Did it?

"Your closest friend and you did not deem it necessary to tell him of me?" John dismissed that with a wave of his hand. "You did not deem it necessary to tell me?"

William's eyes never wavered from John's face as if measuring his response, deciding how best to reveal the name that would change John's life forever. He toyed with him. Rowena wanted to rip the man's eyes out.

"William FitzOsbern is your sire."

There it was! William FitzOsbern. Rowena couldn't release her breath but William was not done.

"Some Northumbrian wench had captured his attention. He'd spent the entire winter bedding her. When he learned she was the daughter of Morcar, he set her aside."

"Why?" Rowena's face heated at her outburst, spreading down her neck when William turned his intense gaze on her. She hadn't meant to demand more clarification but truth be told, being the daughter of some northern earl explained little.

"Morcar had sought to defy me. FitzOsbern's loyalty to me was unshakeable, even in love."

The sudden silence and the way William glanced between them seemed an unspoken condemnation. He knew about Leofrid.

"You are very much like him," William said. "An amazing knight. An amazing warrior. An amazing man." Tears filled his eyes. "I take pleasure in spending time with you, John, on your own right but when I see my dear friend in your mannerisms? Your expressions? Your laugh? I had always considered myself truly blessed."

The heat in the room was rising. There was a knock at the door. William's irritation was ready to explode when the door opened behind them.

"My lord, I have been sent for Rowena. Her babe—"

Rowena was up and turning around without being given leave to do so. "Ruth? What has happened?"

The hefty gray-haired man sputtered. "Noth—no, forg—forgive me, my lord."

"Just answer her question!" William shouted, causing the man to sputter even more.

Rowena curtseyed before the king, "My lord, may I have leave to see to my child?"

"Saxons don't use wet nurses?"

She dropped her eyes, grinding her teeth to keep from defending herself against his condescending tone.

"I wish her to care for our daughter, my lord." John's interruption came just in time. "Surely we can continue our discourse without her presence?"

"Bring the child here!" William ordered. The door closed behind them.

Rowena struggled to draw breath but returned to her seat beside John. Unbelievable arrogance.

William began pacing, his hands together at his back, his eyes downcast. "William was a loyal man. I had thought the same of you. When I hear that a man I had ordered killed took more than a year to actually be killed… well, let me say it gave me pause."

The king stopped and faced them both. "I understand your plight, John. Rowena. But I will be obeyed in all things! Do not doubt that. That I love you dearly, John, and I do love you dearly, is a fact. For all these reasons. So I will turn away from your disregard of my orders. I will not have you strung up for treason. This time."

He bestowed a bright smile on Rowena before continuing. "And I am certain you prefer your husband to be there with your family and in one piece so let me warn you as well. The Godwin's reign has ended. I am rightful king and it will be my sons who reign after me. If you have any other thoughts, you need to set them aside if you wish to enjoy a long life."

The screaming baby could be heard long before the door was opened and Ruth was given to Rowena. Her gown was again dampened and she withdrew to the closest alcove alongside the Great Hall to see to her child.

The sound of Ruth's greedy suckling and gulping made John smile despite his angst at William's revelation. The man knew all this time that FitzOsbern was his father but felt no need to inform John. Was there some harm that could have resulted from his knowing? No! Merely peace of mind which was certainly not a priority, not to William.

"Lovely child, yes?" John's peace was complete and he saw William with new eyes. "Our second girl. Mayhap the next will be a boy."

Rowena gasped and John smiled at William.

"She thinks to hide from me that she is with child again."

William smiled, his manner reserved.

"I am verily pleased at the revelation. I cannot say why she would not want to share her news with me." John sighed, leaning forward a bit. "My lord, I will be your devoted knight and always swear fealty to you. Until my dying breath but I believe you have wronged me."

The king pulled back, his eyes wide with outrage. John raised his hand.

"When I spoke of not knowing from whence I came, you could have easily eased my concern by telling me. When I came to you asking if I might marry Lady Emma, FitzOsbern's daughter, you could have told me then that she was my half-sister and explained to me that what I felt for her was not the passion of a lover but the love of a brother. When I came to you wounded and broken, my body burning with fever, praying to God that my father may know that I lived a valiant life and died honorably, you could have told me you would make it so." John looked upon his mentor for what he hoped would be the last time. "You did not. You allowed me to live not knowing my father and not letting my father know me. You played with my life as if it had no meaning at all."

John went to one knee, bending his head. "I swear my fealty to you, King William, that I will defend you at the cost of my own life."

A loud burp echoed through the chamber. With his head still bent awaiting his lord's leave to stand, John smiled. He had a more wonderful life than he'd ever dreamed of and he would live it to the fullest.

"You may rise, Sir John."

Rowena came to stand beside him, Ruth propped up in her arms looking around with wide, violet eyes. Rowena's eyes searched his. He nodded and hoped she understood he would be fine. He knew it beyond a shadow of a doubt.

"Have we your permission to leave, my lord?"

William nodded. After showing him due respect, John and Rowena exited the hall and right out the front door. John stopped at the guard room and asked word be sent to their chamber that their servants were to follow.

The conveyance barely unhitched was prepared again. They settled into the luxury of the enclosed carriage. Ruth was asleep again. John kissed Rowena gently on the lips.

"How long have you known I was with child?"

"A few days."

"Why did you not just ask me if it were so?"

"I did not need to ask. I waited for you to tell me when you realized it."

Rowena smirked. "You talk a good talk but methinks you enjoy not sharing all that you know."

He sighed. "That is the way of it. But I will share a thing or two with you. More important than anything else."

"One?"

"If need be, there is no torn loyalty within me. It will always be you that I back."

"My thanks, my lord. And two?"

"That I love my dear Saxon bride."

Chapter Forty

The Great Hall was quiet when Tisa and Tadhg came inside. Smells of home drifted to Tisa and she smiled.

"Do ye remember the smell of that sweet bread, Tadhg?"

He breathed in just as deeply. "The best! Where is yer father?"

"There's little doubt that he is sitting beside the cook as she makes this bread."

Roland O'Brien's voice carried to them through the hall. "I dunna need to rest! Now leave me be. If I want—"

The man stopped abruptly at the sight of his daughter. Fergus stood beside him, a wide grin on his weathered face.

"Daughter!"

Tisa went without hesitation into her father's arms. He held her tight against him, kissing her head. "I have missed ye something fierce."

Fergus accepted Tadhg's extended arm then patted him on the back.

"I love ye, da," Tisa said.

Tadhg coughed. "Sir?"

Her father stiffened and his arms quickly fell away when he stepped back. "What do ye here?"

"Father, Tadhg and I are wed!"

"What? How can that be? What of the damn Meic Lochlainn?"

"Damn, indeed," Tadhg said before making eye contact with Fergus who nodded his head in agreement.

Tisa quickly sobered. "Darragh is dead and so is Aodh."

"In battle?"

"One of their warriors turned against them," Tadhg said.

"Darragh's last words to me were to marry Tadhg so I did." She reached to take his hand. "And I am very happy."

"Glad I am that ye've wed the lad. He's had his eye on ye forever."

Her father's smile was genuine despite his teasing but he still looked tired.

"Roland." Tadhg's tone was grave. "We've more to tell you."

"Mayhap I'll go and fetch some of that sweet bread," Fergus said before narrowing his eyes at Roland. "If yer father left any."

"I did! Now go bother someone else." Roland fidgeted on his chair as if unable to get comfortable.

"Do ye have pain?"

"My body aches every time it rains."

It hadn't rained the entire trip home. Tisa and Tadhg exchanged worried glances.

"I have news for ye. 'Tis something I just learned myself." Tadhg sat on Roland's left where he indicated. "I ken why my father broke it off with ye and I ask yer forgiveness for the deed."

"I would forgive that man anything. He was closer to me than a brother."

"Ye'd always been close," Tisa said. "We've heard there was a time when ye all believed Padraig was dead."

Roland leaned his head back and blew a breath. "A terrible time. So much death and dying. Then poor Moira. She was beside herself." He leveled his eyes to look at Tisa. "Yer own mother had passed. She had been ill for a long while so 'twas no surprise, more of a blessing. She was in so much pain. But Padraig. Every day I prayed that Padraig would come home safe and sound."

Tisa swallowed, not sure what to say next.

"Ye took good care of my mother. Of all of us. I thank ye, Roland. Ye're a good man."

Roland nodded but his eyes seemed distant, as if reliving the terrible time.

"And there was a moment when ye took comfort in each other." Tisa fought to keep any censure from her tone. "Ye and Moira had lost so much."

A frown creased Roland's forehead but he didn't speak.

"Nothing ye had meant to have happen but," Tadhg placed a hand on Roland's arm, "a child was conceived."

Roland's eyes widened and he leaned forward as if he might strike Tadhg.

"Father! Moira chose not to tell ye, not to tell anyone, but Brighit is yer daughter."

"NAE!" The big man's voice trembled, his pain so deep. "Dunna say 'tis so! Poor Moira. I dinna ken. 'Twas wrong. We were overcome with grief."

He dropped his face into his hands and wept.

"We are not here to judge ye. I've come to ask that our alliance be restored, Roland." Tadhg waited until Roland had lifted his head. "The alliance between our clans should never have been severed. Can we put back what once went wrong? Ye are a good man. I hold ye in high regard and pledge to defend ye and yer household from any that may come against ye. Now and in the future. Ye have my word."

Roland searched his face before smiling again. "Let it be so!"

Fergus' impeccable timing caused Tisa to believe he'd been listening and waited to enter. She smiled her thanks. Many servants loaded down with fruits, vegetables, and sweets followed him in.

"This is cause for celebration! Fergus, gather the villagers."

"They await a chance to see their Tisa even now. Young Liam ran to spread the news." Fergus winked at her. "They've missed ye. We all have."

"We have a joining to celebrate! A joining of clans and a joining in marriage."

Tadhg's relaxed smile was wonderful to see. Tisa hugged him close, bringing her mouth to his ear. "When will ye tell him that Brighit has returned from England and will be here anon?"

"He will learn soon enough." Tadhg pulled back and kissed the tip of her nose. "We will respect his decision about telling her."

Tisa nodded. "Tadhg?"

He loosened his hold of her so she could step away. "Have I told ye that I love ye? More than life itself?"

"I believe ye have but I will never tire of hearing of it."

Her eyes filled. "Then have I told ye I'm carrying yer child."

He dropped his jaw with his audible gasp.

"What is amiss?" Roland asked. He glanced between the two of them then smiled. "Oh, did ye just learn she was with child?" He slapped Tadhg hard on the back. "Ye've got to be more observant, son."

Her father turned away laughing at his own joke. People were quickly filling the hall as the trestles were set up and covered with as much food as they could hold.

"Sweet, Tisa!" Ignoring everything around them, Tadhg gently gathered her in close, almost as if he thought she might break. "A child! Just as we'd planned."

"I will not break." She hugged him much tighter to prove her point.

He grunted as if she held too tight.

"Oh, stop!"

Tadhg took her mouth, caressing his lips lightly over hers before deepening the kiss into a passionate display of his love for her, leaving her knees weak and wishing they were in a more private area.

"I love ye more than I ever thought I could love anyone. Ye are the fulfillment of my hopes for my life. Not bad for the sixth son."

"Sixth son?" Roland asked. "Aye, the legend of the seventh son. Ye've done well for yerself despite the legend."

Tisa's brows lowered. "My love, ye are wrong."

"Tisa, I ken the legend as well as ye do."

Tadhg's tone indicated his rising irritation with the subject, as if he'd heard about it his whole life. He probably had. It took three generations for the blessing to be fulfilled. To have the hopes of those generations dashed was surely a great loss.

"The sixth son will have nothing but trouble." Tadhg made the pronouncement as if proclaiming a death sentence. "Now, had I been the seventh son—"

"Ye *are* Padraig's seventh son." Tisa was only too happy to interrupt his tirade. "The priest, Matthew, told me yer father had been joined with another before Moira and they'd had a son. Both were lost."

Tadhg's expression went blank. "I am the seventh son?"

"Ye are."

"Hah! And the legend has come true. A toast!" Roland said in a loud voice, lifting his simple mug. "To the joining of my daughter, Tisa, to the seventh son of the seventh son of the seventh son of the MacNaughton Clan, Tadhg. May they have a warm home full of love and children. And to the restoring of our alliance with the MacNaughton. May we continue to have a peaceful existence with all those around us."

All drank in agreement. Tadhg shared his cup with Tisa then kissed her again with all looking on.

"Huzzah!" The united shout of happiness.

"Huzzah." Tadhg whispered before capturing her lips again.

Epilogue

MacNaughton Clan – One year later

The birds outside were loud enough to wake the dead, which was exactly what Tisa was wishing she were. Young Darragh's birth had been easy, the carrying even more so. Not with this one. Sick every morning, tired every afternoon. Being only four months along did not give her much hope that things would be getting better any time soon.

"Oh, ye're awake." Tadhg came in. Little Darragh, wrapped snuggly inside his brat and close to his heart, slept soundly. "Just taking him out for a peek around the place."

She pressed further under the covers. "Sounds like a wonderful day outside."

"That is for certain but methinks having this young warrior with me makes it even better."

Tisa watched Tadhg as he walked around the room. The sheer joy on his face always warmed her heart.

"Tadhg, he is too little to ken what ye're showing him."

"Not true!" He managed to unwrap the babe, tuck him beside Tisa, all without awakening Darragh. "He watched all that was going on around him. That's why he is asleep now. I exhausted him."

"I dunna question that!" Tisa held him close to her.

"Sean and Thomasina have come."

Tisa started to sit up but quickly needed to lay flat again.

"Still sick? Can I bring ye something?"

"Sorry I am to be feeling like this. I dunna want to stay in bed. It has been too long since Sean and Thomasina have come to visit."

Tadhg poured her a drink of water. "Sean taking over as chieftain requires a lot of time."

"He learned well from working alongside ye."

Tadhg nodded. "His mother's clan is more than happy with him as their leader, just as we are to have this new alliance now." Tadhg took a sip before handing it to her."Methinks they have news for us."

"Did young Brighit come with them?"

"She did."

Tisa looked down in the little face of her son. Such a handsome boy with dark, curly locks like his father. "Do ye think Darragh will be upset that his betrothed is older than he is?"

"'Tis Brighit! She will be a lovely lass for him. What matter is her age?"

Tisa took a sip of the water, cool and refreshing. She sighed. "She is not much older. Months only."

"True." Tadhg managed to lay behind her on the bed, pulling her back into his arms without disturbing the babe. "Did ye not wonder of their news?"

"A child?" Tisa raised her eyebrows, knowing she was being a total grouch. "What other news could there be?"

Tadhg kissed her neck before nuzzling behind her ear. "Ye may be correct. Mayhap it is more?"

Tisa could not think of any other news they could bring. They had all been busy with their planting and rebuilding after the winter storm. "I dunna ken what else it could be."

She looked over her shoulder. Tadhg's averted eyes told her he knew something.

"What have ye heard?" she asked.

He shrugged. "Ye are probably correct. With child. That is all."

Snuggling Darragh up on her chest, she turned to her husband with lowered brows. "Tell me."

Tadhg's face split into a wide smile. "They have had word from Malcolm."

"Caireann?"

"They will be down for a visit."

"Oh!" She had expected something more. "No news of a child?"

He kissed her gently on the forehead. "Nae. Not that I have heard."

In all her talks with Caireann, it had always been Tisa's greatest wish to have many children with Tadhg but she couldn't remember her dear friend ever saying as much.

"Do ye think they are happy?"

"I do." Tadhg searched her face.

299

"Mayhap they should have returned with us. Gerrit still lives. A constant reminder to her."

"Hmm, not nearly as arrogant, of that I am certain. And Brian has done very well with his trading to the north. Even in Alba."

Tisa nodded. She had never been to England or Alba and that suited her fine.

"He sends Ian in his stead. The captain deciding to stay on has given Brian a commander he can trust," Tadhg said.

"How fares Breandan?"

"He travels with Ian. Methinks they are happy to be together. That they were able to set aside their jealousy when Darragh died to comfort each other speaks well of them."

"That is very good."

A sudden fluttering in her belly made Tisa place her hand there.

"The babe?" Tadhg asked.

"Mayhap but 'tis more forceful than I would expect so early."

"Mayhap 'tis two babes."

She turned her evil eye on him. "Dunna even say that."

"Why not? If we have two more boys, we will be nearly halfway to another seventh son."

Tisa laughed, the baby wiggled in her arms and she rocked him back to sleep. "And what is the blessing with that?"

Tadhg kissed her cheek. "That they have the seventh son of the seventh son of the seventh son for their father and all will be right with the world."

"Aye and that it will."

THE END

ABOUT THE AUTHOR

Aside from two years spent in the wilds of the Colorado mountains, Ashley York is a proud life-long New Englander and a hardcore romantic. She has an MA in History which brings with it, through many years of research, a love for primary documents and the smell of musty old libraries. With her author's imagination, she likes to write about people who could have lived alongside those well-known giants from the past.

Connect with her online at:

Website: www.ashleyyorkauthor.com
Email: ashleyyork1066@gmail.com
Twitter: @ashleyyork1066

Please enjoy these sample chapters from The Bruised Thistle, *the first book in* The Order of the Scottish Thistle Series.
Ashley

CHAPTER ONE

Dalmally, Scotland 1149

"Where have you been?" Iseabail bristled with irritation at having waited nigh an hour for her brothers' arrival. Trying to look busy alone in an open field was a challenge, especially with the cool autumn wind stinging her exposed skin.

"Getting supplies," Iain answered readily enough, but he didn't sound himself.

Their little brother Calum stood at his elbow, nodding his red head a touch too eagerly.

She glanced between them as her suspicions rose. They were hiding something. "What is wrong?" Iain usually took great care with his appearance, but today he was ill-kempt. His thick dark hair hung limp around his face, and his brown eyes were bloodshot and red-rimmed. Her irritation shifted to concern. "Are you not well?"

"Well enough. See what we've brought?" Iain's tone brooked no discussion.

Iseabail allowed him to distract her with the large basket Calum was carrying. He placed it on the ground and lifted the lid. All manner of cloths, containers, and herbing accoutrements greeted them. Iain pushed this aside to reach beneath and lift the false bottom, showing a good array of cheese, breads, and dried meat for their trip.

A shiver ran down her spine, but she smiled up at him. "Good. We are ready then."

Ready to leave the only home they had ever known, the overwhelming sadness caught her off-guard. She forced herself to remember the abuses they had suffered at the hands of their powerful uncle, the new laird of *their* lands. What he had subjected her to as a female was the most horrendous of all.

She clenched her jaw in determination. "Shall we go?"

"Iseabail." Iain's face was unreadable, but she sensed his hesitation. "I cannot go."

His words knocked the wind out of her. The thought of having to return to the hell she had been enduring left her lightheaded.

She shook her head in denial. "No, Iain, I cannot..." She corrected herself, "*we* cannot go back." Her brothers did not know about their uncle's abuse. There were no visible signs. "We cannot. We must make our escape now, while he is away from the castle."

Iain's eyes rounded with sadness and fine lines creased his forehead.

Iseabail had a terrible sense of foreboding, and the whisper of hope she had been nurturing began to dissipate. The idea of escape had come up so suddenly, yet they had all agreed straight away. Their uncle's plans to be gone for a few days gave them the perfect opportunity, and it was one they could not afford to waste. They needed help ousting Uncle Henry from their lands. Not only was he ignoring their father's last will and testament, his brutal treatment of the local clansmen had weakened them until their fear would not allow them to stand against him. Assistance from those outside the powerful Englishman's control was their only hope.

Iain firmed his shoulders, a determined set to his handsome face. "*We* will not return. You and Calum will travel on without me."

Fear slammed into her chest, and it became hard to breathe. "What do you mean? We cannot go alone. It is not safe."

Iain held her gaze and spoke clearly. "This may be our only chance to go for help. I will stay behind to see that no one follows, and then I will join you."

The look that passed between Iain and Calum made her throat tighten. Something did not seem right. "When will you come?"

"When I know it is safe and you are not followed." Iain's answer came a bit too quickly.

Calum shifted and avoided her gaze.

"How will we know that *you* are safe if you return to the castle?"

"Trust me, sister. I can take care of myself." His smile did not reach his eyes. "Do not worry so."

A thousand scenarios played out in her mind as desperation seeped into her thoughts. "And in the woods? How will we stay safe? Calum is only nine years old." She smiled an apology at her little brother for such a frank statement.

"I have protection. See?" Calum withdrew a dangerous-looking knife from its hiding place in his boot.

"You fight very well, Calum, I know, but..." She turned beseeching eyes on Iain. He had to come with them.

"You must remain vigilant. I know you can do this, Iseabail. Here." Iain held out a dagger. "Take this. Keep it near you at all times."

Iseabail accepted the *sgian dubh* Iain offered. She slid the knife out of the scabbard. Their father had given it to Iain when he turned ten, and she found comfort in its weight and the cold metal of its blade.

This would never work, but there was no other choice. Was it not better to die trying than to live playing dead?

"If you think this is best." She slipped it into the basket.

"Go on, and do not worry about me. I will protect what is ours. Understand?"

"It will be dangerous for you." She wrapped her arms around him and drew him close to keep him from seeing her tears, but he stiffened and stifled a gasp. She drew back. "What is wrong?"

He smiled at her with misty eyes. "I love you, Iseabail. I pray you will be safe. And you," he grasped Calum's shoulder as men do, "you must look out for her. Aye?"

Calum wiped his nose. "Aye."

"We will stay together." She straightened her shoulders and held her head high, feigning a strength she did not truly feel. "And we will get help."

Iain tipped his head, a small smile playing on his lips as his features softened with relief. He glanced around, searching the far-off woods. He pressed his mouth into a thin line, and his eyes almost looked black as he surreptitiously slipped a small leather-wrapped parchment from beneath his tunic. Their father's will.

"This is the only support we have for our claim." With his eye on the document, Iain continued, "You must protect it if we want to take back what is rightfully ours."

She nodded, solemnly accepting his edict. She shifted the silver cross that hung against her bosom then tucked the treatise down the front of her gown. The worn leather was comforting where it rested, snug between her breasts.

"When you get to the Campbell's land, look for the shepherd boy, Inus, in the lower fields. He shall get you to Hugh, who knows of our dear uncle's treacherous way firsthand. Trust no one else. Do you understand? No one."

Her brother's closest friend had always been a thorn under her skin with his constant teasing. That he was her savior now made her want to laugh, but the dire look in her brother's eyes stopped her. He held her at arm's length as if memorizing everything about her. A lump grew in her throat as she fought back tears. She wanted to be strong for him. Make him proud. Despite her concerns, despite the strangeness of his behavior, she trusted him, and she would respect his decision.

"You must promise me, Iseabail. Trust no one else."

"I promise." Despite her best intentions, tears coursed down her face. "I look forward to being with you again, dear brother." She kissed his cheek and hugged him. She did not want to let go, but when Iain made a strangled sound, she released him at once. His breathing was heavy and his forehead glistened with sweat. "Iain?"

He stepped back, his jaw clenched. He shook his head at her to stay away. "Go, both of you."

CHAPTER TWO

Seumas looked up as the two newcomers entered the hall. Frigid air swept across the room with their arrival, but it was not the cold that caught his attention—the large, wooden door opposite the great hearth had opened numerous times since dusk as peasants sought shelter from the suddenly plummeting temperatures. Something about them tugged at him. Their lack of grumbling, perhaps? Or the timid way they moved amongst the rabble? Either way, he seemed to be the only one who took an interest. Glancing at the other soldiers he sat with, he was not surprised they had noticed nothing.

"Ta hell ye did, Miguel! Dere were only five av dem!" The Irishman's indignant retort echoed across the hall. Patrick, always ready to argue, was instigating yet another fight. The bench Seumas shared with the burly man tipped unsteadily as he stood.

"'Tis the truth," Miguel responded to the insult with as much heat. Though he remained seated, he moved his hand to the dagger at his waist. "You had already turned tail and run."

Seumas shook his head and lifted his gaze heavenward. His patience with these men was gone. "Do ye need to get on like this every night?"

"Ye don't care for our company?" Patrick's bloodshot eyes did not appear to focus as he turned his anger on Seumas, his face a little too close. "Bugger off, den!"

As the leader of these men, Seumas knew what power he wielded over them. They knew it, too, but that did not change how they acted. "Methinks not." Seumas lifted the mug to his mouth, his eyebrows raised in expectation as he held the man's glare.

Patrick stumbled backward onto the bench. Seumas caught him before he fell against the wall. "Why are ye such an arse, Seumas? Have ye not got anywhere else to do yer carousing?"

The man was a son of a bitch to be sure. "Nae, Patrick, I have nowhere else to go. Now settle yerself down."

It was true enough. He had believed he would eventually get over what he had been through in Edessa and stop hating himself. Then he would go home. But he had played the wait-and-see game too long. Now his father was dead, and Seumas had even more reason to hate himself.

Needing a diversion from his troubled mind, Seumas searched the crowd again for the two. The hard frost had come too soon, finding many unprepared, and the Great Hall was cramped with villagers and peasants. Nevertheless, he soon spotted them. Covered with grime, from the hoods obscuring their faces to their cloth-wrapped feet, they blended well enough with the others in the hall, but they had a certain bearing that did not match their outward appearance. They did not shy away or shuffle their feet. The one who led the way, the smaller of the two, had a surprisingly noble posture but hesitated the slightest bit before joining the ever-increasing crowd by the fire. Interesting.

He was intrigued by their presence, but, for their sakes, he hoped he was the only one. The people at this castle were as cruel as their overlord, Lord Bryon. Any who did not belong, no matter the circumstances, would be cast out without a moment's hesitation. There would be no mercy, even in freezing weather.

Patrick slammed his cup on the table emphatically as he told his next story, the earlier argument already forgotten. The other men at the table were enraptured by the tale, but Seumas ignored it, intent on his study. The bitter mead dribbled down his chin as he took a deep swallow, and he traced his lower lip with his tongue.

They had their heads down and turned away from the room now, but were not cowering at all. Sitting up straighter, Seumas realized they were trying to avoid being noticed.

"Right, Seumas?" Patrick slapped him on the back as spittle came out with his words. "Damn beauty that one, right?"

Seumas exhaled in irritation. He had not been listening, but he nodded to keep from being drawn into the conversation.

"Not that ye could do anything about it." The man burst into laughter at his own joke. "But do not worry yerself, Seumas. I took care of her. I gave her what she wanted, since ye could not."

Seumas tensed at the insult, giving the Irishman his full attention as he turned toward him, jaw clenched. Patrick was clearly too drunk to notice that the others had grown ominously quiet. Seumas slammed his fist against the thick wooden table. The Irishman locked eyes with him, and his laughter stopped abruptly. The tin cup rolling along the edge of the table was the only sound. It landed with a dull thud on the rushes covering the floor, and perspiration broke out on Patrick's brow. He was very unwise indeed to let his tongue loose every time he drank, and he had the crooked nose and missing teeth to show for it.

The blond man across the table took up the retelling. "You might have taken care of her, Patrick, but was she pleased with what you gave her?"

The rest of the men laughed nervously. Uncertain glances came Seumas's way as he struggled to accept the intervention and let the insult pass.

"I would say ye have the right of it, David." Seumas's voice was tight. He appreciated the man stepping in, but he should not have let it get this far in the first place. He had to control himself. He was their leader not because he had earned their respect, but because Lord Bryon thought it humorous to put "God's soldier" in charge of his pack of mercenaries, and because Seumas had no other prospects. From being a man with integrity and beliefs to a man with no self-respect was a mighty fall. He had to consciously release his clenched fist.

Seumas returned his gaze to the others milling in front of the fire—some sitting, some lying down, all trying to keep warm. The dark-haired woman who had grabbed his crotch last night smiled at him, but he looked right through her. She had been hoping to share his bed, but she had been sorely disappointed, and would be again. Carnal pleasure did not interest him. He had received a wound in the siege of Damascus, and his body no longer became aroused. As such, he neither needed nor wanted female companionship. There was some relief in having his mind in agreement with his body.

A disturbance by the fire startled him back to the present.

"Get your damn dog out of here, Robbie, and do not come back to the heat of the fire until you do." A squat, gray-haired woman smacked the boy's ear as she yelled at him.

"It's too cold, Mum. He keeps slipping back in." Robbie dragged the mangy canine to the wooden door that led outside.

The leader of the newcomers—a young boy, Seumas thought—seemed to freeze in place as he too witnessed the encounter. The lad stiffened, appearing affronted by the treatment of the stable boy. Like a chivalrous knight, he reacted as if he might actually come to Robbie's defense. The person behind the lad gave him a none-too-gentle shove. When the little knight glanced back, Seumas caught a glimpse of his filthy, childish face. It was indeed a boy and not anyone he recognized. As he suspected, these two were not from the area.

The second person remained a mystery of uncertain sex and age. Though there was something about the way he moved and the protective hold the little knight had on his arm. Seumas stroked his beard. It could be a female, but the big cloak effectively hid any sign.

They were pushing through the mob to get closer to the fire when the little knight dropped out of sight. He had tripped over Perceval, the mute who lived beneath the bridge leading to the castle. He was a mean one, and the jab he gave the boy was intended to do harm. The little knight grimaced.

Seumas moved in quickly before a brawl broke out.

Without a word, he pulled the little knight out of harm's way. He kept his eye on Perceval. "Now that is no way to act."

The frantic hand gestures said it all. His mouth flapped of complaints and mistreatment without a sound while the little knight looked on, darting fearful looks between them. Perceval's eyes had dark circles and his cheeks were sunken from lack of food.

"Methinks there is something for ye somewhere else," Seumas said. When he moved closer to whisper to him, the smell of urine and feces was overpowering. "Go see Fran. Ye know Fran?"

Perceval's eyes brightened and he bobbed his head, recognizing the cook's name. He leaned in to hear Seumas.

"She is holding some sweet cakes for me, and I want ye to get them."

The boy's face fell—he no doubt thought he would have to give the morsels up to Seumas.

"But I do not want them. Ye eat them."

Perceval did not hesitate. He bolted toward the kitchen door.

"Now then," Seumas turned toward the little knight, still in his grasp. The mystery companion held back, well hidden. "What have we here?"

"I did not do anything to him." The boy's eyes were wide and round. "I got tripped up and fell. That is all."

"Aye. And yet... I see that ye do not belong here." Better to let the boy know up front he had been found out.

The little knight caught himself as he started turning to his mysterious companion. "I do, m'lord." He tipped his head emphatically, a convincing liar.

Impressed by the act, Seumas smiled at him and included his companion when he spoke. "Stay to the right side of the fire. That is where the young'uns sleep. Ye will be safe there unless they realize ye do not belong... then out ye go. Hear me?"

The little knight nodded.

Seumas glanced at the boy's companion, but the shadowed face turned away. The dirt-encrusted cloak covered him—or her—from head to toe, but the long fingers gripping the edges of the cloak together were just visible. They were also decidedly feminine.

Seumas smiled and returned to his men.

CHAPTER THREE

Someone was watching her. Iseabail woke instantly. Wedged between Calum and the wall, she feigned sleep, keeping her breathing steady though her body tensed. Through half-closed eyes, she scanned the hall. The crackling fire silhouetted Calum's slumped form. He had turned away in his sleep. The overpowering stench of unwashed bodies gave her a strange sense of belonging after being alone in the woods for so long—she probably stank as much as they. The sounds of snoring and breathing surrounded her.

The men carousing earlier could no longer be heard. They had been well in their cups, so no doubt they were either passed out or had staggered to their beds. Female laughter and low, muffled voices drifted to her from the stairs. Or had they found female companionship? She shuddered. They were mercenaries—hard men who did as they pleased and answered to no one. When she passed the group earlier, she had averted her eyes, hoping to avoid their notice. If Calum had not tripped, they would have been ignored. Now she had unwanted attention.

The draft on her leg was her only warning.

Someone clamped a hand onto her bare ankle. She opened her mouth but no sound came out; her gasp froze in her throat. She had been discovered. If Calum were older she could have called for his help, but she did not want him to get hurt trying to defend her. As usual, she was left unprotected.

Her attacker slid a calloused hand up her leg. Fear quickened her breath. He caressed her calf before grabbing on to pull her away from Calum. She bit into her lip and clawed at the ground as she fought against being dragged further. Her assailant's throaty chuckle reminded her of her uncle's, and panic overwhelmed her senses.

I will not be used again.

Determined, she thrashed and rolled, trying to turn onto her back. He bent to grab her legs at the knees, grunting with the effort. The noise made her sick. Her gown slid further up her thighs, and his low sound of carnal appreciation echoed in her head. On her stomach with her ankles held against either side of her attacker, she could not have felt more vulnerable. Or angry. She twisted and pulled, finally wresting one leg free. She tucked her knee to her chest and kicked as hard as she could, connecting with the man's tender area. Hope blazed through her. He groaned and dropped her legs abruptly. Her knees hit the ground with a painful thud, and she pressed her lips tightly together to muffle the hiss of pain.

Finding herself released, she pulled her tattered gown over her legs and dragged herself into a sitting position. The unmoving body of a chunky male lay at her feet. She looked up to find a large man with pitch black hair standing there, the leather-wrapped hilt of his dagger visible in his clenched fist. The smear of blood on the silver pommel where he'd knocked out her assailant marked this man as her defender. His dark blue eyes narrowed in concentration as he searched her face. He was also the man who had threatened Calum earlier.

"So ye *are* a lass." He spoke in hushed tones, his soft Scottish brogue sweet to her ear. Alas this was not her clansman but one of the mercenaries. He wiped the pommel on his leg before placing it back into its bejeweled sheath at his belt and crossing his arms in front of him. Motioning to the body that lay unconscious between them, he added, "I would say I was not the only one who figured it out."

How? She was always being mistaken for a boy at home... Well, maybe not so much of late. But she had been covered from head to toe with the blanket that lay crumpled behind her. It must have slipped off in her sleep. As if reading her mind, the Scot retrieved the blanket.

"Thank you for your assistance." She blanched at the stupidity of her own words, but nothing else seemed appropriate. She just wanted him to go away.

His eyes were intense before he looked down. "Ye were doing well on yer own, I would say."

She followed his gaze. It was quite gratifying to see her attacker still holding his private parts, though the goose egg on his head was clearly the blow that had stopped the assault. Her satisfied smile evaporated, however, when she noticed the Scot eyeing her suspiciously.

"Still, I am in your debt." Her smile froze on her lips. Admitting to a mercenary that you owed them was not the smartest course of action.

His eyes brightened, but she sensed a smirk hidden in that thick, dark beard. "Are ye now? Weel then, tell me what ye are about. I would say ye are not in yer usual sleeping place."

Her heart raced as he hunkered down beside her, his face so close she could see the laugh lines around his eyes. His low voice resonated through her, and he held her gaze.

He stroked his heavy beard before he spoke again. "Ye have chosen a bad place to rest yerself, *if* that is all ye had in mind. Ye have put yerself in harm's way."

She glanced toward the tables, where a few of the mercenaries mumbled and shifted in their sleep. "How, pray tell, have we put ourselves in harm's way?"

"Pray tell, is it?"

Iseabail covered her irritation with herself with a shake of her head. Pray tell was not a term a peasant used. He was making her feel very defensive.

"I told yer friend," the man pointed at Calum, his eyebrows raised in question, "brother, perhaps? I told him to stay to the *right* of the fire." He rolled his 'r's as he spoke.

"We are to the right..." Iseabail stopped herself just short of doing the same. She and Calum were trying to blend in with the local peasants seeking refuge from the cold. It would not do to give herself away as a Scot. His eyes narrowed ever so slightly. Had he heard her slip?

"Ye are not!" His voice had become very forceful, and Iseabail's breath caught in her throat. He glanced around and lowered his voice. "This is the very spot where the women sleep who are looking for a warm bed to share."

He raised his furrowed brows as if expecting some sort of response. An apology? She knew they should never have tried to come in from the cold. The woods were the only safe place. Tears threatened, tightening her throat. She would not show her weakness.

She dipped her head and pushed to standing. He was a little too close, and she stood a little too fast. Her head slammed into his hard chin, nearly making her lose her balance. He grabbed her with strong hands, righting her. His firm touch sent heat through her body.

Iseabail jerked away from him. The warmth remained, unsettling her as it made its way into her belly. His bright blue eyes were clear, and his hands hovered just above her arms as if about to touch her again. He looked her up and down as if seeing her for the first time. Her pulse started to race, anticipating his touch.

He glanced at Calum before he spoke again. "I do not suppose ye are?"

His voice was quieter, reassuring. As a hired soldier, this man held authority here and had every right to throw her and Calum back out into the cold, but she did not believe he would. What had he asked her? Was she in her usual sleeping place? No, for that was a soft bed in her father's castle...

The warmth found its way into her head, turning her thoughts to mush. She fought to clear her mind and think rationally. His expectant look was playing havoc with her innards, but was it fear or that singeing heat? However, when his hands dropped back to his side, there was no mistaking her disappointment. What was she thinking? She needed to protect her family, and this man seemed to be a threat. Underestimating their uncle's need for revenge when they had escaped was her first mistake. She could not make another. If there were any chance she could make him believe she belonged in the castle, she had to take it.

"Aye, I am." She tried to sound as forceful as she dared despite the look of disbelief that spread across his face. Had there been disappointment as well? Now why would that be?

A cloud seemed to pass over his face, shifting his disbelief to a beaming smile that showed off the dimple in his right cheek. He now looked quite pleased with himself, and Iseabail feared that did not bode well for her at all.

Made in the USA
Middletown, DE
12 March 2016